P9-CNH-331

3 1780 00078 9495

The
KNAVE
of Hearts

By Elizabeth Boyle

Novels

The Knave of Hearts

The Viscount Who Lived Down the Lane

If Wishes Were Earls

And the Miss Ran Away With the Rake

Along Came a Duke

Lord Langley Is Back in Town

Mad About the Duke

How I Met My Countess

Memoirs of a Scandalous Red Dress

Confessions of a Little Black Gown

Tempted By the Night

Love Letters From a Duke

His Mistress By Morning

This Rake of Mine

Something About Emmaline

It Takes a Hero

Stealing the Bride

One Night of Passion

Once Tempted

No Marriage of Convenience

Novellas

Mad About the Major

Have You Any Rogues?

ELIZABETH BOYLE

The KNAVE of Hearts

❧ Rhymes With Love ❧

AVONBOOKS

An Imprint of HarperCollins Publishers

AVON BOOKS
An Imprint of HarperCollins*Publishers*
195 Broadway
New York, New York 10007

Copyright © 2016 by Elizabeth Boyle
ISBN 978–0–06–246579–5
www.avonromance.com

First Avon Books mass market printing: February 2016
First Avon Books hardcover printing: January 2016

Avon Trademark Reg. U.S. Pat. Off. and in Other Countries, Marca Registrada, Hecho en U.S.A.
Avon, Avon Books, and the Avon logo are trademarks of HarperCollins Publishers.
HarperCollins® is a registered trademark of HarperCollins Publishers.

Printed in the U.S.A.

10 9 8 7 6 5 4 3 2 1

To JoAnne Thelin
A woman dedicated to helping others,
a generous friend,
and someone I admire with all my heart.
Your smile and spirit are an inspiration.
Thank you for everything you do.

CHAPTER 1

London, 1811

Lavinia walked down the aisle of the London church, her gaze searching every pew.

"Looking for this?" Up near the altar stood the charwoman, who'd come in right behind the wedding party. In her hands she held an elaborate bouquet of roses and peonies.

A bridal bouquet, to be exact.

"Oh, dear, yes. I don't see how that could get left behind," Lavinia exclaimed as she hurried forward to claim the lost treasure.

"Well, there were quite a few tears being shed, my own included," the lady said, "so it isn't hard to see why these beauties might be forgotten." The old woman smiled. "'Sides, 'tis my experience that it's a love match when so many have to reach for their hankies."

"A love match? Oh, yes, decidedly," Lavinia agreed as the lady handed over the mislaid bouquet.

"Still, such a fancy collection of posies. Would be a terrible shame for them to be left behind," the old woman said, not even seeming to mind the petals falling where she'd been sweeping. She looked down at them and smiled. "I do like the roses, even when they leave a mess. Pretty bits of confetti, I like to say. I takes them home and dries 'em."

Lavinia couldn't help herself, she inhaled, and the sweet scent of roses surrounded her.

And just as quickly she found herself tearing up again. She dashed at her eyes with her sleeve, having already ruined two handkerchiefs.

"Oh, there now," the old charwoman told her kindly. "Weddings do that to a soul. Leave one all tied up in knots. Why, when me sister got herself married, I cried for a week."

"You did?" Lavinia began. "I suppose I am still in shock. When we came to London, my sister made it quite clear she had no intention of ever being wed . . . and now . . ."

Lavinia looked over at the altar.

"Glad tears, though," the charwoman said. "Always glad tears at a wedding. Your sister seemed ever so happy when she married His Lordship. And everyone saying him a big brute, but he looked over the moon with her at his side, now didn't he?"

Lavinia shifted the bouquet from one hand to another and looked away. "Yes, they are quite meant for each other." And once again, a sheen of tears rose in her eyes.

Oh, the devil take her! Would she ever stop crying? Louisa had married her beloved Piers . . . and now . . .

"Those are tears of happiness I see, aren't they?" the charwoman prodded.

Really, the woman was a terrible busybody, but having come from the village of Kempton, a place rife with such spinsters, Lavinia found the old lady's inquiry oddly comforting.

So she leaned closer to the woman and said, "I have to admit, as I watched my sister marry her viscount, the tears you witnessed were hardly charitable ones."

The charwoman prodded her toward a place in the pews. "Tell old Tildie all about it." She plopped down in the front row and patted the space next to her.

Lavinia looked down the aisle toward the open door. Outside, the May sunshine shone brightly. Beckoning. "I really should be going—"

"Oh, come now, no one is going to leave without you. Besides, do an old woman a favor and tell her the story." The woman winked with a cheeky glee. "I saw that kiss at the altar. I'd wager my broom there's a bit of scandal and romance to all of this." Then she looked at the door as well. "And more to come if I'm not mistaken."

Lavinia smiled, for Tildie had the right of it. Everything about this wedding and the days leading up to it were filled with scandal . . . and romance.

Truly, what would a quick recap for a lonely old woman cost her?

So she gathered her thoughts and tried to decide where best to begin.

"I suppose you could say it started," Lavinia told her rapt audience, "when Louisa and I came to London for our Season. Our godmother, Lady Charleton, had promised to sponsor us, or so we thought." She paused for a moment. For what had really happened was that they'd arrived in London only to discover that the baroness had passed away over a year earlier, and it was the baron's secretary who had made all the arrangements—including finding them a suitable chaperone, Lady Aveley.

But all those points hardly mattered. And as their dear friend, Lady Essex, always said when a story got long-winded, "Get to the good part."

So Lavinia did. "Our fortunes truly changed the night we went to Almack's and our party was joined by Mr. Rowland—"

At the mention of Lord Charleton's nephew and heir, the charwoman brightened. "Oh, he's a handsome one—the one who stood up with His Lordship—isn't he?" Tildie sighed a little, her smile turning dreamy like a newly arrived debutante's. "Knavish looking fellow if ever there was one," the charwoman happily mused. Then, as if thinking better of her choice of words, she added quickly, "Well, that's what me mum would have said."

Though Tildie appeared to share that sentiment.

"And right she would be," Lavinia advised the charwoman in no uncertain terms. For if ever there was a knave, it was Mr. Alaster Rowland. "None of this would have happened if Mr. Rowland hadn't let go of me in the middle of Almack's. None of this." She looked down at the wedding bouquet in her hands before picking up her story again.

For Tildie's sake, and her own.

For it had all happened so fast, she hardly believed it herself.

For a young lady who had made a study of all things proper, Miss Lavinia Tempest always seemed to find her fair share of mishaps.

The small fire at Foxgrove. The bunting incident of '08. And the rather infamous trampling at the Midsummer's Eve ball two years earlier.

Sir Roger still claimed he didn't miss those toes.

Of course, he was joking. He'd been very fond of those toes.

And worse, every time Lavinia attended a ball, soiree, or even just the weekly meetings of the Society for the Temperance and Improvement of Kempton, someone (usually Mrs. Bagley-Butterton) had to remind one and all of one of her more recent follies.

So when Lavinia entered the hallowed halls of Almack's, it was with, she vowed, a fresh start.

A clean slate.

And so it seemed she was right. No one pulled their hem out of the way as she drew near for fear of it being trod upon or worse, the lace being completely ripped away. No one whispered behind their fan, or laid wagers as to who or what would be broken by the end of the evening.

She was, for the first time in her life, merely Miss Tempest, the daughter of the respected scholar, Sir Ambrose Tempest.

"It is just as I imagined," she said in awe as she and her sister Louisa handed over their vouchers. The perfect place to launch herself into the lofty reaches of London Society.

After all, she'd spent most of the afternoon planning out her evening (when she hadn't been reading her favorite *Miss Darby* novel).

First and foremost, she was wearing her new gown—a demure and respectable dress done in the latest stare of *modest* fashion. And while she had longed for brilliant sapphire silk that had been on the shelf at the modiste's shop, that color would never do for a debut such as this.

After all, the very rule was on her list:

> *Proper Rule No. 3. An unmarried lady always wears demure and respectable colors. Such as white. Or a pale yellow. Or an apple green, but only if the occasion permits.*

So the blue silk could only be eyed from a distance, and she'd consigned herself to the muslin, for propriety was the order of the evening.

That is if she was to gain the highest obligation of every young lady making her debut Season in London:

> *Proper Rule No. 1. Marriage to a respectable, sensible, well-ordered gentleman is the order of business for every proper lady.*

So she had the gown, entrance into the very heart of the Marriage Mart, and now all she had to do was finish the evening without incident.

But this was Lavinia Tempest, and that was easier said than done.

"No dancing," Louisa whispered to her as their chaperone, Lady Aveley, led them into the Wednesday evening crush. Her sister held out her hand, pinky extended, and Lavinia wrapped her own finger around it and the two sisters bound their promise together.

No dancing.

In Lavinia's defense, she had made her promise most faithfully with every intention of remaining safely at the side of the dance floor.

She had demurred when Lord Ardmore had asked. Begging off in a charming fashion that she was "too nervous to dance," this being her first visit to Almack's.

She'd even refused the very handsome and dashing Baron Rimswell—though she had been sorely tested for it was only a simple reel, but then one glance at Lord Rimswell's glossy boots and she'd thought better of it and remained firm to her promise.

No dancing.

But apparently no one had told Mr. Alaster Rowland. Now in his favor, Mr. Rowland's boots hadn't a fine gloss and he was rather squiffy from an indeterminate amount of brandy, so even if she had stepped on him, he was drunk enough that it would most likely dull the pain.

"Come now, Miss Tempest, my uncle expects me to dance with one of you," he said as he came wavering up to her. "You cannot stand here all night."

She looked around for her sister, Lady Aveley. Anyone. "I-I-I, oh dear. Mr. Rowland, I don't believe—" she stammered out, even as Mr. Rowland took her hand, his strong, sure fingers lacing around hers.

No man had ever just come up and claimed her before for the simple reason that Kempton was a small village, and everyone knew (thanks in no small part to Mrs. Bagley-Butterton) that dancing with Lavinia was akin to asking to have your toes trimmed—or those of your neighbors—or to have something valuable broken.

Or a section of your house scorched.

Mr. Rowland, completely unaware of the mortal danger into which he was placing himself and a good portion of London society, just caught hold of her hand and tugged her out onto the floor, utterly and completely deaf to her protests.

"No, please, sir, I don't think this is wise," she told him. And she meant it. This was a very bad notion.

But unfortunately, her protests had no effect on Mr. Rowland, horrible scoundrel that he was . . .

Has that been mentioned as yet? That Mr. Alaster Rowland, the presumptive heir to his uncle's barony, is the worst sort of knave? It should be. And often.

He was also the most handsome devil Lavinia Tempest had ever met. Or had held her hand. Or smiled down at her with a wicked light in his eyes.

Lavinia had never seen brown eyes hold that sort of promise, the kind that sent a shiver of something so delicious, so dangerous, down her spine that she made a note right there and then to add a new rule to her list at her first opportunity:

No. 83. A proper gentleman should not make one's insides get so very warm.

In truth, as Mr. Alaster Rowland slid his hand around her waist, took her other hand in his, something altogether improper happened to Lavinia.

It had to be improper, for it certainly *wasn't* proper.

"Mr. Rowland, I cannot," she protested one last time, when to her horror, the band struck up a cotillion.

A cotillion? The last time she'd tried to dance a cotillion, Lady Essex's house, Foxgrove, had caught fire.

Yet here was Mr. Rowland, laughing and leaning closer. "But of course you can," he whispered in her ear, his breath warm against her skin.

It was as if he had brushed his fingers there—right against the curve of her neck. It was so intimate, so promising a gesture, that it left Lavinia in a blinding daze.

Yet Lavinia, the girl who had made a study of all things proper, knew exactly how to behave when all was proceeding at a proper pace, but right now she was being steered down a path she'd never taken before and assailed by a river of improper desires.

At least she assumed they were desires, for it was a dangerous, heady sort of warmth spreading through her limbs.

That, and something else happened. Her feet—which before had always seemed two sizes too big—untangled. It was as if the warmth of Mr. Rowland's touch, his teasing glance, his confidence in her, awakened a very graceful part of her.

Lavinia straightened, head held just so, and a long-forgotten admonishment from the dancing master Lady Hathaway had hired years ago, tripped through her thoughts.

Dancing is all about elegance.

And right there and then, Lavinia felt elegant. Not because her gown was proper. Or that she was standing on the dance floor of Almack's (though that certainly helped) but because the man gazing down at her held her, not at arm's length and in obvious fear, but with all the proper care and respect of a gentleman.

Moments later, Lavinia Tempest found herself dancing.

Perfectly. Like a lady. Mr. Rowland moved, as did everyone else, and Lavinia moved as well.

And in the right direction.

Once she was able to breathe, she nearly exploded with delight. She could dance. And a cotillion, no less. Yes, here, in the rarified air of Almack's, Lavinia Tempest had found her true talent.

"I'm dancing," she gasped, as she made yet another turn and no one cried out in pain. Nothing crashed to the floor in a thousand indistinguishable pieces.

"Why wouldn't you be?" Mr. Rowland asked, his attention rising from her to something that was happening across the room.

Lavinia didn't dare look to see what had caught his attention, for she was still reining in no small amount of terror that disaster was just one misstep away. "No reason," she replied, deciding it would only tempt the Fates by reminding them that she wasn't supposed to be doing this.

And so they moved through the room. As she whirled around, she spotted Louisa gaping at her, her sister's expression one of absolute terror.

But there was no need. All her years of careful study. All the setbacks. All the unintentional disasters.

It had all been for this one dance. And when it was over, she knew her Season in London would be nothing less than a tremendous success.

Yet Lavinia was to find that when one climbs too high, the fall can be all that much more treacherous. For the fortunes and future of a miss can often come down to one particular moment.

That memorable glance across a crowded ballroom. The first time a gentleman takes his hand in yours.

Even a stolen kiss.

But for Lavinia it became that moment when Mr. Rowland said, "Oh, bloody hell," and, to her horror, let go of her.

He took off across the crowded floor leaving Lavinia stumbling and scrambling to find her footing.

Which she did by crashing into Lord Pomfrey, sending him into Lady Kipps and then the entirety of London society. (Well not *everyone*, but to Lavinia it might as well have been.) For there they all went, tumbling over like well-placed dominos.

Nor did it help that Lady Jersey landed with her petticoat up over her head.

"Oh dear, she really should have been wearing more under that gown," Lavinia remarked to no one in particular. But then again, having tumbled more than her fair share of times, she was always prepared for such a misfortune.

However, not even a lifetime of preparation or lists of rules could save Lavinia Tempest from what came next.

Even before Mr. Alaster Rowland—Tuck, to his friends and just about everyone else—had arrived at White's, the disastrous events of Almack's were already being discussed. Some with firsthand accounts, others just chiming in with their own version so as to be part of the merriment.

"Lady Jersey with her skirt up over her head!" One fellow laughed. "I would have paid good money to see that."

"Most don't have to pay," Lord Budgey added with droll

charm. "But I suppose given your reputation with the ladies, you would, Procter."

This was followed by a round of raucous laughter at poor Lord Procter's expense. The young baron was saved from further ribald comments when the man of the hour himself arrived.

"Rowland!" they cheered, tipping their cups toward him.

Tuck saluted in return with a royal wave of his hand and nodded at one of the servants to fetch him a drink. He had no need to order. Every single one of them knew what to bring Lord Charleton's heir.

Which was good, because he was already well on his way to being half-seas over, and now he wanted nothing more than to finish this night's work by getting good and drunk.

"Come now, Tuck," Lord Ardmore called out. "I was just re-counting the entire tale. Nearly got trapped into dancing with one of those ungainly chits myself. However did you escape un-scathed?"

"Better question would be," Lord Budgey interjected, "what the devil were you doing at Almack's?"

Nods all around from the confirmed bachelors and rakes in the room. Some even groaned at the mention of that hellish place.

"My duty," he told them. Which was the truth. His uncle had all but ordered it.

"And is it true that Wakefield was there?" Procter asked, having recovered from his earlier humiliation.

"Aye," Tuck said. He wasn't going to say much more—he and Piers Stratton, Viscount Wakefield, had been friends since child-hood, and despite the great rift between them, he still felt a fierce loyalty to the man he considered his truest friend.

Even if Piers no longer shared that sentiment.

"Wakefield and Rowland at Almack's," Budgey said, shaking his large head like a mastiff. "That does it. Hell has frozen over. I've a mind to call for my coat."

There was general laughter all around, and Tuck accepted

their jests and comments with good grace. He found a small table to one side and settled down at it.

"Where did your uncle find that fetching pair of colts?" one of the fellows asked, casting a lascivious wink at the crowd. "Cow-handed they may be, but a pretty gel isn't something one casts aside easily."

Tuck eyed the man narrowly. His tone and manners set Tuck's teeth on edge and an odd sense of chivalry ran down his spine. "They are Lady Charleton's goddaughters," he told him with the same cold tone he might use to utter a challenge.

That took some of the wind out of their sails. For Lady Charleton had been respected and beloved by one and all.

And while a few of them raised a silent toast to the deceased baroness, Tuck wondered at his own strange need to rise to these chits' defense.

They weren't his responsibility—that was his Uncle Charleton and Lady Aveley's purvey. Nor was taking the stance of *knight-errant* his usual inclination, but that single word—*fetching*—stirred something inside him.

She had been fetching, hadn't she?

Images of dark hair and a lithe figure flitted through his memory and his body responded with an awakening that all but confirmed the gel had indeed been quite comely.

So why had he let her go tumbling across the dance floor if she was so pretty?

Tuck pressed his hand to his forehead. That was the problem with being middling drunk. If he were dead drunk, he wouldn't care, and if he was only mildly squiffy, he'd know the answer.

Happily for him, his drink arrived then and he tossed it back, deciding the best course of business was to blot the evening out, so he waved for the entire bottle.

Around him, the story of the Tempest sisters and Almack's began anew.

Lord Ardmore was on his feet regaling one and all. "—for

after Ilford danced with one of them, he claimed he'd have to have new boots made. She'd quite trampled them."

There was another round of laughter.

"Your boots, Tuck? What are the state of your boots?" Ardmore demanded.

Tuck laughed and held one out. "As poor as they were when I arrived at Almack's. I'd send them over to your valet to get a proper polish, Ardmore, but poor Falshaw wouldn't be able to show his face in public if I went 'round his back like that."

A few of the fellows nodded in agreement. No gentleman would ever do such a thing to his valet.

"Good thing you abandoned her when you did, Tuck," Lord Budgey said. "A good pair of boots should never be sacrificed—especially when they are probably your only pair."

More laughter followed and Tuck ignored the jibe.

"The real question that needs asking is why ever did you abandon Miss Tempest, Rowland?" This query came from a newcomer, and Tuck turned and for a moment felt the shadow of a grave cross over his heart.

Poldie.

Yet not Poldie—the figure in the doorway was his younger brother, Bradwell Garrick, now Lord Rimswell, for he'd inherited his brother's title when Poldie had perished on the Peninsula during Moore's retreat to Corunna.

Demmed fellow was quite the image of his brother and always gave Tuck a moment's pause.

And regret. *I should have been there. I should have been in Spain.*

But he hadn't gone as he'd promised. He'd remained in England when Piers and Poldie had sailed off. And only Piers had come back—wounded and embittered, shutting himself away and barring anyone from his house.

So in a sense, Tuck had lost both his friends.

Yet Brody was far more proper than his older brother had ever been, and he came into the circle of rabble-rousers and glanced around with an air of disdain. "Why did you abandon Miss Tempest so abruptly?"

There was a youthful air of gallantry to Brody's demeanor. A challenge of a sort.

Tuck hadn't the inclination to get into another dust-up. One an evening was his limit.

Or at least so he thought.

But even as he tried to find a reply that would satisfy Brody's sense of gentlemanly conduct and send the upright young man packing, Ardmore waded in.

"Come now, Brody," the young lordling called out. "Did you see how her sister danced with Ilford? Can't blame Rowland for not wanting to ruin his *only* pair of boots."

This was followed by a loud howl of laughter, which neither Tuck nor Brody shared in.

"Ah," Budgey announced, pointing toward the door. "There is Ilford. We'll have the entirety of it from him."

Tuck groaned. The last fellow in the world he wanted to encounter tonight—yet again—was the Marquess of Ilford.

Quite frankly he was shocked the man was even showing his face in White's, considering the facer Piers had planted on him earlier.

His spirits brightened for a moment, for *that* was it.

Piers had been in some sort of tussle with the Marquess of Ilford and . . . and . . . Tuck had gone to his old friend out of instinct.

Yes, yes, and in his haste, he'd abandoned Miss Tempest. Tuck nodded to himself in satisfaction that he'd puzzled it all out. Save with the memory came the realization that right after he'd gone to help his friend, then it had all gone wrong.

Oh, not the nonsense on the dance floor. But with Piers. One minute it seemed they'd been patching things up, and the next, they were arguing again.

About Poldie. About Spain. About questions Tuck was unwilling to answer.

Couldn't answer.

"Rowland," the Marquess of Ilford said with a sniff as he passed Tuck's table. "Still drinking. What a surprise." He moved into the room and flicked his fingers at Lord Budgey—a mere viscount—to give up his seat.

Which Budgey, being a mild-mannered sort, did with great haste.

Ilford was the most arrogant aristocratic Corinthian if ever there was one. The heir to his father's dukedom, he never missed an opportunity to point out his own lofty status. He claimed the spot he'd usurped with great fanfare and eyed his audience with the disdain of a tyrant. Though with only one eye. The other was noticeably swollen shut.

Oh, yes, the marquess appeared in high dudgeon. And looking for someone to vent his ire upon.

"Looks like you got tapped good, my lord," Ardmore said, peering over at Ilford. "Risky business that, raising Wakefield's ire. Everyone knows he's mad. Might have killed you."

There wasn't a man in White's, save Tuck, who didn't flinch at such a foolish statement.

But then again, Ardmore wasn't the brightest candle. More of a nub with an even shorter wick.

"He is mad," Ilford said, issuing a wave of contempt. "Dashed if I know why he came at me. No reason whatsoever. Should be in Bedlam."

Tuck, who had never been called sensible, pressed the point. "So why did you call him out?" he asked as he refilled his glass with the newly arrived bottle. "Or have you conveniently forgotten that part of the evening?"

There was a moment of silence around the table before a cruel smile spread across Ilford's lips. "I don't challenge cowards."

But that was a lie, for Ilford had challenged the viscount in a fit of pique, but now was going to ignore his momentary lapse of judgment.

Tuck started to get up, but a firm hand on his shoulder stopped him.

He glanced up and found Brody there, his eyes blazing.

Confident in his position, Ilford continued. "I pity poor Wakefield. We all know why he came back from Spain the way he did. It's what happens to men who retreat and don't stand and fight."

"Oh, bloody hell," Tuck began, this time shaking off Brody. "The only reason you're retreating from your challenge is because you know he'll actually shoot you. Not miss like most of the cowards you demand satisfaction from. Then again, you'd have to show up . . ."

He let his implication drift down.

The marquess glared down the long beak of his nose. "Coming from the likes of you, Rowland, that isn't even an insult. You bragged to one and all that you were going to fight in Spain and then . . ." Ilford tugged at his chin as he thought about it. "Oh, that's right, you stayed home and let your friends serve for you. Isn't that right, Rimswell?" The man shot a glance up at Brody. "Wasn't Rowland supposed to be at your brother's side when he died?"

Across the room, a tall figure rose, cutting into the cold fury that had seemed about to erupt from Tuck and Brody. Stately and commanding, Lord Howers was one of the old guard. Lofty in government circles and influential, Howers deplored anything that hinted of scandal. "Rimswell," he intoned, not in a greeting but more as an order. "There you are. Hathaway and I were just finishing up. Join me."

It wasn't a request, and Tuck watched as Brody's teeth ground together. But he did as he was bid.

"Follow your master, Rimswell," Ilford called after them. "Obedient dog," he added for the circle around him. "Just like his idiot brother."

Chaunce Hathaway, a man Tuck knew by reputation, settled into the chair that had been Brody's. Without an invitation, he filled his glass from Tuck's bottle and took an appreciative sip. "He's merely baiting you. Don't give that bastard the satisfaction."

Tuck knew that Chaunce was right. But it was demmed hard to listen to the marquess blather on and not do something, especially when his ears pricked at the tale Ilford was regaling his audience with.

"—don't know what Charleton is thinking. Those Tempest chits will run wild before a fortnight is out. Their mother was a light skirt, and her daughters will prove no different." Ilford paused and glanced over at Tuck. "Tumbling about the dance floor means they are ripe for a tumble elsewhere, eh? Is that what you were doing, Rowland? Seeing which one would suit your appetites best?"

There was some nervous laughter from the fringes of the gathered crowd.

But Tuck was done listening. "Shut up, Ilford."

"Easy, Rowland," Hathaway muttered under his breath.

But Tuck was past reasoning. Something in his memories stirred. An image of Miss Tempest and her bright blue eyes, as surprising as the bluebells that came up in London in the spring in the most unsuspecting places. And in his arms, she'd been a lithesome figure, kindling something within him that had left him a bit off-kilter.

Something far different than just the effects of the brandy.

Something that demanded satisfaction.

He got up and wavered a bit. "Those girls are innocent. Respectable. You'll keep your vile opinions to yourself."

Ilford spat out a laugh, utterly unimpressed. "My opinions hold more sway than you know. Those chits won't be able to set one foot outside your uncle's door by tomorrow morning," he replied, loud enough for all of White's to hear him. "Their mother was ruined goods and now they are as well. Why, I've heard tell that Sir Ambrose isn't even their father. They aren't fit to be seen in decent society. The only thing such gels are good for is—"

"Enough!" Tuck declared, his fists hitting the table.

"Oh, hell," Chaunce muttered under his breath, getting to his feet as well.

"Those girls are innocent of everything you've said," Tuck told him. "My uncle would hardly have taken them in for the Season if anything you said was vaguely true."

Ilford laughed. "Your foolish uncle will find it's a short Season he has to manage. They are done for. Ruined goods."

"You're the fool, Ilford. The Tempest sisters are Diamonds. And I can prove it."

Ardmore sat up, eyes alight. "I smell a wager brewing."

And for once, the man was spot on.

CHAPTER 2

Alaster Rowland woke up with a dreadful hangover and a fore-boding sense that disaster lurked just beyond his door.

In other words, it was a rather typical day.

Even as he began to stir, his manservant came bustling into the room, tray in hand.

"What's the damage, Falshaw?" Tuck asked as he reached for the steaming mug of coffee. No fine pekoe for him. He started each day with a bracing cup.

Most usually out of necessity.

"Your uncle, Lord Charleton, has sent round a note," the fellow told him.

"That bad, eh?"

"So it seems," Falshaw said with an uncharacteristic note of censure. A real valet wouldn't dare such a tone, but then again Tuck couldn't afford a proper valet. However, Falshaw had his own unique talents—like being able to discourage creditors and making ends meet when there were no ends to be had, so truly he was the best man for the job. "And you made a wager."

Nothing new there, Tuck noted as he pulled on his wrapper and strode over to the window.

"Regarding a pair of ladies," Falshaw continued as he began to straighten up the room.

Again, nothing new, Tuck thought, as he parted the curtain and looked out at the bright May sunshine. He'd wagered on more than his fair share of opera dancers and flirts. Why there was once this time—

"Ladies," Falshaw repeated, and this time the censure was more telling.

Ladies? Tuck turned a skeptical gaze toward his employee.

"Lady Charleton's goddaughters, to be exact," the man supplied as if prodding at Tuck's lack of memories.

Ladies? Goddaughters? That all had a decidedly proper ring to it. He scalded his mouth as he took an anxious gulp of coffee. And it rather did explain the note from his uncle.

"Yes, indeed," Falshaw replied, sounding a bit too gleeful as he hung up a jacket.

If Tuck didn't know better, he'd suspect that Falshaw rather liked seeing his employer periodically roasted by his only respectable relation.

"I'm in the suds, aren't I?"

It wasn't so much a question as an utterance, but that didn't stop Falshaw from happily answering, "Oh, aye, my lord."

Lord Charleton's butler, Brobson, barely admitted Tuck to the house. Even then, only to the foyer. "Your uncle will see you momentarily." Then the fellow strode off as if he had just admitted a plague victim into the household.

Yes, indeed. It was as bad as all that.

As he stood there, shuffling about a bit nervously, he heard something. Coming to a standstill, he heard it more clearly.

Weeping. And then a huge sniffle. The sort that would leave a perfectly good handkerchief utterly useless.

He glanced at the front door. The one that led to the street and London beyond. Where perhaps he could start anew. Join a circus. Ship off to parts unknown. Drown himself in the Thames.

He shook his still throbbing head at any of those options. He wasn't overly fond of travel—all the discomforts and inconveniences of being away from one's own bed. And sadly, he was a perfectly good swimmer.

The crying had now risen in pitch and fervor, and jangled at his nerves. Bother, it would weigh on any man's sensibilities.

Besides, it wrenched on his heart. He'd never admit this to anyone, not even if they were to forgive all his debts, but a woman's tears were his undoing.

Against his better judgment, Tuck pushed the library door open and waded in.

He immediately wished he hadn't.

Admittedly he'd been a bit drunk the previous night, but certainly he'd have remembered *this*.

The puffy, red face. The ugly, provincial gown. The dark hair sticking out in a few places.

But to the lady's credit, it appeared she was nearing the end of her torment, for certainly much more and she'd risk flooding the carpet.

Then her gaze became more focused as if she'd finally realized she was no longer alone. And her eyes took on a wild-eyed rage that prodded him to take a step back.

"You!" she gasped, stalking forward with all the fury of, well, a fury. Worse, she caught up a vase from the side table as she approached.

Alaster Rowland was many things. A fool wasn't one of them. He took as many steps backward as he could until he bumped into the wall, having misjudged the angle of his retreat.

Worse yet, the woman hunting him was a veritable horror. A hot, wet mess of tears and scalding anger brandishing a domestic weapon of sorts.

"That vase . . . in your hand . . ." he managed.

"Don't think I won't throw it," she told him.

"I'd duck and it would be a waste of a perfectly innocent vase."

"I won't miss," she told him with all surety.

"No?"

"I'm the best bowler in Kempton. I'm always picked first."

Yes, just his luck. To have found himself facing an angry miss with a penchant for cricket.

Could his day get any worse?

He tried another tack. "You know that's my uncle's favorite vase. And I do believe quite priceless."

He had no idea if it was or wasn't—a favorite or of value—but it was enough of a caution that she thought the better of her actions, and luckily for him, returned it to its former place of glory.

How could this be the same chit he'd met last night? It wasn't possible, for he held a very certain recollection of her having been quite fetching.

"You wretched, horrible man! How could you let go of me?"

So, yes, it was her. Though he hadn't thought he'd been *that* drunk.

"How could you?" she raged, wagging a finger at him.

Yes, well, better a finger than the crockery being cracked over his head. At least so he thought until she hurled her next accusation at him. "You've ruined me!"

This took Tuck aback. Ruined her? He wanted to rush in and assure her, having taken a second glance, that he could say with all certitude that nothing of the sort had happened between them.

He'd have remembered taking this descendant of Medusa to his bed.

She managed a gulping sob that seemed to quell her tears, and then she blew into the poor, hapless square of linen, trumpeting like an ailing swan, a sound that stabbed at the last remnants of his hangover.

"Miss Tempest, isn't it?' he asked, hand pressed to his brow, his eyes clenched shut against the unending pounding within. As his mother liked to tell him, a hangover was merely the brandy's way of trying to get out.

"Of course I am Miss Tempest," she snapped. "We met last night."

He looked again and still couldn't make the connection to the lithesome chit he'd met.

Worse, her eyes widened as she came to a shocked realization. "You don't remember me." To his horror, she took a calculating glance at the vase.

"I wouldn't say that precisely," he offered quickly, hoping to divert her. "But certainly you were wearing a different gown—" Lord, he hoped she was wearing a different gown—for the one she had on was positively hideous.

She snorted and took another step back from him. "Whyever did you let go of me? I was dancing."

Tout au contraire. He was neck deep in a wager that proved beyond a doubt that what she'd been doing the previous night was anything but dancing.

A wager Falshaw had delightedly filled him in on.

"And now you've ruined me," she finished.

"I hardly think I've done all that," he told her, doing his best to glance in any direction but hers.

Yet he found it an impossible feat. Like when one happened upon a carriage accident and everything was in a desperate tangle.

How could you not look?

Nor would the miss be ignored. "You. Let. Go. Of. Me."

Truly, could anyone blame him?

"And now . . ." she began until another bout of sniffles and gulps came choking out. "And n-n-n-ow . . ."

At this seemingly insurmountable impasse, she flopped down on the settee and began to cry anew, leaving him aimlessly adrift in the middle of the room. A litany of unintelligible complaints rose up through this new spate of tears as to all she'd lost—a proper marriage this, a respectable match that, and a lot of other things that seemed of great import to her, including some mention of a list.

"Miss Tempest, I am truly—" he said, trying to make her stop. Indeed, his head was reeling.

"I know what you truly are." *Sniff.*

He thought of advising her to get in line. The rest of London thought of him thusly.

Nor was she done. "We are both ruined." *Sniff.* "My sister and I." *Snuffle. Snuffle.* "We'll be sent home for certain." *Sniff.* "Tomorrow, if not today."

He hadn't truly been listening, what with all the sniffling, but a few words stuck in his ears.

Namely, "sent home."

Sent home? Tuck whirled around to face her. No, no, no, this would never do. Sheer, gut-wrenching panic ripped through him.

"A fortnight, sir," Falshaw had said. *"You've two weeks to prove that your uncle's charges are indeed ladies. 'Diamonds of the first order,' is how Mr. Hathaway and Lord Rimswell phrased it when they carried you in."*

Yet if the Tempest sisters left London . . . however would he win this wager? A wager he couldn't afford to lose.

"Home?" he blustered, raking a hand through his hair and pacing in front of her. "I hardly see why. Besides, uncle wouldn't be so cruel as to send you away so soon—"

"He won't have a choice," she declared, waving what was once a proud white bit of linen that now sagged in surrender. "Did you look at the salver when you came in?"

"Well, no—" Since it wasn't something he usually gave much regard. His always contained notices from creditors and the greengrocer. Barely veiled threats from unhappy husbands. Vowels that needed to be paid.

No, salvers had never been his friend. And now it seemed they weren't hers either.

"It is empty," she told him, with another shuddering sigh of loss. "Empty!"

In his residence, that would be something of a miracle.

"Mr. Rowland, if ever there was clear evidence that my sister and I are ruined it is that empty salver out there. No one wants us."

Somehow, Ilford's words from the night before came haunting

forward. *Those chits won't be able to set one foot outside your uncle's door by tomorrow morning.*

Now it was Tuck's turn to sag down onto the settee beside her, for suddenly he couldn't breathe.

If he didn't win this wager, he'd be forced to . . .

He didn't want to think of what he would be forced to do.

This time Charleton would cut him off. Blame him for this entire mess, just as Miss Tempest was now.

As they rightly ought, but no matter that, he had to find a way to make this right.

For his sake. He stole a glance over at the lady beside him and listened as she went on about all the things that she'd never have now—a decent match, a good home—and knew that this wager was a far more dangerous bramble than he'd first realized.

What the devil did he know about making a lady into a Diamond? Or finding decent prospects? Or even good Society?

All things he'd avoided his entire adult life.

Now all these idols of decorum, these altars of propriety, everything she desired, was suddenly everything he must deliver unto her.

He drew a steadying breath, and, like the good gambler he was (most days), he rallied his wits, his steely nerve.

"All is not lost, Miss Tempest. Never is," he began, Uncle Hero's words coming out of nowhere. Oh, it was a desperate day indeed when he found himself quoting the Honorable Hero Worth.

Who was a contradiction in every way, starting with his name.

"I don't see how—" she began, then dissolved into another spate of desperate tears. When her handkerchief wouldn't do, she caught hold of his sleeve and dabbed her eyes on it, so distraught she didn't appear to even realize what she was doing.

To his best coat.

In his own state of desperation—after all, this was his only decent coat—Tuck quickly intercepted, pulling his arm away and sounding like the veritable expert on the subject. "My dear Miss

Tempest, London society is terribly fickle—one day you are on the out, and the next an Original, a Diamond to be desired by one and all."

"A Diamond?" she managed, gulping at the word, a tiny flicker in her eyes, or was it just the last bit of tears still welled up there, threatening to spill over? In either case, that little spark in her eyes—as tiny and easily extinguishable as it might be— also appeared capable of illuminating even the dark reaches of his heart—the one usually blotted out by a brandy bottle.

For suddenly, that small sparkle, dare he call it "hope," brought with it more memories from the night before.

Good heavens, she could be rather fetching—when one ignored the red nose and blotchy complexion.

Or the mess on his sleeve.

Her eyes, though, puffy and red-rimmed, held something else. Determination.

"Miss Tempest, you must have faith," he told her, getting to his feet. "You must trust me—"

"Trust you?" Her astonishment all but filled the room.

Well, she might have a point in that regard . . . But this was a new beginning for both of them.

"Yes, you must trust me. Because I can put this all to rights. I can." He tried to sound far more confident than he felt.

After all, he only had two bloody weeks to pull off this miracle.

"I don't see how—"

"Believe me, you will," he promised, catching hold of her hand. "Let me be your guide. You came to London to be matched, did you not?"

"Well, yes—" she managed.

"And it would be a shame to have to leave when you've just arrived—"

She gave a shuddering sigh. "I haven't even received all the dresses I ordered."

"No!" He shook his head. "And how pretty you will look wearing them."

"There is no point to any of it, for I cannot dance," she told him.

"Is that all?" Tuck waved his hand at this. "'Tis nothing a good London dancing master can't fix in an afternoon."

The lady shook her head and glanced away, but not before he saw the skepticism in her expression.

"Come now, Miss Tempest," he said softly, coaxing her to look up at him. "Will you allow me the privilege of helping you find your perfect match?"

All Lavinia had ever desired was wrapped up in those three words: *your perfect match.*

How many times had she envisioned how that would happen: She'd be wearing a pale muslin of the latest stare—much as she had worn last night. She be in the middle of a crowded assembly, surrounded by elegant and suitable guests.

And then *he* would come forward, pressing for an introduction. A delighted glow in his eyes over being granted admission into her inner circle. And then he'd take her hand and ask, nay, plead for a dance.

Of course that was usually when her splendid imaginings would come to a screeching halt.

For the dancing part was always a bit of a sticking point.

But still, she knew she would know *he was the one* because his touch would send shivers down her spine.

Wasn't that always how it happened? At least it always did in the *Miss Darby* novels.

And yet, it was happening now.

Which there was no way it could or should be. For here she was, wearing her oldest day gown, and good heavens, whatever must she look like with all these tears? Yet, she was shivering. As she had last night at Almack's.

When *this man* had held her hand.

No, it couldn't be. Somehow he'd managed to draw her to her feet so she stood before him.

She glanced down to where her fingers were held hostage by Mr. Rowland, and she found herself transported back to the night before.

To that moment when his hand closed around hers, sending those traitorous tendrils of desire through her, leaving her utterly witless.

Exactly like she felt right now. This warmth, this dizzy desire to let him stay so improperly close had made no sense then and even now left the very frosty "No thank you, sir," she should be issuing as a useless lump at the back of her throat.

Now there was no denying as she looked down at Mr. Rowland's hand, the one still holding hers, that *his* warmth, *his* charm, or whatever it was that that twinkle in his eye did to her wits left her considering his daft offer of assistance.

And it was daft. As daft as her desire to step a little closer to this devilish rake before her.

"No," she managed, pushing the word past her lips like one might a barrow full of rocks over a steep hill. Besides, she wasn't so naive that she didn't know, as Lady Essex always said, "a girl once ruined is forever so." And so she told him. "What you are offering is impossible."

There was nothing Alaster Rowland could do to help her.

Besides, you've already done enough, she thought, her earlier ire rising yet again, pulling her gaze back toward the vase.

Which didn't look at all as priceless as Mr. Rowland avowed.

"Hardly impossible," he replied, reaching and turning her so her back was to the vase. "Anything can happen. It's London, after all."

London. The very word still gave her shivers—much like his touch.

"Yes, it is," she said, pulling away and returning to her spot on the settee. She settled in, smoothing out her skirts. "Though I thought London would be glorious." She paused for a moment. "Not like this."

Mr. Rowland found his spot beside her once again, catching

up her hands and holding them until she dared to look up at him. "And it will be, if only you consign yourself to my care."

His care. The care of a known rake. A veritable knave.

"Certainly not!" She snatched her hands back even as those dangerous and wretchedly treacherous shivers began to wile their way up her arms.

"A hastily made declaration, Miss Tempest, if ever there was one. You haven't even heard me out."

"I don't need to. You have a very distinct reputation, Mr. Rowland."

She slanted a glance at his handsome features and knew her list would need immediate amending.

> *Proper Rule No. 84. A lady must always be wary of a man who is far too handsome.*

"A reputation? I suppose I might," he offered. One might suspect, proudly. "But I am also welcome everywhere . . . most days."

"Most days?" she echoed. "What sort of day is today?"

He glanced around. "I will admit today might not be my best example. For both of us, I imagine."

"Best example? I was ruined last night."

He shook his head. "Ruined? Hardly." He got up from the settee and took a step back from her. "Ruined, Miss Tempest, usually involves something far more intimate than a clumsy display and a bit of gossip."

Intimate.

Whyever had he used that word? For it whispered about inside her. It was like the mischief that swirled about him. Ever so tempting.

And decidedly not proper.

Alaster Rowland was one of those charmingly handsome devils that Lady Essex had always railed against at every meeting of the Society for the Temperance and Improvement of Kempton.

Handsome men can spare a glance at a lady and have her . . .

And have her what? Lavinia had always wanted to ask, for unfortunately, Lady Essex's admonishments had never gone much further.

But suddenly Lavinia's imagination seemed capable of filling in the rest. For all she could see was a shadowy room. Coals glowing in the grate.

And a gown falling to the carpet. Not a pale muslin. But a dark velvet. The sort of gown she'd always secretly desired. In blue. And not just any blue. But a rich, deep midnight blue. And his hands . . . his lips . . .

Lavinia pressed her lips together and tried to tamp down the heat growing inside her.

What was it about this man that had her wavering so easily from her very proper list?

"Come now, Miss Tempest," he was saying, "you mustn't let one unfortunate night dictate your entire life."

She shook her head, more to push out the last remnants of those very improper, passionate thoughts, but Mr. Rowland mistook her, and continued on, pressing his point. "I'll make you the talk of the Town, Miss Tempest," he added as if he could sense her hesitation, her concerns.

"You already did, Mr. Rowland," she shot back with the same sort of regal air she'd heard Lady Essex use on more than one occasion.

Though instead of cowing the man, it did quite the opposite.

He grinned at her. And it wasn't with humor.

Rather approval.

"Then let's give them something else to say," he said, once again holding out his hand for her.

CHAPTER 3

The next morning, Lavinia awoke to the sound of the front door-bell jangling away. She sat up, her eyes fluttering open with a single hope.

Perhaps Mr. Rowland had been correct. The terrible silence that had filled the house the previous day, had been, as he'd predicted, merely a temporary setback.

There was mail arriving. And mail meant invitations. She heaved a sigh of relief.

And for all Mr. Rowland had offered to make her the talk of the Town, she'd been entirely correct to refuse his offer of assistance.

Thankfully, Lord Charleton had come in the library right as she'd finished her refusal, and she'd been able to make her escape before she got caught up once again by Mr. Rowland's charm.

She was beginning to suspect that Lord Charleton's heir could talk a lady into anything.

Proper Rule No. 7. A lady is always mindful of the company she keeps.

Yes, that was exactly the proper rule she needed to remember. That, and it would be nigh on impossible to find the right gentleman if the wrong one was constantly in her company.

And if ever there was a wrong gentleman, it was Mr. Alaster Rowland.

Downstairs, the bell jangled yet again, and Lavinia smiled as she scrambled out of bed and dressed quickly. On the window sill, her sister's horrid cat, Hannibal, watched with his one eye. Thinking better of awakening Louisa, she left her sister sleeping and went downstairs to discover what glad tidings awaited them, Hannibal trailing in her wake.

Indeed, as she got to the salver in the foyer, it held several notes, including one addressed to her.

Miss Lavinia Tempest.

The confident masculine scrawl stopped her.

She'd never received a note from a man before. She glanced down at Hannibal, who was sitting looking up at her with his usual expression of disdain. Biting her lip, she reached out and snatched the missive off the top of the tidy pile.

Even as her fingers held it, she felt a shiver run up her arm. "No," she chided herself. Mr. Rowland wasn't *the one.* And this note couldn't be from him. Even if it had her heart pounding in an odd fashion.

Besides, he wouldn't dare, not after she'd been most plain with him.

No, Mr. Rowland. I want no part in your mad plans.

Glancing around, she considered marching it to the nearest hearth and consigning the note to the flames, but her curiosity—that dreadful trait that always saw her run headlong into the path of trouble—prodded at her to slide her finger under the plain wax seal.

And yes, apparently Mr. Rowland did dare.

Miss Tempest, before you toss this note atop the coals, please hear me out.

"I thought I already had," she muttered. And bother, how had he known that she'd most likely toss his note in the grate?

Experience, most likely.

Now that you've had some time to consider my offer . . .

Time to consider? Of all the arrogant, presumptuous . . .

I have the most excellent news—I have secured the services of one of London's finest dancing masters, Monsieur Ponthieux.

Lavinia's lips pressed together as she remembered what Mr. Rowland had said the day before.

Nothing a good London dancing master can't fix in an afternoon.

A dancing master, indeed!

Yet, he'd never heard Mrs. Bagley-Butterton declare there wasn't a fleet of such fellows who could help her or Louisa manage a simple reel.

With a sigh, and despite her better judgment, she continued reading.

Meet me in front of Wakefield's house at half past eleven. Rowland.

That was it? Just like that. Meet him? After she'd made it quite clear she wanted nothing to do with him.

She had a much better notion, carrying the note like one of Hannibal's recent kills between two fingers and out in front of her, she was nearly to the dining room when she heard Lord Charleton say from within, "Amy, it can hardly be as bad as all that."

Lavinia stopped just before the door. Hannibal glanced up, then shook his tail a bit, stalking off toward the kitchen.

Apparently, eavesdropping was beneath even him.

Yet Lavinia couldn't help herself, for even now, Lady Aveley let out a long sigh. "It's worse," she declared. "There hasn't been a single invitation arrive since . . ."

Their chaperone didn't need to finish the sentence. Lavinia knew exactly the defining moment in this conversation.

Since Almack's.

She glanced over her shoulder at the salver. How could everything be so dire when there were invitations arriving.

Then a deep, dark cloud of realization settled around her.

What if all these incoming missives weren't invitations?

Lavinia sagged against the wall beside the door. And while she knew she shouldn't listen in and that she should decidedly announce her presence, when Lady Aveley next spoke, Lavinia found herself rooted in place.

"All these others have written to withdraw their previous invitations."

Lavinia's mouth fell open. For as much as she had suspected the truth, hearing it was far worse.

"Withdrawn!" Bless Lord Charleton, his outrage filled the word with furious indignation.

There was a flutter of papers shifting over one another as Lady Aveley was most likely sorting through the earlier arrivals. "Oh, they all have proper excuses, but underlining each of them is the very real fact that they don't want Louisa and Lavinia in attendance."

"Of all the utter—" the baron sputtered.

"Yes, it is," Lady Aveley hastened to say, if only to cut off Lord Charleton's ire. "But it is exactly as I feared."

"Worse, by the sounds of it," he conceded. "Stubborn, dreadful cats."

Lady Aveley agreed with a sad sigh of resignation.

"What of that soiree you mentioned?" the baron asked.

Again there was a sorting of paper, then a pause. "I don't see anything here. Oh, my, Lady Gourley hasn't written." There was no small measure of shock to her announcement.

"Excellent," Lord Charleton declared. "The girls will attend, then all of London shall see them in a proper light, see them dance, and they'll know they aren't—"

. . . see them dance . . .

Those words hit Lavinia with the force of a brick. *All of London.* To witness her next stumbling foray onto a dance floor. Suddenly, her chest began to tighten and the air left the room.

Oh, good heavens. Dance? She couldn't. Not again.

"Dear me, I don't see how. Not unless they—" Lady Aveley's words came to an abrupt halt.

"They what?" Charleton prompted.

"Shine," Lady Aveley said simply.

Oh, that was all. Lavinia shook her head. The only times she'd ever shone, mayhem had followed. And she didn't suppose that was what Lady Aveley meant.

She glanced down at the note in her hand. It teased at her with as much mischief and temptation as the author's eyes might.

Now that you've had some time to consider . . .

Lavinia shook her head, folding the note shut tight. No, she couldn't. She wouldn't.

"Bless their hearts," their kind chaperone continued, "but they are not their mother. Where Kitty could command a room by just entering, her daughters are . . . are . . ."

"I hardly think comparing them to their mother is the right place to begin," the baron told her. "After all, this is more Kitty's fault than anyone else's. Bother her and her licentious inclinations."

"My lord!" Lady Aveley scolded—though even to Lavinia's ears the rebuke was half-hearted. "I have said for years her reputation was only sullied after . . ."

"Yes, well, 'after' then. But you can't argue that 'after' she turned into the worst sort of light skirt. And damn Ilford and the rest of his ilk—they'll go out of their way to nose about that old scandal, if only for their own amusement."

Lavinia could all but see the sad shake of Lady Aveley's head as she said, "I had hoped no one would remember that part. That they'd see those girls and only remember Kitty in her earlier years, when she was so happy, so very much in love."

"It's unfortunate she couldn't have stayed that way, but she made her choices and those are all that matter now. All that anyone will remember." He sighed, and his chair creaked as he shifted about. "And they probably wouldn't have remembered any of it, given how the two of them seem proper enough . . ."

"Yes, and they might have had a chance, if only . . . if only . . ."

"If only Lavinia—it was Lavinia, wasn't it? I have a devil of a time telling them apart. Whichever one it was, it didn't help matters when she tumbled into Pomfrey like a drunken opera dancer."

"Oh, Charleton, don't be vulgar."

"But you do agree."

It wasn't a question, rather a statement. One that, most notably, Lady Aveley didn't argue with.

"There is always their dowries," the baron offered. "Sir Ambrose has written me with their arrangements—demmed generous ones. If it was known what they will come with—"

Lavinia shuddered. Oh, good heavens, to be bartered off like a shipment of damaged silks. The horror of it was too much to bear, and she nearly blurted out a heartwrenching "No!" but Lady Aveley beat her to the punch.

"Don't you dare, Charleton," she scolded. "That will only bring out every wretch and rogue in London. The sort who won't have a care for their welfare . . . their future happiness."

There was a catch to the lady's voice that suggested she was speaking from experience.

Lavinia turned from the door, breakfast forgotten, all her hopes for a London Season now utterly dashed.

And it wasn't the revelations about her mother that had her heartsick. She had heard all those rumors and the associated gossip since she was nine.

Poor Sir Ambrose . . . left to raise her *daughters.*

That was why Lavinia had spent every free moment trying her best to be worthy of Papa's great sacrifice.

Her fingers curled around the note she still held clutched in her hand.

She looked down at it and—much to her horror—found herself considering his offer.

A London dancing master. What if this monsieur could untangle her feet? Teach her left from right?

What if she went to the Gourley ball and managed to give

the *ton* something else to chatter about, as Mr. Rowland had promised?

Lavinia glanced at the clock across the foyer and realized she hadn't much time to find out.

Rushing upstairs to the room she shared with Louisa, she found her sister sitting by the window, staring over at Lord Wakefield's shuttered house.

"Has he stirred?" she asked, knowing her sister had grown fond of the bellicose man across the lane.

"Not unless you count tossing Hannibal into the garden."

"Some might call that a good deed," she replied, hoping to tease a smile from Louisa.

But none was forthcoming.

Instead, Lavinia caught up her pelisse, plopped her bonnet atop her head and took a quick glance in the mirror. Tucking a stray strand of hair back in place, she noticed one other thing.

Dear heavens, gloves! She'd nearly forgotten.

"Where are you going?" Louisa asked, sitting up and finally taking notice.

"Um, the lending library," Lavinia told her, trying to sound as nonchalant as possible. Tuck's note lay on her dressing table, and she carefully palmed it, then shoved it deep in her reticule.

"Truly?" Louisa turned from the window and looked her up and down, lips pressed together. Part of being twins was that it was nigh on impossible to lie to the other. "Where are you really going?"

"To the library, as I said," Lavinia huffed, all the while tamping down the guilt that reared its ugly head over telling a falsehood.

"Is Nan going with you?"

A maid? Oh, bother. The last thing Lavinia needed was Nan trailing along. But still . . .

"Of course," she replied, not looking at her sister. "Actually, if you must know—" she began, trying to find some way to redirect Louisa's scrutiny, "I recalled in Harriet's recent letter that she'd found a new *Miss Darby* novel, and I thought I might see if they had a copy—for you—um, to lift your spirits."

Louisa rushed over and hugged her sister. "Oh, you are too kind. Perhaps I'll come with you," she said, looking around the room for her bonnet. "That would definitely lift my spirits."

Oh, no! Louisa's joining her would never do. She could just imagine what her sister would say to an illicit outing with Mr. Rowland.

Lavinia looked around and saw her sister's hat lying on the bed, half concealed by the coverlet, and quickly flipped the covering over to hide it completely while Louisa continued her fruitless search in the clothes press.

"Aren't you worried where Hannibal might be?" Lavinia asked, making a grand show of looking out the window. "I don't see him in the garden. I do hope he isn't . . ."

Oh, there was a laundry list of things Hannibal could be doing, so Lavinia just let the entirety of that miserable cat's misdoings rise between them like an unholy specter.

Louisa turned from her search. "He's disappeared again? Oh, no. I suppose I should see that he isn't causing more mischief."

"More?" Lavinia asked, though in the next breath wished she hadn't.

"He left something in Lord Charleton's bedchamber yesterday," her sister confessed. "And one of the maids quit because she said Hannibal has an 'evil eye.'" She shook her head. "Have you ever heard such nonsense? Is it his fault he has only one eye?" She fussed a bit, coming to look out the window at the empty garden, her lips pursing in despair.

Lavinia shook her head. "Louisa, you cannot let Hannibal be the cause of any more problems. Lord Charleton has been nothing but kind. You must keep that beast in check."

Her sister paused, then sighed. "Yes, I suppose you are right."

Suppose? Oh, dear heavens, Lavinia loved her sister, but Louisa had a terrible blind spot when it came to that devil-cat of hers.

"'A good guest next becomes an inconvenience to her host,'" Lavinia reminded her, quoting one of her most worn and beloved volumes, *A Lady's Essential and Thorough Guide to Deportment and Genteel Manners*. But still feeling guilty about her deception, she added, "If I don't find this new *Miss Darby* book at the lending library, we can make an afternoon of it—perhaps try some bookshops—how does that sound?"

"Perfectly delightful! You are the dearest sister ever," Louisa told her, giving her another impromptu hug and leaving quickly to find her cat.

Lavinia certainly didn't feel like the dearest sister ever. More like Hannibal's acolyte.

But she had made this mess they were in, and she was determined to fix it all. Even though Louisa claimed to have no desire to marry, in the last few weeks, her sister's heart had proven vulnerable in the form of one Viscount Wakefield, and Lavinia couldn't let Louisa's chance at happiness be ruined.

Even if it meant making a deal with the very devil.

Taking a deep breath, she made her way quietly out of the house and to the spot around the corner, the one Mr. Rowland had designated for their assignation.

Much to her shock, he was there waiting for her—she hadn't thought him the prompt and orderly sort.

Except he wasn't waiting. He'd picked up the reins and the carriage was rolling forward.

Lavinia hurried. "Mr. Rowland, please don't go. Not yet. Not without me."

He turned around, and when he spotted her, he pulled the horses to a stop, his features spreading into a warm smile.

"No maid, Miss Tempest?" he remarked as he climbed down from his carriage. "How daring of you. Then again, it lessens the chances we will be discovered."

Good heavens, he made it sound like they were organizing an illicit tryst. What if someone overheard him?

Besides, in Kempton, ladies often walked unaccompanied even though strictly speaking it wasn't perfectly proper.

But a rebellious part of Lavinia had never liked having some chatty maid trailing behind her.

"Mr. Rowland—" she began as she tried to catch her breath. "You mustn't say such things."

He stepped up on the curb in front of her. "Say what?" he asked, his eyes sparkling with feigned innocence.

Not that she had an answer, for suddenly he quite took her breath away. She hadn't realized he was that tall. Or so very broad in the shoulders. And with his grand beaver hat, his coat brushed just so, and his boots polished, he cut a rakishly grand figure.

Save for one thing.

"You're about to lose that button," she said, pointing at the bottom of his coat.

He glanced down. "Suppose I am. Will have to tell Falshaw." He smiled at her and continued, "I have to admit I didn't think you would come. Was about to drive away."

Lavinia took another baleful glance at the woeful state of his button, hanging as it were by a thread—he was going to lose it, knowledge that pricked at her thrifty and proper sensibilities—but then another part of her realized what he was going on about.

"—just a minor setback. After Monsieur Ponthieux has worked his magic, you shall be the most celebrated lady in London. Invitations to every ball and soiree—"

Invitations. And suddenly the entirety of it burst down on her, and tears welled up in her eyes.

Oh, she was far too sensible for tears, especially tears two days in a row, and tried to wipe them away, but in the blink of an eye, she was a veritable watering pot, as if a chorus of doubt taunted her.

. . . they are not their mother . . .

. . . drunken opera dancer . . .

. . . hasn't been a single invitation . . .

"Oh, good Lord, not this again," she heard Mr. Rowland mutter even as he pressed a handkerchief into her grasp.

"I fear I might ruin it," she managed.

"Better that than my sleeve," he replied.

In between gulps, the entire story spilled out. Lord Charleton and Lady Aveley's doubts—that there wasn't a hope or prayer that she and her sister could repair the damage that had been wrought. And when she'd come to the end, she hiccuped and tried to find the right words to tell him that no matter if he'd found the finest dancing master in all of London, nothing could save her, he caught hold of his handkerchief—more like rescued it—and dabbed at a few stray tears, then tipped her chin up so she looked up at him.

"But you missed the one bit that ought to give you hope, Miss Tempest," he said softly, a warm light in his brown eyes.

"Which is?" she asked between hiccups and sniffs. She couldn't think of anything about this entire situation that might lend her any bit of hope.

"My uncle had the right of it," he assured her.

"That I appeared at Almack's like a drunken opera dancer?"

Mr. Rowland scoffed at that. "Oh, bother my uncle and his opera dancers. When you attend that soiree tomorrow night, and if you look as fetching and pretty as you do this morning, all of London will see how wrong they've been. One session with Monsieur Ponthieux and you shall be ready to dazzle even the most discerning old cat."

"I don't know—"

"What will it hurt?" he asked. "Besides, standing here is giving the entire neighborhood something to discuss." He nodded toward one of the viscount's windows.

She looked up and found two small noses pressed to the panes. Bits and Bobs. Louisa had mentioned that the cook she'd hired for the viscount had brought along her orphaned niece and nephew. Lavinia braved a smile up at them, and one of them waved back.

Looking at the stately residence, she felt a pang of jealousy, for this was exactly what she wanted. A house of her own. A loving husband. A respectable life. She hadn't come this far—all the way to London—not to find her heart's desire.

What had he asked her yesterday? Was she going to let one ill-fated night dictate the rest of her life?

Lavinia took a deep breath. That would never do.

Dashing away the last of her regrets, she let a familiar, stubborn determination straighten up her spine.

Just because her carefully laid plans had come to a crashing halt—quite literally—that didn't mean she couldn't make allowances for complications.

Like Alaster Rowland? a wry voice teased.

She ignored it. She had no place for rakes and knaves, save if they could help her, as this one had promised to do.

"Then a dancing lesson it is," she told him as he handed her up into his carriage.

Yes, Lavinia was quite determined. That is until Mr. Rowland retrieved the reins, and the horses stepped forward in a lively fashion.

If ever there was a headlong course onto the path of trouble, this had to be it.

She caught hold of the rail beside her and hung on, even as she glanced over her shoulder at the retreating vision of Lord Charleton's proper and respectable London town house.

Wherein she was safe. Chaperoned. In good company.

"Oh, dear, I fear I am violating half a dozen rules at the very least," she said.

"Rules?"

"Exactly," she replied. "This isn't proper."

"It probably isn't, but I'm no expert."

She didn't think he would be. But she was.

They wheeled around a corner and drove into the busy thoroughfare. "No, I am quite convinced this isn't proper."

"Are you certain?"

"Yes. I keep a list, you know."

"A l-l-list?" He sort of stammered this out, glancing quickly at her, then back at the road before him.

"Yes," she said, folding her hands primly on her lap. "A list of Proper Qualities."

"Truly, a list?"

"Well, yes. How else would one maintain a proper and respectably ordered life without one?"

He shrugged. "You have me there. Though I will admit, I haven't really given such a prospect much thought."

"You ought to," she suggested. "For if you had, you wouldn't have suggested this outing."

"And yet here you are."

"A moment of weakness and desperation I fear."

He slanted a glance at her. "Perhaps you should regard your list as more of a lofty pinnacle to which to aspire rather than a bridle on your life."

"Abandon my list?" She shook her head at the very notion. "I could never—"

And yet, she had, as he'd so astutely pointed out. "Normally, I adhere to it to the letter."

"Truly, to the letter?" This seemed to amuse him.

"Of course." She tried not to be affronted.

"Then what's changed?"

What a ridiculous question. "You entered my life," she replied as tartly as she could—without being overly rude.

Proper Rule No. 37. Rudeness is not a proper answer to a ridiculous question. But a pert reply may be warranted in extreme cases.

"Me?" He laughed, a rich deep timbre that sent shivers down her spine. "I have a way of doing that."

"A way of—" she stammered, a bit of outrage simmering up. He needn't sound so proud over the fact. "What? Unraveling order?"

He grinned at her. "Perhaps, Miss Tempest, your list is holding you back."

Holding her back? Of all the ridiculous notions. Excellent manners and an adherence to propriety were the very backbone of good society.

But he wasn't done yet. "Take your dancing," he pointed out. "Or your professed lack of skill therein. If you weren't so overly concerned about getting it right, appearing the proper miss, you might find you enjoy it."

"Enjoy it?" This time Lavinia shook her head adamantly. "Dancing is hardly meant to be enjoyed."

"Yes, well, perhaps you should add that to your list," he offered.

She tucked her nose in the air. "I don't believe you quite understand the concept of a list of Proper Qualities."

"Apparently not." And with that, he continued to drive, but the strained silence between them was even worse than listening to his nonsensical notions of propriety.

"Lord Charleton was your father's older brother, and you are Lord Charleton's heir," she said, for a conversation on titles and inheritance could hardly be steered in the wrong direction.

Then again, this was Mr. Rowland.

"Presumptive heir," he corrected. "My uncle could very well set up a nursery, and I'd be on the outs."

"Lord Charleton is far too old to marry again," she pointed out. Not to mention starting up a nursery.

She looked anywhere but at Mr. Rowland. For here was a subject that was definitely not proper.

"One can never assume," he told her, wading into those murky waters without a care in the world. "Besides, with my uncle and Lady Aveley thrown together again . . . you never know. They could rekindle their former romance and . . ." He waggled his brows.

Lavinia's mouth fell open. "Your uncle and Lady Aveley? Oh, do not be ridiculous. Why your uncle is . . . and Lady Aveley is . . ." She waited for him to recant his statement, but when his only reply was to whistle a tune that she would have bet her pin money had a very ribald set of words to go along with it, she continued on. "I can't believe they were ever . . . why they haven't shown the least . . ."

He looked over at her, eyes sparkling wickedly. "You really don't know?"

"No! And I still don't believe it's true," she told him—for it put their entire living arrangements in jeopardy. Lady Aveley had moved into Lord Charleton's house for the sole purpose of being a chaperone for her and Louisa.

She was a mature widow. A respectable lady. Hardly the type to be carrying on some illicit . . .

Lavinia didn't even want to venture down *that* path.

Mr. Rowland must have it wrong.

"How like Aunt Charleton—your godmother—to toss them together again—since she was the one who stole my uncle's affections away from Lady Aveley in the first place. Of course, she wasn't Lady Aveley then. She married the marquess shortly after my uncle abandoned her." He glanced over at her and must have seen the skepticism in her eyes. "Ask her if you don't believe me."

"Ask Lady Aveley if Lord Charleton threw her over for another?" Lavinia shook her head. "That would be beyond the pale."

"Is that according to your list?"

"That doesn't even need to be written down. Every lady knows that rule."

"Still, you might want to write it down when you get back to my uncle's," he said. Once he'd stolen a glance at her and saw the look of utter disbelief on her face, he added, "Then again, maybe not."

"Definitely not," she said. Taking a deep breath, she decided to take the conversation in a different direction. "What exactly does one do when they are a presumptive heir?"

"Good God!" he barked out. "As little as possible."

Her lips pursed together.

"What?" he asked.

"Well, I understand that as a gentleman you can't very well take up a trade—"

"Thank heavens for that."

"But don't you want to be useful?" A notion that had been drummed into every young lady in Kempton from the time they had been old enough to help fill a basket for the elderly spinsters in their village.

"I'm being useful now, aren't I?"

His teasing left Lavinia rather unsettled. She glanced away. "Yes, but I have to imagine you don't make a habit of rescuing ladies."

She had hoped it would work as a set down.

"No," he said, bellowing out a laugh. "I'm usually the one they need rescuing from."

"That is hardly something to be proud about."

"It isn't my only skill," he informed her, but his lips twitched with amusement.

If he thought she was going to ask him to elaborate, he was entirely wrong.

Unfortunately, he seemed determined to press the matter. "Don't I strike you as an industrious and respectable—"

"No."

He turned to face her. "That's it, just 'no'? Just like that? You didn't even hesitate." His brow arched upward slightly. "Nor did I finish, I might add."

"I think the answer was self-evident."

He shook his head and went back to minding his driving. "You are an opinionated handful."

"A regular harridan," she suggested before she could stop herself.

His head spun toward her. "How did you—" He looked her up and down. "That was a private conversation."

It had been. A few days earlier, Viscount Wakefield and Mr. Rowland had been summoned to Lord Charleton's study. And Lavinia had caught Louisa with her ear to the door.

And when she'd pressed hers there as well—well, even a proper lady was subject to a moment of unrestrained curiosity from time to time—she had heard the viscount distinctly telling Mr. Rowland that she and her sister were destined to be a pair of harridans.

"Is eavesdropping on your list of 'Proper Qualities'?" he asked. Now his nose tipped a bit in the air.

"Certainly not," she replied, nonetheless feeling a rosy heat rising in her cheeks.

"But you seem to be prone to it—"

"I am hardly—"

"Were you invited to listen to Lady Aveley and my uncle this morning?"

"Well, no—"

"And was the door closed on the study when you decided to press your ear to it?"

"You know it was." This conversation was hardly going as she'd planned. They were supposed to be discussing his failings as a gentleman.

Not hers as a proper lady.

Mr. Rowland's reply was to pick up whistling that jaunty tune again.

They continued through the streets, and Lavinia made a determined effort to enjoy the sights of London. Not that she would probably enjoy them for long. For if everything that Lord Charleton and Lady Aveley said this morning was true, there was little hope of restoring her and Louisa to society's good graces.

Especially given that now their mother's old scandal was being bandied about.

It would cast a shadow over all of them—including Lord Charleton and Lady Aveley, and might even taint Mr. Rowland, since he seemed determined to help her.

Lavinia's fingers curled into a hard knot in her lap. "You know about my mother—"

If anything, she was giving him a perfectly good way of bowing out.

"Yes."

She felt, rather than saw, the shrug that went with his answer. "That's it? Just 'yes'?"

He kept his gaze fixed on the road ahead. "What else is there to say?" He heaved a deep breath. "Your mother is not you."

He said it with such force, such finality, that for a moment she held the suspicion that he was talking about someone else.

"Unless, that is—" he added after a few moments.

She found his head cocked as he studied her, and worst, that light of mischief was back in his eyes.

Unless, that is, you are very much like her.

"Hardly!" Lavinia exclaimed, smoothing out her skirt though it didn't need it. "I want a respectable match, with a proper gentleman. I would never throw away . . . Leave behind . . . Be like . . ."

He held up his hand to stave her off. "Yes, yes. Never mind the rest. I can see you aren't."

"Certainly not," she shot back. Never like her. All Lavinia had ever wanted was everything her mother had spurned that day when she'd ridden off from Maplethorpe with her dancing master swain beside her.

Standing all alone in the nursery windows, Lavinia had watched her go, her beloved, beautiful Maman, in her pretty bonnet and gay smiles. Watched her run away, leaving behind the broken-hearted man who had given her everything—including a respectable name when she'd needed it most.

As always, when plagued with memories of her mother, Lavinia found herself decidedly out of sorts.

"Truly, Mr. Rowland, do you think a single dancing lesson can restore my reputation—given that everyone would much rather discuss my mother's sins?"

Tuck glanced over at her. No, he didn't think it would. But he could hardly tell her that.

No, he needed her to believe she could be the rarest, finest Diamond in London. And then, perhaps . . . perhaps . . .

Oh, it was the most desperate wager of his life.

He'd spent the previous afternoon and evening gaining intelligence as to the battle before him. And he'd found out quite quickly he was outgunned and outmanned. Everywhere he went, Ilford had been there before him—or one of Ilford's many sycophants, Lady Blaxhall in particular—stoking the flames of public opinion against the Tempest sisters.

Sadly, their mother's scandal turned out to be the perfect kindling to get every tongue aflame as matrons and gossips and cats rehashed the old tattle.

He hadn't found a single solitary sympathetic ear. And more than a few doors had been shut in his face.

This wager would be his ruin if he didn't find a way to change the Tempest sisters' fortunes. Starting with this one and all her proper notions.

But the very fact that she'd shown up, stopped him from driving away, had been like drawing a queen when one held naught but a six and five in a game of *vingt-et-un*.

Hell, he'd have wagered his boots that his note would most likely end up consigned to the flames. Unread. Unopened.

But when Tuck pulled the carriage up in front of the building where his aforementioned and most infamous Monsieur Ponthieux lived, he knew the real battle was just beginning as she glanced around their surroundings, her nose wrinkling noticeably.

Unfortunately the lady wasn't such a country rube that she didn't recognize that this wasn't the finest of addresses.

"I thought you said he was in demand," she remarked as she climbed down from the carriage. "That he is famous."

He could hardly tell her that Ponthieux was more infamous than famous, and then again, for the amount he could drink and his many paramours, but nonetheless, the fellow had once been the finest dancing master in Paris.

Or so the old fraud claimed.

"He is," Tuck told her, then looked around, seeing the place through her eyes. "Miss Tempest, do not let his address concern you. He is an eccentric. And French."

He tried to make it sound as if that explained everything. Including the man's choice of residence.

Which also happened to be Tuck's. Which is how he'd met Ponthieux. The man had the rooms one floor below Tuck.

Nor was he about to tell her that. Even he didn't need a list of Proper Qualities to know that bringing her here—to the same building where he had his bachelor rooms—was in itself beyond the pale, but he was desperate.

"French sensibilities are not the same as yours and mine," he continued, as if this too was common knowledge. He could only hope that she hadn't met all that many French and therefore could not argue the point.

"If you say so—" she began, her feet still planted on the sidewalk and not moving up the stairs.

"He's a rare master," Tuck continued to proclaim. He knew he sounded like some traveling peddler extolling the quality of his questionable goods, but right now, Ponthieux was his only hope. "That he even has an opening to extend to you is a miracle— given the extraordinary demands on his time. Why, it's said he taught at Versailles."

"And yet the French were not impressed enough to let their poor queen keep her head, were they?" she pointed out, looking at him with those very piercing eyes of hers.

How was it that when this chit looked at him like that, he had the strangest compulsion to stand up a bit straighter. Not even his dragon of an aunt, the indomitable Lady Craske, could get him to do that.

That, and her wit surprised him. He'd had it in his mind that she was naught but a simple country miss—and yet today, the lady who had walked out of his uncle's town house was anything but.

Oh, she wasn't wearing the first stare of fashion, but it was her eyes, blue and deep, that told him she could gather much in just a glance.

And now that glance was fixed on him.

Tuck stilled, his hand halfway to the latch on the door, and he realized that perhaps he might have overplayed his hand.

So he resorted to the one thing he knew very well: charm.

"Think of how lovely you will look making a pretty turn about Lady Gourley's ballroom tomorrow night, proving every ugly rumor untrue. The gossips will be utterly shamed, apologetic for mistaking the matter."

His words, the pretty picture he painted seemed to do the trick, for her lips turned up slightly, a sign of hope, before she thought better of such woolgathering and pursed them back together.

"And you think *this* dancing master can teach me?" she asked, skepticism lacing every word.

Her question pricked at Tuck.

Like finding one's powder damp in the middle of the battle-field.

What if his eccentric, half-mad French neighbor couldn't teach her to dance? Instill in her that bit of poise and confidence that she seemed to lack. He could tell her she was the prettiest little minx he'd met in ages, but she wouldn't believe him.

She needed that confidence to live in her bones.

Besides, the one thing he did remember very clearly from that fateful night was being a bit charmed by her.

So truly, how bad could her dancing be?

CHAPTER 4

A half hour later, Tuck had his answer.

"Mam'selle can't dance."

Tuck glanced up at Monsieur Ponthieux. "Whatever do you mean, 'mam'selle can't dance'?"

The Frenchman made an inelegant snort. "Have we not been in the same room, monsieur?"

Sadly, they had. And as much as he wanted to argue with Ponthieux's opinion, he didn't bother wasting his breath.

To his credit, Ponthieux had transformed his large room to make it appear that he did still teach dancing, and had even dusted off the old pianoforte in the corner, which Tuck had been enlisted to play.

It all appeared a legitimate and perfectly respectable enterprise.

Save for the moment Miss Tempest took her first step. Right onto poor Ponthieux's foot.

After she'd trod all over the Frenchman's toes, he'd fetched a compatriot from across the hall to be her partner. After all, the man was a portrait painter by trade, and being hobbled by Miss Tempest wouldn't ruin his livelihood.

"I could teach a pug to do a better reel." Ponthieux flinched as once again the lady on the dance floor went one way and her partner the other.

"Now see here, Ponthieux, you go too far," Tuck told him, but the dancing master wasn't listening, for he had waded back out into the fray, his staff pounding into the floor. Reluctantly, Tuck drew his hands back from the keys.

"*Non! Non! Non!* Mademoiselle, you must go left!"

She glanced over her right shoulder. "This isn't my left?"

Monsieur buried his face in his hands, while his neighbor took the free moment to shake out his bruised and battered feet. Tuck saw his future seeping into the deepest reaches of the Thames—where they would most likely find his body.

If anyone bothered to look.

"Oh, dear," Miss Tempest said, biting at her lower lip as she gazed down at her boots, both of which must seem like her left. She glanced over at Tuck and tried to smile.

"Perhaps if she could just manage a few basic steps," Tuck suggested. "If you were to help her—"

Ponthieux wheeled around on Tuck, and stalking forward, he whispered, "Do I tell you what to wager on?"

"Uh, no." He glanced over toward Miss Tempest to ensure she hadn't heard.

"Exactly. If I did, you wouldn't be in these straits." He threw up his hands and stomped around in a circle, muttering in French about English foolery and ungainly misses.

Tuck began to play again to drown him out, leaving Miss Tempest's partner no choice but to dance with her anew.

But not for long.

"Mademoiselle! That is not your left."

Tuck stopped playing, and a trembling sort of silence filled the room.

The ill-fated painter spoke first. In rapid French. Tuck followed most of it, and wished he couldn't.

Miss Tempest's French appeared to equal her dancing, so thankfully she couldn't understand a word. "Whatever is he saying?"

Before Ponthieux could translate, Tuck got up from the pianoforte, clapping as he came forward. "Monsieur's assistant was just
comparing your dancing to a summer cloud—light and airy."

The other two men in the room gaped at him as if he'd
gone mad.

"Such tremendous improvement," he continued, taking her
hand and spinning her about.

At the same time, minding his boots.

She came to a bit of stumbling halt. "Truly?"

And when she looked up at him, something in her starry eyes
struck him.

Miss Tempest actually believed him.

And then he remembered what the Honorable liked to say in
these situations—*a belief always trumps the truth.*

Of course the Honorable had been teaching him how to bluff
his way through a tough card game, yet Tuck had learned from
more than one bad hand that sometimes everyone else at the table
could be convinced to believe the same lie.

He shot a hot glance over at Ponthieux, enough so to change
the man's dirge-like tune.

"Yes, yes, mam'selle, that last turn was most elegant," the
dancing master managed with smooth grace.

The painter was not as well-mannered and continued to
grumble.

Thankfully, in French.

"Here, allow me," Tuck said, taking her into his arms.

His arm curved around her waist, his palm coming to rest
at her hip, while he caught hold of her hand, letting their palms
meet.

Then, to his shock, something rare happened.

If he was willing to believe in such things, it was as if the stars
in her eyes had fallen around them, illuminating something long
lost and forgotten.

Perhaps it was just the way their hands fit together—like a kiss,
lips barely touching and yet . . .

Tuck stilled. For this wasn't just the sweet twinkling notes of longing that Ponthieux was finding as he warmed up his fingers at the pianoforte, nor was it because he hadn't held a woman in a long time.

He'd held this very one the other night at Almack's.

But until now, the memory of that dance had been relegated into a haze of recollections—after all, he'd been a bit squiffy.

Oh, demmit, he'd been drunk.

Yet suddenly his body remembered, and some other part of him recalled that first time he'd held her.

They'd danced. His eyes widened a bit as he remembered. Good God, they had!

They *had* danced. Perfectly. Elegantly.

With Lavinia Tempest back in his arms, he remembered. And as he looked down at the lady, this time sober as a judge, he realized a very fine distinction: at Almack's he hadn't doubted her.

In fact, he'd been a bit taken aback by his uncle's country miss.

So as monsieur's fingers swiftly found a lively German tune on the pianoforte, Tuck grinned at the lady in his arms and began to dance.

Because he believed.

Lavinia didn't need to speak French to know her dancing lesson was a dismal failure. One look at the poor fellow pressed into service to act as her partner, limping as he was now to the nearest chair, told the sad truth.

She was an utter failure when it came to dancing. That hadn't stopped Mr. Rowland from putting his best foot—literally speaking—forward and praising her attempts. It was kind of him, but she knew a Banbury tale when she heard one.

Yet she had to give Mr. Rowland his due, for here he was, queuing up for his turn. Which she supposed only confirmed his reputation as a foolhardy gambler.

Hadn't he witnessed enough carnage over the last half hour?

Apparently not, for he nodded to monsieur to play—and the Frenchman did, striking up a sweeping tune, much to her horror. He expected her to dance to *that*?

Perhaps this was Ponthieux's revenge on Mr. Rowland.

All Lavinia could do was close her eyes.

But not for long. As Rowland took her in his arms, she shivered. Then panicked a bit, remembering that a proper lady would not find the way he held her, the way his fingers curled around hers so . . . so . . . *wonderful*.

Worse, she tried to still her hammering heart by taking a deep breath, only to find her senses teased with a masculine cologne. Bay rum. Something a bit smoky. A note of danger that had her lashes fluttering open and finding Alaster Rowland gazing down at her with a bewildered expression.

"What?" she asked, for certainly she hadn't trod on him.

At least not yet.

"Nothing," he replied after a few moments, glancing over her shoulder at Monsieur Ponthieux as if he'd just remembered something he'd distinctly forgotten. Then he whispered into her ear, "Just follow me, Livy," and they began to move.

Follow me. Those words lured her. Entwined her.

She should be outraged that he'd used such gross familiarity with her. Livy, indeed! No one had ever called her that.

Why of all the impertinent, scandalous, rakish . . .

And then Lavinia looked up and realized she was doing exactly as he'd asked. Following him.

When Mr. Rowland whirled, she whirled. When he stepped one way, she went as well.

Follow me.

Good gracious heavens, somehow this man had once again worked his knavish enchantment on her, and she was dancing.

"I cannot believe this," she managed as he whirled her about the floor—and nothing toppled over in her wake.

"Whyever not?" he asked, smiling. "I remember distinctly your doing much the same the other night."

"But before—" She glanced over at her previous partner, who was still rubbing his toes.

"My poor performance at the pianoforte," Mr. Rowland told her with a dismissive wave of his hand.

Lavinia wasn't that foolish. "Hardly. You actually play quite well."

"You needn't sound so surprised."

"You don't strike me as a man with the patience to learn to play."

"It was my aunt. Your godmother. She insisted I learn. Said it would give me something civilized to do." He glanced away at the memory. "No one naysayed her. She had a charming way about her that had one agreeing to the most outlandish suggestions."

That explained much as to why Lord Charleton and Lady Aveley had both agreed to honor Lady Charleton's dying wish to see her goddaughters brought out in society—even knowing of the likely backlash they might encounter.

"Still, my previous attempts can hardly be blamed on your playing," she insisted.

He leaned down and whispered in her ear, "Then obviously you only require the right partner to make you the most captivating woman in the room."

Her first thought was to tartly tell him that she was the only woman in the room, but she couldn't do it. Not when she was rather fixed on the other words he'd uttered.

. . . *the right partner* . . .

Even made with an airy jest, they sent her heart racing. For certainly, Mr. Rowland wasn't the right partner. He just couldn't be.

Yet when he made one more grand turn, the entire world blurred around her as she found herself gazing up at his lips—parted just slightly and so very perfect.

Her lips opened as if seeking something, air perhaps, for he seemed to surround her when he held her. Protected her from herself.

Worse, when he looked down at her, his eyes all dark and smoky, a terribly, desperate shiver ran through her.

No, more of a *desire*. To be held so much closer. To be kissed. Thoroughly.

Kissed?

She blinked and realized that the music had stopped. Had been for a few seconds.

"Well done, Miss Tempest," he whispered again, right into the shell of her ear, and his breath teased at her much as his eyes did. "If you look as pretty as you do this very moment, there isn't a man in London who will be able to resist you."

Then he squeezed her fingers and let go of her.

When he did, she stumbled just a little bit, as if suddenly set adrift atop a restless sea.

But the only thing restless, tossing about like hungry waves, was her heart.

Oh, no, no, no! She wanted to protest, much as Monsieur had earlier. *No.*

She turned her back to Mr. Rowland and did her best to compose herself, remind herself that she was determined to find a respectable partner in life. One with a solid inheritance or, better still, already in possession of his title and good fortune.

Still, when she looked over her shoulder at Mr. Rowland, speaking as he was in low tones to Monsieur Ponthieux, she had to admit it wouldn't be so bad if her future spouse was also a bit charming, with a smile that sent a breathless sense of not knowing what was going to happen next, only the knowledge that when it did, it would leave one dizzy.

She shivered and glanced around for her pelisse. The room was warm—but suddenly she had a terrible chill of foreboding. Not to mention she had better sense than this.

No, she was just dizzy from the dancing. That was it. Obviously, discovering that she could dance without causing property or personal damage had rattled her more than she realized.

That was all it was. Exactly.

Yet, as she took one more sidelong glance at Mr. Rowland, her hand, the one he'd held far too long to be proper, tingled, her fingers reaching out for something . . .

And she couldn't help wondering what would happen if he held her thusly again?

"Will you come to Lady Gourley's soiree tomorrow night?" Lavinia asked as Mr. Rowland stopped the carriage at the corner near Lord Charleton's house.

"But of course," Mr. Rowland replied, tying off the ribbons and getting out to help her down. When his fingers took hold of hers, Lavinia was transported right back to the moment when they'd begun to dance. "I wouldn't miss your triumph for the world, Livy."

"You mustn't call me that," she told him, trying to sound as an expert in propriety might.

Yet . . . when he used such easy familiarity, when he took her hand in his to help her down, delicious shivers ran up her arm.

And it was his words, the intimacy with which he spoke. Teasing her. Testing her.

This is what passion feels like. Isn't it wonderful? Isn't it just like dancing?

Lavinia wanted to lean in, as she had when they had come to a stop in the middle of Ponthieux's dance floor. She wanted to dance again. She wanted to feel his hand curl around waist, holding her just so and . . .

She tugged her hand out of his grasp and took a step back. Not daring to look up at his handsome features, she reminded herself as to why she'd come to London.

Proper Rule No. 2. If a lady desires to contract a proper and respectable match, she will comport herself with nothing less than the strictest manners and unassailable propriety. At all times.

That last bit she'd underlined for good reason. And now she knew why.

Mr. Rowland was everything that was *not* on her list.

Rakish. Devil-may-care. Flirtatious.

"Until tomorrow, Livy?" he ventured.

"Yes, tomorrow night," she said, taking another step back from him and ignoring his familiar ways.

"Save a dance for me," he told me, making an elegant bow, then a cheeky wink as if it were all a grand lark. Then he returned to his carriage with all the same confidence that had been penned into his note.

Which, she realized with some consternation, had worked to lure her earlier.

Well, it wasn't going to work ever again, she vowed, as he made a jaunty salute once he'd regained his seat, then drove off.

Yet for some reason, she couldn't find the compulsion to leave the spot where she stood until he was out of sight.

But once the last bit of the carriage turned the corner, she took a deep breath, for she felt a bit out of sorts. Almost empty.

And she couldn't see why. She could dance. She'd done it. And now, all she had to do was prove to all of London that she wasn't as cowhanded as everyone presumed. That she was entirely proper and respectable.

With a renewed air of confidence and purpose, Lavinia strode into Lord Charleton's house.

"*R-r-r-eow. Hissss.*"

She glanced down to find Hannibal sitting in the middle of the foyer like an aged, battle-scarred sentry.

"Oh, shoo, you dreadful wretch," Lavinia told him, waving her parasol at him.

Not that such a flimsy piece of female whimsy would arouse anything less than disdain in such a creature as Hannibal. "*R—r-r-eow,*" he snarled back. And added another *hiss* for good measure.

Lavinia had the sense that the cat knew exactly where and

what she'd been about and wasn't afraid to tell everyone her secret.

"*R-r-r-r—o-eow!*"

It was the sort of clamor that should bring half the household down to investigate. Save most of Lord Charleton's staff held an unholy terror of being in the same room as Louisa's cat.

Not that Lavinia blamed them.

"Shush, you dreadful patch of mange," she told him.

Hannibal hardly took any of this as an insult. She would swear the horrible fleabag actually preened.

"Move," she told him, nudging him with her boot.

The cat took offense at this, swiping at her and letting out another indecent yowl, but to her relief, he seemed to realize that he wasn't going to win this battle and finally stalked off, with what was left of his tail in the air and a swagger to his steps that reminded her a bit of Mr. Rowland.

She'd probably find a dead rat on her pillow in retribution for her offense, but it wouldn't be the first time.

"Oh, dear Lavinia—it is you, right?" Lady Aveley called down from the upper landing. She was still learning how to tell the two sisters apart.

"Yes, my lady."

"Excellent. Louisa told me you went to the lending library." It was more of an inquiry than a statement, and Lavinia, who had never been overly good at falsehoods shifted uneasily.

"Yes, my lady," she replied.

Lady Aveley came down the stairs. "You didn't find anything to your liking?"

I did, came a reply straight out of her heart, and the memory of Mr. Rowland's lips just inches from her own left her feeling a bit dizzy.

"No," she said back, a bit more sharply than she intended. "That is, they didn't have the book I was looking for. I had thought to get the new *Miss Darby* novel for Louisa."

"Ahh, how kind of you," Lady Aveley replied as she got to

the first landing. "Well, while you were out, the new gowns you ordered arrived. Louisa is trying hers on right now."

"Oh, how perfect," Lavinia declared, hurrying forward. Truly her fortunes were lining up. She'd learned to dance today, and now she had the most elegant gown in the world to wear.

Tomorrow night would be a triumph.

She hurried past her chaperone, but as she passed Lady Aveley, the matron stopped her.

"Lavinia, I know that things are different in the country, but in London, you mustn't go out without a maid. A lady must always safeguard her virtue and her reputation. You never know what sort of rogue you might encounter out there."

And from down below, Hannibal had his own opinion on the matter. "*R-r-reow.*"

Which rather sounded like, *I told you so.*

CHAPTER 5

"We shall restore our good names tonight, Louisa," Lavinia told her twin, giving her hand a squeeze. They stood at the doorway of Lady Gourley's town house and Louisa, just seconds earlier, had come to an abrupt halt. "Just you see," she reassured her.

Certainly, Lavinia wanted to prove all the old gossipy cats wrong, almost as much as she wanted to feel as she had in Tuck's arms.

No, make that *Mr. Rowland's* arms.

No more than it was proper for him to call her "Livy"—of all the ridiculous presumption—would it be for her to think of him as "Tuck."

Yet when he had whispered with such intimacy into her ear . . . Oh, heavens, it made her heart flutter ever so oddly.

Much as it had when she'd been dancing with him. Of course, then her heart's unlikely rhythm was understandable—for she'd been dancing—perfectly and elegantly. As if she could fly.

And Tuck had done that. For her.

She tamped down a small smile and looked over at her sister.

"This is a bad idea," Louisa said in a mulish tone.

"Nonsense, my dear," Lord Charleton told her, prodding the two of them forward. "You're borrowing trouble."

Lavinia couldn't agree more. She had tried to buoy her sister's spirits, much as Mr. Rowland had done hers, but Louisa was resolved.

They were ruined, and there was nothing to be done about it.

Though Lavinia suspected that if Viscount Wakefield had poked his nose out his front door instead of remaining holed up in his house like a troll under a bridge, her sister's opinion might differ.

"Yes, indeed," Lady Aveley agreed—even if it was a little too readily and a far sight too brightly. "The *ton* is a fickle lot. I'm sure everything has been forgotten."

Lavinia nodded in agreement, for hadn't Tuck said much the same thing? He had been right about her dancing, and she held every hope he'd be right about this.

After all, he'd promised.

Besides, her new gown and slippers were entirely proper. She checked that off her list. Lady Gourley was a well-regarded hostess, and her kindness would go far. Check and double-check. Finally, she could dance, and certainly that would help when everyone saw she wasn't some cowhanded country miss without a notion of proper behavior.

Check and check again.

Lavinia's buoyed spirits carried her right up to the entryway of Lady Gourley's ballroom, where she reveled for all of two ticks of the large clock behind her in her impending success. Yet in those moments, everything changed.

Their appearance stopped nearly every conversation. The only ones still nattering on were the old cats in the wings who were too nearsighted and/or deaf to realize something scandalous was bubbling up.

Noses rose in the air, backs turned toward them, and any interest in their arrival was shuttered against as quickly as the sudden arrival of a bitterly cold northern gust.

"Oh, heavens, no," Lady Aveley muttered under her breath as she looked across the crowded room—which seemed to be parting into two camps—neither of which appeared to hold a single ally.

At the end of the room stood Lord Ilford. The marquess raised his glass to their party, a wicked smile on his lips.

"What the devil is he about?" Lord Charleton muttered. "I won't stand for it."

The baron began to move forward, a determined and ruthless set to his jaw, but Lady Aveley caught him by the arm and anchored him in place, all the while smiling. "Whatever you are considering, be mindful of the consequences, my lord."

Her words were enough to get the baron to look away from the object of his ire to the stormy waters surrounding them.

He muttered something under his breath, then, like Lady Aveley, pasted a jovial expression on his face and went forward to greet their hostess as if nothing were amiss. "Lady Gourley, it has been far too long. My dear Isobel always spoke so affectionately of you and your social prowess. I can see she wasn't wrong, but then again we both know she rarely, if ever, was."

Lady Gourley opened her mouth, her lips fluttering like the fan in her hand, as if she couldn't quite find the words to reply.

Lord Charleton, for all his bluff and bluster, showed a side of himself that Lavinia had yet to see. All charm, he drew Lady Gourley's hand to his lips and spoke in a confidential tone. "I knew I could count on Isobel's dearest friends to see her god-daughters through their first Season."

Yet his charm was for naught. Nor was his call to old friendships and loyalties. Lady Gourley's brow furrowed like a deep, thick field, and her jaw finally stopped wavering. "Lord Charleton, there seems to be some mistake. I sent a note." The lady flicked a hard, determined glance toward the ballroom doors.

Her meaning could not have been any clearer. *Please see yourselves out.*

Hopes and dreams, Lavinia discovered, were not unlike champagne. For every bubble that rises in that effervescent scramble ends its wayward ascent with a sharp pop, lost forever into the ether.

Frantically, her gaze searched for Tuck. He would make this right.

He'd promised.

"A note? I fear it did not reach my notice," Lord Charleton was saying, managing to look positively bewildered, as if he had no idea why she would have to send a note. He glanced over his shoulder at Lady Aveley, who gave a little shake of her head as if she was equally perplexed.

Lavinia had to hand it to them, they were quite a pair of thespians. Playing willful ignorance, as if that would erase the dire sentence being cast down upon them.

"Come my dear girls, it appears the dancing is about to begin," Lord Charleton announced walking past an open-mouthed Lady Gourley. "Perhaps some punch beforehand." He took a quick glance back. "My compliments, madame. It appears you've managed quite the crush."

"Well, we've stormed the gates," Louisa said in a practical sense. "But have you any notion how we are to win the war when we are surrounded by enemies on all sides?"

And enemies they were. Lady Blaxhall strolled past them, and the widow eyed them both with cool disdain. She whispered something to her companion, and the pair laughed, all while looking at the sisters.

"Jealous, spiteful woman," Lord Charleton muttered. "If ever there is a silver lining, it is that Wakefield is well rid of her."

"She certainly holds no affection for us," Louisa said. "Then again, it appears no one does."

Rather than admit that her sister was right, Lavinia glanced around looking for a friendly, familiar face—perhaps Harriet, or Daphne, or even Tabitha, their dear friends from Kempton who had come to London and made glorious matches.

Taking one more searching glance, Lavinia was loathe to admit that this second time she was looking for a particular gentleman. But any sign of his tall frame and easy smile could not be found.

Worse, the deeper they waded into room, the more fans that snapped shut as they came past, the more backs that were turned toward them, and Lavinia's heart fluttered with a different refrain.

For every *snap* left her feeling torn asunder, because she knew all too well that even if her knight-errant arrived, not even he could save the day.

Tuck arrived at Lady Gourley's late.

Which wasn't unusual for him, but this time he found himself hurrying up the steps in a state of anticipation.

He'd even left what might have been a profitable card game to be here.

To see her.

Well, not to see *her*. Precisely.

But then he envisioned her as she'd looked at Ponthieux's, a bit disheveled, a few stray strands of her dark hair tumbling down and her eyes—those demmed blue eyes of hers—sparkling with a rare delight.

He'd lived too long in London, amongst the jaded hearts of the *ton*, and had all but forgotten what joy looked like.

Pure, innocent joy. She'd quite startled him senseless.

And he was loath to admit, but that was what he feared he would find when he entered Lady Gourley's ballroom.

Lavinia Tempest gazing up at some lordling or gentleman with the same magically enchanting light in her eyes.

He shook his head and told himself he was being ridiculous— because that very sight was the object of his desires—no, not desire, per se—make that the object of his future interests.

She'd catch the eye of every bachelor in search of a wife and have a crowd around her after the first reel.

And then he'd be well on his way to seeing Ilford's ill-made wager wipe away his outstanding debts.

He might even be able to pay Falshaw's back wages. Or at the very least a good portion of them.

All because that winsome little chit had found her footing.

Tuck grinned. For all her claims that she couldn't dance, she'd been light as a feather in his arms, entirely enchanting with that delighted smile on her lips, her flashing eyes bright with joy.

All in all, Tuck felt as if his recent spate of bad luck had turned a corner.

He handed his hat and coat to the butler and strode confidently into the ballroom. A crush greeted him, but almost immediately he was greeted by a familiar voice.

"Surprised to see you here, Rowland."

He turned to find Lord Rimswell leaning against the wall. "Why is that, Brody?"

Having known the man since childhood, Tuck had a hard time thinking of him as Rimswell, the title Brody's older brother had held for a number of years.

"Ilford will be delighted. He'll have someone else to crow over." Brody pushed off the wall and came to stand beside Tuck.

He didn't like the way that sounded. "How so?"

"You know the man. Always relishes a chance to rub salt in a wound. Especially when he smells blood."

"Blood? Hardly." Tuck rose and straightened his shoulders. "I'll have you know I've set this all to rights. Ilford hasn't a chance—"

"I wouldn't be so sure," Brody told him, nodding toward the far wall.

Tuck first looked about the dance floor, confident he would see a certain mahogany-haired beauty being squired by some viscount or other gentleman of impeccable breeding.

But Miss Tempest was nowhere to be found. Not there, at least. Then he looked at Brody again and found the man's gaze fixed on a point farther away.

The spot usually reserved for those unfortunate souls who had managed to gain entrance to the hallowed halls of the *ton* but really didn't belong. If anything, they filled the wings and room to give it that essential volume that enabled a hostess to cry out the next day in feigned dismay that her soiree or ball or musicale was a "dreadful crush."

In truth, the wallflowers were key to her triumph. Thus the invitations.

So Tuck looked beyond the Diamonds and Originals. Beyond the Corinthians and those esteemed few who held sway. Beyond that to the fringes.

And there to his horror stood his uncle and his charges.

Not just pressed to the wall, but in a far, lonely corner.

"No one will pay them any heed," Brody remarked. "Ilford has done his damnedest to see that they are given the cut direct."

"No," Tuck said, the word writhing in this gut.

Then he looked again and found the marquess holding court in the middle of the room, several matrons fawning about him, while the usual gossips and Tulips fluttered about, close at hand to catch any bit of the man's viperous words.

"I'll kill him."

Brody shrugged. "Won't help them," he replied. Then he was more succinct. "Won't help you."

Tuck opened his mouth to argue the point, but the younger man cut him off. "You take on Ilford directly, you will be all but admitting defeat. Then again, since no one is likely to invite them anywhere—certainly not after tonight—the Tempest sisters are finished." He looked over at Tuck. "As are you, I'd imagine."

Tuck tried to breathe. Tried to quell the panic growing inside his chest. But . . . but . . .

"Too bad," Brody remarked. "They are a fetching pair."

Tuck latched onto this like a drowning man being tossed a rope. "Then you go ask one of them to dance."

But Brody was already shaking his head. "I'm not sacrificing my new boots for your sorry wager. You dance with one of them."

"Can't," Tuck told him.

"Can't?"

He shook his head. "Would look like I was desperate to save my wager. Or worse, my uncle had put me up to it. Wouldn't do either of them any favors. Poor girls. They are truly rather innocent in all this."

Brody groaned even as he took another glance in the direction of the Tempest sisters, his all-too-obvious honorable nature taking over.

Just as Tuck had hoped.

"You did call them 'fetching,'" he prodded.

That was all the nudge that was needed. "Demmit!" the young baron cursed. "You'll owe me, Rowland." But he set off across the ballroom, willing to sacrifice the gloss on his boots for a higher calling.

His spot was soon filled by none other than Ilford himself.

"Sad about your uncle's pretty goddaughters," the marquess said in a friendly tone as if they were old friends.

"Sadder still that you've gone and ruined their chances," Tuck replied.

"Ruined their chances, improved my own," the man said in an offhanded manner. "Either way, I come out the winner."

"I wouldn't be so sure, Ilford." Tuck glanced at the dark bruise that marred the marquess's face from where Viscount Wakefield had planted an excellent facer the other night.

And how Tuck wished he'd been the one to land the blow.

And Ilford knew it. "That sounds like a threat, *Mr.* Rowland."

Tuck knew what the man was fishing for—another disturbance, another chance to bring down shame on the Tempest sisters. Still, that didn't stop his fists from tightening.

"I would think you wouldn't want to provoke another scene, Ilford. You'll hardly be welcome anywhere if you keep ending up on the floor," Tuck replied as nonchalantly as he could. "People will think you've taken to drink. Or that you simply belong down there—beneath all our feet."

"I cannot wait to see you ruined," Ilford said, his narrow lips curling. Then he glanced downward, where Tuck's fists were balled tight, and he must have thought better of provoking him, for he smugly retreated, much to Tuck's relief.

For another few taunts, and Tuck wouldn't have been willing to walk the path of restraint. For Brody had been right—he had a tightrope to walk at the moment. One that had to carry him through this wager. Him and *her*.

Miss Tempest. When he looked in her direction all he saw was a girl with a smile that was a tad too bright. Oh, her nose was turned up just so, all defiance and pride, but her smile and her eyes told the real story.

Her heart was breaking.

Damn.

Tuck shoved back a sudden tide of guilt and fury. This was all his fault.

Well, that and Piers. If his cousin hadn't hauled off and tapped Ilford's claret in front of half the *ton*, the man wouldn't have been spouting such foul words at White's, and Tuck wouldn't have made such a foolish wager.

And . . . and . . . and . . .

All water under the bridge, as his Uncle Hero would say. *Spilt milk can't be tucked back into the cup.* Or his most astute maxim:

Don't wager what you can't afford or can't outrun.

But there it was. Tuck was mired up to his neck, and he had to find a way out. As he'd done so many times before.

Yet this time . . . oh, bother, something about this time was all different. Tangled him up in ways he couldn't fathom.

Where before he wouldn't have cared if he'd slighted a debutante, left a lady in some bit of scandal—after all, that was what he did, at least according to his uncle and a good part of society, but this time . . .

Everything was different. He was different.

And right now he didn't have time to consider just exactly what was wrong with him.

Certainly, all of it would be righted when the Right Honorable Lord Rimswell asked Miss Lavinia Tempest to dance. Brody couldn't be more respectable if he tried, and his good opinion would go a long way.

Then to his horror, Brody's progress came to a halt by none other than Lady Rimswell.

The formidable old dowager had her only remaining child in a death grip and appeared to be giving him a thorough wigging.

And worse, it appeared his Uncle Charleton was making a quiet retreat toward a side door.

They were giving up?

No! No! No! Tuck wanted to shout. And yet there they went. One by one, slipping out the side door. The last one to go was Miss Tempest.

His Miss Tempest. *Livy, stop*, he wanted to tell her.

By chance, she took one last glance back at the ballroom. She didn't see him, but he saw the bright glisten of tears in her eyes. And he could well imagine the recrimination there as well.

You promised . . .

"Whoever is it that you seek, Lord Rimswell?"

"Pardon?" Brody glanced up. He had just divested himself of his mother and now yet another was blocking his path. He did his best to be polite. "Ah, Miss Stratton. How are you this evening?"

"Quite well, not that you would notice," Roselie replied sharply.

"How can I not? You look as fetching as ever," he replied, all the while glancing up and toward the spot where Lord Charleton and the Tempest sisters had been.

Had, being the point of the matter. Oh, where the devil had they gone?

"Spanish coin, my lord," Roselie told him with a dismissive flutter of her hand. "But then again, you haven't answered me. Who are you looking for?"

"Miss Tempest," he told her. "Damn this bloody crush. It is nigh on impossible to find anyone. I can't see her anywhere."

"They've left," Roselie told him.

"Gone?" he sputtered.

"Yes, that's usually what 'left' means."

Tart-tongued little minx. She was the devil's own. No wonder she was on her—what—fourth Season?

To his relief, Tuck came wandering up and joined them. "Cousin," he said with a short bow to Roselie.

The lady snorted. "Don't cousin me, you rogue. We are hardly related."

Tuck turned to Brody. "What the devil happened? You lost them!"

"My mother," he had to admit—though he didn't have to stand in shame for long, for it became apparent that Miss Stratton wasn't going to be left out of the conversation.

Much to Brody's relief she turned her razor's wit directly at Rowland. "Whatever are you doing here? Isn't it bad enough what you did to that poor gel at Almack's?"

Tuck took her chiding in stride. "For someone who is hardly related to me, you certainly take a great interest in my business."

"Have you not thought of how this will reflect on our uncle?"

At this, Roselie's adversary grinned. "So you do admit that we have a relation in common."

The youngest Stratton barely even flinched and went right back to lobbing her artillery at her "cousin." "You've ruined her, Tuck, what with that dreadful display at Almack's and now some vulgar wager with Ilford. Really! You've gone and done the Tempest sisters no favors."

Brody felt as if he was watching a tennis match, for here was Tuck firing back, unwilling to concede defeat.

"I can hardly be blamed for Almack's. I wasn't in my right mind—"

"As if you ever are," she returned with alacrity.

Tuck was enough of a gentleman to ignore her insult. "—when I spied Piers having that row with Ilford, I merely came to his aid. I don't see why you aren't—" Then he stopped, for it appeared he'd finally caught up with what she'd said before. "Just a moment. Whatever do you mean by some 'vulgar wager'?"

Roselie looked from him to Brody and back again. Huffing with dismay at their feigned expressions of innocence, she shook her head. "I know you wagered Ilford an ungodly sum of money

that the Tempest sisters could be raised above their current misfortunes—"

"That's putting it politely," Brody muttered.

"I'm a lady," Roselie reminded him. "As I was saying, you bet
those girls would be Originals before a fortnight was out, did you
not, Tuck?"

Unthinking, Brody rose to his defense. "I say, Roselie, however do you know what happens at White's? Those are private
matters."

Then Brody realized what he'd done—he'd unwittingly just
confirmed the truth for the intrepid chit.

For while Roselie might favor her beautiful mother in looks,
she had her father's keen wits. Woe be it to the man who tangled
with her.

Which right now was him.

"Private!" She scoffed again at both of them as if she'd never
met such fools. "There is nothing private in London."

"Oh, I wouldn't say that," Brody muttered, glancing around the
ballroom and feeling finally that he had the upper hand over her.

For there were some matters she wasn't party to. And never
would be.

"And what would you have me do, coz, since you have taken
such a keen interest in all this?" Tuck asked.

"See that you don't lose," she told him. "I despise that horrid
man. It would be nice to see him get his due."

Meaning Ilford.

"I took Lavinia to see a dancing master. Thought that might
help matters," Tuck confessed, then looked as if he wished he hadn't,
for Roselie's brows drew up in a most expressive manner of shock.
"Yes, well, she was quite improved by the end of the lesson."

"A dancing lesson? That was your solution?" Roselie looked
like Lord Howers when he was about to give some new agent at
the Home Office a devil of a time for failing to notice a critical
detail. "And how would that solve anything? Especially given the
gossip about their mother."

Before Tuck could answer, she stopped him by raising her gloved hand. "Tuck Rowland, you know as well as I, probably more so than anyone in this room given the number of ladies you've led astray, that a girl with scandal attached to her name is not forgiven, not like you devil-may-care rogues always are."

Brody would have agreed with her, but that hardly seemed sporting to leave Rowland out hanging.

"No, it is going to take more than a mere dancing lesson to help the Tempest sisters," Roselie told them both. "But that might be a good pretext to begin with—" Her jaw set, and her gaze took on a faraway expression that suggested she was plotting something more. "If this is to be done properly, you both will need my help."

"Me?" Brody sputtered.

"Us?" Tuck echoed, shaking his head.

"Yes. The two of you. Something should be done. Besides, I do believe Piers rather fancies Miss Louisa. And if that particular Miss Tempest makes my brother happy, then *we* need to set this all to rights." She looked them both over while they gaped at her in return. Poking her finger into Tuck's chest, she started with him. "You were his best friend. You two were inseparable. And whatever happened between the two of you, I don't care, I only want to see my brother happy again."

"I hardly see how I—" Brody began, hoping to find a way to extract himself from this encroaching tangle.

"Oh, you will help as well, Baron Rimswell," she replied. "You owe your brother as much. Piers admired Poldie, called him the finest man who ever lived. You can't let that memory be tarnished. Wouldn't be honorable."

Oh, yes, if there was anyone who could pluck at the very heart of something, it was Miss Roselie Stratton. No polite mincing of words or dancing around a subject.

Brody worked his jaw back and forth in consternation because for the life of him he couldn't come up with a single protest. Not one that didn't leave him sounding like a complete ass.

"Bring Miss Tempest around Monday afternoon," Roselie was telling Tuck.

"Which one?" Tuck had the temerity to ask.

"Well, certainly not the one Piers fancies," she told him without missing a beat. "He's probably still a pretty fair shot."

Oh, yes, nothing escaped Roselie.

Then she continued, "Maman is always out on Monday afternoons, so I'll have Herr Fuchs sent round. He's a regular martinet, but if anyone can put the right foot where it belongs, it is Herr Fuchs." She paused for a breath and continued like a general snapping out orders. "Besides, I must get to know her if I am to help her. We haven't much time." Her brow arched at Tuck as if he should have made his wager with far more than just a fortnight in which to bring about a miracle. "In the meantime, cousin, you owe that girl an apology."

"I—I hardly—" Tuck began.

"Don't argue with me," she told him. "Tomorrow. Apologize to her. Flowers are in order as well." She stopped and looked him up and down. "Well, what are you waiting for? You are hardly helping matters standing around here feeding the gossips. Off with you."

And so dismissed, Tuck made a hasty bow and departed.

Brody wished with all his heart he could do the same, but he couldn't for the life of him think of a good excuse.

Nor did it seem that Roselie was done with him. "You've spent the entire evening searching the room for some lady. Who is she?"

He straightened up and looked anywhere but at the lady beside him. "I have no idea what you mean."

She snorted again. "At balls, from your box at the theater, even at Almack's, you spend your evenings searching for someone. I just would like to know who is this paragon you seek. Perhaps I can help you find her."

He continued to feign disinterest. "You've always had the devil's own imagination, Miss Stratton," he told her, folding his arms

over his chest and tipping his nose in the air. "There is no mysterious lady."

"So now I'm Miss Stratton? My dear Lord Rimswell, there
was a time you always called me Roselie, you even for a time
called me Peach—though I've forgetton why."

"Because you would tattle on me," he replied. "That, and you
hated it."

"Oh, I did hate it, but Peach would be a vast improvement
over the stuffy, horrid way you say 'Miss Stratton.' You make me
feel a hundred and five. As if we were never friends, and we were,
friends. Good friends. And the one thing I do recall is that we
never told each other falsehoods." Roselie rocked on the heels of
her slippers. "So who is she, this woman whom you seek?"

"There is no one, Peach," he told her, smiling slightly.

If he thought he'd gained the upper hand, he'd forgotten that
this was Roselie.

She smirked up at him. "Then again, perhaps I've mistaken
you entirely. Tell me, is it a gentleman you seek?"

Oh, yes, that was enough to topple him from his imperious stance. Brody's head nearly spun off his neck, and his mouth
dropped open at the very suggestion.

"Certainly not—" he sputtered out. And after a moment of
consideration, his brows furrowed. "You shouldn't know about
such things."

"And yet, I do," she replied with a smug confidence. "You
would be amazed at what I've learned over the course of three
Seasons, Lord Rimswell. And whom I know." She began to saunter away, but a few steps into her departure, she looked over her
shoulder at him. "When you are ready to find her, Brody, let me
know. I'd be more than happy to help."

That will never happen, Brody would have liked to tell her as she
waded into the crowd.

Mostly because there was a singular problem with his search.

He didn't know who the lady was.

CHAPTER 6

The next morning, sitting in the pew of St. George's Church, Lavinia prayed silently that an errant mail coach would run down Lord Charleton's heir with all due haste.

Now perhaps that wasn't the most charitable of thoughts to be having on a Sunday morning, but considering her recent fortunes, Lavinia didn't think she had much more to lose.

Besides, how could he not have kept his promise?

Save a dance for me.

Bah! He could have had them all given the complete debacle Lady Gourley's soiree had turned into—that is if he'd bothered to show up.

"Wretched man," she muttered absently, which only served to gain her a reproving glance from Louisa.

Lavinia looked around to see if anyone else had noticed, but the lofty congregation at St. George's was either too busy gossiping or had already decided to just ignore their party outright. Not even church had turned out to be a safe haven from the *ton's* scorn.

But Lady Aveley would have no wallowing over the previous night's stunning failure.

None whatsoever.

She'd had them summoned early, chided their maids to see that they were scrubbed, properly dressed, then as one united household they'd come to St. George's.

"They can say what they like," Lady Aveley told them as they crossed the street, "but you are proper young ladies, and proper ladies are above reproach."

Lavinia found St. George's a far cry from their small but beloved St. Edmond's, the ancient Norman relic of a church back in Kempton. She didn't know why the high-backed pews leading up to the large open nave, and the grand stained glass over the altar surprised her—everything about London was done on such a grand scale.

Lord Charleton's pew sat halfway up the aisle, leaving them seated amid the same heartless, mean-spirited gossipy creatures who had uncharitably given them the cut direct the previous evening.

"Pious cats," the baron had remarked as he waited for the ladies to take their places.

"None of that," Lady Aveley had scolded—though from under her breath.

Oh, heavens! When will the services begin, Lavinia wondered, for sitting here under the scrutiny of every member of the congregation was as insufferable as being on display at Lady Gourley's.

Lady Gourley's. She sighed, filled again with dismay.

If only Mr. Rowland had been there.

Oh, bother, she stopped herself right there and made a vow to put that horrid man from her thoughts, absently reaching for the hymnal and paging through it.

"Do stop fidgeting," Louisa scolded, but Lavinia couldn't help herself. She set aside the hymnal, then thumbed through her prayer book.

Having never been the object of such vicious scorn and derision, she had no idea how she was supposed to act.

Every book she'd ever read on manners and propriety were all about keeping a lady out of ruin.

Not one of them had bothered to pen a chapter on what to do when one was in that state.

Such information would be quite useful, especially given her current circumstances.

On the other side of Louisa, Lady Aveley sat like a serene angel, confident in her place and position, and Lavinia did her best to affect the same pose, but at the exact the moment she'd managed the set of her shoulders and a faint smile on her lips, an eruption of whispers came rushing toward them from the back of the church.

Oh, not again, she silently moaned, but then realized everyone had stopped looking at them and had fixed their collective gazes on the back of the church.

Either the services were about to begin, or someone with a more scandalous nature had arrived.

Having her second uncharitable thought of the morning, she rather hoped it was the latter.

The whispers hardly even abated as the organ wheezed to life, filling the church with the first hints that the services were about to begin.

Then a great shadow fell directly down their pew, and Lavinia shivered, as if something had just stepped upon her grave, and when she glanced up, almost immediately her mouth fell open.

Mr. Rowland.

"Am I late?" he asked, coming in without an invitation. "Terribly sorry," he murmured as he passed in front of his uncle, then Lady Aveley. "Yes, if you don't mind," he told Louisa as he continued by her, stepping over her skirt and finally continuing past Lavinia to wedge himself into the last bit of space at the end of the pew. He wiggled into place, as the rest of them adjusted their seating to allow him room.

Lady Aveley looked as pleased as she might to find a snake at her feet. She nudged Lord Charleton, a move that said one thing all too clearly, *Do something.*

Lord Charleton glanced down at his heir and shrugged, as if

having his ne'er-do-well nephew at church was hardly worth his notice.

Tuck, no make that Mr. Rowland, Lavinia corrected, leaned over and whispered, "'Allo, Livy."

Lavinia was still trying to recover from the shock of his arrival, but something else struck her. "How do you know I am Lavinia?"

For it usually took strangers weeks to determine which of them was which.

"I always sit next to the prettiest minx in the room." He grinned. "Especially in church."

"Don't be ridiculous," she told him, brushing aside his compliments. Mostly because his softly whispered words were doing the most improper things to her insides.

Minx, indeed! And inside church, no less.

"Do be forthright, sir. Most people can't tell us apart."

"You seem to forget, I am not most people." His dark, deep eyes fixed their gaze upon her, and his glance teased as if his fingers were brushing her cheek. "And I can tell you apart."

"A lucky guess."

"Hardly. But if you must know—"

"I must."

"I thought you would, Livy. So if you must know, when you turned and looked at me, you were the only one who smiled."

"I did not—"

But she had, and it gave her pause. Oh, not that she had smiled, but that no one else had.

And that Mr. Rowland seemed to expect such treatment. Such dismay. A general lack of welcome at his arrival.

How terribly lonely that must be, and she slanted a glance at him and took a new look at the man beside her.

She who had never been scorned, never been shunned, and now found herself in the role of village pariah. Oh, she was bemoaned for a general lack of grace, but she and Louisa were welcomed because . . . well, because everyone in Kempton was accepted.

But to Mr. Alaster Rowland, such a lamentable status was par for the course.

There was no time to reply—not that she wanted to—for whatever was there to say?

Just then, everyone rose, and the procession began to make its way forward. Worse, now everyone had a fine view of the tall and stately figure of Mr. Alaster Rowland, who, along with the other parishioners, began to sing.

Which, like his playing at the pianoforte, took her aback. For beside her rose a rich baritone, and even more to her amazement, he sang without the hymnal, without any direction, in a clear, deep cadence that carried upward, taking Lavinia's breath away.

When he noticed her beside him, or rather gaping up at him, he took her hymnal, opened it and pointed at the line in the song.

All without missing a single note. And she did her best to join in, but her thoughts had suddenly scattered with the single thought: What the devil is he doing here?

And all spruced up. And shaved. Even his hair was trimmed. Mr. Alaster Rowland looked absolutely proper from head to toe.

Exactly like a gentleman ought. Exactly like the sort of gentleman she had always dreamt of marrying.

Marrying?

Lavinia nearly blurted out an oath but remembered where she was and stopped herself—and thankfully so—for right then the hymn ended, and the reverend, about to start his opening prayer, cast a stern eye over his fluttering flock though even he stumbled a bit as he glanced in their direction.

Lavinia had the distinct impression she was standing next to Lucifer himself, for here was the reverend beginning his prayer with a halting sort of speech, his gaze fixed on their pew as if he were expecting the heavens to open up and smite them all.

"Apparently you don't come to church very often," Lavinia whispered.

"No more than necessary."

No more than necessary? *Harrumph!*

"I would think in your case weekly attendance would be required," she shot back.

Mr. Rowland leaned closer. "What an uncharitable thing to say, Miss Tempest, and in church, no less."

With the prayer finished, everyone sat down, and as Lavinia tried to settle in, she found herself wedged up against Mr. Rowland.

His firm, muscled arm—the same one that had wound around her waist while they had danced—brushing against her own, leaving her with memories that were decidedly not appropriate for church.

Well, perhaps confession.

"Why are you here?" she whispered.

" 'Tis Sunday," he answered, continuing to stare straight ahead. "Where else might a gentleman be?"

Wretched man.

"A proper gentleman attends church on Sunday, does he not? I imagine that is on your list. Number 8 or at the very least, Number 11."

She clenched her teeth together because she couldn't argue that. More so because it was Number 8. But not for long. "And what do you usually do on Sunday morning?"

His angelic expression changed in an instant—his eyes narrowed with wolfish glee, his smile hungry. "Do you really want to know?"

Lavinia couldn't help herself. She shivered. "No. I don't. I doubt it is proper."

"Then don't ask," he told her. After a few moments of feigned interest in the readings, he leaned over. "If you must know, I am here because I promised to help you." He paused, as if measuring each word. "I failed you horribly last night."

Lavinia thought of all the things she'd expected him to say, it certainly wasn't that.

"I owe you an apology."

Nor that. He was apologizing?

"Then why weren't you there?" she blurted out. She blamed her shock that he'd come to, of all things, say he was sorry. Of course now that the cat was out of the bag, she persisted. "Why weren't you there?" she whispered, ignoring a scathing glance from Louisa.

"*I was.*"

Her fingers wound around the edge of the pew, holding on to the only solid thing she could find as she tried to make sense of all this.

He'd been there? He'd seen her humiliation?

For some reason that was worse than if he hadn't bothered to show up.

"As it is, I have enlisted Lord Rimswell and my cousin, Miss Stratton to our cause. I daresay with Roselie's help, we could storm the gates of hell. She's a most intrepid chit."

"She's Lord Wakefield's sister, is she not?"

"Yes," he replied.

"Louisa met her the other night," she recalled, "and said she seems . . . she seems . . ."

"Quite formidable?"

Lavinia nodded. Louisa had described the viscount's youngest sister as a veritable lioness undaunted by her brother's wrath or reputation. "*Fearless*, I believe, is the word she used."

"Then you have the measure of my cousin. She quite scares the boots off of me, but don't ever tell her I said that," he said with a slight shudder. "But mark my words, we need her."

"We?" Lavinia asked. And not for the first time wondering at his insistence in helping her.

"Yes, Livy, we are in this together. I promised."

Yet why had he promised? It was definitely something to puzzle out later.

Her brows furrowed, and if he noticed—which surely he did— he added, "Tomorrow. My cousin requests I bring you round for a visit. I'll pick you up at half past two, just the same as before."

Lavinia was already shaking her head. For countless reasons.

Why she barely knew Miss Stratton and couldn't ask the lady to wade into this mire.

That, and she could hardly continue to jaunt about Mayfair in the company of Tuck Rowland before someone noticed.

Someone always noticed.

"I don't see how——"

As sudden and shocking as his appearance here at St. George's, his fingers wound around hers. Even through her gloves, the warmth of his touch stole her breath away. Stopped her protests.

"Miss Tempest," he whispered in her ear, "have some faith."

Tuck pulled his carriage up in front of Piers's town house and glanced up at the shuttered and dark windows.

He knew what that meant.

Piers was on another bender. Sad thing, that. And such a waste. If only . . .

Tamping down a sense of responsibility, Tuck told himself— for yet the thousandth time—Piers's decline wasn't his fault.

But you could help him out of it, he could well imagine Poldie saying. Nudging him as it were from the heavens.

Yes, well, he'd tell his old friend that the viscount could get in line. Tuck had enough troubles of his own right now, thank you very much.

Especially since Ilford had done his worst—there wasn't a solitary hostess in London who would issue an invitation to the Tempest sisters now. Tuck knew this because he'd tried calling on some of his staunchest supporters. Wry old gels who didn't mind his roguish reputation in the least and had seen hundreds of scandals come and go.

And yet even they hadn't been forgiving.

It was all a disaster. If the chits weren't out, weren't being seen, then however could he find a way to make them into the Originals he'd wagered upon? And in only a fortnight.

Actually, less than that, he realized with a low groan.

Yet this had become more than just the problem of his wager.

More than once of late, he'd woken with a start with Lavinia Tempest's words ringing in his ears.

Why weren't you there?

And it wasn't really her accusation that had him sitting up and trying to catch his breath.

He was used to being accused of worse. Accusations he shrugged off with the least bit of conscience.

But there had been more to her question. Silent recriminations he'd heard loud and clear.

I trusted you.

You promised.

You should have been there.

I needed you.

Oh, that last one had shone clearly in her eyes, piercing his heart.

A heart that most of London would suggest, didn't exist. Even Tuck would have agreed with that.

That is, before Livy had come tripping into his life.

A heart made one vulnerable. It made one susceptible to caring, meant having to hurt those you loved. And those you loved could hurt you in return.

He'd done his best in the long hours of the night to shake Miss Tempest's soft voice out of his head, to tell himself she wasn't really his problem.

But he knew only too well she was very much his.

Problem, that is. And not just because of his foolhardy wager.

Sitting beside her at St. George's, he'd had a dangerous moment of belonging. Of being accepted.

And oh, how it had lured him. Tempted him.

He who belonged nowhere.

Except there, beside her. This oh-so-proper miss. Why was it when she smiled at him, he had the sense that she understood him better than he did himself? She hadn't looked askance at his arrival, hadn't pulled back her skirt. Instead, there had been a flicker in her eyes of relief.

As if he were there to save her. Meanwhile, the rest of the congregation had known exactly why he'd darkened their doors: to save his own skin. And they'd been hardly overjoyed to see him.

And certainly weren't going to offer him a helping hand. But she would.

Livy would. And he knew that with the same certitude that he knew her eyes were like bluebells.

Oh, one day, his uncle's pew might be his, and he'd have the title of Lord Charleton, but he wasn't foolish enough to think he would be welcomed as the prodigal son. That society would accept him simply because he'd had the rare luck to inherit.

And yet, what had he told her?

Have faith.

Ironic that, since he had none. Not one bit.

And as if on cue, he heard a door open and close with a *thud*, then her determined footsteps coming toward him.

Tell her. Tell her the truth and send her home.

But he was too selfish to do that. Especially when he spied a rebellious lock of mahogany hair spilling from beneath her bonnet.

For that was Lavinia Tempest. All proper and well-ordered. Yet not entirely.

She came marching up to the carriage, each *tromp* of her boot more determined than the next. Stomping, one might say, though he doubted that stomping was a proper, ladylike endeavor.

Her gaze fixed on him, her jaw set, brows in a dark line over her bright eyes.

Usually, when a lady looked at him like that, it was because she'd just discovered the jewels he'd been showering upon her were all paste. As worthless as his promises.

"Whatever has you, my dear Livy, in such a pet?" he asked over the side of the carriage.

Her lips narrowed at his familiar usage, then her gaze dropped to the middle of his jacket. "I was going to say Lady Aveley, but now I must add that button to my list. Mr. Rowland, can you not remember to tell your valet to secure that button, or you will lose it."

Tuck glanced down. Her world was crashing down around her, and she was worried over his button? What a funny bit of muslin she was. "I hope it isn't the state of my jacket that has you at sixes and sevens."

"It doesn't help," she told him, sending another woeful glance at his jacket before getting to the heart of concerns. "Lady Aveley tried to make calls on our behalf today."

He scrambled down and came around the horses, pausing before her. "I take it she wasn't well received."

Tuck needn't have asked. He knew what his reception had been when he'd tried to do the same.

"Oh, Mr. Rowland! Her expression was terrible to behold when she came home. She arrived and went straight for her chambers."

Yes, it had gone as well as his attempts. But instead he told her, "Ah, one day's worth of bad company is hardly the harbinger to give up. Come now, let's change all this." He held out his hand, and, after a moment's hesitation, she took it and allowed him to help her up.

"I fear all your efforts will be for naught," she told him in all earnestness.

Enough so that he felt a pang of something sharp inside his chest. Still, he persisted. "Your success will be my greatest reward." Which was, after all, the truth. "With Roselie and Lord Rimswell behind us, we cannot fail."

"Oh, if only it was that. I had a terrible row with Louisa. It was ever so dreadful." At this, Lavinia looked away.

They drove for a bit. Having never had any siblings, he wasn't sure what to say—though he did know what it was like to be at odds with someone near to you.

"Whatever were you arguing about?" he asked quietly.

"Everything."

Tuck quirked a brow. "That narrows it down."

He could see she was doing her best not to smile, nor did her bit of levity last long, for she quickly continued once again in earnest, "She wants to go home. Leave London."

Oh, the devil take him. Not this again.

He shook his head. "Leave? Admit defeat? I hope you told her, 'No, never, not I!'"

"I did," she replied, "but when Louisa starts in, she starts to make sense. Especially after Lady Gourley's."

There would be many such "Lady Gourley's" in her future he feared, and again, an odd pang of conscience nudged at him.

Tell her. Tell her the truth. Even if he could pull off this miracle, and she gained a match, there will always be those who will never look at her with anything but dismay.

"A mere bump in the road," he insisted instead, feeling every inch the knave everyone claimed him to be.

"Also, Louisa is beginning to suspect—"

"Suspect? Suspect what?" he asked in all innocence.

"This," she said, fluttering her hands at him and his carriage. "It isn't easy to hide all this from her."

Tuck saw nothing to worry about. After all, "this" was his forte. "Did you tell her you were going to the lending library?"

"Yes." She hardly sounded convinced. Or convincing.

Then again, not everyone had the benefit of a lifetime of instruction in the noble art of dissembling and lying by the Honorable Hero Worth.

"There you have it. It is an explanation that is always accepted."

"Not when you come home empty-handed," she replied. "Further, I am no bluestocking, Mr. Rowland."

He spared her a glance. No, she definitely was no bluestocking. Far too pretty for that. And too lively beneath that prim exterior.

"—so to continue to disappear and not come home with a book—any book—is going to invite notice," she was saying.

"I can't argue that." Hero always avowed that props made all the difference in a good tableaux.

"The only thing I like to read—other than books on manners and civility—are . . . are . . ." She looked around as if she were concerned someone might overhear her confession.

Good Lord! Whatever was it that that the chit secretly indulged herself in? French novels? Those lurid confessionals his mother devoured?

"What is it, Miss Tempest? You might not realize this, but I am a man of the world. You can tell me anything, I won't be shocked."

She took a deep breath and let her words come tumbling out. "I like to read the *Miss Darby* novels." She looked at him as if waiting for some measure of recognition or horror to set in. When none was forthcoming, she repeated herself. "The *Miss Darby* novels? Oh, heavens, you must have heard of them? *Miss Darby's Darkest Hour*? *Miss Darby and the Curse of the Pharaoh's Diamond*? Oh, certainly you've heard of *Miss Darby's Daring Dilemma*?"

"I can't say that I have. Your Miss Darby sounds like a very busy creature."

"She has the most divine adventures, and always, her true love, Lieutenant Throckmorten, is close at hand to save the day." She sighed, a dreamy, faraway look to her. "He once fought a saber duel to restore Miss Darby's honor. That, Mr. Rowland, is love."

"Love or lunacy." He laughed. "They are two sides of the same coin."

"Hardly so. You shouldn't be so skeptical."

So she *had* detected the note of sarcasm in his voice. "One can't be skeptical when one doesn't believe in love."

"You don't believe in—" Her eyes widened.

Apparently she couldn't bring herself to finish it, so he did for her. "I don't believe in the notion, no."

He couldn't have startled her more than if he'd announced they were going to Seven Dials and he wanted her to take up a life of crime.

"You don't believe in love?"

"No."

"That's terribly unfortunate, Mr. Rowland," she said, shaking her head, her hands fluttering about like absentminded butterflies as she tried to convince him otherwise. "Love is as essential as . . . as . . . well, the stars." She looked up at the blue sky, but he had to imagine she was seeing a glorious collection of constellations given her dreamy expression.

"I live in London, Miss Tempest," he reminded her. "I rarely see the stars or bother to look up for them."

"You should. Every night," she chided him. She paused for a moment, then put her hand on his sleeve. "For without the stars there to remind us, whatever would we reach for?"

Her fingers curled into his sleeve, reassuring him, coaxing him to just try.

To have faith.

"Perhaps if you were to read a *Miss Darby* novel," she offered and began espousing the various merits of each book.

Not that he was listening. Tuck found himself taken aback. Here was a naive young lady, barely into her first Season, leaving him feeling as if he were missing out on the very secret of life. On something so very essential . . . and all he had to do was look up to find it.

Instead, he looked down at her hand, half listening to her descriptions of Miss Darby's foray into a harem, and wondered at her easy familiarity. Whyever did she care?

Because that was who she was. She just did care. Like noticing his button. And he wasn't used to any concern for his well-being, his heart.

It rather left him off-kilter, like the warmth of her touch.

Just then, her words came to a stumbling halt, and she realized she still had hold of him.

Immediately, she plucked her hand back.

And then he did know something—with the very certainty of the heavens—the absence of her touch left him feeling unsettled once again. That perpetual restlessness snaked its way back into his chest.

He knew instead of wallowing over all this, he should take her innocent hold on him as a warning that she could be his undoing.

Or his salvation.

He looked away as well and reached for something familiar. Teasing her, he asked, "Is that what you would like, Livy? Adventure? To be kissed by some impertinent lieutenant? To fall in love under the stars?"

She sucked in a deep breath of indignation. "I'll have you know that Lieutenant Throckmorten is hardly impertinent. He and Miss Darby are very much in love." Her nose tucked up slightly.

Love. There was that dangerous word again. It beckoned with all the appeal of quicksand. Which Miss Darby had escaped apparently, on two separate occasions.

Still, in the face of Livy's outrage, he felt the need to smooth things over. "My apologies. I had no idea that I had completely mistaken the matter."

Sniff.

"Still, your Miss Darby hardly sounds the proper sort. I daresay she's violated most of the rules on your list."

"However can you say such a thing when Miss Darby is—" Then she stopped as she considered her defense. After a few moments, Lavinia glanced away, but not before he spied the furrow deepening in her brow.

Aha. Did he detect a crack in her proper armor?

"Won't admit it, will you?"

Her nose rose a bit higher, all assured defense. "Certainly Miss Darby has led an unconventional life. One can hardly expect her to comport herself with all the proper social conventions when one is escaping a harem." Then she rallied further, rather like Miss Darby's intrepid lieutenant. "Besides, it isn't as if she is real."

"No, of course not," he conceded, though he'd seen the envious, eager light in her eyes as she'd recounted her favorite scenes.

Tuck realized that in those moments he'd seen the door to her heart push open ever so slightly. Miss Lavinia Tempest had yet another secret—a daring, passionate side she did her utmost to keep well in check.

"And what about you?" he asked. "Do you adhere to all the proper social conventions?"

"I must." She shifted in her seat and glanced away. "All I've ever wanted is to find a respectable, sensible gentleman and be married."

"That sounds horribly dull. Not a single saber duel to be had."

"Saber duels never end well," she reminded him.

"No, I suppose they don't."

"Have you ever been in a duel?"

"Good God, no!" He glanced over at her, and if he wasn't mistaken, she looked overly disappointed. "I don't relish the idea of being shot at. Or have a saber run through me."

She sniffed, and he could almost hear what she was thinking. *That never stops Lieutenant Throckmorten.*

Well, it rather stopped Tuck. He liked living. Excessively so.

"You were going to go to Spain—to fight—you might have been shot there."

"Yet I didn't go."

He waited for the inevitable slew of questions. *Why didn't you? What stopped you?* Followed by the look that suggested he was a coward. Gone craven. Hadn't the bottom to face the enemy.

It was what everyone else did. But apparently not Lavinia Tempest.

"I'm sorry to have brought it up. Rather like discussing my mother."

How close she was to the truth. Save it wasn't her mother . . .

Meanwhile, Lavinia rather artfully redirected the conversation. "Tell me about your cousin, Viscount Wakefield."

It wasn't so much a request as a demand.

"Setting your cap for him, minx?" Tuck shook his head. "I should warn you—"

"Oh, heavens, no!" she declared. "Dreadful man. But Louisa

is rather taken with him. I just want to know . . . that is . . . I must know . . . Is he worthy of her?"

"Piers?" Tuck was a bit taken aback. Certainly it had been a shock to see his old friend arrive at Almack's, least of all show an interest in anyone besides himself, but here was Lavinia suggesting that Piers's interest was . . .

Then he recalled that Roselie had said much the same thing at Lady Gourley's.

"You know him well, don't you?" she prodded.

"Yes. I did."

"Quite close, according to Lady Aveley."

"Yes."

"But you fell out."

He shifted in his seat. "In a manner of speaking."

"Was it over a woman?"

That was definitely not the question he was expecting. He couldn't resist teasing her just a little bit. Waggling his brows and grinning, he asked, "Isn't it always?"

"No, please, seriously," she said, shaking off his purported charm as if she were immune.

In fact, it seemed she was.

"It's not so easy to explain."

Beside him, Lavinia settled down in her seat, folded her arms over her chest and looked expectantly at him.

Egad! The chit actually expected an explanation.

"Some matters are not discussed," he told her. "Isn't that on your list? For if it isn't, it should be. In the top five, at the very least."

"Secrets and disagreements should never be allowed to fester," she remarked. "Number 4. They only grow, and very soon you find them hanging over your head like a noose."

"Speaking from experience, Livy?"

"Yes, I suppose I am." She glanced away at the passing scenery. "I should have told Louisa about Maman. Even though it turns out that she knew all along."

"Ah, quite the family muddle," he remarked, a subject he knew all too well.

"Indeed. If we'd been open and forthright with each other—"

"That's a chilling notion," he told her.

"Perhaps if you were forthright with Lord Wakefield, you could repair the breach between you."

Now it was his turn to look away, for he didn't want her seeing into his heart at this moment. *Oh, Poldie, I failed you. Failed Piers as well.*

"There are things that cannot be undone," he told her.

"I don't believe that," Lavinia replied.

"You don't?"

"No. For if I did, I wouldn't be here with you, I'd be on the next mail coach to Kempton."

"But you are still here. Why?"

"You," she said. "You told me to have faith."

When would he learn to keep his advice to himself? Faith, indeed! That word weighed on him. Because Piers and Poldie had relied on him, had faith in him, and he'd failed them both.

Horribly.

They came to a stop before the modest house Lady Wakefield had taken after her son had returned from Spain.

Lavinia, sharp bit of muslin that she was, asked the obvious. "Why don't Lord Wakefield's mother and sister live with him?"

Tuck laughed a little bit. And gave the obvious answer. "Have you met Lord Wakefield?"

She shrugged in agreement.

He didn't know why, but he had to continue. To make sure she understood the truth. "While you might hear that Wakefield cast his mother and sister into the streets like a madman, it was Her Ladyship's decision to move here."

"Yes, well, I suppose one could hardly have a regular afternoon in if the master of the house is having a . . . a . . . bender."

"A bender?" Tuck tipped his head and looked her. "What do you know of such things?"

"Mr. Rowland, London hasn't the only collection of malcontents in England. You might recall I come from a village of spinsters."

As if any man could forget the very image of such a place.

Before she could continue her explanation, another carriage pulled up. Tuck glanced up and spied Brody arriving right on time.

"Miss Tempest," the baron said, tipping his hat to her.

She smiled shyly in acknowledgment, an approving glance that sent a surprising jolt of jealousy shafting through Tuck.

"Rowland," Brody added, clearly not happy about having to make good his promise.

"Lord Rimswell," Tuck replied, trying to appear delighted to see him. For right now he certainly wasn't happy to see the man—since it occurred to him that in Miss Tempest's eyes, the baron was a most *eligible parti*.

Yes, Livy and Brody. That would solve half his problem, but for some reason that sat rather badly in his craw.

Before he could subtly edge the other man away from Livy's side, the front door of the house flew open.

"You are all late," Roselie announced, hands fisted to her hips.

Tuck leaned over to Livy, and whispered. "Warned you."

"Do not listen to a word that rogue says, Miss Tempest," Roselie Stratton told her, coming down the steps and waiting at the curb while—to Tuck's chagrin—Brody had leaped down from his carriage and was now helping Lavinia down with all the proper gallantry of a gentleman.

Tuck pressed his lips together. And while he should be delighted, he had suddenly had the strangest desire to stand across a grassy knoll from the younger man and put a bullet through his chest.

Especially when Livy gazed up at the baron with stars in her very blue eyes. His insides roiled again.

What had the chit said? Oh, yes, he recalled it.

For without the stars there to remind us, whatever would we reach for?

Not that Brody was much of a reach for her. He was a baron and she the daughter of a respected baronet. It would be a good match for both.

No, the real truth of the matter was that if anyone would be reaching when it came to Livy, it would be he. For Tuck knew that to reach in her direction would only mean dragging her into the mire that was his life.

And eventually, as the truth would come out, his world would extinguish that irresistible light in her eyes.

And that, of all his crimes, Tuck knew would be unforgivable.

CHAPTER 7

Lavinia knew immediately that she was going to like Roselie Stratton excessively. The viscount's sister had hurried them into the house, dispatching their coats and hats with the footman and ushering them into an airy sitting room. The furniture had all been moved against the walls and the carpet rolled up.

At the pianoforte sat a tiny woman, and beside her stood a tall, solidly built man with impeccable posture. He stood at attention like a wooden soldier.

"I am so glad you asked me to help, Tuck," Roselie was saying. "This Season has to be the dullest in years. I needed a project that would require some subterfuge just to keep me from dying of boredom."

If ever there was a living and breathing example of Miss Darby, Lavinia had the sense she was meeting her. That, and Roselie also reminded her of Lady Essex—the most indomitable of all the Kempton spinsters.

Lavinia glanced around and spied an elderly lady dozing in the corner.

Roselie noticed and winked at her. "That is Mrs. Pratt, the companion my mother hired to keep an eye on me. Actually, she came very highly recommended from a dear friend. Mostly because she is always and ever on the alert."

There was an indelicate snore from the far side of the room, and the lady's head bobbed as she slept.

Roselie grinned happily. "And, of course, this is Herr Fuchs."

The dancing master clicked his heels together and nodded slightly at the new arrivals, but even so, Lavinia could feel his gaze taking a full measure of the work ahead of him though he barely moved, that is until Roselie began directing the proceedings.

"Now Tuck," she announced, "you partner Miss Tempest, and I'll dance with Brody."

Herr Fuchs struck his walking stick to the floor. "*Nein! Nein! Nein!*" he protested after taking one scathing glance at the couples before him. "This will not do," he declared, marching up to them, all the while shaking his head. "You and the young lady do not suit. Not in the least," he told Mr. Rowland, who had come to stand beside Lavinia.

"Actually, we rather get along quite well," Mr. Rowland replied.

"That has nothing to do with dancing," Herr Fuchs shot back, nudging Tuck aside with his walking stick and prodding Brody to stand beside Lavinia.

Lavinia knew she should be thrilled to be partnered with Lord Rimswell. He was everything an eligible *parti* should be. Handsome. Titled. Wealthy.

Yet as the music began, and Lord Rimswell politely took her in his arms, all Lavinia could do was steal a glance over at Roselie and Tuck. Her lips pursed together as she realized that the pang running through her with a jolt was jealousy.

Ridiculous, she told herself, and turned her full attention on the baron.

And promptly stepped on his boot.

"I am so sorry, my lord," she hurried to apologize.

"It is to be expected," Lord Rimswell replied politely. "Why this German martinet of Roselie's has even me on edge."

Lavinia laughed a bit—at least until Herr Fuchs shot her a scathing glance. She straightened hurriedly and tried to concentrate on her feet.

Yet all she could think about was how dancing with Lord Rimswell was nothing like the magic she felt when she danced with Tuck.

Again, she stole another glance in that direction.

"They dance quite well together," Lord Rimswell commented.

"Yes, they do." Then again, everyone danced quite well together if they weren't partnered with her.

"Not that it's a surprise, we all learned to dance together."

"We?" she asked.

"Me, my older brother, Poldie, Tuck, and Piers—Viscount Wakefield, his older sister, Margaret, and, of course, Roselie." The baron said her name with a bit of resigned annoyance.

"Whatever is the matter with Miss Stratton?" Lavinia asked. "She seems quite lovely."

In fact, she looked quite fetching in Tuck's arms. The pair of them striking together.

Another jolt of jealousy shafted through her as Tuck whirled Roselie in a perfect circle.

"I suppose it sounds foolish, but Roselie and I are the same age, and all the others were a few years older. My brother, Piers and Tuck were inseparable, while I was deemed too young to be included in their adventures and was left behind with Roselie. Utterly humiliating."

"Yet Miss Stratton has turned out quite pretty," Lavinia noted.

Lord Rimswell barely spared the other lady a glance. "Yes, I suppose so. But I fear, she'll always be a dreadful handful to me."

"Mr. Rowland seems to find her diverting," she said aloud before she could stop herself.

Lord Rimswell smiled and leaned down to whisper, "I would wager they are arguing."

Lavinia hardly thought that was fair, but as she took another glance at the other couple, she also came down hard on top of the baron's foot. "I am so sorry," she managed.

"No, that was my fault," he said, even if it wasn't.

"*Nein! Nein! Nein!*" Herr Fuchs said, pounding his walking stick and marching over to Lavinia and Lord Rimswell.

From across the room, Tuck sent her an encouraging glance. *Courage, Livy. You can do this.*

The dancing master stopped right in front of her, his face a stern mask of disgust. "Can you not count, fraülein?" The walking stick came down hard against the floor, and the man struck an imperious pose before her.

Lavinia felt every bit of her resolve crumble in the face of this martinet. "Yes," she sniffed, and glanced away. Oh, dear, she was going to turn into a watering pot. This was more humiliating than the time she had nearly burned down Foxgrove. And yet despite her best efforts, her eyes welled up.

Herr Fuchs remained unmoved. "What? Are you crying? There is no crying in dancing!"

"You weren't the one dancing with her," Brody muttered as he limped back a step from her. Abandoning her to Herr Fuchs's tirade.

And yet it was Tuck—the knave, the rake—who stepped in to rescue her. "However is this helpful, Herr Fuchs? Making a young lady cry? Villainous!" he declared, taking Lavinia by the hand and turning her so her back was to everyone.

"Steady on, Livy. I'll dance with you." He glared over her shoulder at Herr Fuchs, and the dancing master made an exasperated noise and stomped back over to let loose a flurry of complaints at Roselie. In German, thankfully.

"He said we do not suit," Lavinia reminded him, dashing at the tears now falling to her cheeks.

Tuck pulled a handkerchief from his pocket. "I disagree. We rub along most excellently. Don't you think?"

Lavinia looked up at him and found herself nodding in agreement. They did rub along well. It made no sense, for here was a man who didn't fit anywhere on her list, but oh, how he fit to *her*.

Like when they'd danced at Monsieur Ponthieux's. Or when he'd sat next to her at St. George's, her shield against the scrutiny of the *ton*.

Or today. For there in the carriage, she'd thought he was going to say something, ask her something, tell her something very important, or when she'd put her hand on his sleeve, it was because somewhere, deep inside her, she just knew that was what she should do.

Never mind his teasing ways (which, if she was being entirely honest, she rather liked), he'd nearly had her confess that yes, she loved Miss Darby because the girl lived exactly the life Lavinia desired with all her heart.

Adventurous. Passionate. And oh, so improper.

And she suspected he would never disapprove of such a dream. Such a desire.

Any desire, for that matter.

Yet to take that step into such a world, would be her ruin. And Louisa's as well. Worst of all, it would break her father's heart to see her follow in her mother's footsteps.

Still, the lure of Tuck Rowland was nearly irresistible. She knew now why Lady Essex and every book she'd ever read on ladylike comportment warned of such men.

But there was more to all this than just the way he made her feel—beyond forward and passionate—there was a wounded and desperate man beneath all this Corinthian veneer.

And that part of him tugged at her heart. Felt they shared something deep and unspoken—a sense of being outside the rest of the world.

She couldn't imagine what it was like to be him—what with the whispers and pointing she'd seen at St. George's.

In church, no less.

For while she'd put her hand on his sleeve to press her point—

that he did need to know that love was real—but once her fingers curled into the wool of his jacket, the heat of his arm rising into her fingertips, she had the sense that as much as she needed his help, he needed hers as well.

She just didn't know how.

"Perhaps you could teach us something new?" Roselie was saying. "I hear there is a new French—"

Oh, just the mention of that land across the Channel was enough to send Herr Fuchs into a fury.

"Did the French compose the great music? *Nein!* Did they create the waltz? *Nein!* What do the French know of these things? Music is the very heart and soul of a German!" He pounded his fist to his chest, his face red with emotion.

"Oh, do teach us to waltz," Roselie begged. "My father learned how when he was in Vienna and would dance it with my mother."

After sending a skeptical glance at Lavinia—most likely because the man was certain he was about to see the dance of his beloved homeland tromped all over—Herr Fuchs nodded in agreement and waved his hand at his poor beleaguered accompanist, who began to play a wonderfully sweet arrangement—the sort of notes that were meant to awaken the very soul.

Tuck already knew the dance—of course he would for it was a scandalous thing. He caught hold of her hand, and his other came to rest on her hip—ever so intimately. And they began to move together, just as they had at Ponthieux's.

"Thank you for rescuing me," he told her. "My cousin was ringing a peal over my head."

"For what?" Lavinia asked, growing dizzier by the minute. And it wasn't just the circles they were dancing.

It was Tuck.

"Everything," he teased back.

"That narrows it down."

"Minx," he whispered in her ear, sending tendrils of delight through her.

"Knave," she replied with just as much passion.

He grinned at her, then something over his shoulder caught his attention. He glanced back at her. "And what were you and Lord Rimswell discussing? And in such earnest, I might note."

He'd been watching her? She shouldn't be, but the idea thrilled her. "Mostly I was apologizing for stepping on his feet. "

"Then Brody can't be that much of a partner, for I think you are a perfect handful." And as if to emphasize the point, his hand, the one on her hip, curled slightly, caressing her.

Somehow, the world slowed around her. "Truly?"

"Decidedly," he whispered into her ear.

And there it was, all those shivers, and she couldn't help herself, she leaned closer to him. And as she fit against him, she could feel him flinch, ever so slightly.

But he didn't move away, only pulled her closer, as if he was testing the same theory.

That something magical, something impossible was happening.

"Does it always feel like this?" she whispered up to him.

"No, Livy, it doesn't."

There was an emotion behind his confession, his words, that she'd never heard him use. As if the truth surprised him as well. Yet before she could ask him another question, from beyond the music room, there was the sound of the front door opening and closing.

"Roselie! Oh, Roselie, where are you?"

The music stopped, and all four of them came to a halt, even as a woman came rushing into the room.

What followed was a very uncomfortable moment. The matron—whom Lavinia had to assume was the dowager Viscountess Wakefield—came to a fluttering stop, and her eyes blinked a few times, the scene before her coming into focus.

If she had questions or objections, the only sign was the slight uptick of her brow and the quelling glance she shot her daughter.

Her *unmarried* daughter.

"Roselie, I didn't know you were entertaining,"

"Just a dancing lesson, *Maman*," Roselie replied, leaving Brody's side and smiling as if there was nothing wrong with having two unmarried gentlemen in attendance without anyone proper to chaperone—well, other than her hired companion, who was dozing in the corner.

Her mother glanced around, until her gaze lit on Herr Fuchs, who executed a precise and measured bow of respect.

"You said the other night that I could stand to improve my steps a bit," Roselie rushed to add, "and it was ever so kind of Miss Tempest—and Mr. Rowland and Lord Rimswell—to aid me and agree to keep my secret. Terribly embarrassing to be twenty and four and still unable to remember such a simple measure. And besides, dear Bernie has been here the entire time."

When they all looked at once over at the corner, there to Lavinia's surprise, was a completely awake and for all accounts, alert Mrs. Pratt, who was not only awake, but on her feet. She bowed her head to her ladyship as if to say that nothing untoward was going to happen on her watch.

Roselie, for her part, beamed at her co-conspirators. *Follow my lead, or we are all done for.*

But there was no need for that, for Lady Wakefield was now fixed on another subject.

Or rather person.

"Miss Tempest? Truly?" The lady gazed at Lavinia and shook her head. "That cannot be. I have it on good authority that not thirty minutes ago Miss Tempest was seen getting into Piers's carriage. Lady Gourley was quite convinced."

"Then it must be the other Miss Tempest, *Maman,*" Roselie explained. "This is *Lavinia* Tempest. The one I met the other night is her sister, Louisa."

"Truly?" She gave Lavinia another once-over as if she wasn't quite convinced that she had it muddled. But then she brightened. "Oh, yes! I do recall now. Twins, isn't it? In the excitement of the moment, that quite slipped my mind."

At this, Lavinia stepped forward. Though her thoughts were reeling at this unexpected news.

Louisa was out riding with Lord Wakefield?

"My lady, my sister and I are identical," she told the dowager viscountess. "We are often confused for each other."

The lady looked her up and down. "Identical, you say? How perfectly delightful! But more to the point, it would seem I do indeed have the correct Miss Tempest, for you can tell me all about your sister. I must know everything." The lady stalked forward, smiling widely, but her piercing gaze had Lavinia pinned in place.

"*Maman!*" Roselie protested. "You are terrifying poor Miss Tempest."

"Nonsense. She strikes me as a miss who knows her own mettle," the dowager declared. Then, like a cat, came pouncing forward and folded her arm into Lavinia's, catching her tight.

Lavinia had a horrible moment of knowing exactly how Hannibal's prey felt when that wretched beast went hunting.

Meanwhile, Lady Wakefield began to tow Lavinia from the room, saying, "I know we are going to get along famously! You are going to be at Lady Grayson's tonight, are you not?"

"No, my lady."

This halted Lady Wakefield in her tracks. "Whyever not?"

Lavinia drew a steadying breath. "The invitation was withdrawn."

"Withdrawn?" The dowager paused and looked Lavinia over, then her eyes widened as if she were collecting, cataloguing and plotting all at once. And more to the point, her gaze lifted to Mr. Rowland, a sharp, narrow accusation that Lavinia suspected could pin the man to the wall.

"It isn't as if you are missing much, Miss Tempest," Roselie rushed in to add—and obviously familiar with her mother's moods. "Lady Grayson rarely sets a proper supper."

"No, not in the least," Lady Wakefield echoed. "Roselie, I've changed my mind. You and Mrs. Pratt walk Miss Tempest home. You are staying with Lord Charleton are you not? With Lady Aveley as well?"

Lavinia nodded.

"Yes, inform Lady Aveley I shall be calling in the next day or so." Lady Wakefield once again raised her glance to Lord Rimswell. "You may leave now, my lord. My best to your mother."

Her tones held a warning note, which turned out to be enough to send Lord Rimswell bowing and beating a hasty retreat.

Not that Mr. Rowland was as easily cowed. "But my lady, I thought to see Miss Tempest home myself."

At this, the matron snorted. "You thought wrong, Tuck. Roselie and Mrs. Pratt will see her home. *Properly.* Besides, I would have a few words with you before you scurry off."

Roselie tugged at Lavinia's hand, and whispered, "Come along before she changes her mind yet again."

And Lavinia went, following the remarkably spry Mrs. Pratt and the much-chastened Roselie out the door.

But at the doorway, Lavinia took one last glance back and found Tuck watching her.

And she had the sense that suddenly their roles were reversed.

For his last glance seemed to cry out, *Save me, minx.* Why, the poor man looked terrified.

Lavinia pressed her hand to her mouth and stifled a laugh. And she almost wished she could stay.

Well, almost.

After his own mother, Tuck counted Lady Wakefield as the second most conniving and cunning woman in London, which hardly boded well for him considering she had her sharp gaze currently fixed on him.

Leaving him with the unsettling notion that he should check his wallet and his watch. But that was more his mother's strong suit. And he was pretty certain Lady Wakefield hadn't taken to crime.

At least not yet.

"Come out in the garden with me, Tuck," she said, smiling kindly.

Rather, he suspected, like Henry VIII had invited Anne Boleyn to a garden party.

At the Tower.

And while the small bower behind the house was a lovely spot, the roses and vines did nothing to soothe Tuck.

Nor should they have, for the rosebush beside him was in full thorn.

"Whatever do you think you are doing?" Lady Wakefield demanded.

"I-I-I," he stammered.

"Yes, well, I know of your wager," she told him, sitting down on a bench and waving her hand at him to sit on the other half.

He rather sank down beside her. What had happened to the sacred sanctity of silence as to the doings inside White's? Now it seemed every miss and matron knew exactly what was happening within its walls. The club needed to take another look at its membership and issue muzzles to the more chatty subscribers.

"Yes, well, you are going about it all wrong," her ladyship continued, smoothing out her skirt and her countenance.

Then to his surprise, Lady Wakefield sighed and shook her head. "Oh, Tuck, this is a terrible muddle."

"I can't argue that," he admitted.

"And I hardly see why you think you can save these girls. They are quite ruined. Kitty saw to that years ago, and what Charleton and Amy thought by introducing them—well, I will never understand."

Tuck couldn't argue the later part, but one name stopped him. "Kitty?"

The lady looked up and nodded. "Their mother. Lady Tempest."

Then it struck him. "You knew her?"

"Yes, of course. Isobel, Amy and I were all friends with her. We went to school together. Came out together." Lady Wakefield glanced across the garden and, he suspected, across the veil of years. "Don't believe everything you hear about Kitty. She was not the light skirt all claim her to be, though unfortunately Society has handed down that judgment, and there is nothing to be done about it."

"Hardly seems right," Tuck said, prodding at a loose stone with his boot. He knew quite well what it was like to be unfairly labeled.

"Never is. It is always difficult when men are cruel, but when women turn on one another, point fingers and whisper such foul names, it is a grave thing. A terrible curse. As it was for Kitty." She glanced over at him and probably divined what he was thinking. "Oh, she was as selfish as they say—but she was so very pretty and spoiled—and a terrible flibbertigibbet, but she loved only one man. And for that she should hardly be condemned."

Only one? Tuck looked over at Lady Wakefield. "Her history rather contradicts that statement, my lady. She married, then ran away with her lover."

"Oh, I'm not talking about Sir Ambrose or that horrid dancing master, but her true love." Lady Wakefield reached toward the rose bush and her fingers brushed over a newly opened blossom. "She loved Lord Eddows first and always."

"Lord Eddows?" Tuck shook his head. "Isn't he a bit—" He stopped there, for he could hardly find the right words. The Lord Eddows he knew of lived in the country, rarely came to town, and also had an affinity for Italian dancing masters.

"No, no, not Lucius," Lady Wakefield said, laughing a bit. "I am speaking of his older brother, Ewen—he's been gone so long most people have forgotten him. But Kitty, oh, she loved him desperately, and Ewen loved her in return. They planned on marrying—there was a bit of a tangle about it all—I don't remember what exactly—but before anything could be arranged or agreed upon, he died of a sudden fever."

"And yet she married Sir Ambrose in all due haste." It didn't sound like this Kitty's affections were as deeply rooted as Lady Wakefield seemed to think.

A pensive expression crossed over the older woman's features. "And whyever, do you think, a lady would do that?"

It didn't take Tuck long to come up with one reason. "Are you suggesting—" He paused there for a moment. "Poor Sir Ambrose."

"I don't think Sir Ambrose minded—at least not at first. He had loved Kitty from afar from the first moment she made her curtsy. He would have taken her broken and destitute. Which in a sense, he did." Lady Wakefield shrugged and smoothed her skirt yet again.

The magnitude of it all weighed down on Tuck. "And now her daughters—"

"Yes, her daughters are here." She looked over at Tuck, and he realized now it was his turn to share. For having been the wife of a diplomat, Lady Wakefield knew that information was something that came with a price.

"If Piers is—" She said the words both hopeful and with a bit of trepidation.

If Piers is in love with one of them . . .

"As I said earlier, he was seen out riding with—" she prodded.

"Louisa Tempest," Tuck offered.

"Louisa," the lady murmured as if trying out the name. "I do like the sound of that. What is she like?"

"I can't say that I know Miss Louisa, but her sister, the one you met today, Lavinia, I do know."

Lady Wakefield's gaze turned sharp yet again, but all she could say was "And is she like—"

Like her mother . . .

Tuck laughed. "Oh, hardly. Lavinia Tempest is a walking encyclopedia of all things proper. She even keeps a list. Can cite lines from any number of volumes on manners and propriety."

"A list?" Now it was Lady Wakefield's turn to laugh. "Oh, how diverting. I ought to encourage Roselie to spend time with her. I fear my daughter is as headstrong as her father and her brother."

And her mother, but Tuck wasn't going to add that to the lady's list. Still, Roselie and Livy plotting together? Dear God, he feared for London.

No, make that the entirety of England.

"Yet, explain this to me, here is Miss Tempest—whom you claim is an expert in propriety—and yet she is gallivanting about Town in your company." Lady Wakefield made a *tsk, tsk.*

Whether that was over him or Lavinia, Tuck wasn't too sure. Probably both of them. "Yes, well, Miss Tempest is a bundle of contradictions. While she goes on and on about the need for proper rules and order, she is utterly fascinated with some series of novels about a Miss Darby."

Lady Wakefield groaned. "Oh, those books! They are the bane of every mother in London. Miss Darby this, Miss Darby that! Why Lady Shelby's daughter insisted on wearing the most ridiculous feathered headdress last Season because Miss Darby favored the fashion. Half the young ladies in London were donning those dreadful creations by summer."

Tuck recalled the gaggle of debutants parading about the previous year and laughed a bit—for at the time he'd thought them a mad collection of muslin.

But Lady Wakefield's expression changed, as if something began to dawn on her. "Though you might also recall Lady Shelby's daughter married the Marquess of Scorton."

"Oh, yes. I remember her now. Forward chit, wasn't she? Always laughing, and I think she even joined a card game at Almack's." Tuck shrugged. "Her antics nearly got her ruined."

"Nearly," Lady Wakefield agreed. "However, she did catch the marquess's eye with all her parading about. And her, the daughter of a baronet. Imagine that." She paused and looked at Tuck "Helped that she was so pretty . . . rather like your Miss Tempest."

"She isn't 'my Miss Tempest,' " he said, shifting on the bench.

"Perhaps Miss Tempest's fascination with the *Darby* novels isn't such a bad thing—" Lady Wakefield began. "Perhaps it might be the perfect way to help her."

"Perfect?" Tuck blurted out. "Oh, yes, that would fix everything if she were to start parading about Town—"

Lady Wakefield said nothing, just cocked a brow and smiled slightly, as if encouraging him to see past the point that was stopping him.

He shook his head, as he imagined Livy—his Livy parading about in some feathered headdress. Catching the eye of some marquess. "No-o-o . . . And here I've always thought you a sensible woman, my lady."

"I am," Lady Wakefield told him.

"And so you think I should—" Honestly, he wasn't too sure what the dowager was suggesting.

"I think you should introduce Miss Tempest to your mother."

CHAPTER 8

"I'm ever so sorry my mother came home," Miss Stratton said, slanting a glance first at Lavinia, then back at the elegant house they'd just left. Behind them, Mrs. Pratt followed. "I can't imagine what *Maman* is saying to Tuck."

The girl looked as if she would give up her dowry to go back and eavesdrop.

Then again, so would Lavinia, but one glance at the stern-looking Mrs. Pratt stopped her from making such a suggestion.

"Then again, bother Lady Gourley and her gossipy ways." Roselie huffed as if the indignation was hers to bear. "And especially when Tuck seemed so—"

Lavinia glanced sharply at her. "When Mr. Rowland seemed so what?" she prompted. She wasn't sure wanted to know the direction of Miss Stratton's speculation.

But Miss Stratton was ever the diplomat's daughter. "Just that it seemed as if you and Tuck were making such excellent progress." She paused to nod at a matron who was just coming out of her carriage. "With your dancing, that is. Why you two appeared perfectly suited"—again the significant pause—"when you were dancing."

Perfectly suited, indeed. That was the last thing Lavinia wanted to hear.

Even if it seemed true.

"I hope she isn't too disapproving," Miss Stratton said with a sigh.

"Your mother disapproves of Mr. Rowland?"

At this, Miss Stratton laughed. "My dear Miss Tempest, everyone disapproves of Tuck Rowland."

"How unfortunate for Mr. Rowland, when he is only trying to help me."

Mrs. Pratt made a noise that sounded very suspiciously like one of Lady Essex's snorts of derision, but when she glanced back, their chaperone was busy watching a wagon go by.

"Yes, well, *Maman* has complained for years that Tuck is a terrible influence on Piers, but I think it was the other way around—Tuck was always there to pull my brother out of one coil or another."

"And yet you disapprove of him as well," Lavinia persisted. She found it rather unfair that the man was judged for simply being himself.

"Only on principle," the girl replied. "And because he broke his word to Piers and let him go off to Spain with only Poldie at his side. If Tuck had been there—well." She shrugged, for what were wishes and things that might have happened—only that, a mere slip of the shoulder.

"He must have had a very good reason," Lavinia replied, though she half waited for another snort of disagreement from Mrs. Pratt.

But this time there was none forthcoming.

"Perhaps," Miss Stratton agreed, albeit reluctantly. "Though I will say, Aunt Charleton loved him dearly. Then again, she always saw the good in everyone—even when no one else could or would. *Maman* used to say her sister was far too kindhearted, too forgiving."

"Those are hardly sins," Lavinia pointed out.

"Then you have yet to fully understand my mother." They continued on down the block, but silence was apparently not Miss Stratton's friend. "Tuck admires you."

"Me?" Lavinia said, nearly stumbling to a stop.

"But of course," Miss Stratton asserted. "Didn't you notice how he put Herr Fuchs squarely in his place when the man was bullying you? No one naysays Herr Fuchs."

"Perhaps they should," Lavinia replied. Dreadful man.

"He got you dancing," Miss Stratton noted.

"Mr. Rowland did that." And the moment the words spilled out, Lavinia regretted them, for she'd unwittingly dropped a baited, irresistible hook into the conversation.

One Roselie Stratton eagerly caught hold of, saying, "Tuck? However did he do that?"

Oh, there was no mistaking the seemingly innocent tone to her new friend's question. Lavinia realized that here was someone with a lifetime of experience in the London *ton* and three years of wading through the Marriage Mart.

If anyone could understand the growing dilemma inside her, Miss Stratton was her best hope.

Lavinia leaned a little closer so her words would not spill beyond the two of them. "It is the oddest thing. When Mr. Rowland takes my hand, my feet untangle."

"And not with anyone else?" Miss Stratton asked.

Lavinia shook her head.

"I don't believe that is odd at all," the girl assured her. "Tuck admires you."

"Oh, hardly," Lavinia demurred.

"And if his careless heart is tempted, then any number of truly eligible *partis* are just a dance away, Miss Tempest," Miss Stratton said with all confidence. "That is, unless—"

There it was again, that telling pause.

"Unless?" Oh, botheration, Lavinia couldn't help herself. She had to ask.

"Unless you find him—"

"Him?" Lavinia shook her head. "You mean Tuck? I mean, Mr. Rowland?" Lavinia shivered right down to her boots. "Not in the least! He hardly fits my list."

This time it was Miss Stratton who faltered a bit. "You have a list?"

Why did everyone in London find this so odd?

"But of course," Lavinia replied, doing her best to sound as it were the most casual and normal of things to do. "A list of Proper Qualities."

"Proper Qualities," Miss Stratton repeated, as if Lavinia had just broken out in Dutch or Greek, and she was trying to sound out the words. "Such as?"

"Oh, the usual. Titled, well-to-do, a man of property and integrity."

"You should have remained with Lord Rimswell," Mrs. Pratt muttered from behind them.

Both girls turned and stared at her.

The lady shrugged, and they continued walking.

"Bernie is right. I would think Lord Rimswell would suit you perfectly," Miss Stratton replied, though to Lavinia it sounded as if she were unwillingly surrendering something of great value and at a high cost.

"Oh, heavens no," Lavinia assured her. "He's nice enough and kind, but if I didn't know better, I'd say his heart is otherwise engaged."

"You could say that," Mrs. Pratt agreed.

Beside her, Miss Stratton stiffened but then continued prattling on. "Well, if we must, we'll cross Mr. Rowland off your list, as well as Lord Rimswell. But that doesn't mean we shouldn't be able to find one gentleman in London who meets your requirements and will fall head over heels in love with you."

"Do you think so?" Lavinia asked. For now her list had one other requirement: the gentleman must make her feel as wonderful as she did when she was with Mr. Rowland.

"I don't see why not," Miss Stratton was saying, "and if *Maman* has a hand in it, this ridiculous situation you find yourself in will be over before Wednesday, and you'll be back in Almack's."

Almack's?

"Oh, must I?" Lavinia burst out without thinking.

Miss Stratton laughed and reached over to squeeze her hand. "Sadly, we all must."

"You shouldn't be encouraging a match a'tween the two of them," Mrs. Pratt said, even as the door to Uncle Charleton's house closed.

"Whyever not?" Roselie replied to her plain-speaking companion as the two of them turned to walk back the way they'd come. "They seem to suit. Did you see the way he looked at her? Or how she stammers when she speaks of him?"

"Suit or not, that knavish cousin of yours will run through her fortune in no time, poor gel." Bernie's lips pursed together.

"Fortune? Whatever do you mean?" Roselie shook her head. "Miss Tempest hardly strikes me as an heiress."

Bernie snorted. "You've had money all your life, gel. When you grow up like I did, you learn to spot it in others. That gel will come with a rich purse."

"So you say," Roselie said, feeling a bit outfoxed. Miss Tempest had a fortune? How had she missed such a thing—when she prided herself on seeing beyond the obvious.

No, Bernie must be mistaken.

The older woman laughed. "Have I ever been?" she asked, having correctly guessed the reason for Roselie's creased brow.

Oh, botheration. For there was the rub.

Bernie was rarely wrong.

Tuck left Lady Wakefield's house in a bit of daze.

The dowager couldn't be serious. Introduce Livy to his mother? Why it was utter madness.

"Whatever was that about?"

The question jolted him out of his musings, and he looked up to find Brody there, standing beside his carriage—waiting for Tuck to emerge from the dragon's lair, apparently.

"I don't usually get so summarily dismissed." Brody straightened his coat, then went to work tugging on his gloves. "But I do like to know why. Whatever did Lady Wakefield have to say?" He glanced down at his boots. "Oh, and you owe me a new pair of boots."

"Yes, well, take that problem up with Herr Fuchs. He was the one who paired Livy with you," Tuck pointed out. And he deliberately left out any mention of his conversation with the dowager.

"Monstrous fellow. I don't know what all the clamor is about over him." With his gloves now on, Brody gave his hat a rakish tilt. "Going to take a jaunt through the park. Care to follow along? We can see if Budgey got that new phaeton he was going on about."

Tuck shook his head. No, he'd had enough censorious scrutiny for one day. "Rather not. But thank you."

Brody nodded and went to climb up into his carriage. He paused and turned back to Tuck. "What do you make of that— that bit about Piers?"

"Piers out driving with one of my uncle's charges?" Tuck shook his head. "Or any lady for that matter. Lady Gourley needs to get a new pair of spectacles."

"I suppose," Brody agreed as he climbed into his carriage. "But if he were, that would be good news for you, don't you think?"

"A miracle would be more like it," Tuck offered.

Brody laughed. "You haven't a chance with this wager, you know that, don't you?"

Tuck didn't reply. He never liked to admit defeat, but it was certainly looking like he'd be taking an extended vacation— somewhere far from England.

"They are pretty gels," Brody told him, trying to sound encouraging. "But sadly, pretty isn't what you need right now."

He chirped at his set, and the horses trotted off, leaving Tuck standing stock-still on the curb.

. . . pretty isn't what you need right now . . .

Tuck tried to breathe. For that was right along with what Lady Wakefield had said. Well, nearly.

Still, Brody's offhanded remark only gave the dowager's suggestion some weight.

Oh, but he couldn't. It was far too scandalous. Dangerous, even.

Introduce the sharp-eyed and all-too-proper Miss Lavinia Tempest to his mother? One wrong step, one wrong word and . . .

Tuck dragged in a deep breath and let it out. Giving over Livy to his mother was akin to putting a dove in the hawk's reach.

Then again, what else did he have left to try?

"Anything but that," he vowed, his fists clenched to his sides.

But Tuck wasn't usually one to keep his word.

Almost as soon as Lavinia entered Lord Charleton's house, feeling as if the entire world was once again opening up to them, here was Louisa coming down the stairs like a storm cloud.

"Where have you been?" her sister demanded.

Lavinia came to a blinding halt. Oh, bother, however could she tell the truth—for to do that would mean she would have to admit to being in league with Mr. Rowland.

Something she knew her sister, and Lady Aveley, would not approve of. Not. In. The. Least.

"Why, at the library. You knew that," she said, hurrying toward the stairs and daring not to look her sister in the eye.

Louisa stepped in her path. "You were not at the library–"

Something about her tone made Lavinia bristle. "Why of course I was."

"You were *seen*, Lavinia."

This stopped her in her tracks. Oh, bother. Double bother. But still, she didn't like Louisa's tone.

So Lavinia chose to stand her ground. "Seen? Whatever does that mean? I went to the library."

"Lord Wakefield saw you getting into Mr. Rowland's carriage, Lavinia."

"And how would you know that? Were you over there again? With him? *Alone?*"

"No!" Louisa sputtered quickly retreating. "He and I . . . that is, he offered—"

"Yes, I suppose he did," Lavinia said, grasping the upper hand quickly. "He always seems to be on hand to offer."

Louisa's lips fluttered as she sought the right retort, but it was to go unsaid. For right then, Lady Aveley appeared on the landing above them.

"Girls! There you are. I had hoped to find you together. Excellent." She smiled at them and began to come down the stairs.

Both sisters shot the other hot glances, vows that this was hardly over.

But it was, in ways that they could never have suspected. Lavinia least of all.

"However was the library?" Lady Aveley asked Lavinia.

Smiling at her sister—who she knew would never carry tales—Lavinia turned to the matron. "Delightful. Though I am afraid I lost track of time—I started reading Homer's *Odyssey* and couldn't put it down. Such a gripping tale."

She might not tattle, but that didn't stop her sister from groaning.

Not that Lady Aveley noticed, for she only smiled brighter, as she came to a stop in the foyer. "I have had a letter from your father." She held up the note. "He has asked Lord Charleton to provide you with a carriage as far as Tunbridge Wells, and he will have your coachman meet you there."

"Leave London?" Lavinia whispered.

"Yes. Your father thought these arrangements would be the most expedient," she told them.

"No-o-o!" Lavinia sputtered, backing away. "I won't go."

"My dear, I know this is—" Lady Aveley reached out to her, but Lavinia jerked back, her eyes already brimming with tears.

"No! I won't go," Lavinia repeated. She backed into the post at the bottom of the stairwell and used it to support herself. "You cannot make me. The Season . . . It isn't fair—" She thought to tell them of Lady Wakefield's promise, of her plans, of Tuck's resolve to help her, no, them, but even that seemed futile given Louisa's expression—dear heavens, her sister appeared relieved at the news.

Of course she would be—she had never wanted a Season to begin with.

"Dearest, it is over. At least for us," Louisa told her.

"Not for me. I refuse to go. I won't leave. Not yet," Lavinia shot back before she burst into tears and went running for the refuge of their room.

"But if your father sent for you, however did your sister manage to get herself betrothed and married to his lordship so quickly?" Tildie asked.

Lavinia glanced up, so lost in her story that she'd all but forgotten that she was here in St. George's. Oh, yes, where was she? She glanced down at the flowers in her hands.

Louisa's hasty marriage to Wakefield.

However could she tell the charwoman her suspicions about Louisa and Lord Wakefield? How they had spent a ruinous amount of time alone together. Perhaps even a night together?

Given that kiss when they'd been pronounced man and wife—well, it was one that spoke of experience.

By both parties.

Lavinia pushed such a scandalous thought aside. Now that Louisa was married, it all hardly mattered.

Besides, she was already in much the same situation with regards to Tuck.

So instead, she went with what she did know of how the match came to fruition.

"Mr. Rowland," she announced. "It was all his doing."

"Him?" Tildie shook her head. "It's my experience that men like that are hardly the ones to be prodding a fellow bachelor into the parson's trap."

"In any other case I might agree," Lavinia said. "But as it turns out, Mr. Rowland isn't quite the heartless knave he appears."

CHAPTER 9

Tuck arrived at his rooms later in the day—his thoughts jumping from one piece of advice to the other.

Pretty isn't what you need right now.

I think you should introduce Miss Tempest to your mother.

Yet he knew right down to the soles of his boots what he must do. Soles that were getting thinner and thinner by the day.

Still, he just couldn't bring himself to do it. To do *that*. To her. To his Livy.

Town had a way of changing people as it was, but when he thought of Lavinia Tempest, he found he rather liked her just the way she was. Cowhanded. A bit sharp-tongued. Well, very sharp-tongued.

But the part of her that coiled around his heart was that starry bit of innocence about her that suggested the world was a magical place—if one only paused to take a glance—even when she stood amid all the grime and grit of London.

He suspected she held the secret of how to do just that—pause and see the stars in the sky, that single bluebell pushing up through a crack in the pavers, how to find the light that was the very spark of life to everything.

Livy stood apart from every woman he'd ever met, extraordinary in her innocence, in her bright blue eyes, in her unguarded manners.

And if he was to do what must be done, all of that could be lost. No, *would* be lost.

For the first time in his life, Alaster Rowland wasn't sure he wanted to take that wager.

For if ever there was a line that just shouldn't, just couldn't be crossed, it was this one.

But then again, he was desperate. And running out of time and options.

He'd sought some solace at White's, but he'd been plagued the moment he arrived by the curious and the "well-wishers" with a litany of questions as to his "progress" and false consolations of "heard about Lady Gourley's" and "sad luck, that."

Sad luck, indeed.

Wretched bad luck that had his neck in a noose was more like it.

And then to make matters worse, there was Ilford holding court in the salon upstairs as if he were the wounded party in all this, decrying that he was the one who was going to pay for all this, for he'd never collect when Tuck lost—not unless he wanted to venture after him to the northern reaches of Canada.

All had laughed, long and hard, that is, until one of the servants had come in with a note for the marquess, one that had left the color draining out of the florid man's face.

Tuck had heard the words, "Wakefield" "in a rage" and "murderous over it," then seen Ilford leave as if the devil were at his heels.

Bloody coward. Oh, Ilford would do his best to ruin others, but when he got called out for his misdeeds, he always conveniently had a prior engagement to see to—usually in Scotland.

Still, with Lord Ilford gone, that hadn't stopped the speculations from running rampant in the room over Tuck's wager and the now-infamous Miss Tempest.

Tuck looked around at all his boon companions, the ones who

had abandoned him since the first indication that he was about to lose his shirt. And his boots. And everything else he possessed.

Lofty and noble gentlemen all.

Yet as he stood in the doorway and listened to them boast and brag, something else struck him.

Not one of these fine examples of all that was good and proper had stood up for Miss Tempest and her sister. Not one of them had decried Ilford's villainous gossip.

Worse, he had to find a likely husband for Livy amongst this collection of gilded liars and rogues.

He'd left White's feeling out of sorts with the world. With *his* world.

And that mood hadn't improved much when he'd entered his rooms and found Falshaw waiting for him like a gargoyle.

With *that* look dragging the man's thick, heavy brow into a single line and his wide chin jutted out. The one that said all too clearly he didn't like to be the one left to defer the landlady on her overdue rent. Or the greengrocer. Or the tailor.

But no, Falshaw's news was worse.

The man straightened, like Black Rod at the House of Lords about to announce some unholy disaster.

"Lord Wakefield has been here," he intoned.

"Piers?" Tuck sputtered, for it was the last name he expected to hear.

Falshaw drew a deep breath, as if gathering patience and perseverance along with a lungful of air. "Yes. As I said, *Lord Wakefield.*" His withering tone implied that he hadn't thought there would be any confusion on the matter. Then to make his point, he added. "His Lordship called twice."

Twice? What the devil? Piers never set foot out of his own house. Well, that is until of late.

Until the Miss Tempests had arrived.

"What did my dear cousin want?" Tuck asked, trying to sound nonchalant as he plucked off his gloves and tossed his hat up on the shelf.

Falshaw's brow furrowed as the hat bounced around a bit before it finally landed—he was after all a valet, at least he tried to be one. "I would hardly know, sir. He didn't mention anything specific," he said with a sigh of resignation.

"He said nothing at all?" It was hard, if not impossible, to imagine Piers being circumspect. The viscount had never been one for subtlety.

"It would be indelicate for me to repeat what he might have mentioned," Falshaw admitted, though grudgingly.

"Out with it, my good man! Indelicate, indeed. When I found you, you didn't even know what that word meant."

Falshaw, who before, in his previous employment at a Seven Dials' gambling hell, had been known as Johnny the Breaker, had the audacity to look affronted.

Dear God, this is what happens when one meddles with the natural order of things, Tuck realized. Falshaw was taking on Mayfair airs.

He didn't want to imagine what would happen to Miss Tempest if he turned her over to his mother and asked her to . . .

No, he couldn't consider that. Not right now. Not when there was this baffling matter of Piers to contend with first. "Out with it, Falshaw."

"I fear he was rather in a state—"

"When is my cousin not?"

"Yes, well, be that as it may, he might have made mention of a young lady. And something about a lending library." Falshaw paused, brow drawn into that line again as if he were waiting for some explanation of these curious utterings.

Tuck wasn't about to offer up explanations. Really, the man was getting as gossipy as a Berkeley Square housekeeper. Besides, he suspected Falshaw of holding back the real heart of the matter—a tit for tat situation.

But with another moment of waiting and adding a withering stare, his manservant became more forthcoming. "Oh, yes, he also said you aren't fooling anyone, and he desires a full accounting of your intentions toward the lady." Falshaw looked as if he would like the same.

A full accounting.

Tuck shook his head. What the devil? Piers was starting to sound like their uncle. "Did Lord Wakefield say he was going to return?"

Falshaw shook his head. "No, he didn't mention it, but he did seem rather determined to find you. I suggested he try Boodles."

"Good man, Falshaw," Tuck said, slapping the fellow on the back. Boodles was their agreed upon diversion if someone came looking for him.

As it was, Tuck never went to Boodles, but most debt collectors didn't know that. And since Piers had been out of society for years, he probably wouldn't remember that either.

Yet avoiding Piers wouldn't be as simple as sending him off to the wrong club. This was Piers. And the only reason Tuck could think of was that he'd heard about the wager and taken exception to it. Especially if what Roselie said the other night was true.

Besides, I do believe Piers rather fancies Miss Louisa.

Piers in love? Oh, that would be dangerous.

"Have we any supper tonight?" Tuck asked as he moved quickly, retrieving his hat from the shelf and gathering up his walking stick. He already knew the answer.

"Not unless you've come into your inheritance, sir," Falshaw replied, the crease in his brow caving into an even deeper crevice. "Sir, may I ask, where are you going?"

"To the one place Piers won't look for me," he replied as he went to the door.

"And where is that, sir?"

"His house. And I know there is supper there," he said with a cheeky grin.

Falshaw hardly looked amused. That, and he had one other thing he'd been holding back. "Sir, there is one other matter . . ."

Tuck paused at the door, hand on the latch. "Yes?"

"A letter," Falshaw said, nodding to the salver on the table.

"Is it of consequence?" Tuck asked.

He was under no delusions that Falshaw, given his background, wasn't so indelicate to be above opening his employer's private correspondence.

"Sir, I would never—" Falshaw began, taking one furtive, guilty glance at the innocuous-looking missive.

"Falshaw, we both know you always do," Tuck told him. "Now, what is it?"

"It is from a lady, though she didn't sign it, and it is rather bad news, I imagine."

"Worse than having my cousin hunting my hide?" Tuck asked, for plaintive, dire notes from ladies weren't exactly an unusual occurrence.

Falshaw nodded toward it, a movement that meant he wasn't going to touch it. At least, not again.

More than he already had, Tuck would point out. Still, he returned to the room and opened the note, the plain white paper folded neatly and crisply, the writing clear and direct.

It has been decided. We are leaving London.

Tuck had two choices—avoid Piers for as long as possible or go find Livy and get this straightened out immediately, but one glance at his pocket watch revealed that he'd have the misfortune of arriving at his uncle's during supper.

Oh, yes, that would make for a painful hour of Lady Aveley's glaring across the table at him and no opportunity to speak privately to Lavinia.

Lady Aveley would see to that. Come to think of it, so would his uncle.

So, unfortunately, Livy would have to wait.

Besides, speaking of supper, Piers had a new cook. The talented Mrs. Petchell. Oh, her steaks were said to be a marvel, perfectly turned and a delight to cut into.

Then again, he'd been all but summoned by Piers, so truly

Tuck was doing his cousin a favor by coming to him instead of forcing the viscount to go blustering about London in search of him.

So it was to Piers's he went, where he found himself being welcomed into the house by the viscount's butler, Tiploft, who greeted him with an effusive, "I am ever so glad that you are here, Mr. Rowland."

And the fellow meant it.

"You are?" Tuck wasn't able to contain his surprise. Most times, Tiploft looked like he should be hurrying to lock up the silver when he arrived.

"Bless her heart, she's done His Lordship a world of good— what with hiring more staff, cleaning up the house, and finding Mrs. Petchell, but I don't know now—His Lordship may ruin everything if he hasn't some guidance with this—"

The man paused and sent a significant glance at the salver near Piers's usual spot. Atop the gleaming plate sat a pile of well-thumbed letters tied up in a blue ribbon.

Something about them, something so very familiar drew Tuck closer, that is until he saw the handwriting. He stumbled back, a cold river of shock rushing through him. "Dear God, those aren't from —"

"Aye, sir," Tiploft said. "Lord Rimswell."

"But where the devil—"

"Miss Louisa brought them over. I didn't mind when she fired the cook, and I haven't complained about her cat, and bless her heart, she's gotten him up and out of the house, but this—" Tiploft shook his head. "It may be too much."

Tuck swallowed. Hell, they were too much for him. Poldie's bold handwriting staring up at him like a specter rising from the grave coming to exact a debt.

"Where did she get them?"

"Lord Rimswell's heir."

"Brody," Tuck said under his breath more as a curse. Then he drew in a deep breath. Brody had said he was going to the park—

somehow he'd managed to intercept Lavinia's sister and pass along his brother's letters from Spain.

"So you can see why I am so glad you've come," Tiploft was saying.

Like a sacrificial lamb to go beside the roasted potatoes and ham already on the table, Tuck mused as his gaze strayed back to the letters.

Those demmed letters.

Tuck sunk into the chair before them.

Tiploft cleared his throat and left, mentioning something about telling the cook that there was to be a second for dinner, leaving Tuck all alone, staring down at the lines—the words blurring and after a moment he realized it was his eyes filling, so he dashed at them with his sleeve.

"Why are you crying?" a child's voice whispered from behind him.

He twisted around to find a pair of imps gaping at him. "Who might you be?"

"I'm Bob, and this is my sister, Bitty. Our aunt is the cook."

The little girl, whose red hair stuck out of the two braids that came down either side of her head, regarded him with the same air of mistrust as Lady Aveley at church.

And then he discovered why.

"You aren't going to make His Lordship mad, are you?" she asked.

"I rather hope not. Devilish temper, my cousin."

"He's yer cousin?" Bob asked, taking a step closer, head cocked and examining Tuck like one might a questionable horse favored in the second race.

"Yes," he told the lad. "Of sorts."

The boy's expression turned skeptical again. "How sorts?"

No one would ever call this child eloquent, but Tuck got the gist of what he was asking. "My uncle, Lord Charleton—"

"The fancy old toff next door?"

"Yes, but don't use that word around him," Tuck advised.

"Which one?" Bitty asked.

He thought about it. "Fancy or old."

"Well, he is," Bob said, clinging to his choices.

"Yes, but I think he'd prefer 'dignified gentleman.'"

The boy shrugged liked he didn't see the difference but there was no accounting for the vagaries of the aristocracy.

"Now where was I?" Tuck asked, liking the pair immediately.

"Your uncle," Bitty prodded. And then added quickly, "The gentleman."

"Yes, yes, thank you," Tuck told her. "My uncle, Lord Charleton was married to your viscount's aunt."

Both children considered this, and it was Bob who came to a conclusion first. "Don't seem like yer related in the least."

Yes, well, there were plenty of times that Piers, his parents, and his sisters had wished the same.

The door creaked a bit and slid slightly open, having been prodded not by Piers but by a large, mangy-looking cat.

"There you are!" Bitty scolded. "Bad Hannibal."

Miss Louisa's infamous cat hardly looked chastened. Instead, it walked into the room, stubby tail waving in the air, his only ear cocked up at a jaunty angle, and with his one good eye, he took in the scene before him with a quick, furtive glance.

Dropping the rat he carried, he headed straight for Tuck.

Having met this beast before, he drew back in his chair.

He rather liked all his fingers and hadn't any desire to lose some to this animal.

"Don't you like cats?" Bitty asked.

"Why, is there one about?" he replied, as Hannibal proceeded to rub and wind around his legs. Then, with one quick, assessing glance at Tuck, he jumped up into his lap, settling down immediately and making a mangled sort of sound that he surmised might be purring.

At least he hoped it was.

"Never heard him do that before," Bob remarked with a bit of awe in his voice.

"What does he usually do?" Tuck asked.

"I don't think you want to know," Bob told him. "Not with him sitting on your lap and all."

"Aunt says he has fleas." Bitty said this as both a caution and as if she was glad to have something to add to the conversation.

Tuck glanced down at the cat in his lap and tried not to shudder. "Lovely."

Nor was Bitty done. "You won't put His Lordship in a state, will you? He was right angry at you earlier, and our aunt just got him sober."

"Your aunt could quite stop Bonaparte if she managed that," he told her.

The little girl beamed at such an opinion, but her expression turned back to one of serious intent. "You shouldn't be squiring about with Miss Tempest."

She couldn't have said anything that would have shocked him more.

"Pardon?" he managed, getting to his feet, dumping Hannibal in the process. The offended cat hissed and stalked from the dining room.

"We saw you," Bob said, coming to stand next to his sister. "With her. In your carriage."

"Well, yes, I was with Miss Tempest."

"Have you been kissing her as well?" Bitty asked.

"Have I been—" Tuck stammered, feeling the conversation had taken a very wrong turn. Then it struck him, sending a rather ugly current of shock through him. "As well? Who else has been kissing Miss Tempest?"

Both children regarded him with an air that said he had their votes for the village idiot.

Then it struck him and he sat back down as it all came together. "Has my cousin been kissing Miss Tempest?"

"Yes," Bitty told him, eagerly really, as if the secret had been bubbling inside her for days ready to burst. "In the linen closet."

"Bitty!" Bob said, rounding on his sister.

"Well, he did. Kiss her."

"But you weren't supposed to tell." Bob heaved an aggrieved sigh. "Mr. Tiploft said so."

Not even this stopped the unrepentant little busybody. Bitty shrugged as if it had been old news to tell, and besides, was being wasted residing in silence.

But Bitty wasn't the only one with a penchant for gossip.

Now it was Bob's turn. "Have you been kissing Miss Tempest as well?"

Tuck was glad he was seated again. "No! I barely know the lady."

"But we saw her—" Bitty said, diving back into her part of their interrogation, "getting into your carriage."

"Twice," Bob added. "What were you doing if you weren't—" The boy stopped there, unable to bring himself to mention an act so repugnant to a lad of his age.

A pair of Lincoln's Field's barristers, these two, Tuck mused. But they had managed to arrange all the facts for him and answer all his questions as to Piers's ire.

"You do know there are two of them," he offered.

They looked insulted. "Of course," Bob huffed.

"And that they are identical?"

"I—what?" Bob asked, his brow furrowed with questions, while a bright light lit up Bitty's face.

"Identical," Bitty informed him. "They look the same."

Bright little minx.

"I was out with the other Miss Tempest, Miss Lavinia Tempest, not your Miss Tempest."

Bob still regarded his assurance with some measure of suspicion—but Bitty seemed quite relieved.

"She's not ours," Bob told him.

"No, she's his," Bitty told him with a nod toward the ceiling, meaning Piers.

"That's excellent news," Tuck told them both. And though his gaze strayed for a moment over toward that demmed pile of letters, he couldn't help himself, he turned his attention back to the children. "Now tell me more about my cousin and Miss Tempest. Especially the kissing part."

Tuck was well into his third helping of lamb and reading the last of Poldie's letters when he heard the front door slam shut.

Ah, Piers. And in his usual good mood. There was a muffled conversation with Tiploft, then his cousin's hard steps came crashing toward the dining room.

When the door plowed opened, Tuck glanced up and grinned. "Where the devil have you been, cuz?"

"Looking all over Town for you," Pierson said as he strolled into the room. But he got no further than the table when his gaze fell on the salver of letters.

There was no mistaking the shock in his eyes—for he knew that handwriting as well as Tuck.

"What are those?" Piers managed, taking an unsteady stance as if he needed confirmation that he was seeing things.

"Letters," Tuck replied, setting the one he'd been reading down amongst the jumble.

But if he thought his cousin would have the same curiosity, he was quite mistaken. For Piers lurched forward, gathered them all up as quickly as he could and carried them toward the fireplace.

Tuck knew he should stop him, do anything to keep those letters from going into the flames, but for the life of him, he couldn't get up. It was almost as if Poldie's calm presence and sensibilities had settled into the room. All Tuck could do was make the same sort of quiet, solid request that their long-lost friend might have.

"Please don't. If you bear any bit of love for Poldie, don't do that."

Piers stiffened, his back still to Tuck. "I can't. I can't read them," the viscount confessed, the words faltering over his tongue.

"Then let me tell you what they say—" Tuck got up and

walked over to where Piers stood. He took the letters from him, sighing with relief that the precious missives were safe.

For now.

As he looked down at Poldie's scrawling handwriting, a desperate sort of need filled Tuck. Piers needed to hear this. Tuck knew that Brody had tried over the years to get Piers to see him, to listen to Poldie's version of the events—which right now, more than ever, Piers needed.

Quickly sorting through them, Tuck smiled at one in particular. It had made him bark aloud with laughter.

"*Wakefield found us a rare cook,*" he read, using Poldie's northern accent and affable tones. "*A fellow from Bristol who can make a feast out of a rat. Though he had the nerve to try and convince us it was rabbit.*"

Pierson had much the same reaction as Tuck and laughed.

So far, so good. Tuck set it down and chose another. The one that had left him with an icy cold lump of foreboding in his chest.

Wakefield saved my life tonight. Pulled me off my horse and down behind a tree just as the French snipers began picking us off again. I never noticed a thing before that moment, but he did. I'll get him killed before this march ends and I'll never be able to live with myself.

He glanced up and found Pierson dashing at the tears welling up in his eyes.

"The next day it was him," the viscount said quietly. "He saved me. But—"

But. Tuck knew what that meant. That "but" had jolted him awake with guilt more times than he could count.

If I had been there, it might have been me, and not Poldie.

"Yes, indeed," Tuck said instead, glancing away, as he dashed at his eyes with his sleeve and went back to reading.

You should see him, Brody. Wakefield is magnificent with the men. He can rally them through chaos, and has held our unit together these long days of marching. The people of England will be well served when he takes his seat in the House of Lords.

Pierson's gaze flew up. "No more," he told Tuck, reaching for that letter.

"No," Tuck said, shaking his head. "This is the last one he wrote to Brody, and you will listen."

Promise me, that if I don't make it, you'll follow his example. Seek his advice. He's the finest man I've ever known. He deserves every honor, every happiness.

"No more, please, no more," Pierson told him.

He couldn't argue with that. More than once he'd put Poldie's letters down, determined not to read another word. But this time it was different. "As you wish. Couldn't read anything more if I wanted to. Those were his last words, Piers. His final wish. That you find happiness."

Pierson shook his head and turned his back to Tuck, unwilling to let anyone see the tangle of emotions roiling inside him.

Much like the ones inside Tuck. He'd read every word. Including a number of passages about himself.

I am sure there are some who have spurned Tuck for abandoning us. For not buying his commission and staying behind. I won't. I trust he had his reasons. Good reasons. If I can forgive him, there isn't a man alive who shouldn't.

"Why did you bring those here?" Piers's question pulled Tuck out of his reverie.

He shrugged. "I didn't. They were here on the table when I came in."

"So you—" Piers's mouth snapped shut, his annoyance leaving him at a loss for words.

Perhaps Tuck shouldn't have pried—after all, Brody had sent the letters for Piers to read, not him. But then again, Tuck believed in luck and fate, and perhaps this was Poldie—reaching from beyond the grave—trying to see this estrangement between his two best friends put to rights.

If Tuck was being honest, he missed Piers—the man who had been more brother to him than chance relation. He missed their routs. He missed the companionable silences that could slide along all evening over a bottle of whisky—and for no other reason than there was nothing that needed to be said.

And he knew that now. Was willing to even admit it, if need be. For when Miss Tempest had asked him that simple question, "What do you do?" he knew he needed to find an answer.

Perhaps it was as simple as being a friend.

So he shrugged off his cousin's sharp words. "Of course. I knew that hand immediately. Knew you might go into one of your stubborn tempers and burn them." He paused and looked Pierson directly in the eye.

He wasn't going to let Poldie's words go up in flames all for one of Piers's irrational flares of temper.

"Where did they come from?" the viscount asked, taking his chair and collapsing into it and pointedly ignoring the jab about his temper.

"According to Tiploft, your Miss Tempest brought them by earlier."

"How the devil—" he began, looking up.

Tuck let him figure it for himself. Besides, his cousin probably knew better how Miss Tempest had gotten hold of letters written to Poldie's brother, Brody.

Piers reached for the decanter Tiploft had brought in earlier, pouring himself a glass of wine, then, after a second, refilling Tuck's glass. "Did you know?"

"Yes," Tuck told him, picking up his glass and letting the wine swirl a bit. "Rather, I suspected. He wrote me as well, you know. Never one to hold a grudge, that Poldie."

"Never," Pierson agreed.

Suddenly, the room seemed to close in around them, and Tuck felt as if they weren't alone. For years it had been the three of them. Him, Piers and Poldie. Inseparable since childhood. Gone to school together. Gotten into more scrapes than he cared to recount.

Piers the adventurer, the headstrong leader. Tuck, madcap and equally driven to find trouble, but savvy enough to save their hides when need be.

And then there had been Poldie. Quiet, solid Poldie. Always there. Always game for whatever his friends proposed.

Yet, the one thing Tuck had never understood, at least until this very moment, was that Poldie had been the glue that had kept them all together. And when he'd died, he and Piers had wrenched apart, fallen away.

In some odd, unforeseeable way, Poldie's calm words had brought them back to this place, and they stood on a precipice. At a moment of choice.

And they both knew it for what it was—a rare opportunity.

A gift from a long-lost friend.

Piers raised his glass, and Tuck followed suit.

"To Poldie," they said together.

And in that moment, a good portion of the estrangement between them melted away, something they both acknowledged in a nod, in silence.

"Yes, well," Tuck finally said, pointing toward one of the covers on the table. "Do try the roast lamb. Mrs. Petchell has outdone herself."

"You mean there is some left?" Pierson teased back.

"Always," Tuck told him. "Always."

And while Pierson filled his plate, Tuck leaned back in his chair, glass in hand, considering how to broach the next subject.

Not that he needed to. Piers, never one to mince words, got to the point. "Why are you here, Tuck?"

"Thought I'd save you the trouble of all that driving and come to call. Heard you were looking for me." He paused and shook his head. "Don't like the idea of anyone nosing about my rooms. Simply not done, my good man. Not without an invitation." He sat up and passed a platter of pork chops—not before taking one. "These are most excellent."

The viscount's gaze rolled upward. "Thank you."

"You're welcome," Tuck said. "Demmit, Piers, what did you think to find?"

"Not 'what.' Whom," Pierson corrected. "What were you doing with Miss Tempest's sister?"

"Which one?" Tuck asked, feeling a bit mischievous. It had been too long since they'd talked like this. "They are devilishly hard to tell apart."

"It doesn't matter which one," Pierson told him. "Whatever you are about, stop."

"Can't," Tuck told him, cutting into a chop.

"Can't?"

"Won't," he insisted.

"Now see here," Pierson told him. "Charleton will have you staked out on the nearest piling on the Thames and leave you for the tide and the fishes for leading one of Sir Ambrose's daughters astray. And nor would I blame him."

Tuck glanced down at his nails, turning his hand one way then the other, completely unmoved. "So is that why you went bolting out of your house to go looking for me? Didn't want me stealing a march on you, eh?"

This took Piers completely aback. "How did you—"

"You need to remind those urchins of yours under whose roof they live before they start gossiping."

God bless the pair, Tuck silently toasted. They had given him fresh hope for his cause.

Pierson had closed his eyes and brought his hand to his forehead.

Given this was Piers, Tuck guessed his cousin was considering a long, laborious punishment for the two imps. Then again, he should probably help them out a bit, at the very least to save them from having to scrub the cellars.

"Yes," Tuck said, raising a glass in a mock toast. "You can't imagine how well informed those two imps are—but you cannot blame them for their indiscretion. I am rather adept at getting what I need." He paused for a second, taking stock of the set of Pierson's brow. "Well, perhaps you can."

"This isn't about me," the viscount told him, sitting up straight and for the first time in years, looking like his old self.

And given that Tuck had known the man all his life, he had to imagine Piers was trying to change the subject, for he never liked being caught out. But this time he wasn't going to get out of a scrape that easily.

Besides, Tuck wasn't the one who'd been caught kissing some innocent gel. He might have sent Lavinia Tempest spinning out of control in Almack's, but what Piers had been doing was irreparably ruinous.

"Not about you? Oh, but it is," Tuck replied. "What the devil are you doing, Piers, kicking up a fuss to find Ilford? You've gone and sent that fox to ground what with all your stomping and saber rattling in all the clubs and his dreary haunts." Tuck leaned forward. "Going after Ilford all by yourself? *Tsk, tsk, tsk.* Badly done."

Piers ruffled with indignation. "You don't think I could?"

Tuck held up both hands. "Oh, I know you could. That's the problem." He reached for his napkin and settled it on the table, then pushed his empty plate forward. "Once you found him, then what were you going to do? Kill him?" He shook his head. "Then once you'd put him to bed with a shovel, what do you think would happen?"

No one was more surprised than Tuck at his own sensible advice. Having read Poldie's letters had given him a fresh perspective. And so armed, he pressed forward.

"You have a chance here, Piers." Tuck needn't say what that chance was.

They both knew what that was. Or rather whom.

The one you've been kissing, Tuck would have liked to add. But he took another tack. "What are you thinking? Letting the likes of Ilford ruin it for you?"

Piers glanced away, trying to hide an expression of grief that Tuck had managed to glimpse. "There is no chance there. She's bound for the country—"

Yes, he knew that as well, but Tuck was never one to give up. He couldn't.

So he laughed. "Don't try some bouncer on me. You went racing out of this house today because you love that gel."

"I hardly raced."

"Yes, well I got my information from those brats of yours."

"They are not mine."

"Tell them that," Tuck replied, smiling as he poured himself another glass of wine. "As for the other Miss Tempest, you have to trust me when I say I have that chit's best interests at heart. You'll see."

"I doubt it. They must leave town now, Tuck. There is no other way of it," Pierson told him—resorting to the gloomy countenance that had become far too familiar on his old friend.

"Bother that," Tuck declared. "I'll make those two the talk of the Town before the Season is done."

"I think Ilford already managed that," Piers pointed out.

"He can go to the devil," Tuck told him, half hoping the man was already there, imagining a dozen or so endings for the foul fellow that hardly seemed good enough.

Now it was Pierson's turn to laugh, for he probably knew exactly what Tuck was thinking—just as he had when they'd been younger. "You told me I couldn't kill him."

"So I did," Tuck admitted. "Sometimes I forget myself."

Just then there was a scratch at the door, followed by Tiploft's entrance. He came in carrying a tray and wearing a somber expression. "You are summoned to Lord Charleton's."

Pierson glanced over at Tuck. "Told you. You're in the suds now. Charleton will cut off your quarterlies, if not your—"

"My lord," Tiploft said in an uncharacteristic interruption. "It isn't Mr. Rowland."

The viscount looked up at his butler. "Pardon?"

"It isn't Mr. Rowland who is summoned next door," Tiploft told him. "You are, my lord."

Tuck reached for the decanter and topped off his glass, raising it in a mock salute. "In the suds now, cousin."

Wakefield rose, his brow furrowed.

"Care for some experienced advice?" Tuck offered.

Piers only glared.

Never one to back down from his friend's temper, he grinned. "Don't bother denying the charges. Uncle rarely has his facts wrong."

To this, Piers cringed.

That bad, eh? Tuck mused.

Then, when the viscount turned to leave, he added one more sally. "In the linen closet? Truly? Cousin, you need this gel more than you realize."

CHAPTER 10

Lavinia sat stubbornly on the bed, arms folded over her chest as Louisa continued sorting and folding her clothes. Her open trunk was half full, and she kept slanting significant glances in Lavinia's direction that said all too clearly her sister should do the same.

Resign herself to leaving London and do her packing.

Lavinia refused. Even though the hour was growing late. Even though Mr. Rowland hadn't answered her summons.

She'd waited all through dinner for Brobson to come into the dining room and announce an addition to their party.

But Mr. Rowland had not come. She was starting to fear he hadn't gotten her note.

Or that he'd given up entirely. No longer cared for her.

For some reason, those two notions stung more than the thought of going home.

"Vivi, no need to frown and dwell on these matters," Louisa said, her voice full of false cheer. "Going home means we won't have to endure another night like Saturday or ever have to set foot in Almack's again."

"But Lady Wakefield promised to call tomorrow, and I am most certain she will be able to help us."

Louisa's reply was only a sad shake of her head.

So Lavinia curled tighter into a ball and chose to ignore her sister's industry.

Nor did she do much more than glance at the door when one of the maids scratched at it and popped her head in.

"Miss," she said, looking from Louisa to Lavinia. "Ur, His Lordship would like to see you in the library."

This got Lavinia to her feet. "He does?" Tuck! He'd come to rescue her.

Rather, *Mr. Rowland* had come to her aid.

"Um, well, he asked for Miss Louisa," the girl posed carefully, looking again from one sister to the other.

Louisa? Lavinia stilled, then dropped back down on her narrow bed.

"Me?" her sister asked. "I don't see why—"

"His Lordship is in the library," the girl said, rushing along now that she'd found the right miss.

"I hardly feel like a game of chess with all I have to do, but it would be rude to turn down the baron when he's been nothing but kind to us," Louisa said. Then, with a sigh of resignation, she nodded to the maid and turned to Lavinia. She looked about to say something more, but then changed her mind and left in silence.

Which was just as well. Lavinia didn't want to hear it.

Glancing about the room, the heavy weight of resignation fell down upon her. Truly, there was nothing to be done but pack, but oh, how she hated giving up.

Losing all she'd ever wanted since that fateful day—the one the beautiful and vivacious Lady Tempest had chosen to leave them.

How was that her one and only memory of her mother?

And why did it have to be so clear? So piercing in the detail. She'd stood all alone at the nursery window, watching as her mother had come dashing out of the house, valise in hand, and climbed hastily into the open carriage that had pulled into the drive just moments earlier.

And then the pair, Mama and the man who'd been coming to the house to give Lady Tempest dancing lessons, had driven off.

Her mother hadn't even looked up at the house. Bothered to check the nursery window. Just put her back to her children and husband and left.

And even at that tender age, Lavinia had known what it all meant. Not that it had stopped her from wishing with all her heart, *Look back, Mama, look back and see me, so you will know you've made a mistake.*

But Lady Tempest never had. Looked back. Or returned, for that matter. Rather there had been the story put about of her being lost in a carriage accident, but even that hadn't carried a ring of truth to Lavinia.

Later, the whispers at social gatherings and such had all but confirmed what Lavinia suspected.

"Accident indeed!"

"Poor dears. So blighted by that woman."

"It's a favor she did, never returning. Such a shameful business."

And when her mother had finally perished—in Italy, of a fever, all alone, having been long since abandoned by her lover, Louisa had seen the post when it arrived.

And later found it, tucked in the far back of Papa's desk drawer.

She knew she shouldn't, but she'd stolen it and secretly translated what the priest from Verona had written, the Italian dictionary in the library helping her make out the gist of the man's words.

Signore, I regretfully write you to tell you of the passing of your wife.

Instead of feeling the shame of her mother's actions, her mother's scandal, what had torn Lavinia's heart in half was the shock and grief on her father's face when that letter had arrived.

The quiet fortnight retreat he'd made into his own private hell had aged him more than the past ten years of shame ever had.

Lavinia had vowed, after she'd put all the pieces together, that she would atone for all those sins. She would go to London, make

a brilliant match—just as their mother had done—then she—
Lavinia—would be the perfect wife, with never a thought to
desert her children, her house, her husband.

She would erase the pain and disgrace her mother had caused.
By her own good example, she'd show them all that she hadn't an
iota of her mother's taint to her, there would be no more need to
whisper behind a flutter of fans every time she entered a room.

Thus was born her list of all that was proper and ladylike. Like
a mariner's compass, it pointed her life in a direction that would
never allow for error, a single misstep.

That is, until she'd arrived at Almack's. And everything she'd
worked for, every lesson, every adherence to propriety had been
lost in just that—a single misstep.

Granted, more like a colossal tumble—but nonetheless now
she was branded with the sins of her mother.

Punished to a spinsterhood that would leave her as a caution-
ary tale to all young ladies and a subject of conjecture and suspicions rather than the example of good sense and proper principles
that she'd always strived to be.

Her list. Her beloved list, all that hard work, all those lessons,
for naught.

Worse, there was Roselie's suggestion that she and Tuck suited
each other.

She pressed her lips together. Why, that was utter madness.
They. Did. Not. Suit.

Tap.

Lavinia paused.

Tap. Tap.

She turned toward the window. *Tap.*

Puzzled, she went to it and pushed open the curtain. Down in
the garden, she could see a man prodding around in the dirt with
the toe of his boot. Retrieving a stone he'd dislodged, he looked
up and paused when he saw her standing there.

A wicked grin lit his face. A decidedly improper one.

And she knew just how improper such an expression that was, for to be a proper lady, one needed to know exactly what wickedness looked like.

And Alaster Rowland was the epitome of everything that was scandalous about a man—standing there in the moonlight—his cravat loose and open, his coat unbuttoned, and his boots now muddy from the garden.

He looked more like a highwayman come to steal the silver than the gentleman he was purported to be.

Besides, gentlemen didn't come throwing stones at the window of a lady's bedchamber.

How utterly indecorous, she told herself. *How very Tuck.*

So why did she want to climb down the drainpipe and dash across the bit of lawn toward him?

Doing exactly what her mother did . . .

Setting her jaw, she pushed the window open with only one thought. *Send the rogue packing.*

"Come down." His request—it wasn't so much a request as a command, an expectation—teased her with temptation.

"I will not." She wouldn't. She couldn't. She stole another glance down at him, telling herself she needed to confirm to herself who he was—a rogue. A knave. Not to be trusted.

And yet he called to her. Loosened a part of her that had been buried deeply ever since the day her mother had taken flight.

"I have good news."

She doubted that—at least the sensible part did. Her heart, on the other hand, chimed happily at those words.

Good news.

Oh, but being a proper lady meant one had to listen to sensibility and propriety. Not the wavering and fickle breezes of a suddenly unreliable organ.

"Have you found me a likely match?" That was after all what their agreement was: for him to find her a suitable *parti.* "Well, have you?"

"Um, no," he admitted, his boots shuffling in the dirt beneath him.

"Are my vouchers to Almack's to be restored?"

His gaze rolled toward the stars. "Don't really see why anyone would want them in the first place. Almack's is nothing more than a den of dreadful—"

"Have you or haven't you?" she pressed.

Again, he shuffled uncomfortably. "No, I haven't got any vouchers."

Harrumph. She crossed her arms over her bosom and frowned. "Have you come with a salver full of invitations?"

He groaned as well, one hand raking through his hair, leaving it all tousled. At the sight of him thusly—bareheaded and anxious—her fingers flexed in a desire to straighten the untidy curls at his brow, smooth out the furrow.

Which was hardly a proper thought, she realized, banishing it to the dark reaches of her heart and tightening her fingers into a hard ball.

There wasn't a single reason to become softhearted over the perpetually unrepentant likes of Alaster Rowland.

None. Whatsoever.

Save when he looked so undone as he did now . . .

"Sir, I asked—"

"Yes, yes, I heard you. And you can very well see that I don't have any bloody salvers or knights in shining armor tucked up my sleeve." He shook out both arms just to make his point. "Besides, you summoned me."

Lavinia's lips pursed together. He would have to bring that up.

Nor was he about to let it alone. "So it is only good and proper that *you* come down *here*."

"I don't see how you can say you come bearing good news. No suitors. No invitations. No vouchers." She paused, suddenly distracted. "Oh, good heavens, is that button still loose?"

"Wha-a-a-t?"

"The button on your coat—is it still loose from earlier?"

"I imagine it is," he told her, looking down and, to her horror, plucking the poor thing free of his coat. "It is in worst straits now." He held it up for her to see, looking most woebegone.

Oh, heavens no. The only thing worse than a button hanging by a thread in her estimation was one tugged completely free. Now it just begged to be lost.

Botheration, considering everyone said Tuck Rowland had pockets to let, it only figured that they would also have holes in them.

Why didn't he just cast that perfectly good silver button into the gutter and be done with it?

Lavinia shuddered, thinking of Proper Rule No. 23.

One must keep one's garments in a state of proper repair to avoid an appearance of dilapidation.

Down below, Tuck coughed to get her attention. "Forget the demmed button, will you? Just come down to the garden." Each word was bitten off as if he was barely holding in his frustration.

He was frustrated? He wasn't the one being sent off in disgrace.

"Just come down and hear me out." After a pause, he added, "Please. After all, you did ask for my help."

Bother that horrible moment of weakness, she cursed.

"Why would I want to do something utterly ruinous and improper as all that?" It was an irrational argument considering she'd been sneaking off with Mr. Rowland for days, but she was in a mulish mood.

Hence her refusal to pack. Or vacate Lord Charleton's house. Or quit London.

But to his credit, he didn't point out the fault in her logic. No, he went back to what he did best. Coaxing.

"Livy, I have a plan," he said offhandedly, his words rising with all the right notes of a piper meant to lure her astray. "You won't have to leave London. I promise."

Not leave? It was too good to be true.

Still, wasn't that exactly why she'd written her desperate note in the first place? So he would come and rescue her?

"This won't take but five minutes, Livy. Please. Hear me out."

Lavinia wavered. Why was it every time he called her "Livy," something unfurled inside her.

An unwilling surrender of sorts.

"Though," he added, "what I have to suggest might be slightly *improper.*"

Oh, there was something about the way he said that word, *improper,* that left her shivering. Much as she did when he held her in his arms.

Improper and Tuck seemed to go hand in hand. The man probably knew every way to define it. Act upon it.

Lead her to it. She shivered anew, her knees quaking slightly.

"Then again," he was saying. "I was wrong to come to you. Given your strict adherence to your list. Perhaps it is best that you return to Kibble."

"Kempton," she corrected without thought. But how that word and all it meant jarred her. *Kempton.*

Her eyes closed, but all she saw before her was a spinster's cold and lonely existence.

It was also enough to nudge her past her pride, past her list— but just this once more. Slowly, she opened her eyes, only to find that he had turned to leave. "Is this new plan anything like your last one? The one that left me alone and humiliated at Lady Gourley's?"

At least at this he had the decency to look properly contrite as he glanced over his shoulder. "I will admit that wasn't my best-laid endeavor."

Harrumph. An utter shambles would be a more accurate description.

"But this time," he continued as he returned to the spot under her window, "I have a proposition I know will work. At least it's worked before."

"A proposition?" Oh, she just bet he had one of *those*. He probably had half a dozen or so such propositions planned for the remainder of his evening.

Harrumph. She went to close the sash.

"No. No. No. Miss Tempest, you misunderstand. Please listen."

Not Lavinia. Not Livy. But Miss Tempest. All proper and quite respectable.

For some reason, that left her even more vexed. She rather liked being his Livy. Not his, precisely, but . . . well, it was hard explain.

Or understand.

But it was there. That desire. That need. To hear him call to her in that terribly familiar, overly improper manner.

For it suited. More than she cared to admit.

"I don't need to do anything but finish packing," she told him, turning to look over her shoulder as if she had mountains piled about her.

Not that he could see she hadn't even opened her trunk, or the clothes-press, or even a drawer.

"Livy, sweet Livy, you cannot give up. You haven't it in you."

And there it was. Livy. She was his Livy again. Her heart pattered rebelliously.

He stepped closer to the house and looked up at her. "Packing is a waste of your time. Come down, and I'll tell you why." After a moment, he glanced up again, a wry grin on his face. "Please, Livy?"

"You shouldn't call me that," she muttered under her breath. Because when he did, oh, how it tugged at her in the most dangerous ways.

She glanced over her shoulder at Louisa's half packed trunk and her own unopened one sitting at the foot of her bed.

Truly, what were her choices? Give up and fold gowns or go listen to whatever outlandish nonsense Tuck Rowland had come up with now.

You did ask for this . . .

Lavinia shook away that thought and told herself that she certainly hadn't asked him to show up so late and in such an unsuitable fashion.

Why couldn't he knock at the front door like a gentleman?

Because he's a knave, and right now, that's exactly what you need.

Needed? At that, Lavinia took a step back from the window. "Perhaps it is best if I just left London and saved you all the trouble."

"Leave? Heaven forbid!" Tuck declared, trying his best not to look as panicked as he felt. Leave? Was she mad?

With her sister all but matched to Piers, he was halfway to winning his wager.

All he needed was a bit of luck, a likely gentleman to shower some attention on Livy, give her an enviable boost up in society, then . . .

Something icy knifed through him at that thought, but he had to push it aside.

No, he must play the hand he'd been dealt. Besides, Brody and Lady Wakefield had passed him the winning card.

One he'd be a fool not to play.

"Don't see why I would want to stay," she was saying.

"What is all this?" Tuck wasn't a gambler for nothing, and he had the sense she was bluffing. "You hardly strike me as someone who gives up so easily."

"I'm not," she told him, bristling a bit at the implication. "But—"

"No 'buts.'" He began to dig into his jacket and fished out the note she'd sent. Holding it up like the most damning bit of evidence ever produced, he said, "The lady who wrote this had no intention of being sent home in disgrace."

She flinched. Good. She should.

"That was hours ago," she shot back. "Speaking of which, what took so long?"

"I had a matter to take care of with Piers, then I came straight-away."

She hardly looked impressed. Which meant his most proper, list-at-the-ready miss was girding herself for battle.

As she ought to. For she had a battle in front of her.

Yet when she didn't so much as move or reply, or toss down another parry, he continued his explanation. "Yes, well, it would have been a shameful waste not to partake in dinner at Piers's when it was all laid and waiting to be eaten." He sighed with pleasure as if recalling every bite. "How the devil did your sister get the infamous Mrs. Petchell to cook for my cousin?"

"I believe Lady Aveley helped. But then again, Louisa can be quite persistent."

"She'd have to be to charm my cousin as she obviously has."

"Charmed him? Whatever are you implying?"

He grinned at her. "Come down, and I'll tell you."

She wasn't so easily persuaded. Instead, she sniffed and crossed her arms over her bosom in a stubborn declaration.

Impossible minx. But he had a few tricks up his sleeve. Including a few improper ones.

Shrugging off his jacket, he tossed it aside and came stalking through the flower garden to the side of the house.

She might be a stubborn miss, but she was also incurably curious, for she leaned out the window almost immediately. "Whatever are you doing? You'll trample Lord Charleton's prized peonies if you aren't careful."

"Then he will have only you to blame. If you won't come down and have a civil conversation with me," he told her, spitting on his hands and rubbing them together, "then I shall just come up." He caught hold of the drainpipe and put his foot on a stone that jutted out a bit and hoisted himself up.

She leaned out the window, gaping at him. "What? You mustn't! You shouldn't!"

"It isn't like I haven't climbed into that window before."

THE KNAVE OF HEARTS

"You'll fall. Quite possibly break your neck."

He shrugged. "Not to mention the state I'll leave the peonies in."

"Mr. Rowland, you climb right back down this very moment."

"What? Don't you want some help packing?" He climbed a little higher.

"No!" She heaved a sigh. "Oh, sir, you'll leave me ruined."

"I already did," he reminded her.

"Worse than ruined," she protested.

He wasn't too sure what was "worse than ruined," but he suspected if he asked, she'd tell him.

She probably had a bloody list.

"I am going to continue climbing until you agree to come down and hear my plans."

"Not if I lock the window," she said, hands going to the window frame. "Or throw a vase at you." She disappeared for a moment and returned, brandishing yet another vase.

Oh, hell. She would.

Leave him clinging to the drainpipe a good two floors above the ground or worse, laid low by a well-flung piece of crockery.

"Then I'd have to call for help," he told her. "It would be devilishly embarrassing to explain how you wrote me a note and pleaded for me to come to you . . ."

"No one will believe you."

"I have a missive that begs otherwise."

"That is blackmail!" she declared, but, notably, she relinquished the vase.

"I suppose it is," he told her.

"And hardly proper."

"Decidedly improper." He winked and began to edge a little higher.

And apparently high enough for her. For she made a loud *harrumph*, crossed her arms again and in a sense, surrendered. "I will come down. But for no more than"—she seemed to be considering the scenario—"well, five minutes—you can hardly cause much scandal or ruin in that amount of time." With that, she turned and left the window.

Tuck sighed with relief and climbed back down.

Nor did he point out the real flaw in her logic.

There were plenty of ruinous things he could do to a lady in five minutes.

He'd even give her a list.

CHAPTER 11

Lavinia turned from the window and considered picking up the chamber pot and tossing it at his head.

Of all the infuriating, horrible, dreadful knaves!

Threatening to climb up into her bedchamber.

Why it was a ruinous notion. Not that he seemed to care. Apparently, climbing into a lady's private room was nothing to him.

No more than the proper care of peonies.

Or jackets, she suddenly recalled, having had the nagging suspicion she'd forgotten something. Oh, bother, he'd lose that button if it wasn't promptly sewn back on.

Cursing that weak moment when she'd agreed to his schemes—that, and her abhorrence of missing buttons—she dug around in her drawer for her sewing kit, and with it in hand, caught up her shawl and readied herself to hear him out.

And then point out the flaws in whatever madcap scheme he'd suddenly devised.

No, she wouldn't be lulled this time. She'd stick to her list. Everything had gone wrong the moment she'd deviated from her carefully wrought plans.

She only hoped five minutes would be enough time, for if

she was being honest, it wasn't so much that she didn't trust Mr. Rowland—more to the point she didn't trust herself.

Not with him.

With his charming ways, that grin that took her breath away, the merry way he looked at the world.

Looked at her.

Lavinia brushed at the gooseflesh rising on her arms. Willed her heart to resume a normal, level rhythm.

Yet when she got outside, Mr. Rowland was no longer standing among the peonies. Good news for the budding blossoms but leaving her with a darkened yard to search.

"Bother the man," she muttered as she quietly and warily went down the steps.

And when she got to the end of the graveled path, she paused, having finally spotted him, standing in the shadows, his face turned to the house beyond the garden wall.

Lord Wakefield's residence.

She couldn't see what Louisa saw in the bellicose viscount or his dreary house. But then again, Louisa also loved Hannibal.

Certainly there was no accounting for another's sensibilities. Or the lack thereof.

Speaking of lacking in sensibilities, she opened her mouth to begin the lecture she'd been compiling since she'd left the sanctuary of her room, but the censorious words stopped in her throat.

If she was willing to admit such a thing, she might have acknowledged that it was her heart that put a stopper in her ire.

For of all the times she'd looked upon Alaster Rowland— bosky at Almack's, rakishly bowing to her at Monsieur Ponthieux's, grinning as he'd driven up in the carriage today, winking at her as he'd been about to climb up the drainpipe, she'd never thought of him as anything but devilishly carefree.

The epitome of a rake. Knavishly handsome, without a care in the world. No thought other than to his own pleasures and his own desires.

That is until she saw him standing before her in his shirtsleeves and a bit disheveled from his scrapped climb up the drainpipe.

His expression laid low every conviction she held about him. For there on his face was a mixture of emotions, so raw, so deeply personal that she nearly gasped.

No amount of censure could match the pain she saw in his eyes. The regret. The loss. Deep, personal loss.

All of it played out in the crease of his brows, the hard set of his jaw. But it was his eyes, pleading and searching as they looked at the dark house beyond Lord Charleton's garden wall, that told the story.

If that wasn't wrenching enough, her own reaction left her trembling.

Go to him. A voice from deep within her soul nudged. *He needs you.*

She couldn't even argue the fact. She'd never seen a man so lost in his own reverie. In a place so bleak that she wondered if she were to wrap her arms around him, lend him her own warmth, would she be able to pull him back from the abyss upon which he seemed to be teetering.

Be able to find some way to bring solace to the pain in his expression.

Suddenly, the path beneath her feet became a crossroads of sorts.

If she dared, if she went to him, put her hand upon his sleeve, everything would change.

For this would be a very different sort of dance. A pledge of sorts.

Because now she knew the truth.

Inside this knave, this beast of a man, this wretched and intolerable rake, beat a broken heart.

Oh, she knew a broken heart only too well.

She also knew the cure for such an ailment.

One she dared not offer. Not to this knave.

For that would be her ruin.

*   *   *

Tuck had watched Livy turn from the window, and he'd turned as well, only to find himself looking over at the house across the garden wall.

Piers's house.

He didn't know how he felt now when he looked at it. For in the last few hours, everything had changed.

He'd changed.

He walked across his uncle's lawn, toward the house he knew as intimately as he knew his own rooms—and tamped down a familiar bit of envy.

Pierson Stratton, the fifth Viscount Wakefield, had everything, in Tuck's estimation. A title. Wealth. A comfortable London house. Profitable estates in the country.

While Tuck . . . well, he had his wits and an inheritance that might or might not be his one day.

An inheritance that went to him because his uncle had yet to have a son, and there was no one else between them.

Growing up, Tuck had never thought much about the differences in their stations—his and Piers's—until the day Piers had come into his inheritance, and a gulf of sorts had opened between them.

Not so much on Piers's part, but Tuck suddenly had seen how very different their circumstances would be—a realization that had only been magnified on the night before they were to buy their commissions.

Those long, dark hours had changed everything.

It had begun weeks earlier with a reckless decision—he, Poldie and Piers—all vowing to join the army in Spain. To fight Napoleon. To win for King and country.

"And," as Poldie had drunkenly added, "to put a good thousand miles between us and every busybody, matchmaking mother bent on pushing her cowhanded daughters into our path."

They'd all had a grand laugh over it.

Lord Charleton had reluctantly given his blessing (and the money to buy the commission) to Tuck—claiming he didn't like the idea of his only heir running off to war, but for the first time in his life, Tuck had seen a hint of pride in his uncle's expression.

And he'd fully intended to do all of it. Buy his commission. Go to war. Fight with Poldie and Piers.

Make his uncle proud. Be the heir worthy of the old and venerable barony that had been in his family for centuries.

And then it had all gone wrong.

He shook his head at the memory, trying yet again to dislodge it, leave it behind once and for all.

But it clung to him stubbornly, refusing to let go, towing behind him like a great anchor.

He hadn't gone. The money for his commission wiped out. His friends sailing away without him. Piers furious and Poldie, dear Poldie, forgiving. Endlessly forgiving.

If only Tuck could do the same for himself.

A crunch on the gravel pulled Tuck out of the darkness of the past.

There, he spied Miss Tempest stealing back toward the house.

"Livy," he called softly, "please don't leave."

She stilled, then slowly turned around.

Nothing could have prepared him for what happened next.

For there in the garden stood the most beguilingly innocent creature he'd ever seen. Her mahogany hair lay in a thick braid, falling over one shoulder. Her plain gown and fair countenance gave her the appearance of some tempting creature Shakespeare might have conjured—a rare and perfect nymph sent to tempt a mortal man astray.

If there was anyone in London alive who knew how to be led astray, it was Tuck.

And this was Livy. His Livy.

His heart made some odd clutch. A rusty, unfamiliar lurch.

No, he reminded himself, he mustn't think of her as Livy. Rather as Miss Tempest. All sensible and proper and practical. With a list.

A bloody list! That was it, think about that wretched list of hers. If that wasn't enough to send a fellow shying for high ground, he didn't know what would.

Yet as he looked again at the reserved creature standing there, even her demmed list seemed to have its endearing points. And as Tuck struggled to find the right words to say, even the heavens above seemed to grind to a stop, offering up one last whisper.

Pretty is not what you want . . .

Then again, Brody hadn't seen her like this.

For that matter, how was it that he, Tuck, had not seen *this*? The luster of her hair—even in the dim light, the curve of her cheek, the rich, deep color of her lips, the starry light of her eyes.

His gut tightened, and he was struck—flabbergasted really—by how tempting Lavinia Tempest appeared.

If only he could trot her down to White's right now—there wasn't a single man who wouldn't demand her hand in marriage.

They'd all want her.

Right now, any man who looked upon her—standing there like a doe caught at the edge of a meadow—would hand over Tuck's full portion of the wager and not care a wit about the state of his boots for the next fifty years.

Would make her *his Livy.*

No longer Tuck's. Never again his.

Tuck wanted to celebrate, and yet his gut clenched as he came to the sudden realization that at the end of all this, she would belong to another.

Oh, he'd known that all along, but why did it matter now?

Because that someone would not be him. No more dancing lessons, no more lectures on propriety.

No more late night meetings in the garden.

Nor would he be treated to the sight of those fair, ripe lips turning up in a rare smile—one meant just for him.

Like when he'd danced with her at Ponthieux's. Or today, when she'd waltzed in his arms.

"Mr. Rowland, are you attending me?" she was asking. "You didn't strike your head when you climbed down, did you?"

His gaze rose to meet hers, and whatever she saw reflected in his eyes startled her.

For her eyes widened, and her mouth opened slightly—perhaps to protest, or maybe to acquiesce. Whatever her reaction, she shivered a bit and took a step back.

"Perhaps this was a bad idea," she said hastily, turning to leave. "I should go back inside."

"Go?" he reached out and caught hold of her hand, stopping her escape. "No, you mustn't. I haven't told you my plans."

"Ah, yes, your plans. The ones you lured me out here with." She glanced down at his hand holding hers and back up at him, her brow arching enough to get him to release her.

Reluctantly so.

"Lured. Hardly." He glanced around and realized this was rather the perfect scenario for a luring. The secluded corner in the garden. The household behind them all dark and quiet.

How easy it was to imagine her in his arms, looking up at him with those wide, innocent eyes, and whispering the words she said the other day in his uncle's study.

I've never been kissed.

Oh, that wouldn't take long to rectify.

"You spoke of a plan?" she prodded. She with the list of the perfect characteristics of a gentleman. She with her proper *this* and *that*.

Certainly, there wasn't a single column where his name might be added. Not even in pencil.

"Oh, yes, my plan," he said, tucking his hands behind his back, where they would stay out of mischief. "I know someone who found themselves in much your circumstances."

"Ruined and an object of scorn?"

"Beautiful and overlooked," he corrected.

Her response was a spinsterly *harrumph*.

No Spanish coin for Miss Tempest. So he continued, "This lady"—a term he was using loosely—"was able to elevate herself to a perfectly respectable marriage and place in society."

Yes, it was the perfect plan. One that would put her far from his sudden, unnerving temptation to have her.

Keep her all to himself. His Livy.

"And?" she prodded again. As if the answer wasn't self-evident.

"And what?"

"There must be an 'and' or a 'but' in all this. For if it was above board and entirely respectable, might not you have thought of it before this?"

"Yes, well, her means . . . well, they aren't entirely—"

"Proper?"

Of course, Miss Tempest had the right word at the ready. Conveniently, it was also her favorite one.

"Well, not precisely. Let's just say her methods aren't exactly taught in your average Bath school."

At this, the lady melted a little. "Oh, if only Louisa and I could have gone to school in Bath, but Papa quite forbade it."

Or couldn't afford it, Tuck mused. For hadn't his uncle been rather circumspect before about the Tempest sisters' dowries.

Which usually meant there wasn't much to be had. Besides, what little Tuck did know of their father, Sir Ambrose, he was merely a scholar—though one of some note—but given Tuck's experience with that sort, he knew it was a polite way of saying the fellow wasn't suited for much else but nosing about dusty books.

"The trappings of a Bath education are overrated," he told her. "This lady did well enough without so much as setting a foot inside one of those schools, and so can you if you are willing to give yourself over to her tutelage."

Miss Tempest appeared thoroughly skeptical.

He continued to press his case. "I believe with her guidance, you would rise quickly above your current situation."

"How?"

"You needn't sound so suspicious," he told her. Not that he blamed her. The entire plan was madness, but other than carting her down to White's right now and auctioning her off to the highest bidder, he didn't have many other choices. "But if you want to follow your sister to the altar, you had best seize this opportunity."

"Are you mad or exceedingly bosky?" Lavinia leaned forward and sniffed, catching a whiff of the sweet scent of Madeira. "Bosky!" Oh, whatever had she been thinking coming down here to listen to his promises and exaggerations. "My sister is not getting married. We are going home." She turned to go back inside.

"Wait! It's true," he told her. "My cousin is madly in love with your sister."

"Oh, I don't believe it—" she began, glancing over the wall at the dark house across the lane.

Certainly, she knew Louisa had developed a *tendre* for the viscount—her sister had said as much the other night—but she'd also been quite adamant on the point that her feelings were not returned.

But if what Mr. Rowland was saying was true . . .

A spark of something flared to life inside her.

"However do you know all this?" she asked. No, make that demanded. "From what I understand, you and the viscount aren't exactly on speaking terms."

There was something in Mr. Rowland's expression that flickered at this, flinched as if she'd poked at an old wound.

Whatever had happened between the two of them? she wondered as she remembered Lady Aveley's words the other day.

The pair of them—Piers and Tuck—couldn't be separated. Trouble, both of them. How their mothers despaired.

"Piers and I just finished a very illuminating supper." And he told her what he'd learned from the cook's chatty niece and nephew.

That the Viscount Wakefield was very much in love with Louisa.

She made her way over to the bench and sat down, feeling

suddenly both light-headed and bowled over. It was all too much to believe—though given her own current schism with Louisa—obviously there was plenty between the two of them that had gone unsaid.

That, and Lavinia realized she'd been so busy with her own concerns that she truly hadn't been paying much attention to Louisa.

Meanwhile, Tuck continued on. "Trust me. You won't be returning to Kittleton—"

"Kempton," she corrected absently.

"Yes, yes, that place any time soon. Not if Piers has any say in the matter. He's over here right now explaining himself to my uncle. He was summoned."

"Over with Lord Charlton?" Lavinia shook her head. "No, no, I hardly see how that's possible, for His Lordship summoned Louisa down to the library not fifteen minutes ago." Then Lavinia paused as she saw that request in an entirely new light. "Oh, my heavens, if the viscount is there, and Louisa is there . . . you don't think—"

"I do," Tuck said, grinning from ear to ear.

"Are you suggesting my sister and the viscount have been—"

"Improper?" he posed. "Most definitely."

"Oh, good heavens," Lavinia sputtered. For certainly that was the only reason she could think of for such a hasty match, but she hadn't wanted to believe it.

Yet hadn't Louisa said as much the other night? After the fiasco at Almack's? That the viscount had driven her home in his carriage. Alone.

Her gaze flew to look at the dark house across the lane. Oh, this was ruinous.

"I would wager Falshaw's wages for the remainder of the year that your sister will be the Viscountess Wakefield before the week is out."

"You should pay the poor man his wages instead of wagering them," Lavinia remarked tartly even as she knew this news should make her deliriously happy—Louisa to be married. But it seemed so very ironic that her sister—who had not wanted to be matched, who hadn't wanted to come to London in the first place—was now to be wed.

"You are too concerned for my valet's welfare," he teased. "Falshaw soldiers on very well, wages or no."

"I would think he would prefer not to—soldier on, that is." She sighed a bit. "I know I would."

"What's this?" Tuck asked, sitting down beside her and tipping his head so he could see her downcast face. "Your sister is as good as betrothed. You should be happy. I know I am delighted."

One glance at him revealed a bright light in his eyes that she hadn't seen before. In fact, he looked overjoyed.

For a moment, she wondered why—why was Tuck Rowland, of all people, so happy to see a fellow bachelor caught in the parson's mousetrap?

Perhaps because it wasn't him being led down the aisle.

Setting a nagging suspicion that there was more to Tuck's *bon vivant* than met the eye, she tried to rally. "Oh, yes, it is most wonderful," she managed, hoping that hid how at odds she felt over her sister's good fortune—no, make that unexpected and meteoric rise in circumstances.

And when Louisa married—where would that leave her? Still in disgrace. Still ruined. And worst of all? Still a spinster. All alone.

Oh, it was unbearable.

She turned toward Mr. Rowland and told him the truth. "Yes, but I hardly see how this all helps me. Even if what you say is true, and Louisa is to be married, my situation remains unchanged, and it will be better for everyone if I just go home as planned."

Livy turned to leave, and Tuck gaped after her. But not for long.

"I won't hear of it," he told her.

"I don't believe it is your decision to make."

"At least hear me out. "

She shrugged. "I have heard your vague plan and hardly see

how this woman can help me," she told him, then continued toward the house.

Tuck knew women well enough to know when one had set her jaw and wasn't going to listen, but when he jammed his hands into his pockets and his fingers curled around the button there, something else came to him. "You've hardly listened to my plans. It will take no more time than it will for you to sew on my button." He held it up for her to see. "You'd be as guilty as Falshaw for sending me off in such a state of *dishabille.*"

It was a gross misstatement of the truth, but he knew her.

Miss Lavinia Tempest loved nice tidy lines and buttons all in a row. His missing button would put her carefully ordered world into a dangerous tilt toward the realm of the disheveled.

She turned around, her brow furrowing at the sight of it. "Oh, botheration." She came back down the path and held out her hand. "Give it to me. As it is, I brought my sewing kit."

And he would have expected nothing less of her. "How fortuitous for me," he said as he handed the silver bit over and retrieved his discarded jacket.

She immediately *tsked, tsked* over the state of his wardrobe. "Oh, good heavens," she muttered as she smoothed the wool with her hands and examined the button band. Having surveyed the task before her, she sighed and sat back down on the bench, drawing out her small sewing kit.

"Won't your valet be put out if I do his work?" she asked.

"Falshaw?" Tuck shook his head. "He's a most excellent fellow but not the most adept with a needle and thread."

Harrumph. "He doesn't sound like a very capable valet. Perhaps you should—"

Tuck knew that tone and look. It said all too clearly she was about to start managing his life much as her sister had with Piers's household . . . Though not for the worse, he had to admit. After all, Louisa Tempest had put the spark back into the viscount's house and life.

But female meddling was still meddling to Tuck's way of

thinking, so he was quick to respond. "Don't you dare fire him—like your sister did Piers's cook. I can't do without Falshaw."

"As I understand it, my sister did the viscount a tremendous favor getting rid of that horrible cook of his. Why, that dreadful Mr. Bludger is wanted by His Majesty's navy for desertion."

"Yes, well, I rather need my horrible valet. And I can assure you, Falshaw is wanted by no one but me."

"He isn't taking very good care of you," she told him as she threaded a needle.

"I suppose not, but even if you were to try to remove him from my service, he wouldn't go."

She glanced up. "That loyal?"

"Oh, no, not at all. Rather, I owe him nearly a year's wages."

"Poor fellow," she told him.

Tuck was under no misunderstanding that her sympathies were all with Falshaw and not his poor employer.

She caught hold of the button band and poked the needle into the spot where the button belonged, digging the needle into the fabric and making a quick knot.

He drew back a bit. "Rather glad my coat is off."

"Why is that?" she asked.

"You look like you want to stab me," he teased.

She made a snorting noise.

"Whatever is so funny?"

"If I wanted to do that, you'd already have the wound," she replied.

Tuck laughed. Tart-tongued minx. And if he wasn't mistaken, she was smiling.

"You are rather deft with that needle," he said, watching her work. He'd never paid much attention to such things, but she did seem to know what she was doing.

"I like sewing," she told him, slanting a glance in his direction. "I usually redo most of my gowns and Louisa's as well, though she never cares if her gown is the latest stare or has the right color of rosettes."

"Scandalous," he agreed. "The wrong color of rosettes could consign a lady to the furthest reaches of society."

"You are a dreadful tease," she told him. "Actually, there is much that can be done to a gown to make it over with the right touches for very little expense."

"Truly?" He shook his head in wonder, thinking of all the times Piers had complained about his sisters' bills. "Now I wish I had a pen and paper."

"Whatever for?"

"Why to begin drafting my list of your qualifications—"

"You rogue," she said, swatting his arm.

"Hardly. I don't see why you can keep a list and I cannot."

"It doesn't sound proper," she told him.

"You haven't seen my list," he shot back, leaning back on the bench, his hands folded together behind his head. "What if I happen upon a gentleman who matches your exacting expectations? If I had a list at the ready, I could easily rattle off your qualities to see if he is interested."

"I hardly see—"

"I have my first three entries at the ready. Economical. Handy with a needle and thread—"

"When you say all that, I sound rather dull," she shot back.

"Oh, Livy, you are never dull," he told her.

Her lashes fluttered for a moment as if she were taken aback by his words, but she recovered quickly. "You mustn't call me that."

"Why not?"

"It's overly familiar," she told him.

"And let me guess, not proper." He laughed. "I think when a lady has ruined the better part of a gentleman's collection of handkerchiefs, it allows him certain rights."

"When I meet this gentleman, I will remember that," she teased back. Then, as if remembering herself, she went back to inspecting her handiwork. She took one last stitch and tied her thread off. Pulling her snips from her bag, she quickly and efficiently cut the thread.

If only all life's tangles could be finished off so—with a quick snip.

"Now for the remainder of my list," he said, sitting up as if he were a clerk in the court. "How do you stand on cats?"

Her nose wrinkled. "Have you met that beast my sister insists on keeping?"

"I don't think that animal counts as a cat," he replied, making a tick mark on his imaginary list. "I suppose I should put a grand Mayfair mansion on this list."

To his surprise, she shook her head. "I would prefer to live in the country."

"You would?" This rather surprised him.

Lavinia nodded. "I miss the grass. The quiet of the evenings. Being able to go for a long walk."

"That sounds lovely," he said. "My uncle has a country house—a wonderful old Tudor pile. I've been to it a few times. I've never understood why he would live in London when he could live there."

"But you like it," she said, smiling shyly at him. "Why?"

"Much the same reasons—it smells good, it has wide meadows and paths—all perfect for good amble or a nice ride. And . . ."

"And?"

He leaned closer. "I've always wanted a dog. One that isn't fond of cats."

They both laughed.

"So a house in the country it is," he noted, glancing down at the imaginary list in his hands. "There, that about does it."

She glanced over at him and asked almost shyly—well shyly for Lavinia, "Isn't there anything else that should be on your list—" Her brows rose noticeably, as if prodding him to offer up his further thoughts on her qualifications. "Perhaps something romantic?"

"Romantic?" He shook his head. "What is all this? I thought you rejected such notions."

"Normally I would. But perhaps I have been mistaken on that account."

"And what do you suggest I say?"

She carefully put away her sewing implements, the needle, thread and snips as she thought about it. When she finished, she glanced up. "That I am not opposed to the notion."

Tuck couldn't help himself. He laughed. "Ah, yes, that will mark you for an incurable romantic."

Her nose notched up a bit. "Hardly. I just want a little bit of romance. Since I haven't any experience in the matter, how am I to know what I would like or wouldn't. Or how much is the right amount? What if there are expectations?" She paused, then after steeling herself with a deep breath, she finally added, "How can I know if I've never been kissed?"

CHAPTER 12

Lavinia wished the words back the moment they came out.

I've never been kissed.

Yes, well, that would make a nice addition to his list. *Will beg for kisses.*

She bounded to her feet, only to take herself out of his horrified scrutiny.

Whatever was worse? The fact that she'd just sounded like a regular simpleton pleading for a bit of romance or that he hadn't even offered to help her out.

Was the idea of kissing her really so repugnant?

This, she had to believe, was even more mortifying than that dreadful mare's nest at Almack's.

Well, thankfully, her only audience was Tuck and not the entire *ton*. And she wasn't a spinster from Kempton for nothing. As always, Lady Essex's staid advice carried her through.

Head up, nose tipped just so, she did her best to pretend those words had never left her lips. Holding out his coat like the veritable wall of Jericho between them, she said, "There. You are as good as new. Perhaps better."

But he didn't look better. He stared up at her as if she had suddenly grown a second head, and she found herself wavering as their gazes locked, and some inexplicable warmth spread through her.

Lavinia knew what she should be doing, tossing him his coat and fleeing for the house.

Instead, her thoughts were awhirl with discordant images . . . of tossing aside his coat . . . moving closer to him . . . letting herself be pulled into his arms . . .

How his hair needed to be trimmed and brushed back just so.

Her fingers curled together, all too willing to do the task, but oh, it just wasn't done, she told herself. Yet how she wanted to trail her fingertips along the line of his jaw where a hint of stubble was already darkening.

It was all so confusing—whyever would she want such things?

Tuck Rowland was everything that wasn't on her list. No income to speak of. He hadn't a title (at least not yet), and he hadn't two farthings to his name.

Heavens, his poor valet hadn't been paid in months. No, make that nearly a year.

Alaster Rowland was a devil and a rogue and a knave.

Yet after a lifetime pursuit of propriety and respectability, all she wanted was to be in his arms again. Feel his warmth surround her. His lips on hers . . .

She wanted him to kiss her. Damn her foolish desires, she wanted *him* to kiss her.

Thoroughly. Recklessly.

"Yes, well, you are as good as new," she repeated, looking anywhere but into his eyes, for she suspected he would be able to see the desire in her gaze, the want behind her confusion.

"I suppose I am." He rose slowly, took a step closer to her, then turned his back to her. Glancing over his shoulder, he explained himself. "I do hate to impose, but I can't get that jacket on by myself."

She glanced down at the coat in her hands. The one tailored for a gentleman.

And a valet.

"So once again, I must do poor Falshaw's job," she teased awkwardly, shaking out the jacket and reluctantly stepping closer to him.

As he held out his arms she found herself—in a sense—surrounded by him. How he smelled—like a man ought, she realized. Not some perfumed Corinthian but like a man. Raw and ready, with a bit of bay rum, and something else . . . something so primal she didn't quite know what it was.

Tuck . . . That was what it was. Him. And the scent had her insides quaking.

Because she wanted to inhale. Bury her nose in his back and breathe deeply.

Her fingers twisted into the fine wool of his jacket when what they really wanted to do was fan out over his shirt and explore the hard muscles beneath.

To touch him. To feel him.

Slowly she guided first one arm, then the other into the sleeves, pulling the coat up and onto his long limbs.

"Yes, like that," he said over his shoulder, his face close to her ear as she worked to tug his jacket into place.

She was so close to him, more so even than dancing, for while dancing was proper, dressing a man, she discovered, was far more intimate.

As she went to bring his coat all the way up and over his shoulders, she came right up against him, her breasts pressed into his back, her hands sliding over the very muscles she longed to caress.

She wasn't touching him *that* way, she told herself, she was merely helping him on with his jacket.

Yes, that was what she was doing.

And then, with one last tug, a last shift, the coat fell into place, and Lavinia found herself stepping back on unsteady feet, her legs wobbling a bit.

He turned around, and even in her inexperience, she knew what the light in his eyes meant. The turn of his lips, the very way he looked at her.

What he wanted. Which, startling enough, was rather the same thing she wanted.

Tuck stepped toward her and caught hold of her elbow, steadying her.

Yet if that was his intent, it failed utterly, for his touch—warm and sure and steady—sent her heart racing, the air in her lungs caught as if twisting in the same confusion as the rest of her senses.

Her passions.

Lavinia, proper, staid, steady, Lavinia Tempest, found herself inside a whirlwind of her own making.

"You make a lovely valet," he said quietly, his voice smooth and coaxing.

And all she truly heard, all that mattered was that one word. *Lovely.*

He thought her lovely. Perhaps that was exactly what she'd wanted him to put on his list.

The air, trapped in her lungs, fled in a soft sigh, as he brought her in closer to him, then it was exactly as she had wanted—he was surrounding her.

And now that he was, her gaze locked with his, a passionate light full of promises.

Did you want to be kissed? Allow me . . .

His hand slid around her waist, his fingers curving around her, guiding her closer, while his head began to dip down.

He was going to kiss her.

Protest, push him away, don't do this, her sensibilities raged, but in the face of the storm inside her, their disapproval was drowned out by the wayward hammering of her heart.

Her need to know. Whatever was it like to be kissed? How ever could she have this on her list if she didn't know the truth.

Yes, kissing Tuck Rowland was a practical thing, she told herself. A necessary evil. At least, so she told herself for the next half a second.

For then he kissed her, and the deed began, in the touch of his lips, in the warmth of his Madeira-laced breath.

Intoxicating her. His lips were at first just a mere brush, then they were there, against hers, teasing her, tasting her.

This unknown, this forbidden taste, sent a raft of passions racing through her.

Chasing off any last whisper of propriety.

Come, follow me, his lips seemed to whisper, tempting and dangerous.

So she did. Follow him. Lavinia no more, she was suddenly Livy. Alive and lovely. And passionate, oh so passionate.

Her mouth opened to him, and his tongue brushed against hers, past this opening, tasting her.

His arms curved around her, tugging her closer, drawing her up and against him.

All of him, and she was breathless.

This was what it was like. To have him holding her, one hand pressed against her back, the other curved around her . . . Dear heavens, he was holding her by her backside . . . And it was delicious and wonderful all at once.

She clutched at the front of his jacket and barely gave a thought to the buttons there.

And she wondered in that moment if they were hanging on by a thread as she seemed to be doing. Dangling over an unknown abyss, as her breasts and that spot between her legs tightened, throbbed, ached to be given the same indecent attention that he was paying to her mouth—kissing her, deeply, exploring her.

Then, true to his reputation, as if he could hear the need inside her, he moved away from her lips and began to kiss the nape of her neck, a tender spot behind her ear that had her knees wobbling like a barely set pudding.

But it wasn't enough for him, for his lips returned to hers, this time demanding, and she was ready for him now, ready to kiss him in return, when the wrenching *creak* of the kitchen door broke through the silence of the garden.

"Get out with you, you nasty beastie," the cook complained,

followed by a *yowl* of protest from Hannibal as he was hurried out the door by the end of the broom.

Lavinia and Tuck skittered apart, unraveling the passionate thread that had woven them together.

Nearly.

With Hannibal dispatched, the cook peered into the darkness, then, as if satisfied that she hadn't heard anything else that needed taking care of, slammed the door shut with an aggrieved *thud*, the noise snapping Lavinia out of her heated reverie, and she took another step back, leaving the graveled path between them.

A small chasm, but a wide enough one to bring her to her senses.

Good heavens, she was already in dire straits as it was—but kissing Tuck Rowland?

A ruinous deed that seemed to prove everything the gossips were saying about her.

See if she isn't just her mother's daughter—wild and reckless.

No list would help her now, that she knew. No amount of propriety would change something very fundamental that she'd learned in the last few minutes.

Her mother's impulsive fire was hers as well. And this man would be her downfall.

Her ruin.

Meanwhile, after such an ignominious exit, Hannibal had come stalking down the path, tail in the air, head cocked just so, yowling and complaining with every step. He stopped in front of Lavinia and looked at her, then turned his one good eye on Tuck.

He shot one more censorious look at Lavinia before heading to the garden wall and making his escape up and over and into Lord Wakefield's garden.

If only Lavinia could escape as easily. For that was what she needed to do. Escape.

She should never have come out into the garden—whyever had she?

For the life of her, she could barely think, barely catch her breath, her lips still warm from his kiss, and it took her a moment to remember why.

Ah, yes, his plan.

. . . if you want to follow your sister to the altar, you had best seize this opportunity.

And seize it, she would. If only to find a proper match as quickly as possible. Before . . . before . . .

"You said there is a lady who can help me," she asked, not daring to look up at him.

"Yes, but—"

"Can you arrange a meeting?"

"Yes, but—"

"Excellent. Tomorrow, if that is possible," she told him and, gathering up her skirt, she quickly set off for the kitchen door. But she only went a few steps before she paused and turned to him. "Mr. Rowland—"

"Yes, Livy?"

"I want to be married. Properly so." And with that, she hurried inside, wishing she could just as easily leave behind all the very improper thoughts that chased her back up to her room.

And it was then, when she'd closed her door, that she realized something else.

In her hand was a silver button.

One she'd plucked from his coat without realizing it.

Tuck left his uncle's garden in a bit of a daze.

Good God! He'd kissed Livy. What the devil had he just done?

One moment she'd been helping him on with his jacket, and the next, she'd been in his arms.

His desire for her—had shaken him to the soles of his boots. And he couldn't truly blame Piers's wine cellar for this unexpected passion.

For he'd left one thing off his list.

She was utterly desirable. And he'd been a fool. Tempted and trapped.

Tuck groaned. Oh, no, this would never do. He was already in a mire—now he was merely filling his pockets with stones so he could sink faster.

And yet, when he'd kissed her, tasted those innocent lips of hers, he'd found himself breathless, caught.

That is until that demmed door had opened.

Then the moment had been lost.

Oh, and what had she said as she gone back into the house, stalking up the steps with the same ruffled dignity as her sister's bloody cat.

I want to be married. Properly so.

And since he and "proper" were rarely on speaking terms, and that other word, *married*, left an icy pit in his stomach, he knew the only course of action was to see her matched as quickly as possible; and then, he supposed, he'd take an extended trip to the wilds of Scotland.

Or Ireland. Or Canada. Canada might be in order. From what he understood, it froze there.

Often.

Would definitely cool his ardor. Or so he could hope.

But still, Canada. Tuck shuddered.

Which left him only one choice, to move ahead with his reckless plan and see her matched as quickly as possible—but to do that, he needed to find a particularly elusive lady.

But luckily, he also knew her habits and preferences as well as his own, and so he went directly to the most likely of spots.

The most crowded social event of the evening. Lady Menley's soiree—a sort of who's who of the *ton* would be there, and it was always a crush.

But Tuck wasn't interested in the exalted company or being seen. Instead, he made his way to the back of the house and slipped into the servant's entrance and continued up the backstairs. From there he made an educated guess as to which room he sought and slipped inside.

"Ah, I thought you might be here," he said, as he closed the door to Lord Menley's private study, blotting out the noise from the crush of guests on the floor below.

Across the shadowy room, a woman in an elegant, yet simple black gown whirled around.

"Dear heavens, Tuck!" she scolded. "Announce yourself if you intend to move about as silent as a cat."

"You have only yourself to blame," he told her. "It was, after all, you who taught me that trick."

"Nice to know you listened to something I had to say," she said, huffing a bit and giving him a slip of the shoulder. "Now, state your business and leave. I have my own matters to attend to."

"I can see that," he replied, looking around the room. "But as you may have guessed, I need your help."

"I imagine you do," she replied, turning back to the wall of paintings behind her and studying them.

"So you've heard?" He had rather hoped she hadn't. But then again, there wasn't much in the *ton* that she didn't know.

"About that ridiculous wager? Yes." She let out a huffy sigh. "When will you ever learn?"

He had the feeling of being once again in short pants and having been caught out at some mischief. "I was a bit bosky at the time."

"A good reason to steer clear of the bottle in the future."

Tuck shrugged. Good advice, but hardly relevant now.

"Is she as cowhanded as they say?" the lady asked.

He shrugged. "She's pretty, which is far more important."

Her nose curled a bit. "Oh, my. You are in the suds."

"You could help." Tuck hoped he sounded convincing.

"Me?" She laughed.

"Whyever not?" he asked. Then, moving around the great desk in the middle of the room, he stopped beside her and did his own perusal of the paintings before them. After a moment, he reached out and took one of them off the wall, revealing a deep cubby in which a strong box sat hidden.

"How do you do that?" she asked, as she moved forward to tug the strongbox out of its hiding place and set it on the table. Opening up her reticule, she pulled out a set of picks. "Always know which painting hides the treasure?"

"Simple," he replied. "It is always behind the ugliest piece. A copy. Something easily overlooked and hardly worthy of note."

She shrugged, as if the entire collection was rather ugly and hardly worthy of note, then went to work opening the lock. "What do you think I can do for you? Or rather for that poor, unfortunate girl?"

This was a good omen. He'd piqued her curiosity. "Well, you did a rather excellent job of rising up in Society," he said slowly. "And you are the most elegant creature I've ever met."

"Flattery and Spanish coin won't work with me." Then she glanced at him and frowned. "I haven't the time."

"Of course you do. And you will help me because you love a challenge."

Sniff.

Yes, well, apparently flattery really wasn't going to work. So he got to the point.

"I've taken her to two different dancing masters. Neither of them could help. Nor do I have time to find another."

"What about that dreadful fraud from Buxton?" she suggested. "The one who claims to be an exiled Russian prince."

Tuck shook his head. "In Newgate. Stole a bracelet."

The lady sighed. "Truly, I don't have the time. Get the Honorable to help you. He's the best there is."

Tuck's head was shaking even before she finished. "No, not Hero. I cannot risk—"

Again that snort, that bit of derision. "Cannot risk! I'd say you already have."

She had a point there. Tuck ran his hand through his hair and shuddered.

Introduce the very proper Miss Lavinia Tempest to the most dishonorable, improper man in London? Madness.

Not that the lady before him wasn't above pointing out the obvious. "What was it? A monkey you wagered? And how much do you have on hand? A few pence, I'd guess."

He nodded, not all that happy to be reminded what was at risk. Or that the sum was actually four times that.

She straightened and looked him in the eye. "Lord Ilford will be all too happy to put a bullet in you. He's a dangerous enemy. And word has it that he's been nosing about the Dials. Wants to make trouble for Wakefield."

"I won't let him," Tuck told her.

"You won't have much say in the matter if he shoots you first." She went back to work on the lock, and, after a few moments, she spoke again. "I don't see that you have any choice in the matter— you need me *and* the Honorable. I'll send word to him tonight, and you bring her by the house tomorrow afternoon. Not before three—I have a long evening planned."

Tuck nodded.

She smiled at him and, taking another glance at the box, plucked a hairpin free from her elaborate do, then, with a twist of the hairpin, the lock sprang open; and now her grin was triumphant as she reached inside the strongbox and pulled out a large ruby necklace.

Tuck admired it, then said, "I don't know why you are bothering. It's paste. As is everything else you'll find in there."

"Paste? I don't think—" Still, she held up the piece and studied it in the light. After turning it this way and that, she muttered a very unladylike phrase and set it aside. As she plucked out one jeweled treasure after another, Tuck's pronouncement turned out to be all too true.

She pushed away from the table and heaved a sigh. "You might have said something before I went to all this trouble," she chided, arms crossed over her chest.

"But, Mother, it is always such a pleasure to see you at work," he told her as he gathered up the discarded worthless bits and put them carefully back in their box for safekeeping.

She sniffed, for she knew his words were a lie. "Whyever do people keep such worthless baubles locked up?" she asked as he returned the strongbox to its hiding place. "It is really most disheartening."

"Appearances, *madame*, appearances." He paused, then went to work putting everything back to rights. Just as he always did. "Wasn't that the first lesson you ever taught me?"

CHAPTER 13

Tuck's note arrived early the next morning.

Lavinia didn't know if she was relieved or insulted by the hasty scrawl and the prompt response to her edict.

All arranged. Meet me in the garden at two.

Well, she had laid out her demand. *I want to be married. Properly so.*

And Tuck—make that, Mr. Rowland—was going to do his utmost to see the task done.

How kind of him, she thought as she made her determined way to the bench in the garden just as the clock struck the designated hour.

Oddly, there was no sign of him, so she sat down, folding her hands in her lap and doing her utmost to maintain a calm and unruffled demeanor. Never mind that he'd kissed her last night.

She'd kissed Tuck Rowland.

Thank goodness Louisa hadn't been in their room when she'd returned—all undone by the touch of that roguish devil. She didn't know what she would have said to Louisa.

He kissed me, and I would have let him do more . . . anything . . .

And she would have, for he'd quite opened her eyes. Who

would have thought kissing could be so utterly perfect? Especially with the wrong man.

For she was utterly certain of that—Tuck Rowland was the wrong man for her. Feckless, improper. Why he probably finished his evening by kissing half a dozen other ladies.

A thought that had her lips pressed together for a very different reason. Had he? Left her and gone to another? The toe of her slipper gouged into the gravel.

Not that she cared, she told herself. She should be giving Hannibal a plate of kippers for saving her from certain ruin.

And now she was going to meet a lady who could help salvage her Season, and she'd be married in a thrice.

Yes, that was all well and good. Exactly what she'd always wanted. What she'd planned when she'd come to London. As she'd told Tuck the night before, a comfortable home in the country. A quiet sort of life.

Much like he wanted, she realized. She wouldn't have thought it of him, but there it was. Tuck longed for the quiet life.

And yet, why did that notion suddenly leave her feeling horribly out of sorts?

Because she realized that the man who'd inhabit that bucolic haven she'd put on her list would not be the one she wanted.

Behind her, the gate opened and even before she could turn around, she heard a hopeful voice call out in relief, "Louisa?"

Lavinia flinched. It wasn't the voice she was expecting. And when she turned, she found herself face to face with Lord Wakefield—and finally she got a good look at the man who'd stolen her sister's heart.

She watched as first his face was alight with love, then a quizzical realization that perhaps he had the wrong lady in his sights.

Two things struck Lavinia immediately. The viscount could see she wasn't Louisa. That was telling enough as it was—for very few people could discern between the two of them.

No, with Lord Wakefied, his heart was his guide—for she had

seen all too clearly the love in his gaze and the desire to let it fall upon one and only one woman.

"My lord?" she posed, smiling slightly even against her better judgment. She hadn't wanted to like him—given all the talk about his terrible temper and reclusive ways, but there was no disputing one very telling thing.

He was madly in love with Louisa.

"You aren't her." He took two steps closer—his brow furrowing deeper.

Lavinia rose. "Lord Wakefield," she said, nodding slightly and making a quick curtsy. "I must commend you, not many can make the distinction between me and my sister so handily. I can only surmise that you love my sister very much to be able to tell us apart at first glance."

"Where is she?" he asked, looking around the garden. "Where is your sister?"

In love he might be, but that hadn't diminished the viscount's capacity for being overbearing and demanding.

"Over at your house, I imagine," she replied, for she'd seen Louisa leave earlier with Bitty, the cook's niece. But still his question rather put that at odds. "Isn't she?"

He shook his head.

"Lavinia! There you are," came a greeting from the mews. "Prompt and eager to begin our new . . ." Tuck's words trailed off as he came the rest of the way into the garden and spied the viscount standing there.

"Tuck," Lord Wakefield acknowledged. Or rather questioned.

Both men straightened as if they had both caught the other out in some mischief.

Then they both looked at her—the viscount with a wry cock to his brow and Tuck looking slightly guilty.

Oh, good heavens, she had hoped she would be able to slip away yet again unnoticed.

"You were saying you wanted to see my sister?" Lavinia shook out her skirt and avoided looking at Tuck, for indeed she knew her cheeks were flaming. "I can go get her," she added, nodding toward the house.

"Yes, if you would, please," the viscount asked.

Lavinia stole a glance at Tuck, at his scuffed boots and his hair that needed trimming, and ignoring the odd lurch in her heart, hurried into the house and up the backstairs to find Louisa.

There she found her sister face down on the bed, sobbing.

Oh, good heavens, what was this?

"Lala, what is it?" Lavinia asked, using an old nickname. She sat down next to her, and Louisa began to sob harder.

"I—am—unfit," she sobbed. "I've—ruined—everything."

"I hardly see how," Lavinia told her, glancing at the window and wondering what had happened. "Your viscount is down in the garden demanding to see you."

The sobbing paused. "He is?"

There was a hopeful note to her question. "Of course he is," Lavinia told her. "He loves you."

"He can't—he doesn't," she said, the sobs starting to wind back up. "Lady Blaxhall told me—"

Lady Blaxhall? Lavinia shook her head, having stopped listening to whatever that horrible woman might have said.

Whatever it was, it hardly mattered.

For she had seen the light of love in Viscount Wakefield's eyes, and that trumped whatever poison that vindictive woman had been spooning out.

Lavinia wasted no time. She caught her sister by the shoulders and gave her a good shake. "Stop wallowing," she told her, doing her best to sound as commanding as Lady Essex.

It actually worked, and Louisa's sobs immediately subsided, save for a hiccup or two.

"Lord Wakefield is down in the garden demanding to see you. He loves you. I'm certain of it."

"He can't," she began to protest.

"He does," Lavinia asserted. For she had seen the truth herself—felt once again that moment of jealousy. "He knew I wasn't you."

That was enough to get Louisa's full attention. "What?"

"He knew immediately I wasn't you." Lavinia heaved a sigh. "And if that isn't proof enough that he loves you, wants only you, and is about to propose marriage—unless he's already done so—"

At this, Louisa shook her head, but her expression had stopped looking so utterly despondent.

Lavinia got to her feet, towing Louisa with her. Digging a handkerchief out of her pocket, she dabbed up the last of Louisa's tears. "Then you had best hurry downstairs before he changes his mind. Or worse, he comes up here."

"Oh, he wouldn't," Louisa said almost immediately, and then after a second, thought better of her statement. "Oh, heavens, he would."

With that, Louisa hurried away, with Lavinia following closely behind but clearly forgotten. For the moment her sister stepped into the garden, it was as if all of London faded away, and the two of them, Louisa and her viscount from the across the lane, were the only two people in the world.

With a wry smirk on his face, Tuck caught Lavinia by the hand and led her down the garden path and out into the mews, where he had his carriage waiting.

"Is it proper to leave them alone?" she asked, glancing back over her shoulder, ignoring that once again she was running off with Tuck. Alone.

But oh, that was ever so different.

Was it? Was it *now*? Since they'd kissed . . .

She pressed her lips together and vowed to push such thoughts, such delicious memories out of her mind.

Tuck stepped into her view and handed her up into his carriage, and while he came around to climb in, she stole another glance back at the garden.

"Leave them be," he chided. "I suspect when we return, it will be to the sound of wedding bells."

Lavinia barked a laugh. "Oh, hardly. Louisa is far too proper to make some scandalous runaway marriage."

Tuck shrugged. "I don't know. Piers has never been known for his patience."

"Louisa will want banns read, a respectable marriage," Lavinia declared.

"Ah, yes, a respectable marriage," he repeated, glancing over at her.

"Whatever is wrong with a respectable match?"

"Nothing," he replied. "If you want that sort of thing."

"'That sort of thing'?" She shook her head. "You make marriage sound like catching the plague."

He shrugged as if he didn't see the difference.

"I know it shouldn't surprise me that Louisa has found love," Lavinia said. "She is the pretty one."

Tuck shook his head. "The what?"

"The pretty one," she repeated.

Not that it cleared up matters. "I don't see how she can be—"

"Because we are identical?"

"Not to me," he told her, and there was a decisive air to his statement, much as there had been when the viscount had looked upon her. And nor was Tuck done. "I clearly see the differences between the two of you."

"Such as?"

He laughed a little. "Well, for one thing, you are rather forthright. And determined. And your sister hasn't a penchant for lists. At least I don't think she does—"

Lavinia shook her head.

"There you have it. That alone is a significant difference."

She knew he was joking, but she hardly found it funny.

"And I can't see that you'd barge into a fellow's house and take charge of everything."

She sighed. "That's just it. Louisa is so good—she always knows the right thing to do—what to put in a spinster basket, or what color a bunting should be. She's utterly perfect—look how she's helped Viscount Wakefield put his house to rights."

"I think some might use another term for her 'help.' Such as an 'incurable busybody.'"

Lavinia had the decency to be slightly affronted. But only out of a sisterly sense of loyalty. For while she'd never admit it, she did find Louisa a bit of a busybody. But more importantly, she reminded Tuck of one thing. "The viscount doesn't seem to mind."

"No, I don't think he does; still, she must have some terrible, secret flaw?"

Lavinia bit her lower lip and considered her sister's few faults and came up with the most grievous one. "Hannibal. She claims he's perfectly amenable." After a moment, she added, "Though he is rather tame around her."

"So your sister is also capable of taming beasts, my cousin included."

"It appears so."

Tuck slanted a glance at her. "And you haven't any devil's spawn that you profess an affection for?"

She smiled at him as sweetly as she could. "Other than you?"

"Very funny, Miss Tempest," he told her.

"I thought it rather witty," she replied, preening a bit, wishing she could give him the real set down that sat at the back of her throat like a giant lump.

However could you kiss me like you did last night, then be willing to hand me over to another?

But since she couldn't, wouldn't, broach that subject, and he certainly didn't appear willing to raise it, she decided to approach the matter in a more circuitous fashion.

"You never did say who you were taking me to meet." She looked at him with her nose tipped in the air.

He did not rise to the bait. "No, I didn't, did I?"

Oh, bother, her curiosity was going to win out. "Might I know?"

"Yes."

"When?"

He looked up at the road before them. "My mother always says never rush an introduction. It is the mark of poor manners and low associations."

"What does she say about your associations?"

"Remarkably, very little," he replied.

"She must be a veritable model of restraint."

"I believe she prefers not to waste her time." He turned off the thoroughfare, then, after a few blocks, turned again onto a quiet street. "Here we are," he announced, as they pulled up to a small house.

Lavinia glanced around at a block that featured neat, tidy houses. All in all, the residence appeared to be a very respectable address.

Her brow furrowed, and she tamped down a sense of disappointment.

Tuck glanced over at her. "Whatever is the matter?"

"Nothing," she said, hardly wanting to tell him that this was not the sort of place she'd been expecting.

It was so terribly bourgeois. So very proper. She glanced back at him.

"Something amiss?" he asked. "If you have changed your mind—" Tuck reached for the reins as if he was just as happy to call this all off.

Lavinia acted before she even thought and caught hold of his arm to stop him, her fingers curling around his forearm.

Immediately, she wished she hadn't, for to touch him was to rediscover his warmth, his strength, his heat.

So just as quickly, she let go. "No, no, I agreed to this," she told him, taking another glance up and down the street. Perhaps he had the wrong address. "It is just—"

"Just?"

"This isn't what I was expecting," she told him in a huff.

Now it was Tuck's turn to look about. "I know it isn't the loftiest of addresses—"

She shook her head. "Oh, heavens, you misunderstand me. This house is entirely respectable."

He stared at her as she had at him earlier, looking for more of an explanation.

Unlike him, she was willing to elaborate. "Too respectable."

It didn't take Tuck but a moment to get the gist of her dismay, and he began to laugh.

"I hardly see why this is funny," she told him, folding her hands primly in her lap.

"You said you wanted a respectable match, did you not?"

"Yes," she admitted, "but I rather assumed—" She looked around again, her lips pursing together. Oh, bother how to explain this . . . "That is when you said you knew a lady . . . Well, I rather thought you meant a '*lady*.'"

Tuck continued to laugh as he climbed down. "My dear Miss Tempest, hold on to your assumptions."

"Why is that?" she asked as he helped her down.

Then he told her, and she couldn't have been more shocked if he had driven her to Seven Dials.

"You are about to meet my mother."

"Your mother?" There was a decided note of panic in her voice.

Tuck didn't see what she had to be alarmed about. He was the one risking everything by bringing her into his world.

Not that he didn't trust Livy's discretion, for she was as decorous as one of his Uncle Charleton's Holbeins—but glancing over at her, this very proper and innocent miss, he wondered at the wisdom of handing her over to his mother's care.

But what else was there to do? As Lady Wakefield had so wisely pointed out, this might be his only hope.

Tuck suppressed a groan. If only the *ton* would see past Livy's misstep, the shadow of her mother's scandal, then they would see her as he had over the past week.

A breathless little vision. A siren meant to tempt a poor mortal man to take desperate steps . . . to cast aside his freedom.

Any man who had seen her as he had last night would have thrown himself in front of a mail coach to save her. To have her.

'Cept him, he thought. He'd fled from the garden last night as if the devil were at his heels, scurrying off like a rat.

Chased by her unyielding list. Her proper constraints.

I want to be married. Properly so.

And there it was. Properly so. A notion that was definitely not his forte. He was no hero, no knight in shining armor, he wanted to tell her. He was here because he was teetering on the brink of financial ruin. He must find someone to marry her, make her a proper wife, or all would be lost.

Save marrying the chit himself, there was no other way.

Marry Livy.

Tuck stumbled to a stop at the bottom step. Where the devil had that thought come from? But he knew. For to hand her over to his mother was as good as handing her over to another man.

A proper one. One who wouldn't blanch at the idea of being leg shackled.

"Whatever is amiss?" Lavinia asked.

"Nothing, but I don't know if this is the best notion," he said, glancing back at his carriage. Ruin or marriage? Neither side of the coin appealed.

And yet, her kiss, that spark of passion he'd felt last night with her in his arms, gads it was the oddest thing.

He'd found himself holding her with one very single-minded thought.

Mine.

"Not the best notion? Nonsense," she was saying. "If as you say, your mother raised herself up and is inclined to help me, whatever could be wrong with asking her help?"

He didn't have a chance to answer—not that he would

THE KNAVE OF HEARTS

have—for just then the door opened, and his mother appeared, looking the paragon of a modest and respectable widowhood, a role she'd been born to play.

"Alaster, my pride and joy, as punctual as ever," she said, coming down the steps and placing a motherly kiss on his forehead. "And is this *your* Miss Tempest?" She turned to Livy, and smiled brightly. "Dear boy, you were utterly correct when you said she is a perfect beauty."

At this, Livy turned and looked at him. *You said what?*

And if that wasn't bad enough, then a second figure came to the door. "Ah, my dear nephew. Always a pleasure to see you. And Tuck, who is this angel? Surely not the girl your mother says is in dire need of our assistance. I do believe the entire *ton* has gone blind. I do say! Why I can see from here, she has prospects. Fine prospects, indeed."

Tuck wanted to groan. Thought quite possibly he had, given the questioning glance Livy shot at him.

Miss Tempest, meet the Honorable Hero Worth.

Tuck turned to his mother, but it was too late to protest the Honorable's arrival in their midst, for the pair of them had Miss Tempest between them and were leading her into the house, as if it wasn't the den of thieves he knew it to be but rather the most respectable address in London.

Which, he knew all too well, it had never been.

Lavinia found herself being led into a very simple room, devoid of any fancy trappings, not that she had much time to look around, for she immediately found herself being peppered with questions.

"I understand you cannot dance—" Mrs. Rowland stated, though it felt like a query.

"No, I cannot," she admitted wearily.

"Excellent!" Mrs. Rowland declared.

"Excellent?" Lavinia echoed. She'd never heard her lack of grace being described with such enthusiasm.

"What my mother means—" Tuck began, that is until he was pushed aside by the well-dressed older gentleman.

"I echo my dear niece's sentiment, as well. Excellent news!" he was saying. And then looking at her, he paused. "We haven't even been properly introduced." He shot an aggrieved glance at Tuck and continued, catching up her hand and bowing low over it. "Dear, sweet girl, I am Mrs. Rowland's uncle, the Honorable Hero Worth. At your devoted service." With a flourish of his other hand, he rose, like some grand gentleman from another age.

Lavinia found herself enchanted by the old devil—still striking in his appearance and so perfectly mannered. Tuck, she thought, could learn a thing or two from his great-uncle. "Thank you, Mr. Worth."

"No, no, my dear child. Call me 'The Honorable,' everyone does."

"That hardly seems proper—" she began.

"Proper!" Mrs. Rowland said with a bit of a laugh. "Oh, Tuck, she's perfectly charming."

Lavinia twisted to look at the lady, for she didn't know what was so funny about being proper.

Mrs. Rowland continued circling around her like a hawk, and now Mr. Worth did as well.

Lavinia turned, trying to catch up with Mrs. Rowland. "Most find my lack of the finer graces off-putting. Which is how I've ended up—"

Mrs. Rowland waved her hand in dismissal. "Foolish, jealous hens is why you have ended up in these straits. Forget them."

"How can I when they have turned their collective backs to me?"

At this, Mrs. Rowland paused and smiled at Tuck. "She has spirit and is forthright." Then the lady turned to Lavinia. "You have rather strong opinions?"

Tuck muffled a cough.

"So I've been told," Lavinia replied.

"Excellent," Mrs. Rowland declared as she continued to

circle around her, with the Honorable Hero Worth half a turn behind her.

The two of them began to banter back and forth in their own baffling language.

"I hardly see why we are needed," the Honorable declared. "Especially when she has such delightful prospects."

"No, Uncle," Tuck told him. "You are mistaken."

Mrs. Rowland shrugged at this. She had stopped her dizzying rounds of prowling and now stood with one finger tapping at her chin as she studied Lavinia from head to toe.

"Never," the Honorable declared. "I am never wrong about these things, my boy. Prospects, I say."

Now it was Tuck's turn to shrug and looked about to argue the point, but his mother stepped between him and the Honorable. "Dancing, Miss Tempest, is an utter waste of time."

The Honorable nodded in agreement. "Though a lovely diversion," he did note, which his niece conceded with a quick tip of her head.

"But we shall leave the dance floor to all those other girls. Those dull Originals and false Diamonds . . ." She turned to her son. "That is what they are called these days, isn't it?"

"Yes, but I thought perhaps you could help her rise to the top of the shelf. Be the shining light of them all."

"Oh, no, no," his mother protested with a grand shudder. "Miss Tempest is none of those things, nor would she want to be—"

"Well, I would like—" Lavinia began.

"No! No! You are far too intelligent and sharp to be another in a long line of mere beauties," Mrs. Rowland told her.

"Coupled with your prospects," the Honorable hastened to add.

Lavinia hadn't the least notion what the man meant by "prospects," so she made a note to ask Tuck later what it was his great-uncle kept going on about.

"Exactly," Mrs. Rowland agreed. "You have no time for such fleeting fame. You are too far above such vulgarities."

"I am?"

But Mrs. Rowland wasn't listening; instead, her eyes were alight with a faraway brilliance.

"Are you thinking what I was thinking?" the Honorable asked her.

"Salzburg," Mrs. Rowland told him.

The Honorable shook his head. "Too daring. I would think Tourney."

At this, Mrs. Rowland emphatically shook her head. "Takes too long to set up. We've only a sennight."

Her uncle shrugged in concession, but then eyed Lavinia in a sweeping glance. "Brussels."

"Brussels? Heavens, no!" Mrs. Rowland protested, then said in an aside, "You never remember Brussels correctly."

"Oh, so you say, but it might work," he pointed out, undefeated by her vehemence.

"Yes, if we had a willing Russian," she told him, as if prodding at his apparently failing memories.

"Oh, yes, the Russian. You don't think a good Spaniard would do in a pinch? I know a fellow who would make a passable—"

"Certainly not! He wouldn't have the gravitas."

"No, I suppose not. And with only a sennight, you are correct, we haven't the time for a decent Russian. Ponderous fellows, but so handy when one has more time," he agreed, and went back to scratching his chin. "Might I suggest a more subtle ploy. Antwerp, perhaps?"

"Antwerp, indeed! Can't you see this gel is worthy of a duke?" Mrs. Rowland crossed her arms over her chest.

Their rapid-fire banter had left Lavinia feeling a bit dizzy, but one phrase had stood out. "A duke?" she managed.

Not that they were listening.

"Well, if it is a duke she wants, then it must be Salzburg," the Honorable was saying, glancing over Lavinia one more time. "Hmm. You may have the right of it. She's got a certain air about her. Salzburg it is. I don't know why I didn't see it straight off."

Mrs. Rowland smiled in triumph. "But you do now?"

"Perfectly. You haven't lost your touch, my dear," the Honorable told her, rounding the settee and catching up his hat and gloves and grand walking stick. With his belongings collected, he went to the door. "Proper gowns will be required."

"Of course," Mrs. Rowland agreed.

"And does she play cards?"

They both looked over at Lavinia.

"My dear?" Mrs. Rowland asked with a gentle, but firm nudge. "Do you play?"

"Um, yes," Lavinia said. "Quite well, in fact—"

Mrs. Rowland was done with her and had turned to the Honorable. "Well, we will have to evaluate her skills, but I do think we have everything we need."

"Save gowns and the other necessities," the Honorable said in agreement. "I shall get started on the others, while I leave the frippery in your capable hands, Jenny, my dear." He then bowed to Lavinia, tipped his hat to Tuck and was gone.

"Yes, the Honorable is ever so correct. There is much to do," Mrs. Rowland announced. "Now, out with both of you. I have calls to make."

With that, she gathered up their belongings and shooed them toward the door. "Dear Miss Tempest, I am ever so delighted that Tuck has brought us together. I will come and fetch you as soon as I have everything in place." She turned to her son. "Tuck, you were right to bring her to me when you did. If only I had another week to work with, but—" She shrugged. "No matter. When I am done, every man in London will desire her."

Those words—*every man in London will desire her*—shot through Lavinia like an arrow, cutting her open, pulling out of her one immediate and shocking realization.

I only want the one.

Unbidden, her gaze lifted to Tuck. No, he wasn't a duke. Nor even a gentleman. But oh . . . She couldn't help herself, she was back in the garden again, and he was kissing her. Deeply, thoroughly, and she couldn't think but one thing.

This man. This is the one I want.

But she found his expression masked, utterly unconcerned that his mother was about to offer her up to every man in the land, save him.

Had he truly kissed her so passionately last night only to hand her over to another? To someone else?

The door closing behind her with a decided *thud* woke Lavinia from her daze. To her amazement, Mrs. Rowland had efficiently and unceremoniously nudged them out onto the front steps and closed the door on them before they could turn around.

"My goodness, she is rather good at that," Lavinia remarked as she tugged on her bonnet and set to work to get her gloves on before someone saw her outside without them.

"What is that?" Tuck asked, getting himself assembled as well.

"Getting rid of guests. I do say, she's better at it than Lady Essex." Lavinia looked up at him. "And what is Salzburg?"

"A city," he remarked as he held out his arm to her.

Lavinia wound her hand around his sleeve and told herself the soft shiver that ran down her spine at being connected to him meant nothing.

"I know Salzburg is a city—"

"Then whyever did you ask?"

"She doesn't expect me to go there, does she?" Lavinia paused and glanced over her shoulder at the very respectable house. Goodness, that was all very odd. Perhaps not as respectable as she'd thought. "I would prefer my husband to be English."

"And ducal?"

She shook her head. "Oh, nothing as lofty as all that. But a proper baron wouldn't be amiss."

"I might be a baron one day," he reminded her.

"I said 'proper.'"

"Oh, yes. How could I forget?" he teased in return.

They stopped before the carriage, and Lavinia took another glance at Mrs. Rowland's front door. "Your uncle and mother seem well traveled."

"Great-uncle," he corrected. "And a distant one at that."

"Have they been to all those places?"

Tuck sighed. "Unfortunately."

Rather than question this odd answer, she went back to her original line of thought. "Mr. Worth appears quite mannerly. A gentleman of the first order. Is he related to the Lancashire Worths?"

"Depends on the day of the week," Tuck muttered.

Well, that was hardly the answer she expected, but she would have wagered her pin money that there was more to this respectable address and the forthright widow than met the eye. "Whatever do you think your mother has in mind?"

If she was hoping for answers, Tuck was not very reassuring.

"Something ruinous, I have to imagine."

Lavinia didn't say a single word the entire drive back to the mews behind Lord Charleton's house, Mrs. Rowland's promise seeming to chase the carriage back to Mayfair.

Every man in London will desire you when I am done.

And to her chagrin, Tuck sat beside her in a moody silence. More to the point, he hadn't made any objection to this notion of making her desirable for every man in London.

Save him.

I only want the one.

Had he kissed her last night and found her completely lacking? Was that what was wrong?

Could he really kiss her like that, hold her so close, touch her as he had, then quite willingly hand her over to someone else.

Apparently so.

She didn't know whether to shove him out of his seat or burst into tears. She did neither.

She hadn't a handkerchief with her, and she doubted she could handle the high-stepping pair of horses he was driving.

As they came to a stop in the alley behind Lord Charleton's

house, the carriage lurched to a halt and Lavinia found she couldn't contain herself. Something had to be said.

"Tuck—"

"Livy—" he said at the same time.

They turned to each other just as a voice came over the gate. "Oh, Miss Lavinia, there you are. The entire household is in such a state. His Lordship is beside himself. But here you are and with Mr. Rowland—oh, this solves everything." Brobson, Lord Charleton's butler opened the gate and looked out at the pair of them, appearing more relieved than scandalized.

"Brobson, what is it?" Lavinia asked.

"Your sister and Lord Wakefield are to be married."

"Married?" Lavinia said in an exhale. Despite Tuck's earlier prediction and her own suspicions, hearing the news was an entirely different matter.

Louisa, married. Oh, it was so final.

"Excellent!" Tuck declared, climbing down from the carriage and giving Brobson a slap on the back.

"Hardly, sir," the butler replied, as one of the stable boys came out of the mews to collect the carriage and horses. "They are to be married within the hour."

CHAPTER 14

All too soon, and with no amount of indecent haste, Lavinia found herself standing up inside St. George's beside her sister as Louisa made her wedding vows to the viscount.

Louisa, starry-eyed with happiness, had all her attention on the tall, handsome man beside her who was promising to care for her for the rest of his life.

Louisa. Married. To a viscount, no less.

Lavinia was in shock, to say the least.

After having spent most of her life trying to be distinguished from her identical sister, now . . . now . . . they were going to be utterly separated, and a great sense of loss seemed ready to swallow her.

Lavinia struggled to find the right words—ones that didn't make her feel like a jealous worm, ones that matched the tightness in her heart—when she realized that the entire church had gone silent.

She glanced up and found Louisa smiling at her, the bouquet in her hands held out for Lavinia to hold.

"Oh, yes, so sorry," she whispered, as she took the bouquet and watched the viscount put his ring on Louisa's finger.

There it was. The deed was done. Louisa was a Tempest no more. Now she was Louisa Stratton, Viscountess Wakefield. Lady Wakefield.

Lavinia felt as if she'd been cut adrift and was floating away from the steady ground she'd always known. She looked down at the flowers in her grasp and realized the petals were all trembling with the same question.

Whatever will become of me now that Louisa is gone?

And for whatever reason, Lavinia's gaze rose and came to rest on the one place that seemed not to be moving, not to be so very unfamiliar.

On the handsome, rakish knave across from her. Tuck. All brushed and cleaned, wearing a borrowed jacket from Piers, though that didn't stop the rogue from winking at her, as if to say, *Better them than us, eh, Livy?*

Still, whyever did she suddenly feel like she was no longer lost? As if she had found what she had come to London to gain.

Oh, hardly. Tuck Rowland possessed not a single, solitary qualification on her list. He was the most improper man she'd ever met.

Still, perhaps she should have composed her list after she understood what it meant to fall in love.

Tuck found himself standing up beside Piers as the viscount made his wedding vows.

While it might seem a time to make a joke about the parson's trap, he'd never seen his cousin look so happy—a happiness reflected on nearly every face in the church. Lord Charleton. Lady Aveley. Lady Wakefield. Roselie. Even Brody, who'd slipped into one of the back pews.

Yet all this good cheer still had Tuck unable to fathom why it was *his* chest felt so tight or why *his* cravat seemed to be cutting off every bit of air in the vast church. He wasn't the one being leg shackled and yet . . .

His gaze rose and fell on Livy.

He was struck by how pale she looked. Rather like how he felt. A bit stricken and shocked. As if their world were being turned upside down.

It was all he could do to stay in place and not go to her, to remind her that very soon she would be in much the same circumstances.

Standing up in a church and pledging her troth. Getting everything she'd wished for. Everything on her demmed list.

Yes, if everything went according to plan, the next wedding he'd attend would be hers. And then Tuck would be the one standing in the back pew.

And instead of making him feel jubilant, the very suggestion of Livy—his Livy—being led away by another, left him a bit unsteady, off-balance.

But that was what he wanted, wasn't it?

He looked away, for once again his cravat had grown too tight and his gaze fell on Lady Aveley, who sat beside his Uncle Charleton. For her part, the lady sat ramrod straight, yet her gaze was tipped slightly as she stole a glance at the man beside her.

And if he wasn't mistaken, there was a bit of a telltale blush to her cheeks that made her look almost maidenly.

Charleton and Lady Aveley?

For his part, the baron turned slightly and winked at the widow.

Actually winked, like some cheeky lad just out of university.

Tuck looked back at both of the sisters and wondered what sort of magic they'd brought to London with them, for surely the pair had brought mayhem to his world.

Before he could even consider the consequences of such a match—his uncle and Lady Aveley, that is—the reverend intoned the final words, and Piers caught hold of his bride and kissed her fiercely. The two of them tangled together scandalously, and everyone in the room felt the sudden need to glance away and give the happy couple a moment of privacy.

Then he realized that Livy had come to stand beside him.

"No one will ever want to kiss me like that," she said, more to herself than to him.

It wasn't so much the wistful want in her voice that stopped him, but the response tolling through him with the force of the church bells overhead.

I would. I'd kiss you, Livy.

He glanced over at her, and something, a nudge, the urge to take her in his arms again, in front of everyone caught him unaware, but it was something else that stopped him. For out of the corner of his eye, he spied a new arrival to the happy celebration.

Ilford.

Standing in the open doorway of the church like Lucifer himself.

"Wait here," Tuck told her, setting Lavinia behind him, where she was out of Ilford's line of sight as he strode down the aisle.

With the rest of the gathering distracted by their felicitations and well-wishes for the happy couple, Tuck moved quickly toward the interloper—for the marquess could hardly be here to extend his compliments.

Anything but.

"Aw, *Mr.* Rowland—" Ilford sneered.

"My lord," Tuck murmured. He was willing to be polite—up to a point—if only to avoid a scene.

The marquess stepped into the sunshine outside, leaning on his elegant walking stick. "Surprised to see me?" he asked with droll arrogance.

"Rather," Tuck remarked, instantly forgetting his determination to remain civil. "I had heard that you'd run to ground. I would have thought you in your hunting box in Scotland by now."

A flicker of annoyance passed over the man's cool features, then he glanced back in at the church. "So it is true. Wakefield's gone and married one of them."

The way he sneered that last word, "them," set Tuck's teeth on edge. His fingers curled tightly into a fist, and, remembering himself and where he stood, he willed his hand to unfurl.

"News travels fast," Tuck remarked.

"I manage my interests with a careful eye. Nothing escapes me, Rowland, for I have no tolerance for losing. I intend to see you and your cousin ruined."

The hairs on the back of Tuck's neck stood up. But he'd met far rougher characters than the marquess to be undone by his snakish threats. "I would think you'd be worried, my lord. I'm halfway to winning."

"You've only a week left," the marquess reminded him, as a carriage pulled up, and a rough-looking fellow jumped down from the back and opened the door for the marquess.

"Only took a week to find Miss Louisa an advantageous match, certainly another won't be very difficult to find one for the remaining Miss Tempest. She's a rather delightful creature. Pretty as a picture."

"I wouldn't be so certain. Remember, I don't leave these things to chance," Ilford told him, a sly smile turning his lips, then he doffed his hat and strolled down the steps.

Tuck followed if only to ensure the man was well and gone before Piers came out of the church with his bride.

"Perhaps seek a groom for the gel at Bedlam," the marquess offered as he got into his carriage. Glancing over his shoulder at the wedding guests who were now coming out of the doors, he added, "If one sister is willing to marry a madman, another might do in a pinch."

Tuck stepped forward, ready to haul the smug man out of his richly appointed carriage and pummel him into the pavement with the silver-tipped walking stick the marquess always carried, but a steady hand on his shoulder stopped him.

"Not today," his uncle said quietly and firmly. "Not now."

The marquess smiled as he tapped the roof with his walking stick, and the carriage lurched forward. The arrogant fellow waved at the bride and groom.

The new Viscountess Wakefield stared at the two fellows hanging on the back.

"My lord," she said, looking up at Piers. "Isn't that Mr. Bludger and that dreadful Charlie he had working with him?"

Piers's head turned quickly, and his eyes widened with shock. "How the devil—"

Tuck looked as well. "You know them?"

"Unfortunately," Piers said, nodding toward the well-appointed carriage as it went down the block. "That's my former cook and his associate in thievery. I would certainly like to know what the three of them are doing together. That doesn't bode well."

Tuck nodded. He couldn't agree more. "Then let me find out."

He went loping down the block, hugging the side of the buildings and rounding the corner just after the marquess's carriage turned into the slow-moving traffic beyond.

"Do you think that's a good idea," Louisa asked. "Mr. Bludger is a dangerous man."

"Tuck can hold his own," Lord Charleton assured her.

"Aye, he can." Piers nodded in agreement.

Into their midst, Lavinia arrived. "Where is Mr. Rowland going?"

"He had another matter he must attend to," Piers told her.

"Yes, other business," Lord Charleton agreed. "I do believe weddings have an ill effect on Tuck."

Everyone laughed, save Lavinia, who stood watching Tuck depart until he was gone from her sight. When she looked up, she realized everyone in their party had already gone down the steps and were dividing up into the carriages.

"Lavinia?" Louisa called to her. "I forgot my bouquet."

"I'll get it," she promised. "You go on ahead."

Because at that moment, Lavinia, like Tuck, found that weddings had an ill effect on her as well. So she made her way back into St. George's.

"I hate to tell you I told you so," Charleton said later that night as he handed Lady Aveley—Amy—a glass of wine.

She took it, lips pursed. "Then don't. But I will concede that both the bride and groom looked well pleased."

"That gel has worked a miracle with Piers," the baron said, raising a glance in a toast.

Amy did the same.

Their glasses touched just at the rims with a quiet *clink*, and she looked away. "I just don't think—"

"What, Amy? What don't you think?" He reached for her, but the lady slipped past him.

They'd known each other since childhood. Been all but betrothed, then he'd married another. Amy had found Aveley, and the years had passed. Now . . . well, now . . . He reached for her, hungry to have her in his arms again.

Last night had been . . . amazing, he realized. He should have known having grown up with Amy that she would be a passionate handful in bed—she'd always been a headstrong and impetuous minx when they'd been younger.

"We mustn't," Amy said quietly, shaking her head and stepping away. "Not again. It isn't proper. Some chaperone I've turned out to be."

"Not such a bad one," he teased. "You've gotten one of them married off."

"I think that had more to do with you distracting me last night so Wakefield could be alone with Miss Tempest."

"Don't look so formidable," he told her. "It worked. He married her."

"Thankfully," she told him.

"Shall we go for two nights in a row?" he teased, closing the distance between them. "See Lavinia married off on the morrow?"

"If you still mean to marry that girl to your heir, then no," she told him. "They will not suit."

"I disagree."

"Then you don't know Lavinia very well. She has very strict notions of propriety. She has expectations of a good match. And Tuck, well . . . " She paused. "And you know as well as I do, that he'd run through her dowry and inheritance without a thought for the future."

He ruffled a bit at this—hearing his nephew and heir disparaged, but he couldn't argue the fact. Not and reveal the truth. He doubted Amy would even believe him—that Tuck was far more honorable than anyone knew. Or would ever know. That for now, Tuck must remain the less-than-sterling example of propriety.

But that didn't mean he was unworthy of Miss Tempest.

Yet when he looked up, he found Amy ready to cross swords again. "She keeps a list."

"A list?"

"A list gleaned from every manual, treatise and tract on manners and propriety."

"Hardly seems fair," Charleton told her, raking his hand through his hair as he considered this. "Isn't a man in London who could stand up to such scrutiny."

"No, I daresay you are correct in that." She smiled—a simple thing that seemed to illuminate her features.

And once again, he stepped toward her. He couldn't help himself.

And this time he caught hold of her hand and pulled her close, only to have the door to the study come open.

Amy moved first, taking two steps away from him and turning her back to the door.

"Do forgive the interruption, my lord," Mrs. Rowland said, glancing at the pair of them, one dark brow rising as she studied the tableaux before her. "Brobson was under the impression you were alone."

"Madame," he said, bowing slightly. "We were just toasting the happy couple." He reached for his glass, a prop to give his statement some proof.

"Truly? A toast?" The quirk of her brow and her knowing smile acknowledged his lie, but the lady said no more on the subject, instead turning toward the baron's companion. "Lady Aveley, how nice to see you again."

"Mrs. Rowland," Amy replied tightly.

Strolling into the room, Jenny Rowland set her reticule down on the nearest chair and began to remove her gloves. "I feel positively terrible to have interrupted your . . ." She paused and looked around the room again, "*cozy celebration*, but I have a family matter that must be discussed, Charleton."

Amy straightened. "I don't like your implication."

His sister-in-law turned like a cat—smoothly, a smile on her lips. "What ever would be implied, Lady Aveley? I've simply found two unmarried persons drinking alone at a very late hour and standing in close proximity to each other. What does one make of such a scenario?" She glanced over at her brother-in-law. "Charleton?"

"Can't whatever it is be discussed tomorrow?" he asked her.

"No." She shrugged off her pelisse, then settled into the chair next to his by the fire.

"Isn't it rather late for a lady to be out calling on gentlemen?" Lady Aveley asked.

This time Charleton did groan. Amy had always been an intrepid minx, but she was outmanned and outgunned when it came to tangling with the likes of Jenny Rowland.

"Yes, it is very late," Mrs. Rowland agreed, glancing over her shoulder at Lady Aveley. "Then again, aren't chaperones supposed to keep respectable hours? A decorous example and all. Or is that how you managed to get that dear, sweet girl married off so quickly?"

When the color drained from Amy's face, Lady Rowland laughed. "So I thought."

Lady Aveley came marching across the room, looking ready to do battle, hands balled into fists at her sides, but Charleton caught her by the elbow and towed her toward the door. "Please, Amy. Let me finish this, and I'll be—" He stopped himself there.

Right up.

There was a polite cough from the chair by the fire, and Amy tried once again to get to her.

Yes, Jenny had that way about her. Two hundred years earlier and she'd have fed a bonfire for certain with her sharp tongue and knowing glance.

But she was family, *his family*, and Charleton took a deep breath, if only because he'd promised his younger brother he would never forsake her.

No matter what.

"Please, Amy, let me settle this quickly," he told her as he led her from the study, all but towing her to the stairs. "I'll—"

Come find you . . .

There she shook off his grasp and marched up the steps. The look she shot him from the first landing had only one meaning.

Don't bother.

"Oh dear, Charleton," Jenny said as he came back into the study. "I fear I've made things difficult for you."

"You have that way about you, madame."

He sat down in the chair opposite hers, feeling entirely out of sorts.

"I suppose I do," she replied with an unrepentant shrug. Jenny Rowland had a knack for walking into a room and summing up the contents and the people therein within the blink of an eye.

Mostly for summing up the contents. But that was a discussion for another time.

"I think you know what I've come to discuss," she said, holding her hands out to the fire. Her only adornment was the plain wedding band on her finger—the one his madcap younger brother had put there so many years ago.

That she had never taken it off was, he supposed, her most redeeming character.

"You've come about Tuck."

"Of course it is about Tuck. What else would it be?"

It wasn't like Jenny to be quite this sharp, so Charleton realized this wager of Tuck's wasn't his nephew's usual bad run of luck. Jenny looked positively worried. And probably with good reason.

"Ilford," he said simply.

"*Ilford*," she repeated, spitting out the name like a sharp pit. "If only that foul man would meet with some well-deserved accident."

Charleton sat up. "You haven't—" He wasn't entirely unaware of his sister-in-law's less-than-savory connections.

"Oh, don't be foolish," she shot back. "Though the Honorable has quite a different opinion. But I keep reminding him that Ilford is the heir to a dukedom, and I suspect there would be some uproar if he was found floating in the Thames."

Some, Charleton would have told her, but not as much as she would imagine. Even Ilford's father deplored him. But he didn't say as much.

It wouldn't do to encourage Jenny.

"Tuck is in deep, my lord. Something must be done."

"I know," was all he could add.

"We both owe him a great debt," she said, bringing up a subject they had never discussed. "He thinks we don't know what he sacrificed that night, but I do. And I suspect you do as well."

Charleton inclined his head. Tuck had done his own reputation in to keep the Rowland family name out of the suds.

"We can't tell him we know. He's ever so full of pride." She paused, then added, "Rowland pride."

The baron's brow quirked at this.

"He sacrificed his honor for me," she said with more humility than he'd ever heard come out of her. She glanced up at him, a pleading light in her eyes.

He hadn't seen her look so desperate since his brother's passing. It wrung at him, for he'd failed Granville, but he'd vowed then that he wouldn't fail his brother's only child, Tuck. Still, Charleton felt a bit of shame that he'd neglected so much since Isobel had died. That he'd let it come to this.

"He sacrificed much for both of us," he agreed. "What do you propose?"

"My lord?"

He wasn't such a fool that he didn't know that if Jenny Rowland was here, she had a plan. "Madame, don't be coy with me.
We've known each other too long. You've come here with some
mad plan and expect me to go along with it, don't you?"

Now it was her turn to nod. "It is time we repaid him."

And once she explained what she had in mind, George Rowland, the fifteenth Baron Charleton, knew not only was Mrs.
Rowland's plan mad and entirely ruinous, it was also nothing
short of brilliant.

CHAPTER 15

Lavinia spent most of the night sitting on her bed and staring at her window. She'd never spent a night without Louisa nearby. The room was quite empty without her sister, and Lavinia felt hollow inside as well.

She had thought that perhaps . . .

Well, never mind that. It had been a foolish, reckless hope.

That Tuck would come, tossing pebbles at her window and tempt her out into the night.

But even the garden had remained quiet and lonely.

Save when Hannibal had set up a dreadful racket in the wee hours, howling on the fence as if his serenade was his rightful and honorable song.

But morning had finally come and with it, Lady Aveley, throwing open the curtains and clapping her hands together to add to the urgency. "Today we will start anew. Shopping is the best way to begin."

Lavinia had opened her mouth to protest—for she knew not even a new gown would cheer her spirits—but there was a brittle set to Lady Aveley's smile and a sharp light in her eyes that stopped Lavinia's protests.

Something was wrong—beyond the current straits. But what it was, Lavinia had no idea.

So, at the ungodly hour of eleven in the morning, Lavinia found herself being hustled from shop to shop.

At the modiste's—the one Lady Aveley favored—the assistant had brought forward a muslin for Lavinia that the girl thought would be perfect for "the young miss." While Lady Aveley and the assistant looked at the newly arrived collections of prints, Lavinia drew back, as if seeing it all for the first time.

Oh, the muslin was perfectly proper, but something told her such a modest, respectable gown was not what she needed.

Just then, the Frenchwoman who ran the shop came out from the back room. "My lady! Exquisite timing. A silk came in just yesterday—*mais oui*—I thought instantly of you. Come back, I would have you see it in the best light and share a cup of tea—for I have an idea as to how to make it up just so."

Lavinia, who had wandered over to one side, lured by a red velvet that took her breath away—both for the rich color and the price—smiled at her chaperone. "I'll wait here, my lady. I have yet to decide which pattern will suit."

Nearly the moment Lady Aveley disappeared into the back of the shop, the front door opened.

"Mrs. Rowland," Lavinia said in surprise.

"My dear girl, there you are. What a time I've had finding you."

"Me? Whatever for?"

She puffed out a little sigh. "Didn't Charleton tell you this morning?"

Lavinia shook her head. "I didn't see him. We left the house rather early."

"Of course you did," Mrs. Rowland said, coming farther into the shop. She stopped in front of the same velvet that Lavinia had been admiring, her eyes alight with appreciation and the same sigh over the price as Lavinia had made. But the widow was a whirlwind unto herself and turned back to Lavinia. "I've come to claim you, my dear."

Tuck's mother walked over to the counter and picked up an order sheet and the bit of pencil there, dashing off a note and handing it to the assistant, who fluttered about as if she wasn't too sure what to do about such high-handed behavior. "Do give this to Lady Aveley when she comes out—but not before."

The assistant sent a searching glance at Lavinia, as if she had an answer to all this.

But Lavinia was rather baffled until Mrs. Rowland brushed her hands over her skirt and turned to her.

"Come along, my dear, we have much to do today."

"But Lady Aveley—"

"Her Ladyship won't mind in the least," Mrs. Rowland told her, tucking her hand into the crook of Lavinia's arm and towing her toward the door. "Lord Charleton had no objections last night to my offer of assistance, and I told him I would be picking you up this morning." She sighed and glanced over her shoulder at the door to the back room. "Apparently, he didn't have the chance to tell Lady Aveley, but my note will explain everything. She'll understand."

"I really should tell—"

"Come, come, time is of the essence," the woman declared, her back to the shop and her determined gaze set on the street beyond.

And with that, Lavinia found herself being tugged out of the store and toward a waiting carriage. Lord Charleton's carriage, to be exact.

That seemed to confirm what Mrs. Rowland was saying, that Lord Charleton had given his blessing to all this, but at the same time it hardly seemed proper to leave Lady Aveley behind without giving an explanation.

The door to the carriage swung open and it was then she realized that Mrs. Rowland was not alone.

"Ah, my lovely child! How delightful to see you again, and looking so fair this morning," the Honorable declared, jumping down from the carriage to help her in; then once Mrs. Rowland was settled in, they were off in a trice.

"Sir, how nice to see you again," Lavinia said. She was growing rather fond of Tuck's great-uncle. He had a *bon vivant* about him that lifted her spirits.

"Indeed! Indeed!" he declared. "And I am most pleased we were able to find you. If I've said it once, I've said it half a dozen times this morning—that you will brighten our day, our very prospects. Didn't I say that, Jenny, my girl?"

"You did, Uncle," Mrs. Rowland agreed. "You did." Tuck's mother turned to her. "Good thing I arrived when I did—Lady Aveley is a lovely woman, but she lacks an eye for true fashion. What the right gown can do for a woman. I nearly died when I saw that muslin on the counter. She didn't think to have that for you, did she?"

It hardly seemed polite to agree—for it was disloyal to Lady Aveley, who had only been kind to them, but secretly, Lavinia agreed.

But she didn't need to. Mrs. Rowland said it all. "Dreadful choice. Just dreadful."

Lavinia had thought much the same thing but hadn't had the heart to tell the kind woman that it just wouldn't suit.

Not anymore.

"If I had your coloring! Oh, I would be a duchess," Mrs. Rowland declared.

"Should have been," the Honorable added. "Could have been if you'd listened to me."

"A duchess?" Lavinia asked.

"Yes, but sadly the heart wants what the heart wants, and I had already fallen in love with my dear Granville."

The Honorable snorted, arms crossing over his chest. "Devil of a cheat that fellow. Intimating vast connections, claiming a grand inheritance. Bah!"

Mrs. Rowland smiled indulgently at her relation. "You wouldn't understand. You've never been in love."

He *harrumphed* at this. "Bah! Love rarely brings prospects. A fool's fancy is what it is."

Mrs. Rowland winked at Lavinia. "You mustn't listen to him. Love might be blind, but it is divine while it lasts."

"You must have cared most deeply for Tuck's, er, Mr. Rowland's father to give up a duke."

"A duke?" the lady asked absently, that is until her uncle nudged her with the toe of his boot. "Oh, yes, right, a duke. I hardly remember it all now. I would have made a grand duchess, but I am most content being Mrs. Rowland."

There was another snort from the Honorable.

Ignoring him, Mrs. Rowland continued on, "Now that I've rescued you from that gown, I must tell you my plans—"

"About those," Lavinia began. "I'm not sure—"

"Not sure? My dear, you must always be sure. And confident. And quite convinced of your place. That is how I nearly secured the affections of a duke."

"Yes, well, Lady Aveley was just saying this morning she would be working most diligently to secure—"

Mrs. Rowland waved at all this. "I am certain she is trying her best, my dear child, but I have such grand plans for you, magnificent plans."

That stirring inside her, the one Tuck had ignited the other night in the garden, sparked to life. It whispered of a world far beyond the proper one she had so dutifully planned.

"What plans did Lady Aveley have in mind?" Mrs. Rowland was asking.

"She mentioned making calls," Lavinia offered.

Mrs. Rowland's expression was one of horror, and when she seemed to recover, she asked, "And on whom did she propose to call?"

"A Mrs. Clementson."

That did not improve Mrs. Rowland's expression in the least.

From across the carriage, the Honorable groaned.

"Yes, well, I understand Mrs. Clementson isn't the most lofty of personages," Lavinia rushed to add, once again feeling that twinge of loyalty. "But she was willing—"

Oh, it was rather lowering when she had to admit it like that. Out loud.

She was willing to let me enter her house.

Not that Mrs. Rowland or the Honorable appeared to notice. "Good heavens, Tuck wasn't exaggerating for once, now was he, Uncle?"

The Honorable shrugged. "Seems rather low in the instep, but I suppose one must start somewhere."

"If one is to ascend to great heights, it is always best to start far higher up the mountain," Mrs. Rowland declared.

"Indeed it is," the Honorable agreed, sagely nodding.

"The advantage of Mrs. Clementson," Lavinia began, feeling the need to defend the choice, "is that she is willing to welcome me."

"Yes, but not much more, I imagine," Mrs. Rowland said. "My dear, Society will never invite you in because they already know you."

"I don't see how they can know me when they've never met me," Lavinia replied, thinking of the fleeting hour or so she'd had at Almack's before everything had gone so terribly wrong.

"No, my dear, they *know* you. At least they think they do. Do you see the difference?" Mrs. Rowland asked.

"Not precisely," Lavinia admitted.

"We need to show them they knew nothing of the Miss Tempest they coldly—and wrongly—"

"And foolishly," the Honorable added, hands folded over the top of his walking stick.

"Yes, entirely foolishly," Mrs. Rowland agreed enthusiastically, "gave the cut direct. While your sister's marriage to Wakefield is perfectly timed—it creates a curiosity—you must be more than that—a mystery, a puzzle, a divine creature they scorned and now will fall all over themselves to anoint with their blessings."

While it sounded glorious—in fact Lavinia could nearly see it, glimmering before her—she was now well versed enough in the London *ton* to ask the obvious. "How can we do all that when I am relegated to calling on the likes of Mrs. Clementson and no one else?"

"Leave that to me and Uncle Hero," the lady told her. "But first, we must get you a gown."

"I was just about to order one," she pointed out.

"That was a dress," Mrs. Rowland said in lofty tones. Much like the duchess she might have been. "I said *a gown*."

"But I have—" Lavinia began.

"*Tsk. Tsk.* A gown, I said," Mrs. Rowland said as they left Bond Street.

Tuck arrived at his uncle's house just as Lady Aveley's carriage came screeching to a halt behind him. He had gained some leads on Ilford and his mysterious accomplices, terrible whispers of what the marquess had planned, but nothing credible. What he needed was a bit of gold to move along reluctant tongues that refused to wag without an incentive.

But his plans were immediately put on hold as Her Ladyship bolted to the sidewalk, and she turned on Tuck. "You! I blame you!"

"Blame me?" Tuck immediately drew up in a defensive stance, but for the life of him he couldn't think of what he'd done. Recently, that is. After all, he'd spent a good part of the night prowling about the Dials trying to find a lead on this Bludger fellow and his accomplice.

But before he could ask what transgression the lady was referring to, she'd already marched into the house and was calling out his uncle's name.

No, make that yelling.

"Charleton! Charleton! Where are you? I demand you come out now!"

Tuck stood in the doorway, utterly dumbfounded. For he'd never seen the cool and serene woman in such a state—and wondered if he was about to come into his inheritance a bit earlier than expected given the murderous light in Lady Aveley's eyes.

Bludger and company forgotten, Tuck rather feared for his uncle's safety.

Even Brobson had left his post, shooing the gaping footman before him. The man hadn't served the *ton* all these years not to know when it was best to abandon ship.

"Charleton! Come out this instant." Lady Aveley stomped her foot to the marble floor.

Actually stomped her foot.

His uncle appeared at the top of the stairs. "Amy? Whatever has you in such a fettle?"

Amy? Tuck's brow quirked. It seemed his uncle and Lady Aveley had moved beyond a polite detente.

At least on his uncle's side.

Not so Her Ladyship. "Don't you try to cozen me, you wretched scoundrel!"

Tuck nearly flinched, for usually that was the invective being tossed in his direction. Certainly not his uncle's.

Nor was the lady done. "That woman snatched Lavinia right out from under my nose. Mrs. Rowland absconded with my charge in the most high-handed and nefarious way!"

"Just a moment," Tuck sputtered. "My mother?"

Lady Aveley whirled on him. "Yes. *Your* mother."

Now this time he did flinch.

"Oh, so Jenny found you," his uncle said, having come down the stairs, boldly wading into the fray with a wry smile on his lips. "I rather thought she would."

"I merely went into the back room of Madame Poirier's shop, and when I came out—" Words failed her, but she held up a crumbled note. "This! This was waiting for me."

"I hardly see how this is my fault," Charleton told her. "I told you last night that Mrs. Rowland was going to be by this morning for Lavinia."

While Lady Aveley tried to find the words to argue with him, Tuck waded in.

"Are you saying Miss Tempest is with my mother?" A ripple of panic ran through him. Not just from the thought of what his mother and uncle could do without any restraints to be had—but more from what he'd learned of Ilford's plans.

Now it was his uncle's turn to look a bit sheepish, but he rallied quickly, like an old campaigner. "I don't see why you, of all people, are surprised, Tuck. You did after all, demand she help you."

"You did wha-a-at?" Lady Aveley stammered, now whirling to face Tuck.

He shot a furious glance at his uncle, who looked entirely unrepentant now that the tide had turned from him.

"At the time, I thought it might be—"

"You thought!" Lady Aveley scoffed.

"And Lady Wakefield," Tuck hastened to add. "It was actually her suggestion first."

It was a cowardly thing to say, but right at the moment, Tuck's concerns for his uncle's life had transferred to a genuine fear for his own neck.

"I hardly see what you have to object to, Tuck," Charleton said, having used his brief reprieve to rally. "Whyever would your mother's assistance be a problem?"

Tuck set his teeth together, gaze fixed on the ground, rather than give his uncle any hint of an answer.

"Yes, so I thought," his uncle said, turning to Lady Aveley. "And you? What are your complaints as to my dear brother's widow offering her assistance?" When Lady Aveley did the same—setting her jaw—Charleton nodded. "Yes, indeed. That is better." He stood a little straighter and looked them both over. "Are we done now?"

"Yes, sir," Tuck agreed—having seen that look on any number of occasions and knowing better than to voice another complaint.

Lady Aveley opened her mouth, but then must have had the

same experience and thought better of saying anything further. Rather, she simply nodded, a short, curt gesture.

But to Tuck's way of thinking, it also very clearly said, *This isn't over yet.*

"Yes, well, I am off to my club. Try to keep the dramatics to a dull roar—the two of you have quite frightened off Brobson." And with that, his uncle continued out the front door.

The door closed, leaving a terrible silence in the foyer.

But not for long.

Tuck moved into his uncle's wake, headed for the door.

"Where do you think you are going?" Lady Aveley demanded.

"To fetch her back." He paused and looked over his shoulder at the lady. "I don't suppose you are going to object to that."

Lady Aveley drew in a deep breath. "Thank you."

He nodded and opened the door.

"Tuck—"

He paused but didn't turn around.

"I'm sorry," she said kindly.

She didn't need to explain why. He'd been apologizing for his mother all his life.

Tuck arrived at his mother's house almost afraid of what he would discover.

But to his amazement, he burst into the sitting room to find Livy comfortably curled up on the settee, sewing.

It took his eyes a few moments to adjust to such a cozy scene of domestic bliss. In his mother's house.

Hell, he didn't even know his mother owned a sewing basket.

But here was Livy, and save for nipping at the thread with her teeth, looking like a proper miss.

Thank goodness.

And no sign of his mother or the Honorable. Even better.

His relief, however, was short-lived.

For her part, Livy looked up at him in a mixture of bemused

humor and surprise. "Mr. Rowland, what a surprise. Your mother said you were previously engaged today and wouldn't be joining us."

"I imagine she did." He continued into the room warily. He didn't trust his mother—and as for the Honorable?

That went without saying.

"We've had such a lovely afternoon," Livy continued, setting aside the gown. "Thank you ever so much for bringing me to her attention. You can't imagine what we've been doing."

That was the problem. Tuck could.

"Such as?" he ventured, almost afraid to ask.

"Shopping and sewing, and oh—" She paused and lowered her voice. "I played cards with Uncle Hero."

Uncle Hero? Now the Honorable was "Uncle Hero"? Then the rest of what she said came echoing back. Tuck's heart walloped to a *thud*. "You did wha-a-a-t?"

"Just some shopping," she replied, looking into the basket and pulling out another spool of thread. "And just this bit of sewing—"

Tuck waved his hand to get to that last part again. "No, no! You played cards—"

"Oh, yes, with dear Uncle Hero." She shook her head slightly, like one might over a toddler in need of a nap. "I fear your uncle is not a very good player."

Not a good player? What was this? Tuck paused, his eyes narrowing. Maybe he'd mistaken the matter. Which uncle were they discussing? Or had he suddenly come into a new one?

Given his mother, that wasn't an impossibility.

"I hope he isn't put out with me," Livy whispered. "I did try to return his money—but men can be so overly proud about these things."

"Return his mon—ey?" Tuck said each word slowly, more for his own benefit.

She heaved a sigh. "He lost a fearful sum. I tried to let him win it back."

He struggled to get this straight. "The Honorable lost money. In a card game? Against you?"

"I fear so." She sighed and began to thread her needle. Pausing, she glanced up at him. "As I've told you before, I always win."

"Always?" He looked again at the woman before him, trying to reconcile this sure-footed creature with the innocent miss he'd come to know.

Or had he truly taken her measure? Apparently not.

"Yes, I fear I'm rather good," she admitted with the same resignation that she exhibited about her lack of agility on the dance floor. "No one in Kempton will play with me. I suppose, if I stay in London for much longer, no one in the *ton* will either."

Tuck felt as if he'd fallen down a rabbit hole and was now lost in the warren. "Tell me again about Uncle Hero," he asked. "You say he lost to you?"

"Well, yes," she said, looking at him quizzically.

"What were you playing?"

"*Écarté.* Which he asked to play—at first—but once I'd won several hands, he suggested *vingt-et-un*—"

Which was the Honorable's ace in the hole choice. Quite literally.

She shrugged and leaned over her sewing, lowering her voice yet again. "I did let him win a few hands, then . . . Well, I fear the thrill of the game got to me, and I trounced him."

She bit her low lip and did her best to look repentant, but Tuck had grown up around gamblers and sharps and thieves, and he knew a lie when he heard one.

Livy hadn't been able to resist winning, the lure of the hand too tempting to ignore.

And then she all but confirmed his theory when she said, "He made an impetuous wager, and I won all his ready coins."

"And you won?" Tuck still couldn't quite believe it.

"Yes," she said, glancing at him with an exasperated flash of her blue eyes that said all too clearly, *haven't you been listening?*

"Did my mother see you playing?" he asked, wondering what she'd make of this.

Or rather how she'd use it to her advantage.

"Yes, but only a hand or two—and one of those I let your uncle win. Then she was called upon to help an acquaintance." She tied a knot in the thread and nipped the thread. Setting aside her tools, she shook out the gown she'd been working on.

The deep blue velvet beckoned like the night sky, touched as it was with brilliants at the hem and on the sleeves. Tuck found himself slightly entranced by the seductive waver of the velvet as it fell in place.

A gown worn when a lady wanted to catch a man's eye.

Tuck stilled and eyed it suspiciously. "What is *that*?"

Livy smiled. No, make that grinned. "A new gown," she admitted. Breathlessly. Dreamily.

Passionately.

She'd sounded like that when she'd danced with him, when she'd been lost in his kiss.

Or maybe that had been him.

He shook his head. He had a far greater problem before him.

"We went to the most amazing modiste shop," she was saying. "It was quite out of the way, but your mother was more than happy to share its location with me." She gazed at the dress.

Tuck found himself taken aback by how contented and happy she looked—something he'd never seen before—well, save that moment in the garden.

Dear heavens, he had to stop thinking about that.

Yet, it was impossible not to be drawn by her smile—it lit up her entire face. That, and the long tendril of dark hair that fell from her usually tidy coif. Its wayward path gave her an innocent air, and he thought Lavinia Tempest a nonpareil in that moment, that is until he widened his view to include the entire gown and the lady holding it.

"*What the devil?*" The words exploded from him.

The navy blue velvet fell against her fair skin like a deep curtain of night. What he hadn't seen was the plunging neckline and around the short sleeves where a twining string of brilliants that cast their seductive flickers like elusive stars—tempting anyone looking upon them to come closer.

And while she might be merely holding the gown up, the fabric clung to her in all the ways that made it easy to imagine her in it.

Oh, the devil take him.

Clinging to her curves, setting off her mahogany hair with traces of color he'd never seen before—illuminating hints of chestnut and rich, dark shades of midnight—this gown, this lady, paired together made for a seductive dream.

He'd asked his mother to help him make Lavinia Tempest compelling, a woman no man could take his eyes off of.

And she'd done it. In one afternoon. With one gown.

Tuck wanted to groan.

He wanted to possess her.

In that velvet sheath of temptation, there wasn't a man in London who would care a whit that Lavinia Tempest's mother had been a terrible scandal.

All they would want was to be *her* path to ruin.

"You aren't going to wear that!" he said, stalking over and taking the gown from her.

Even holding it, the soft fabric crushed in his grasp gave him a tempting glimpse of the future.

Livy. His Livy. Naked in his bed. Her skin as soft and as teasing as the gown he now held.

"You aren't going to wear that," he repeated.

Livy rallied quickly, retrieving her gown and shaking her head. "Your mother said you would say that. And that I was to ignore you. She says for a terrible knave, you can also be a terrible prude."

Her glance said all too clearly she now shared her mother's opinion.

And he clamped his teeth together if only not to shoot off the retort, the promise biting at him.

I'll show you what sort of knave I am, you reckless minx.

But, instead, he drew a deep breath and remembered his promise to Lady Aveley. To bring Livy home. Safely. "Speaking of my mother, where is she?"

"A friend of hers came by, mentioned that he was having some difficulty—"

Hardly a surprise there.

"—and she was most attentive to his concerns."

"That sounds like my mother," he remarked.

Livy paused. "I don't like to judge—"

Tuck coughed, and she had the decency to blush.

"But as I was saying, this man who came to call . . . well, he hardly seemed proper."

"Truly?" Tuck did his best to sound utterly shocked.

He also utterly failed.

For Lavinia shot him a quelling glance. The sort that said he wasn't taking this seriously. "Yes, well, he was quite young. At least to be an associate of hers—"

He didn't want to explain to her that his mother's associates got younger every year.

"Nor did he seem . . . Well, he had a bit of an air of—"

"Impropriety about him?" Tuck ventured.

"Yes, that." She breathed a sigh of relief. "I am so glad you understand."

"When it comes to my mother, understanding is rarely possible."

Just then the door to the kitchen opened and in strolled—not his mother—but the Honorable.

"'Allo there, Tuck. Fancy you dropping by. Any good word?"

"Uncle," Tuck acknowledged, bowing slightly for Livy's sake. "I've been hearing of Miss Tempest's adventures today. How kind of you to entertain her when I know your time is so very taken up with other matters." He made a pointed glance toward the door.

The Honorable—always on his best behavior when there was company about—deliberately ignored the hint about leaving.

"Don't you think Miss Tempest looks utterly divine today?" the Honorable prompted, subtly changing the subject.

Tuck took a vague glance in her direction. "Yes, of course."

"I think she shows a particular glow about her."

And by "glow" his uncle meant "prospects."

As in a large dowry and an income to boot.

Which Tuck knew Miss Tempest had neither. Charleton had been most clear on the subject.

"Glowing, I say. Glowing with prospects," the Honorable was continuing, as if he were once again on the Continent working another of his shady cons.

"She always glows, Uncle," Tuck told him.

"Excellent. I feared you hadn't noticed. Gotten all rag mannered up there in Mayfair. Forgotten what I taught you."

Tuck had always thought his uncle's advice ran more toward, *always keep an ace in your pocket and never pay for a Vestal without laying eyes on her first.*

"We've been working on her skills," the Honorable was saying. He held his hand out to Livy, and she took it, rising slowly and elegantly from the settee.

Skills? Oh, that could hardly bode well.

"What skills in particular?" Tuck managed, well aware that he wasn't going to like the answer.

"How to walk," Livy told him.

"The walk is where it all begins, my boy!" the Honorable declared.

Livy glanced at Tuck, a sly sort of tip to her lips as she began a slow turn around the end of the settee, then wandered past him with a confident air. From her first step, her gaze had locked upon his, but he couldn't say the same. His gaze had wandered down to where her hips were swaying, hypnotically, leaving his mouth suddenly dry and his heart hammering erratically.

"Bloody hell," he managed, as she brushed past him, her hand trailing across his chest. His uncle had done this? In just an afternoon?

"She's the quickest study I've ever met, Tuck," his uncle told him. "Divine, my dear. Utterly divine," he said to Livy. "Ah, what I could teach you in a fortnight."

Teach her in a fortnight? Tuck swung around. "Uncle! She came here to learn to be a *lady*." He hoped his uncle understood what he meant when he emphasized that last word.

And his uncle, mesmerized by his own success, suddenly snapped to attention. "Oh, yes, Right. *A lady.* I fear I got carried away."

"Not in the least," Livy said, holding up a pocket watch but grinning at his uncle, "Oh, I do believe I did it, didn't I, Uncle Hero?"

"Indeed you did, my dear gel! Indeed," he said, applauding with gusto. "And look there, Livy, at his expression! The poor lad doesn't even realize you took it."

Tuck looked from his uncle to Livy. Why the minx was holding up his pocket watch. "What the devil?!" he exclaimed, patting his waistcoat, then turning to the Honorable. "She's here to learn the graces of a lady."

"Oh, yes, right," Uncle Hero agreed, scratching at his brow as if that knowledge needed to be soothed back into place. "But remember, my good boy, the true graces can be nothing more than an illusion, and our Livy is such a quick study." The Honorable smiled at her. "Did you not see how intoxicating her carriage can be."

Both men turned to look at her, for Livy was back to prowling about the room like a . . . a . . .

Well, Tuck was too much a gentleman to admit what she looked like.

But certainly if she'd sashayed like that into Almack's, no one would have bothered to ask her to dance.

Tuck stepped back, partially in a panic. Another hour—nay half an hour—in the Honorable's company, and she'd be capable of replacing an entire harem.

And absconding with all the sultan's gold.

"Miss Tempest, we need to go."

"Oh, but Tuck—" she began.

"We are leaving," he said in no uncertain terms.

"Before your mother returns?" she posed, then glancing over her shoulder toward the kitchen door as if she expected the long-delayed Mrs. Rowland to magically appear.

"She's right, my boy, that wouldn't do," the Honorable rushed to add. "Jenny would be terribly put out, for I believe she had more things to discuss with our dear, dear Livy."

And to his horror, Livy beamed.

Smiled actually. Happily, as if fitting in here, in his mother's house was the only place she wanted to be.

Proper, practical Lavinia Tempest no more. She'd fallen into this den of thieves like she'd been born to it.

For the sake of every man in England, he had to get her out of here and quickly.

"My mother will understand," Tuck told her, nodding toward the front door. "Now I must insist. You'll be missed, and there will be a need for explanations."

That got her attention. But then she did the unthinkable. She began to gather up the velvet gown.

"Oh, no," he told her. "I don't think Lady Aveley will approve of such a choice."

She bit at her lower lip again, a light of regret in her eyes. "What about the other one?" She tipped her head toward a pile of sapphire silk thrown over the back of the chair. He hadn't noticed it before—but now that he had . . . Oh, good God, where had his mother taken her shopping?

At a house of ill repute?

Tuck stopped himself right there. This was his mother. Not even she would do *that*.

Now the Honorable, on the other hand . . .

"Where did you go shopping?" Because this still had his mother's hand all over it . . .

Livy brightened immediately. "Oh, such a lovely, unusual shop. Uncle Hero, where was it precisely?"

"Uncle Hero," indeed! Tuck thought his head would explode.

For his part, the Honorable grinned widely. "Madame St. Vincent's? A perfectly respectable address, my dear boy, if that is what you are worried about."

In the meantime, Livy was gathering up the silk gown.

"That will have to stay as well," Tuck told her.

She sighed with some reticence and finally, albeit reluctantly, nodded in agreement. Then, after a protracted farewell to the Honorable, and with Uncle Hero's grand and elongated praise in return of her qualities and prospects, Tuck was finally able to extract her from his mother's house.

But halfway to the carriage, the Honorable called after him. "My boy, about that matter—"

Tuck got Livy into the carriage and hurried back to the old rogue's side. "Did you find out anything?"

"Yes, I fear so. You've made some rather dangerous enemies," the Honorable told him. "Grave caution is warranted. Do you remember my associate down by the wharves?"

"Old Kelley?"

"Yes. Go find him. He prefers to take his afternoon ale at the *Dog and Spoon*. With a bit of gold, I'm certain he can help you."

Tuck nodded. "Thank you, sir."

"Caution, my lad. Ilford has gathered some dangerous fellows to his cause. It is no longer a simple wager but a vendetta. He means to win, but mostly he means to ruin you and Wakefield." He gave Tuck's shoulder a gentle pat, like a blessing, and sent him on his way.

A vendetta. That word put a cold, icy pick into his heart as he returned to the carriage and set out for his uncle's house.

Though if he was being honest, he'd known that it had always been more than a wager to Ilford.

"I think I've made a terrible mistake," he told her when they were halfway back to Mayfair.

"Oh, no, not in the least," she assured him. "I've had the most enlightening day."

"Learning to lighten gentlemen's pockets?"

She fluttered her hand at him in a dismissive wave. "It is merely a skill to gain my true potential and prospects."

Tuck groaned. Good heavens, now she was quoting the Honorable.

Worse yet, she continued. "It isn't like I am going to start working a bulk and file in St. James's Square."

"A bulk and file? Do you even know that means?"

Oh, how he wished he hadn't asked.

"Of course, your uncle explained it. You have two people, and the first pickpocket—"

Tuck groaned. "Lavinia, I thought you wanted to be a proper lady?"

"I do, but Uncle Hero says—"

"Oh, stop right there," he told her. "Nothing out of the Honorable's mouth is proper."

"Then they would hardly call him 'The Honorable,' now would they?" She shook her head and dismissed his protests as utter foolishness. "Your uncle only taught me so I would have a unique skill. Like a parlor trick. Uncle Hero says 'every lady should be able to do something magical.'"

Tuck supposed he should be relieved that in this instance, the Honorable had left the magical part to merely picking pockets. Then again . . .

He thought of that seductive saunter she'd managed.

No, make that mastered.

"How long were you in my uncle's company?"

"All afternoon," she replied. "He is so charming."

"You can say that," Tuck agreed. Charming ladies out of their fortunes. Charming unwitting country rubes into card games. Charming yet another magistrate into releasing him.

Oh, yes, *very* charming.

"Weren't you supposed to be shopping with Lady Aveley?"

Livy flinched and glanced away.

Good. At least she had a modicum of guilt left in her.

The Honorable hadn't plucked that out of her.

Yet.

But to his surprise, Lavinia then raised a counterattack. "Actually, your mother and uncle rescued me from Lady Aveley's clutches."

"I might be inclined to argue that point," Tuck told her.

"You wouldn't if you saw the shop your mother took me to—no dreary muslins there. The most spectacular gowns—all of them at such wonderful prices—you cannot believe the opportunities to economize by buying a gown secondhand."

"Truly," he said. "And my mother taught you this?"

"No, I don't think she even gave the price a second thought," she replied. "She merely likes the expediency of buying an already made gown."

That made sense. Economizing to his mother usually meant taking only half of someone's jewelry case or only the lesser pieces.

"Of course, she agreed with me as to the advantages when I pointed out that with what we were saving, the hat and the slippers to match were practically free."

"A rare bargain," he noted wryly, having no desire to see the hat or slippers that went with such a gown—for it all rather made his head spin. And other parts . . .

"Mr. Rowland, you sound like the new rector in Kempton—"

Tuck had to imagine this was the first time in his life he'd ever been compared to a man of the cloth.

"—he is always droning on about frippery being a path to sin, but how can such a beautiful gown lead one astray?"

Tuck's head swiveled and looked at her, for he thought at first she was joking, but no, innocent Miss Tempest was quite sincere.

All she had seen were lovely, elegant gowns, the likes of which she'd probably never seen in her small village.

But in London—well, such gowns were not worn by young ladies. Well, not by proper young ladies, and he was about to explain as much to her when he realized he would sound as boorish as her rector.

Besides, how much harm was there in her having such a gown when it was safe and sound at his mother's house? It wasn't like she was going to be wearing it out in public.

He paused and glanced over at her. She wasn't, was she?

He had a feeling he was going to wake up in the middle of the night in a cold sweat, or worse, hard as iron, recalling the image of her holding that velvet gown up for him to admire.

"That velvet would be quite fetching on—don't you think?"

He tried to breathe, for suddenly he saw her, cloaked in night, a sashaying temptress, her mahogany hair unbound, leaving him with only one thought.

How quickly could he get her out of it?

"Are you fishing for a compliment?" he managed.

"Well, yes I am." She paused, brow furrowed. "Was I too obvious?" Her lips pursed as she appeared to be sifting through her afternoon of lessons. "Uncle Hero said—"

"Would you please stop calling him that," Tuck said, blurting the words out.

"Whyever not?" she asked. "It would be rude not to. He quite insisted, since we are practically family—"

"He is not your family," Tuck told her, more harshly than he probably should have, but hell's fire, the Honorable was no more her family than he was Tuck's.

"Yes, yes, I suppose you are correct," she agreed, "but it would have been most impolite of me to argue with him when he was bestowing his years of accumulated knowledge upon me."

The Honorable's words, to a letter.

Oh, how had this gone all so terribly wrong? She needed to be proper. A lady. A Diamond.

Not the Queen of Seven Dials.

And mostly, she needed to be kept safe. Well away from Ilford . . . and now it seemed a pack of unsavory accomplices.

"Miss Tempest, I fear we must change our plans."

CHAPTER 16

All these hours later, Lavinia was still in a pique.

Certainly, the Honorable's suggestions and lessons had been anything but proper, and as Papa always said, she was a quick study, nor had Lavinia held any notion of putting the kindly man's suggestions into practice.

That is until Tuck had walked into the room and looked at her. And then . . . well, all she'd wanted was to put them to immediate good use.

Especially if she could get him to kiss her again.

When that had failed, she'd held out some hope of being alone with him on the drive back to Lord Charleton's, yet much to her chagrin, Tuck had spent nearly every minute lecturing her on propriety.

Propriety, no less!

He'd prosed on like the vicar at Kempton, so much so, she hadn't managed to get a word in edgewise, or point out that the only one (thus far) who had tried to ruin her was *him*.

Oh, the very irony of him extolling her to exercise "practical restraint" and "all due caution"?

She paused in her distracted pacing. Good heavens, she was starting to think his reputation as a knave was a complete fraud.

Until she thought about his kiss. For when she did—something made her toes curl a bit in her slippers and her tongue wet her lips as if waiting for him to return—she decided perhaps he might know a thing or two about knavery.

Perhaps . . .

That was, until, adding insult to injury, he'd handed her over to Lady Aveley, who had spent a good hour ringing a peal over her head—abandoning their shopping trip without a proper chaperone . . . leaving Her Ladyship in a panic over her well-being . . . spending the afternoon in the company of Mrs. Rowland and the likes of the Honorable Hero Worth.

All grave sins, according to Lady Aveley.

And Tuck? Her Ladyship had sent him on his way with a kiss on the cheek and thanked him profusely for "rescuing dear, innocent Miss Tempest."

Rescuing! Bah! Lavinia puffed out a breath, impatient and furious and . . . and . . .

She turned slightly and caught a glimpse of herself in the mirror.

Oh, yes, she was mad, and furious, but more to the point . . . she was changed. Ever so much.

She turned slowly toward the mirror, gaping at her own reflection, for staring back at her was certainly not the miss who had come from Kempton all buttoned-up with lofty notions of proper manners. Somehow, at some point, all those rules and obligations and restraints had fallen away, one by one—and that flicker inside her, the one she'd done the best to extinguish all these years, had become a torch.

One that, if she dared pick it up, would light her way. Let her shine. Let her breathe. Deeply and with passion.

"I don't want to be proper," she whispered to the creature in the mirror.

"And you don't have to be," came a voice from behind her.

*　*　*

After Tuck had returned Livy to his uncle's house, he'd borrowed an old jacket from one of the footmen and gone straight to the *Dog and Spoon* and sat down at the corner table, the one near the window. This was where Old Kelley had held court for nearly thirty years—gathering information and sharing it—all for a price. As luck would have it, Old Kelley was already well in his cups, so the required gold wasn't as much as it might have been earlier in the afternoon.

"Bludger!" Old Kelley spat out the man's name and shook his head. He leaned back in his chair, the cup of ale Tuck had purchased for him cradled in his hands. Hands that trembled a bit with age.

Or might it be fear?

Given that Old Kelley was a fierce, bear of a man, this didn't bode well.

Kelley leaned forward, lowering his gruff voice. "That there is a murderous black-hearted devil if ever there was one. What are you doing, Tuck, me lad, with the likes of that sort of company?"

"He's been following a friend of mine."

"Your friend hasn't long to live then," Old Kelley declared, heaving a sigh and taking a long drink.

"And the man with Bludger?" Tuck had already learned that Mr. Bludger was a naval deserter, wanted by both the Royal Navy and Bow Street. No one had yet been able to apprehend the thief, and his string of crimes grew daily.

"Charlie," Old Kelley told him. "Grew up in the Dials—had a regular education there."

Which Tuck knew meant picking pockets, burglary, even murder.

"Not the brightest lad," Old Kelley continued, "but he does what he's told, Charlie does. *Whatever he's told to do.* Good with a knife—so be cautious."

"And this man who's hired them—the Marquess of Ilford? What do you hear about him?" Tuck slid a coin across the table, and Old Kelley took it in a flash.

For the true value of Old Kelley was that he didn't discriminate as to whom he gathered information about—the denizens of London's underworld or its loftiest jewels—there was always a buyer when there were secrets to hide.

"Ilford." Old Kelley's rheumy eyes narrowed as he considered his words and pocketed his payment. "That one might as well have grown up in the Dials. Nasty bloke. For all his high-and-mighty titles, he's the worst of the lot. Wondered when you were going to bring him up. Thought that was why you were here to begin with. What were you thinking, boy? One never wagers when it comes to a woman's character. Might as well wager on the wind—they'll change on you just when you get your sails set."

It shouldn't surprise him that Old Kelley knew about his wager, but what touched him was the note of concern behind his reproach.

The man continued, leaning across the table as he spoke. "Whatever did you do to the fellow to have him swearing vengeance up one side of the river and down the other?"

"My cousin tapped his claret at Almack's. I might have found it a bit amusing and offered to help."

"Seems a trifling thing to get all lathered over. What man doesn't get rapped a time or two? And some days, you deserve it. But Ilford, he isn't right—not in the head—not where it matters. He's out to take his full measure in return, and it doesn't matter who he hurts in the process—lady or child—just so you and that milling cousin of yours feel the sting."

"That's madness," Tuck declared, his chest tightening as he thought of all the people he and Piers loved, cared for . . . his mother, Uncle Charleton, Lady Wakefield, Roselie, even the Honorable, and now, the new viscountess, Louisa.

But Tuck's heart pounded only one name.

Livy.

Across from him, Old Kelley emptied his tankard and set it on the table with a practiced *clank* that broke into Tuck's reverie. "That's not the half of his story. A marquess he might be, but he's a marked man." His smile crooked at his own turn of phrase, and those words held all the lure of a siren's song, begging Tuck to seek deeper into what the man meant. The secrets he held.

But like everything with Old Kelley, it came at a price.

And Tuck was willing to pay. He tossed a coin to a passing barmaid to refill Kelley's cup and dropped another one on the table. When Old Kelley didn't take it up, Tuck knew what the man had to say was worth a lot more.

Old Kelley was a lot of things, but he was honest in his dealings.

So Tuck added the entirety of the gold coins his uncle had given him to the one on the table. It was a stack that would keep the man in ale for the rest of year, if not well into the next one.

"Ilford is as mad as they come. Someone would be doing the world a favor if they were to—" The man drew a line across his throat.

Tuck pulled back. For as much as he hated Ilford, he drew the line at outright killing him. Not that it wouldn't give him satisfaction to stand across a grassy field and put a bullet in his heart—all done with seconds and honorably—but what Old Kelley was suggesting was a different sort of death.

It spoke of dark alleyways. A quick thrust of a knife. Plainly said, it was cold-blooded murder.

"Mark me words, someone will," Old Kelley told him, obviously seeing the shock on Tuck's face. "Maybe not soon enough for you, but he's not long for this world."

Tuck shook his head. "He's the heir to a dukedom. There would be hue and cry if he were found to have gone on to kingdom come."

"Not for a man who's been dabbling in treason."

"Treason?" Charleton exclaimed not two hours later. "That's utter madness."

"Not according to my source," Tuck told him. The two men stood in the baron's library, while an ashen-faced Lady Aveley sat near the fireplace. Tuck had refused his uncle's offer of a glass of brandy.

Given what he'd learned, he needed to keep his wits sharp.

"What evidence is there?" the older man asked, staring moodily into the flames, hands folded behind his back.

At this, Tuck drew a deep breath. For he'd pressed and pried at Old Kelley, but on this the man had been as closed as an obstinate old clam. "Nothing. At least nothing that would hold up—in the manner you'd prefer."

That left the baron shaking his head. "Without good proof, evidence, something actionable, our hands are tied."

"Yes, I know," Tuck agreed, feeling the same frustration.

Charleton looked directly at Tuck. "How dangerous is this?"

Tuck glanced over at Lady Aveley.

His uncle drew closer, and said quietly, "She needs to know. She's got a right to know."

Tuck nodded in agreement. Everyone would need to be told. Protected. "We must keep an eye out for this Bludger fellow and his accomplice, but at the same time, we must be mindful—these two are cunning. Dials-bred and black-hearted as they come."

Lady Aveley shuddered. "To think that man was living next door. In Wakefield's house."

"Yes, well, we all owe Louisa a debt for sending him packing," Lord Charleton agreed, but his glance to Tuck told another story. "Piers needs to be told. Immediately."

"Everyone needs to be warned," Tuck added.

"They'll be watching the house, most likely," Charleton said, drawing a deep breath.

At this, Lady Aveley sat up. "Oh, my! One of the maids mentioned something like that just the other morning. That there was an odd man lurking about the mews. I thought it nothing at the time."

Both men turned to her.

She paused for a moment, as if dumbstruck by the realization, then rose to her feet. "Have Brobson fetch Nan immediately. You should question her more thoroughly. Oh, heavens, I feel such an utter fool now not to have realized—"

Charleton went to her and folded the lady into his arms. "There now, Amy, how were you to think such a thing? How would any of us have known such a desperate thing?"

Just then there was a scratch at the door, and Charleton called for them to enter, but not before Lady Aveley stepped a proper distance out of his reach.

Brobson appeared in the doorway and cleared his throat. "My lord—"

"Ah Brobson, perfect timing," Lord Charleton began. "I need you to fetch one of the maids—" He turned to Lady Aveley.

"Nan," she supplied.

"Yes, fetch Nan. I need to ask her about a fellow she saw the other day."

"Yes, my lord, but—"

"Oh, and Brobson, there have been some reports of prowlers and some unsavory characters about, so I want you and all the footmen to keep a sharp eye about and all the doors and windows locked."

"Yes, my lord. Of course. But I—"

"And have Miss Tempest summoned. I must speak to her immediately."

"When she returns, my lord," Brobson replied, "I will advise her that you would like to see her."

"Returns?" Tuck said, pushing past his uncle. "You mean she's not in the house?"

"No, sir," Brobson said. "She left with your mother, Mrs. Rowland, about an hour ago." Poor Brobson looked over all the stunned faces, and added, "I thought you knew, my lord."

"My lord?"

The Marquess of Ilford looked up from his desk. He did not like being interrupted, and here was this low creature boldly coming into his private study.

Bludger was becoming far too familiar. And that was some-thing Ilford wouldn't tolerate. But for now the man was useful. Most useful. And when he was no longer that . . .

Ilford set down his pen. "What do you want?"

Bludger grinned. "The girl. The one you were willing to pay for."

Ilford rose to his feet. "You have her?"

"No. But I've been watching that toff's house like you asked. And I got some information that might be worth the while." His hands rubbed together.

Money. Of course, this rat wanted more money. Ilford glanced down at the papers before him and quickly turned them over. "I've already paid you. To catch her."

"Yes. But I've got her cornered. Not the one that got me tossed out, but the other one."

Lavinia Tempest. Ilford nodded for him to continue.

"And with only a lady with her."

"Ladies go out all the time," Ilford told him with a dismissive wave of his hand.

Bludger remained planted where he stood. "To the Earl of St. John's house? To that big fancy party of his?"

Ilford slowly raised his gaze. "No. You must be mistaken."

"No mistake," Bludger told him, all confidence. "Got Charlie there making sure they don't leave. 'Cause if I can't see her sister get what she deserves, then I say let her twin pay the debt, if you know what I mean."

Ilford did. And Bludger could have her *when* he was done with her. Had destroyed her innocence. But still, he found it impossible to believe that Lavinia Tempest was attending one of St. John's bacchanals.

"You must be wrong," he told the man, sitting back down.

Bludger took another step closer, so close Ilford could smell the dark reaches of the man—a stench of the Dials so deep, so ingrained, that no amount of soap or deception could ever erase.

"No, milord. I'm not. The little bird is at St. John's house. And there ain't no one there to protect her. If you know what I mean."

"Mrs. Rowland—" Lavinia began, as they made their way up the steps of the house. "Whose ball is this?"

"I don't think I said," she remarked.

That hardly addressed Lavinia's growing misgivings.

Though she'd been quite confident back in her room when she'd turned around and found Mrs. Rowland slipping into her bedchamber, valise in hand, Lavinia had known what she should do—refuse the lady's offer to attend the most coveted affair of the evening.

But when Mrs. Rowland had pulled the blue velvet out and given it a grand shake, holding it so the brilliants sparkled in the candlelight, that flame of temptation had flared to life inside her.

Oh, the dress was a vision of temptation. It prodded her to recall Tuck's expression when she'd held it up for him to see.

His first expression, not the look of panic that had followed.

One of desire, of passion, of longing.

Yes, he'd been imagining her in the gown.

And perhaps her without the gown. As improper as such a thought might be, Lavinia couldn't help but shiver at the notion.

"Come now, however will you practice what the Honorable taught you if you remain hidden away?" Mrs. Rowland urged, pressing the velvet into her hands, the soft fabric offering its own seductive whisper.

You'll be as tempting as the night . . .

And before she knew it, Lavinia was begowned, her hair piled and pinned in place, and finally a mask tied on—obscuring her features yet turning her into a beguiling mystery.

The vision in the mirror had smiled back wickedly, and with that rebellious spark now blazing, she'd followed Mrs. Rowland out of the house and into a waiting carriage in the mews.

But now, as this adventure became so very real—and with no mirror to cast an approving reflection—Lavinia's heart fluttered with panic. For looking at the other guests who were arriving—in a colorful parade of fashions—boisterous and full of laughter—she realized this was a far cry from the staid world of Almack's.

A veritable continent from the quiet ways of Kempton.

"Yes, but whose house is this?" Lavinia persisted as she carefully made her way up the steps in the jostle of the other guests.

"You needn't fret—you look lovely," Mrs. Rowland told her, nodding in greeting to a tall man in an elegantly cut coat and a brightly embroidered waistcoat. "Why, no one will have any idea who you are. Tonight you can be anyone."

Anyone . . .

So why was it when she thought of that, she imagined herself in Tuck's arms. In his bed.

Tempting and so very dangerous. Very dangerous.

Oh, heavens. What was she thinking? Frantically she reverted to her old familiar habit of silently reciting her list of Proper Qualities.

> *Proper Rule No. 1. Marriage to a respectable, sensible, well-ordered gentleman is the order of business for every proper lady.*
> *Proper Rule No. 2. If a lady desires to contract a proper and respectable match, she will comport herself with nothing less than the strictest manners and unassailable propriety. At all times.*
> *Proper Rule No. 3. . .*

Oh, bother, she couldn't recall number three as a trio of ladies hurried up the steps, their gowns a scandalous collection of brilliant reds. Why, if Lavinia didn't know better, she'd think they were a trio of Cyprians.

And when one of them kissed a gentleman thoroughly—right there on the front steps, her hands caressing the front of his breeches, without any restraint or discretion, as if that were the accustomed way of greeting a man, Lavinia rather had her answer.

"Mrs. Rowland, I think it is important that I know who my host is," she insisted, thinking of Lady Aveley's earlier admonishment about being on fragile ice.

One misstep and . . .

"This is the Earl of St. John's masquerade ball." Mrs. Rowland tossed this out as if it were nothing more than a respectable garden party, but even Lavinia in faraway Kempton had heard of this annual affair and what the respectable and proper members of the *ton* called it.

St. John's Folly.

Lavinia's mouth opened as all the air escaped her lungs, and her feet came to a halt. "But Mrs. Rowland, I cannot—" She caught hold of the railing and looked around, hoping she would suddenly wake up and find herself back in her room.

Oh, yes she wanted to be "Anyone," but not *"Anyone."*

"Mrs. Rowland, Lord St. John's . . . entertainments . . . are entirely improper."

"Oh, not entirely. Though they do seem to have their fair share of scandals. But all the right people are invited, and everyone comes."

"I don't know—" Lavinia began, digging her heels into the stone steps.

Mrs. Rowland was just as determined. "But I do. You need a venue in which to practice your arts," she told Lavinia, catching her by the elbow and steering her up the rest of the steps. For a small woman, she had the grip of a blacksmith. "And this is the perfect way to start. You will be seen and wondered at, and by tomorrow, all of London will want to discover who you are—"

While that made perfect sense, still, Lavinia couldn't help but see the very real potential for disaster as they entered the grand house and half the company—the male half—turned in unison to eye the latest arrivals.

Never in her life had Lavinia felt like a lamb being led to the slaughter.

And if she were discovered . . .

Mrs. Rowland seemed able to read her mind. "No one will know who you are, Livy. Nor will they care once they are besotted. All it takes is the right *parti* to turn his eye toward you, and no one, not even that odious Lord Ilford, will be able to naysay your ascent into the highest reaches of society."

With Mrs. Rowland's hand on her elbow, the woman led her deeper and deeper into the house, through rooms where couples could be spied scandalously entwined in alcoves. Some shielded partially by curtains, and others openly embracing each other.

This was certainly not the Midsummer's Eve ball in Kempton. Or even Almack's.

"Now, here is the perfect spot," Mrs. Rowland told her, as they came to stop near the stairwell that led upstairs. "Wait here, and I'll be right back before you miss me."

"Can't I come with you?" Lavinia whispered back, slightly panicked at the thought of being left alone. A parade of people flowed past them—some moving toward the ballroom where the musicians had just struck up a new set and others seeking the room just behind them—the one set aside for gaming.

"I'm just going to visit the lady's retiring room. I'll be right back." And then she was gone, slipping effortlessly into the crowd like an eel.

Lavinia thought of trying to follow her, but the lady had just vanished into the peacockery of colors and elaborate costumes. She had no choice but to stay put until Mrs. Rowland returned, for however would the woman find her if Lavinia strayed from this spot?

I can be Anyone, she reminded herself, doing her best to convey the indubitable confidence the Honorable had proclaimed as indispensable for a lady of consequence.

Confidence. Yes, as Anyone, she was the most confident lady to be had. Until a pair of Cyprians swayed past her—and while

Lavinia had never actually met a Cyprian, she had no doubt this pair was very much familiar with the Vestal life—and suddenly Lavinia felt herself right back at her first ball.

No, no, that would never do, she told herself as a kaleidoscope of butterflies took to feverishly batting their wings about in her stomach.

When she got nervous, things got broken. She doubted that the earl would be pleased to find an antiquity of value shattered. Certainly the sharp memories of Lady Broughton's ire over the bunting accident of '08 was enough to leave Lavinia with a keen interest in not repeating that mishap.

Ever again.

She glanced around. Thankfully, such a disaster seemed unlikely to be repeated as the earl hadn't hung any. But to her critical eye, a party was not an event without a bit of bunting.

Then again, she thought with a sigh of resignation, the earl had not spared any expense when it came to candles. They glowed everywhere, and one slight mishap, and it could be Lady Essex's cotillion all over again.

Or as the gossips about Kempton liked to call it, "The Fire Ball."

Which Lavinia thought was entirely unfair. For the damage had been nearly inconsequential.

And Lady Essex had forgiven her. For the most part.

So perhaps Mrs. Rowland had the right notion. Lavinia should stay put. Yet as she looked around, her gaze fell on a tall fellow across the foyer. There was something most familiar about him, and when he tipped his mask up trying to get a better look around the ballroom beyond, she realized why.

Dear heavens, it was Lord Rimswell.

At first, Lavinia was relieved, but then a bit shocked. She had thought the young baron a proper gentleman, but if he was seeking company *here* . . . She pressed her lips together and frowned, Proper Rule No. 28 coming to mind.

A gentleman's pursuits should be of the highest order, with the noblest of intent.

Then again, she was here, so she was hardly in a position to judge, but still . . . She took another glance in his direction, but he was already gone.

"Oh, bother," she muttered. For with the baron near, she'd felt a bit safer, but then someone else came into view, a man in an elaborate mask and richly done coat. Like Lord Rimswell, he was giving the company a thorough scrutiny, but it was his voice that sent a chill knifing through Lavinia's breast.

"Ah, as always promised on this night, St. John has gathered together the most exquisite collection of fallen goddesses for we mere mortals. And tonight I am looking for one in particular."

Lavinia stilled. *Lord Ilford.*

And worse, his sharp and calculating gaze lit on her.

Lavinia turned her back to him and frantically searched for some means to escape his attention.

His most unwanted attentions.

And then it happened—the thick crush of guests parted ever so slightly and Lavinia Tempest—the girl who couldn't dance, who left fires and wreckage in her wake, who hadn't a social grace to her name save one—saw an escape that was perfectly suited for her.

An empty seat at the Earl of St. John's personal gaming table.

Lord Charleton turned to Tuck. "This is all my fault."

Tuck shook his head. "Yours? Hardly, sir. My mother is the one to blame."

His uncle glanced away, and it was Lady Aveley who spoke up. "Tell him everything."

"I gave Jenny *carte blanche* to help Lavinia get noticed." He sighed. "She most likely took her somewhere where she thought she could slip about unnoticed. A masked ball of some sort." Then he looked up at Tuck. "Have you any notion where your mother might go?"

Unfortunately he did. "St. John's Folly."

Lady Aveley gasped. "No! Why she'll be ruined. Utterly."

Tuck had already thought much the same thing. "I'll go get her."

"We all must go," Lady Aveley said, determination and steel in every word.

"Yes, we'll all go," Lord Charleton agreed.

"No." Tuck shook his head. "If the two of you arrive, it will draw suspicion upon us."

"But—" she began to protest.

"My lady, have you ever attended one of the earl's gatherings?"

"I should say not!" she replied with all the indignation of a proper matron.

"Exactly," Tuck told her. "And if I were to guess, neither have you, Uncle. I, on the other hand, will fit right in. No one will think it amiss if I am in attendance."

Lady Aveley wasn't convinced. "But Lavinia will need—"

"—Tuck," Lord Charleton told her. "She needs Tuck. He's got the right of it, Amy. He's the only one of us who can go in that den of snakes and move about without notice."

"Yes, well, my lesser qualities have finally come to some use. Slithering about with the snakes," Tuck joked, albeit a bit weakly.

"Never thought I'd say it, but I suppose it is a good thing you're a bit of a ruin," his uncle relied. "Go get her, my boy. Bring her home. In the meantime, I'll warn Piers."

Tuck nodded. While his first instinct was to rush off to rescue the maiden, he paused and considered lessons he'd learned at the foot of the Honorable. "Uncle, do you have a mask I can borrow? And I'll have that bit of brandy after all."

CHAPTER 17

Tuck arrived at the Earl of St. John's not long after, reeking of brandy and as affable as if he'd consumed half a bottle—and most importantly, as if he hadn't a care in the world but to continue his pleasure-seeking evening.

But his sharp eyes didn't miss the fellow lurking just beyond the light of the streetlamp or the way the man was watching St. John's house as the guests came and went.

Drawing a deep breath, he tried to tell himself he was seeing hobgoblins everywhere, but the telltale shiver down his spine was warning enough.

Livy was in danger.

He hurried up the stairs, and it was no surprise that the earl's butler admitted him without question.

Once inside, Tuck spied a fellow he knew from the clubs coming toward him and feigned a stumble into the man as he passed. "Downing!" he exclaimed with great joy.

"Oh, aye, Tuck," the man said, reeling back a bit. "Haven't seen you about lately. Thought you'd left Town."

"Never," he replied. "Got Ilford on the run," he confided with a broad wink.

Downing smiled, more politely and with a bit of sympathy, as if to say, "poor misguided fool." Then he tossed his head toward one of the rooms off the ballroom. "Don't bother, my good man."

Tuck looked around. "Pardon?"

Downing leaned in a bit. "If you're thinking of finding a bit of luck at the tables tonight, you won't find it here."

"No? Demmed shame that. I had heard the pickings were rare and easy tonight."

"They were," he lamented. "Until the most divine creature arrived. She's taken over Lord St. John's private table." Then the man lowered his voice. "She's cleaning up. Picked my pockets in only three hands of *vingt-et-un*." He shook his head. "Pleasure is all mine, though. She's a rare beauty—at least I suspect that is what lies behind that mask she's wearing—a rare beauty— why, every man here is mad to know who the devil she is."

Tuck had stopped listening after "divine creature," for hadn't those been the same words the Honorable had used.

His eyes narrowed as he looked over Downing's shoulder toward the gaming room.

No. Not even his mother would set an innocent like Lavinia down among the hardened gamesters that St. John kept company with. It couldn't be Livy.

He straightened and looked over at the crowded doorway to the salon, which was attracting the attention of everyone. With all eyes on the tables . . . Tuck's gaze shifted to the empty stairwell up into the private reaches of the earl's house.

Oh, yes, his mother would use a lamb to distract the lions.

"I'll have to go find this creature and try my luck," he told Downing, and patted him on the back before he began to push his way through the crowd.

"I'd think twice about that," the man warned.

Tuck nodded his thanks and went past Downing, but in his distracted state, he collided with a masked woman in a yellow gown.

"My pardon, madame," he said politely as he caught hold of

her elbow to steady her. From behind her mask, her eyes widened as if in recognition, and then ever so quickly, she shook off his grasp, murmured something in French—a curse, he thought—and hurried past him into the ballroom, where she quickly disappeared into the throng of guests.

Some former paramour, he supposed, but he paused for a half second longer, caught by the sense that she was utterly out of place and that he knew her. But then again, the only woman he knew with hair that dark was Pier's sister, Roselie.

But that was utterly ridiculous.

Besides, another glance over his shoulder only confirmed that the bit of muslin was gone, and it wasn't like Tuck had the time for saving any more impetuous chits. The one he had to carry off tonight was handful enough.

When he got to the doorway to the salon, Tuck found the room a crush. Not surprising, for Lord St. John loved his cards and was known to play deep, but they were all gathered around a single table in the middle of the room, every other game—some half-played—all abandoned.

And then he spotted it. A dark, rich navy velvet set against the glittering rainbow hues of the other guests. He pressed his way through, rudely even.

He didn't need to see her—his imagination went straight back to the lascivious image of her holding the velvet gown up for him to see.

He'd known only too well then what she would look like in it—but his imaginings and the real thing could hardly compare.

Gone was the proper miss he'd come to know, that bossy minx with her list. For sitting front and center at Lord St. John's personal table was the most breathtaking creature he'd ever beheld. The velvet clung to her like night itself, the brilliants sparkling lures to draw a man into her trap. Her mahogany hair was done up, but loosely enough that a man could see how easily it could be undone.

How it would fall over her bare shoulders into a beckoning

river of curls, as soft as the velvet that begged to be undone as well.

Tuck found himself unable to breathe, a bit off-balance really, as if he had consumed an entire bottle of brandy rather than just splashing a bit on his jacket to make himself smell like he was half-seas over.

Good God, Livy, what have I done?

For she wasn't Miss Lavinia Tempest any longer. She was Livy, his Livy. This beguiling, mysterious *demoiselle* he'd created.

He glanced around and realized how right Downing had been. Every gaze was fixed on her with the same covetous desire.

To unmask her. To have her.

But if anything, he was thankful for that mask—it did an excellent job of utterly concealing her features—and when she looked up, her gaze meeting his, her eyes widened in surprise—eyes lined with kohl that made her seem all that much more mysterious. Experienced, even.

And if there was ever a damning note to all this, evidence of his mother's hand in Livy's newfound persona, it was the single adornment she wore, a sapphire and diamond pendant hanging from a blue velvet ribbon, one he knew all too well. It belonged to his mother, her sole piece of jewelry that wasn't paste or purloined.

When and how his mother had gained such a treasure, Tuck had never learned. But he did know this: His mother never wore it.

So he was a bit taken aback at the sight of it hanging just above Lavinia Tempest's generously displayed décolletage.

So caught up was he that he hadn't even noticed who else was at the table. Not until one of the gentlemen spoke. Or rather cursed.

"I don't see how you can keep winning," the man burst out, throwing his losing hand to the table in a fit of pique.

Tuck sucked in a deep breath. *Ilford.* Seated right across from her and completely unaware of who exactly the woman trouncing him might be. As he glanced around, he realized—to some relief—that no one knew who this mysterious lady might be. He could see the whispers, the guesses being made, but no one knew.

Including Ilford, who had no idea that his irrational revenge sat right within his grasp.

And if there was any consolation to be had in all this, it was that there wasn't a single hint of the ungainly miss who had tripped her way into infamy at Almack's. Not a single member of the *ton* would put this *Incognita* and Lavinia Tempest together.

Save him.

"Shall we play another hand, my lords?" she asked, her voice huskier than he'd ever heard it sound.

No, he had heard it sound like that before—when he'd held her in his arms and kissed her.

Smoky, and passionate, and full of desire.

No wonder these fools were pushing fortunes into the middle of the table, all eyes on the lady with the cards.

His mother had chosen the perfect diversion for whatever she had planned above stairs. He sent a wry glance up at the ceiling.

Leave it to his mother to both help him and help herself.

When the play returned to Livy, she took a furtive glance around the table. Three of the players had already been broken, having taken cards they shouldn't have—including her host—but she still had Ilford and the Marquess of Gosforth in the game.

Ilford, so confident in his hand, added a mountain of coins to the wager. A sum far above what was gambled even in this fast company.

She pushed all of her winnings into the middle of the table and reached up and slowly undid her necklace, laying it atop the king's ransom that made up the pot. "I assume, gentlemen, that this will suffice."

Gosforth nodded, a gentleman through and through, but Ilford reached out and fingered the gems roughly as if he was already contemplating handling the woman who had worn them in much the same way.

She added another card to the one in front of her.

A knave. The knave of hearts to be exact. Standing alongside the deuce of hearts that had already been there.

Tuck glanced around the table, and counted—five of London's most notorious gamblers. Masks or not, he knew them all. Had played against them on many an occasion. Including the one seated across from her.

"Ah, how unfortunate, my dear," Ilford said, as he laid down his hand—a king of spades and a ten. Smiling as the others groaned, he reached across the table to gather in his winnings.

Certainly, from all appearances, he held the winning hand.

But Lavinia set down the cards she'd held. A five and four. Twenty-one. She tipped her head just so, looking first at her hand, then across the table. "I believe, my lord, the game is mine."

She spoke with a cultured voice, a hint of French and something else. Italian, Tuck guessed.

"Good God, Ilford, she has you! Well done, madame! Well done!" exclaimed one of the observers. There was a chorus of well-wishes and cheers.

The rest of the table watched in disbelief as she quickly gathered together her winnings, pulling them toward her and donning her necklace with all due haste.

Lord Gosforth pushed back from the table "You've cleaned me out, you devilish minx!" He glanced around at the others and laughed a bit. "Which one of you fools suggested we let her play?"

St. John laughed and bowed his head to Livy in concession. Every man at the table had to concede the lady had outwitted the lot of them.

Save one. And as if on cue, the man proved his ill-temper once again.

"You bitch," Ilford cursed, as Lavinia scooped up the last of the coins into her reticule. It now bulged with her winnings. The marquess shot to his feet, his chair shooting out behind him. "Who the hell are you? I'll have you unmasked and whipped for cheating."

Ah, yes, the marquess truly hated being bested. Especially in public.

Lavinia rose as well and backed up a few steps. "It was a fair game."

"And now it is over," Tuck announced, catching her by the elbow, tugging her quickly into the crowd, the swarm of guests swallowing them from sight. "What were you doing?" he whispered into her ear as he towed her out of the room.

"Playing cards."

Yes, he'd quite gotten that. "Where is my mother?"

"She went up to the lady's retiring room," she said, then she paused for a moment. "Oh, heavens, I daresay she's been gone for some length of time. Do you think she might have met with some mishap?"

His mother? That was nearly guaranteed. "Let me guess, she suggested you go play cards."

"No never, that was my idea. I saw Ilford, rather he spotted me—for a moment I thought he knew exactly who I was, so I panicked a bit." They had made their way out of the card room and across the ballroom toward the garden doors.

Behind them, Ilford's voice rose in complaint. "I demand she be unmasked."

Tuck was about to make their escape when a flicker of movement in the garden stopped him. There, just in the shadows, stood an ill-dressed man in a dark coat, his cap pulled low.

All those years of living around coves and swindlers had left Tuck with a keen sense of when something was amiss, and immediately he steered Livy away from the doors and along the wings of the crowded ballroom.

"We cannot leave without your mother," Livy was saying.

And she was right.

Nor could Tuck shake Old Kelley's warning. *He's out to take his full measure in return.*

No, he couldn't leave her behind—even if Jenny Rowland was probably as dangerous as any dockside ruffian.

"Do you know where she might have gone?" Livy asked.

"Yes," he told her, steering her along the wings of the room and through a servants' entrance. Down the corridor they went and up the stairs, deeper into the house, where the true festivities that St. John's Folly was known for were practiced.

"How is it you ended up in there?" he asked.

"Like I said, I panicked."

"So you invited Ilford to play a few hands of *vingt-et-un*?"

"Not at first. He took up Lord Norley's spot after I—" She paused there, her lips pursing together.

"Left him under the hatches?" Tuck supplied. "Good God, you cleaned out Norley? You've got pluck to the backbone. I don't think even the Honorable could have managed that."

"Truly?" She had picked up the hem of her gown so she could keep pace with him. "I thought the man a bit of a braggart."

"Oh, he's that," Tuck agreed.

"Not any more," she told him with all the cheek of a seasoned Cyprian.

He came to a stop on the landing and faced her. "You've a remarkable talent."

She fluttered a bit, as if his praise, his admiration took her utterly aback.

For indeed it had.

"You don't think it off-putting?" She glanced away, the minx chastened.

"Not in the least," he told her, reaching out and curling his fingers around her chin. He raised it up so she looked at him. "Why would I?"

"Well—" She tried to turn away, as if admitting the truth was too painful.

"Well, what?" Then Tuck saw it—as he had so many times with her over the past week. "It isn't proper to play cards, is that what it is?"

"Oh, playing cards is all well and good, but a proper lady should let a gentleman win."

Tuck knew he was gaping, but that was before he started to laugh. "Livy, my girl, when you find a gentleman in this company, by all means, let him win." Then he winked at her.

She grinned and turned to continue upward, her reticule jangling like an entire carillon of bells. She'd catch the attention of anyone they passed. Tuck leaned forward and snatched it from her wrist.

"Those are my winnings," she complained as he tucked the silk bag inside a large ornamental vase.

"We'll come back for your treasure trove," he promised.

"I would say so. I've quite run through my pin money— London is ever so expensive." Her eyes flickered from behind her mask. "Though I never imagined one could win so much so quickly."

"Yes, and marked yourself as a knight of the elbow in the process. And for that, we need to find my mother and get you both out of here."

That and other reasons, but he wasn't about to go into all that. Not until she was safely ensconced back in his uncle's house.

"I played fairly," she complained. "I don't see how anyone can argue the point."

"Believe me, Ilford will. He's a poor loser."

"And rather dimwitted at cards," she replied, as they came to the upper foyer, with only two choices.

Left or right.

Just to their right, a door opened, and a couple came out, the lady's hair tumbling down in a mess of curls and both of them laughing drunkenly as they continued their amorous interlude entwined against the wall and oblivious to anyone else.

"Oh, my," Lavinia whispered, her eyes wide beneath her mask.

From down below came an all-too-familiar voice. "I'll find that thief and get my money back. She cheated, I tell you."

They shared a glance. *Ilford.* And in hot pursuit.

The couple to the right was still completely lost in each other, having not even noticed they were being observed, the woman pressed to the wall by her swain, his hands exploring under her gown.

Livy leaned close, and asked, "Is that why they call this a folly?"

"Not if he's doing it right."

And about then, the woman began to moan loudly.

"Oh, yes, quite right, apparently," Livy quipped, as he caught hold of her again and took her in the opposite direction. Halfway down the hall, he opened a door, and they went blindly into the room, closing the door even as Ilford and his mob of sycophants crested the stairs.

The room Tuck had picked in his haste was entirely in shadows, the thick curtains by the window letting in only a little shaft of light from the streetlamp below.

"Search all the rooms," Ilford could be heard saying, as doors began to open.

Tuck took a quick, assessing glance around the chamber—a small, dark parlor without any other doors and only the window. They had reached a dead end.

"What do we do?" she asked.

"Gamble," he told her, leading her over near the window and tucking her behind the overhang of the curtains. The thick velvet hangings concealed most of her very unmistakable gown.

There was only one way to cover the rest.

Tuck glanced down at her. "Do you trust me, Livy?"

"No, not in the least," she told him.

"Good," he said, pressing her into the wall and covering her. His head dipped down, and his lips brushed against hers, while his hands caught hers, pulling them up and over her head so she was pinned.

She made a sort of *mew* of protest, but then he leaned in, letting his body slide against hers, and suddenly it wasn't Livy who was caught, but him.

Utterly.

For in a second, he was rock hard, his groin pressed against the curve of her hips, her breasts pillowed against his chest, her protest lost as her mouth opened to him.

Livy.

That bastard Ilford had been right about one thing. *This minx was a thief.*

For she was robbing him of every bit of good sense he possessed.

Lavinia couldn't breathe. How could she, with Tuck stealing every breath away with his kiss? That, and with her hands pinned over her head, she was utterly his to do with as he pleased.

As she desired.

For his lips, hot and hard upon hers, left her opening up to him. Letting him explore her mouth, tease her tongue, over and over again.

The curtain all but encircled them, and they were in a cocoon of their own making. The entire world seemed to spin around them until it blurred, leaving only her and Tuck and this hot, blinding passion that had been simmering between them for nearly a fortnight.

He pulled her hands higher, as if to stretch her, leaving her body in a taut line that his other hand explored like a gypsy's violin, plucking wild notes of desire from her—cupping her breast, teasing the nipple into a hard bud, pressing himself against her so she could feel how hard and ready he was.

This is only an illusion, she tried telling herself. For somewhere, far away it seemed, she could hear doors opening up and down the hall and voices getting closer.

This . . . this kiss, his hand roaming over her hips, cupping her breast, it was all a trick meant to deceive.

But she knew one thing: The shafts of desire, the fire of passion blazing inside her were no fraud, no bluff.

It was like magic made real, and she gasped as he pressed his lips to her neck and nibbled at her.

Just then, the door did open, and Tuck raised his head slightly, glared at the intruder, and growled a sharp and angry, "Get out!"

There was a hasty apology, then the door closed.

After a few seconds, he let go of her.

"I believe we've deceived them," Tuck told her, but even to her innocent ears, his voice sounded ragged. Full of need.

A need she wanted to answer. Explore.

"Not quite," Lavinia told him, catching hold of his waistcoat and pulling him back into the shadows. "I think we ought to wait until we are certain."

And then she raised her lips to his and begged another kiss.

"Livy, I—"

When he hesitated, she looked up at him, pulling him closer, letting her hips rock toward him, brush against him. "Tuck, undo me."

He swallowed and gazed down at her, as if seeing her anew.

Lavinia didn't care. "Undo me."

And he did. His lips crashed down atop hers, and his hand found a bit of her skirt, edging it higher until his fingers found the curve of her now-bared thigh.

As he got closer, as his hand moved higher, he paused as if gauging her reaction, and she smiled at him, her teeth nibbling at her lower lip especially when his fingers came just that much higher.

Almost, but not there. *There.*

Lavinia arched like a cat, delirious to be touched, the need to be teased blotting out any thought of modesty.

Of restraint.

"Touch me," she gasped. "Touch me *there.*"

It wasn't as if she didn't know how it would feel—but she'd never had anyone else touch her there, and she had to know.

And then she did. For, oh, bless his knavish heart, he knew exactly where "there" lay, and his fingers expertly brushed at the curls, before easing into the cleft between her legs.

When his finger crooked around the nub there and . . . and . . . oh, yes, he touched her . . .

Her mouth opened, and a mew of desire slipped free. "Oh. Oh, yes."

His fingers pressed deeper, then he was inside her, and she rose on her tiptoes, first in shock, but then because she just knew, knew she wanted to rock against him, feel every bit of his touch sliding in and out of her.

She was ever so wet and hot, for he knew exactly how to tease, when to go deeper, harder.

Yes, this was so much better with him.

A strangled sort of sound escaped him, and his mouth covered hers again, this time almost savagely, as suddenly his own hunger, his own need had overtaken him.

He kissed her deeply, his tongue thrusting over her lips as his fingers began the same frantic dance over her sex.

Tormenting her.

"Yes," she gasped, as her body began to tighten, as the world began to encase them, as everything seemed to spin out of control, as if it would all fly apart. "Yes, Tuck, oh, yes."

And then she did career out of control, pleasure wrenching through her, filling her, flooding her in waves that only served to fan the flames of her desire for him.

Tuck held her in his arms as her release came shattering over her.

Livy undone was a sight to behold. Her eyes alight. Her cheeks pinked. Her mouth opened in surprise and delight.

He kissed her brow, her neck, the top of her breasts, until she found her footing again, drifted back down from the heavens.

What had he done to her? Had he done this? Taken a very proper miss and turned her into this vixen, this tempting minx in a complete state of *dishabille*, looking so utterly tumbled.

She arched against him.

Like a greedy cat seeking to be stroked again. And again.

"We need to leave," he whispered in her ear. For if they stayed much longer, if he held her much more, touched her again, this would indeed turn into a folly.

One that could not be undone.

"Oh, must we?" Again she shifted against him. So temptingly.

"I need to see you safely home."

"Must you?" She looked up at him, and that was a mistake, for the wicked light in her eyes held a smoky promise.

"Yes," he said, more for himself. *Take her home. Now.*

"Just one more kiss," she told him, rising on her toes and pressing her lips, her body to his.

And she was back in his arms, and he was lost.

"Uh, hum." The slight cough was enough to tear them apart.

And Tuck didn't need to look to know who had discovered them. Who else could slip into a room like a thief?

"Ah, Mother," he said as he turned around. "There you are."

"Yes, well, the entire house is in quite a stir over some card cheat," she complained.

From behind him, there was a loud *harrumph.*

"I didn't cheat," Livy declared, stepping into plain sight, fists to her hips, followed by a slight stomp of her slipper.

That was his Livy. *His.*

Oh, God, he couldn't think of her like that. Not even now.

"You?" Mrs. Rowland asked as she came farther into the room. "You're the card cheat?"

Livy looked about to repeat her protest, but Tuck waded in. "After you left her alone, Livy, er Miss Tempest, had to improvise. She ended up in a card game with Ilford, and—"

His mother waved her hand at the mention of the marquess's name. "Say no more. I can see that it is imperative that we leave."

Always the obvious one, his mother.

"And how exactly had you planned to do that?" Tuck asked, then quickly explained the situation below.

She nodded, then looked him directly in the eyes. "Exactly as I entered. Through the front door. Now turn around and no peeking." She pushed him out of the way, turning him so his back was to the pair of them. "As we discussed, we need to change things a bit," she said to Livy.

"I can see now why you had me alter this gown as you did," Livy replied. "Quite ingenious."

"An occasional necessity," his mother replied.

"What the devil are you talking about?" Tuck demanded, turning around to find his mother pulling Livy's gown up and over her head.

A glimpse of long, bare, coltish legs stole his breath away, but another cough from his mother had him turning back around.

Demmit. This was all his fault. All his doing. He should never have asked her to dance. Never wagered on her. Never offered to help her.

Never kissed her. Yes, that was when it had all turned into a mare's nest. He'd kissed her, and he'd stopped thinking rationally. Introducing her to his mother. To the Honorable.

Now the very proper Miss Lavinia Tempest was in the middle of one of St. John's Follies, up to her unwitting neck in larceny after having done her innocent best to unman him.

He paused for a second. Hardly innocent now.

Good God! What would an experienced Livy do to him?

Put him in an early grave, he had to imagine.

"If you must know—" Livy had begun to say.

"Oh, I insist," he told her, wiping at his brow. Suddenly, the room was too hot and too close.

"Your mother had me alter the gown—don't you recall—I told you about it the other day," Livy told him, as the rustle of silk begged him to steal another glance.

Reminding himself he was a gentleman—most of the time—he didn't. Not that his imagination wasn't doing a randy enough job as it was.

"There, my dear, no one will recognize you," his mother was saying, with a hint of laughter in her voice.

And when Tuck turned around he barely recognized the lady

before him, for now she wore a gown of pale pink, and her hair, which had been done up, now fell down past her shoulders.

Even her mask was changed, the color of a blush, almost lending the lady an innocent air. Almost.

"How the—" Tuck said, tipping his head and looking for some evidence of the passionate creature he'd been kissing. The unrepentant gamester who'd cleaned up the tables.

"It was your mother's idea," Livy told him, turning up a bit of the hem to reveal the deep blue velvet. "It is two gowns in one. I thought it rather odd at the time, but now I see how clever your mother was to think of this. Who would have known we would need to leave in such a hurry and so anonymously?"

"Yes, who would have thought such a thing?" he replied, taking Livy by the hand and shooting his mother a censorious glance.

Not that the lady noticed, for she was too busy giving an unwitting Miss Tempest more lessons in larceny. "Now Livy, dear, the key to all this is to walk out as if you are completely bored and haven't the time for such a dull affair."

"Yes, but I've had a rather exciting evening," Livy told her.

"So I noticed," Tuck's mother replied, this time sending her own withering glance in his direction.

Tuck did his best to ignore her, instead leading them to the hall, where he realized he was holding his breath, and taking a lesson from his childhood, he let it out and took another as they crossed the short foyer to the stairwell.

Nothing was going to go wrong. He'd get Livy out of here and home, and no one would be the wiser.

If only he could get rid of the pit in his gut that told him that everything was about to go wrong. Very wrong.

"This evening has been a dull affair," his mother was saying with an airy wave of her hand. "Oh, dear, I forgot one thing." She paused and unhooked the necklace around Livy's neck.

Diamonds and sapphires so distinctive that few would forget it—or the wearer. It was quickly tucked away in the large pocket of her gown—the pockets his mother always had sewn into her clothes—convenient hiding places for the incidental treasures that came into her grasp.

With Livy now utterly changed, they continued down the stairs, sedately and regally, his mother bantering on. "Such a vulgar crowd tonight. St. John's standards are hardly what they once were," she told Livy offhandedly. "I would wager that the stones you were wearing, my dear, were the only ones not paste in the entire assembly." She continued down the steps a few paces ahead of them.

Livy's hand went to where the necklace had been and her wide-eyed gaze flew up. "Those were real? Oh, heavens, I never would have—"

Tuck shook his head slightly to stop her from saying the rest.

. . . *wagered them if I had known that.*

He leaned in close. "I wouldn't mention that fact to my mother."

They had come to a stop on the landing, and indeed, the party below did seem to be in turmoil—people in knots whispering and glancing around, while others continued a determined search of the guests.

For a lady in blue velvet, Tuck had to imagine, not the fetching pink-clad minx beside him.

Meanwhile, Livy had other thoughts. "Oh, goodness. I nearly forgot. My winnings." She crossed over to the vase, and after taking a glance around to make sure no one was looking, tipped it over, pulling her reticule out, the fat bag jangling like a market hog.

"Your what?" his mother asked, whirling around.

Oh, yes, now she was paying attention to her little protégé.

"Your diversion had quite a run at the tables," he told her, as Livy gave her reticule a slight shake—counting her winnings as the Honorable was wont to do.

"You truly won all that?" his mother said, coming forward, her eyes all alight. Her voice turned from hawkish delight to more motherly pride. "My dear, girl, why didn't you tell me you *played* cards?"

"I'm surprised the Honorable didn't mention it," Tuck remarked. "She quite cleaned him out."

His mother's eyes widened. "That rather explains why he didn't mention it. He takes great pride in his acumen."

"Oh, heavens," Livy rushed to say. "I hope I didn't offend him."

"I don't think that's possible," Tuck said under his breath.

Both ladies ignored him.

"Don't you fret about such things. Men need reminding that they're mere mortals every once in a while," his mother advised her as she took to the stairs again now that the crowds below had thinned a bit. "All that matters is that you enjoy playing."

"Lady Essex says my skills are unseemly. No one in Kempton will play with me, not even a hand of whist."

"Never mind that," his mother told her as they went down the last set of stairs and waded into the crush making a beeline for the front door. "London is a large place, and there are always new fools, er, eager players to be found—if you know where to look." She made an imperious nod to the footman at the entrance, and he quickly opened the door.

But not quickly enough.

While his mother was already out the door, from behind them, a loud voice rose, a drunken greeting. "Ilford! Is it true? You're halfway to losing that wager with Rowland? That Wakefield went and married one of those cowhanded chits?"

In front of him, Livy froze, the words catching her as sure as a well-baited hook, tugging her back and around.

Even if she had wanted to continue, she was caught fast.

"We must leave," Tuck told her, but she wasn't listening.

She pushed away from him, suddenly rooted in place.

"Rowland!" Ilford spat out like a curse. "He's got two days to bring the other one up to snuff—" He laughed, the evil bark sending a chill down Tuck's spine, as if the man had just tromped over his grave. "As if he can. I'll win this wager, Budgey, and see him ruined."

Tuck glanced over at Livy—her eyes opened slightly, her mouth forming one word.

"Wager."

A whisper. A breath of disbelief. Shock. All in one word.

One damning, horrible honest word.

He went to explain, to try to tell her it mattered not, not now—but her attention was fixed on the trio discussing her fate.

"I don't see why you bothered," the other man was saying, a fop from the previous century who looked as if he had lived his entire life on the fringes of society, his existence bound up in the misfortunes of others. "Not like you will collect. Everyone knows Rowland's craven. He'll cry off and disappear—run scared, just like he did to Wakefield and poor Rimswell. Bragged all over town he was to buy his commission, then gambled away the money and let his friends rot and die in Spain."

"I well know it," Ilford said. "I've been ill-used from the start on all of this. He won't pay, but don't think I haven't got my ways to exact what I am due. He'll not run coward on me, not this time."

Budgey shrugged as if he wasn't too sure that was even possible. As if Tuck's cowardice was a given. "Still, never thought he'd be able to get Society to notice either of them, let alone Wakefield marrying one. Wakefield, indeed! Must be something quite rare about the chit for her to catch his eye. Twins and all, goes to figure that the other one must be just as much a Diamond, don't you think?"

This question was directed to the newest arrival. The Marquess of Gosforth.

"Who might be?"

Meanwhile, Lavinia turned back to Tuck. "A wager? You did this all for a wager?"

He reached out to catch her hand, to explain, but she yanked her arm out of his reach.

Ilford hadn't given Gosforth the time to answer, launching into another rant. "—and mark my words, Rowland's about to lose the rest of his miserable shirt and what's left of his tattered honor—especially once I nose it about that light skirt's daughter is here—at St. John's—"

Tuck burned to put his fist into the man's smug face, but he could hardly do that and not prove every word.

The old fop was laughing. "Here? Unlikely!"

Ilford straightened and glared at the man. "I say she is here. And I suspect she is the same cheat who sat down at St. John's table and gulled every last one of us."

At this Budgey chortled. "If that charming minx is Miss Tempest, *I'll* marry her. She'd keep my pockets plump for the rest of my days."

"That gel is Miss Tempest, I tell you, and I'll prove it. See if she'll be received then."

Budgey began to laugh at Ilford's wild claims even as Livy sucked in a deep, indignant breath.

While Ilford didn't hear her, Gosforth did. The older man glanced over in their direction, his gaze flicking over Tuck but lighting on Lavinia with all the accuracy of a sharpshooter.

Yet it was his expression that baffled Tuck. The man's eyes widened, his mouth slowly falling open until he was gaping at her, looking at Livy as if he were seeing a ghost, seeing something so unexpected, that he took a step back from Ilford and Budgey, leaning heavily on his walking stick.

By now his mother had come back up the steps. "Oh, good heavens. This doesn't bode well," she said, surveying the tableaux before them.

Nor was Ilford done—and worse—he was drawing a crowd around him. "He'll lose, I tell you. That girl will never be accepted into Society, not as long as I breathe," Ilford's voice carried the chill of death with it. "Rowland has made his last wager. *His last.*"

Tuck's mother shook her head and caught Lavinia by the hand. "Come along, my dear. You've heard enough."

That was enough to break the spell, and Lavinia let his mother pull her out the door.

"Is it true?" she asked in a voice so small and icy, Tuck thought his heart would crack.

"Not now," he told her.

Not here in front of the lingering guests and waiting servants. Gossips all.

But this was Lavinia, and she would have her answer. She came to a halt and planted herself so firmly, Tuck knew not even Napoleon's best troops could rout her.

"Is it true, what they said?"

"Yes," Tuck shot back, the weight of what he'd done, all the half-truths and lies he'd told crashing down. "Yes, it's all true. There you have it. Does it matter?"

The hurt in her eyes nearly ripped him in two—bringing with it a startling realization.

Tuck Rowland, the Knave of Mayfair, had lost a far bigger wager than the one with Ilford.

For he was head over heels in love, and he'd ruined everything.

"Does everyone know?" This, Livy asked his mother.

She nodded, a curt tip of her head that conceded both the truth and her complicity.

Livy's hand fisted to her mouth as if it could stopper back the hurt and shock.

Or perhaps to prevent the blistering scold he so rightly deserved.

But whatever she had been about to say was all lost when another came to stand behind them.

"Madame," an elderly gentleman said, bowing low to Mrs. Rowland. "Do you need a carriage to assist you?" And when he rose, they all gaped open-mouthed at Lord Gosforth. "I would recommend leaving with all due haste." He glanced over his shoulder, back into the house, where Ilford's rant could still be heard.

"My lord," Mrs. Rowland said, curtsying with all the grace of a duchess. "How kind of you. That would be most helpful."

The marquess nodded, then, with one wave of his hand, a carriage pulled up—a plain though well-appointed one. A servant jumped down from the back, despite his lack of the usual livery, the unadorned fellow looked like he had been hired because he didn't mind a bit of trouble. He tipped his head to the ladies and had the door open before Tuck could even manage a protest.

Livy and his mother were handed up into the carriage, and the marquess closed the door.

But Gosforth didn't get in. Instead, he gave quiet instructions to his driver, a nod to the fellow at the door, and returned to Tuck's side as the carriage turned into the night.

As they watched the coach until it rounded the corner, the marquess said, "Miss Tempest will be taken home, and I assure you, not a word of her attendance tonight will be noticed or repeated."

"Thank you, my lord," was all Tuck could manage. He should have apologized to Livy. He should have said something. But he hadn't known what to say.

His usually glib tongue and ready excuses had failed him the one time that he had truly needed them.

"I don't suppose you have a carriage?" the marquess asked.

"No. I walked. I knew that if I brought my uncle's rig, someone might put the two together."

The marquess nodded his approval. "Perhaps you aren't such a wastrel after all. Come along then, we'll find a hackney and make our way to Boodles. I've lost my taste for White's of late—as I suspect you have. Besides, I'd like to hear more about my remarkable granddaughter. Especially how it is you intend to win her back."

CHAPTER 18

Mrs. Rowland said nothing the entire ride home to Lord Charleton's. Just sat silently staring out the window with a faraway look, an expression of profound sadness and loss that spoke of so many secrets.

Perhaps she hadn't known about . . . about . . . Lavinia didn't even like to consider it.

And yet how could she not?

The rumors that swirled about Tuck were true. He'd promised to buy a commission and fight.

And he hadn't.

He'd let his friends go, and he'd stayed in London as pleasure bent as ever.

But it can't be so. It isn't so, a quiet, determined voice inside her declared.

Yet what had Tuck said? *Yes, it is all true.*

"Mrs. Rowland—" Lavinia began as she went to climb down from Lord Gosforth's plain carriage, the door to Lord Charleton's house already open, Brobson, His Lordship and Lady Aveley all coming out onto the steps. She glanced over her shoulder, then back at the lady who still had her face turned away. "Yes, well, I am so sorry."

She didn't know what she was apologizing for, but suddenly she felt as if Mrs. Rowland carried as much of Tuck's shame as she could bear.

And then some.

That she would take it all on her shoulders if she could, if only to see her son free of such a stain.

And in that moment, Lavinia envied Tuck. Envied him his mother—oh, she wasn't so naive that she didn't know that Mrs. Rowland had her faults, but that she loved her only child, her son, was in no doubt.

Lavinia got down and was about to turn and leave, when she heard the lady say, "Livy, he loves you. You must believe that."

Tears sprung up in her eyes, for it was the last thing she wanted to hear. Somehow—that he loved her—made it all that much worse, all the more unforgivable.

And yet . . .

How could he?

All she could manage was a tight nod of acknowledgement before she hurried up the steps and into the house.

Not that she could escape that nagging question. It haunted her all through a long lecture from Lady Aveley on propriety, another one from her maid—this one more of a complaint that she was going to be put out on the streets if her mistress continued to abandon all good sense—then into a sleepless night.

She lay in her narrow bed for hours, her gaze fixed on her reticule perched there on the nightstand, a heady reminder of all that had passed—winning a fortune at the tables, Tuck there to rescue her, the treasure of a different sort she'd discovered in his arms.

Tuck kissing her. Bringing her to that place . . . to that blissful point . . .

Hugging her pillow to her chest, she sighed and rolled away

from the sight of her reticule and realized why so many women wandered from the safe and narrow path of propriety.

When morning came, Lavinia was jolted awake. Rather it was the curtains being yanked apart, a swath of brilliant sunlight pouring over her, and a forthright "get up" that wrenched her out of her dreamless sleep.

She couldn't remember when she'd finally drifted off—but she had, and she had no more answers to her questions than she had when she'd started.

But that wasn't her only problem.

For there at the foot of her bed stood Louisa . . . and worse, she was holding up the blue velvet gown. "Where did you get this?" she demanded, looking down at the dress as if she had never seen such a creation.

"I . . . that is . . ." Oh, yes, this was going to be easy to explain. *I bought it at a secondhand shop that caters to Cyprians and ladies of questionable pursuits.*

"I want one," Louisa told her, arranging the dress on the nearby chair. "That is the most divine thing I have ever seen."

"Pardon?" Lavinia sat up, swiping at her still sleepy eyes. Was this the same sister who couldn't tell a flounce from a pin tuck?

"You must have been quite stunning in it. So I have to imagine I would look just as pretty."

It was an old joke between them, and they both laughed.

"Now, as I was saying, you must get up."

"No," Lavinia told her, pulling the covers over her head. She wanted to spend the day hidden away, feeling sorry for herself and reconciling her suspicions that there was more to Tuck's story than just a tale of cowardice.

"You must get up," Louisa told her plainly, pulling away the covers. "Lady Aveley is in a state."

"So she summoned you over to continue ringing a peal over my head?"

"Why should I do that?" Louisa paused. "Whatever did you do?"

"I wore that—" She poked a finger out from beneath the coverlet and pointed at the dress.

"Where?"

"Lord St. John's Folly." She peered out from the pillow.

Louisa's mouth opened, followed by big sucking sound. "You didn't?"

"I did."

"Did you go with Mr. Rowland?" This wasn't really a question but an accusation.

Lavinia rolled over and gaped at her sister.

"Well, did you?"

"No! Whyever would you ask that?"

Louisa shrugged. "You just seem to be in his company more than is proper, so I thought, rather I hoped . . ."

"Louisa Tempest—"

"Louisa Stratton, or 'my lady,' if you prefer," she teased back.

"I'll 'my lady' you," Lavinia told her, throwing a pillow at her sister.

Louisa ducked. "So if Mr. Rowland wasn't there—"

"Well, I didn't say he wasn't there—"

Louisa sat back down on the corner of the bed. "Tell me more."

"No," Lavinia said, scooting out of the bed and pulling on her wrapper.

"Ooooh, that good," Louisa said. "Now I must have all the details."

Goodness, marriage had made her sister an overbearing busybody.

"You'll tell Lady Aveley, and I will not listen to another of her lectures."

"I never tattle," Louisa shot back, clearly annoyed. "I can hardly believe it—St. John's Folly! Do you remember what Lady Essex said about him?"

"All true," Lavinia replied with a negligent shrug.

"What has come over you?" Louisa demanded, more out of

habit. But then her curiosity got the best of her. "Was there gambling? Were the stakes as ruinous as it is rumored?"

Lavinia's gaze flitted for a moment toward her reticule and Louisa, sharp-eyed as ever, caught it up, and even as she did, nearly dropped it.

"Good heavens, how much is in here?"

"A ruinous sum."

Louisa pulled it open and looked inside, then back up at her sister. "I've never seen so much gold."

"Nor I."

"However did you find yourself in such a game?"

And since there would be no escape from her sister until she told all, Lavinia related what had happened, from Mrs. Rowland's arrival, using the lady's necklace as a stake in the game, and her escape—though she heavily edited the events in the room upstairs.

Still, Louisa knew better. "As I suspected. Mr. Rowland was a part of all this."

"I went with *Mrs. Rowland*," Lavinia pointed out. Yet again. "She's has been so kind . . ." she began, thinking more of the lady's son. "And I had no notion she'd take me there—"

Oh, bother, she'd left the house last night in a pique and not for any other rational reason than she had half hoped that wherever they went it would be somewhere scandalous enough that Tuck would arrive to rescue her. Take her in his arms and . . .

And, well, do just as he had.

For a blissful moment, she was back in his arms, and he was holding her, touching her, kissing her. But that image was all too quickly replaced with Ilford's ugly words and how it had all gone wrong.

So very wrong.

Her misery returned tenfold, and she turned toward the window. "Louisa, why are you here at this early hour? I thought you and Wakefield were going to the country for the rest of the month."

"Wakefield is closeted away with Charleton on some business, and I came over to deliver this." She held out a letter.

"What is it?" Lavinia asked, looking down at the impressive seal atop even richer paper.

"Read it and find out," Louisa told her with a nod toward the note.

Her brows furrowed as she opened it, imagining the worst, but the lines inside quite surprised her.

"She wants us to attend her afternoon in," Lavinia said. "I can scarcely believe it."

But while Louisa grinned from ear to ear over the news, Lavinia felt only horror.

Louisa retrieved the note, and reread the lines as if to reassure herself the words were all still there. "Lady Gosforth has asked us to attend her afternoon in—this very day. I cannot fathom how this has come to pass." Her sister set down the note and shook her head as if it was unbelievable.

"Lady Gosforth?" Lavinia said, eyeing the note warily. "As in the Marchioness of Gosforth."

"Oh, you've heard of her?" Louisa asked. "I don't doubt it— you pay attention to these things. Lady Aveley says the marchioness is a most particular hostess. Even the patronesses of Almack's look to her for guidance. This is a social coup of sorts by getting her to receive us."

"Perhaps your marriage to Wakefield has made her curious."

Louisa shrugged. "This can only help you."

"Why is that?"

The door to the room opened, and Lady Aveley came bustling in. She looked first at Lavinia. "You aren't dressed!" Then she turned to Louisa. "Haven't you told her?"

"I was just getting to the good part," Louisa told the matron. "Lady Gosforth is holding the ball of the Season tomorrow night. I imagine she wants to meet us and see if we are worthy of invitations."

"Worthy?" Louisa thought of Lord Gosforth, the lady's husband, and what she had to assume he knew.

What all of London could discover if he chose to reveal the previous night's events.

"The marquess," she said, trying to sound nonchalant, "he won't be at Her Ladyship's afternoon in, will he?"

"Lord Gosforth? Oh, heavens no," Lady Aveley told her, having moved to the clothespress and taken out a modest afternoon gown. "I imagine he'll be at his club or about Town. Why?"

"No reason," Lavinia added hastily, glancing at her reticule, which held a measure of Lord Gosforth's losses.

"Now hurry along," Lady Aveley advised. "We are about to take the first step in getting you both back in Society's good graces. I'll have Nan press this. A perfectly respectable choice." Her brows arched slightly as she slanted a disapproving glance at the velvet displayed on the chair.

Lavinia made a note to have Nan put it away for safekeeping. Not that she could ever wear it again—not and escape the notice of every libertine and gamester in London.

No, the woman in that gown, the mysterious sharpster who had appeared at Lord St. John's Folly would have to remain just that . . . a mystery.

But Lavinia was not so naive that she didn't know well enough that a secret—when more than one person knew it—never stayed under the table for long.

And while Tuck, Mrs. Rowland, Lady Aveley and Lord Charleton had no reason to reveal her identity, the Marquess of Gosforth was another story.

"Yes, yes, this afternoon will change everything—once you are properly gowned and placed amidst good company," Lady Aveley was saying, her face set with a gracious, determined smile. "Your fortunes are destined to change, I just feel it."

Lavinia was afraid she was right.

And not the way Lady Aveley seemed to think.

*　*　*

Tuck's head was still reeling from his night out with Lord Gosforth. For an old roué, he certainly still knew how to throw back his fair share of brandy. And it wasn't just the copious amount of illicit French bottles that had Tuck's thoughts awhirl but the confidences the marquess had shared.

Dear heavens, would the secrets that swirled around this pair of sisters never cease?

And here he'd always thought his family history reckless.

So it was, when Tuck arrived the next morning at his uncle's residence, flowers in hand and so lost in thought as to how he could manage an apology, that he nearly bowled over a well-dressed young woman coming down the steps.

"She isn't in," the lady told him in a pert fashion as she sidestepped around him.

"Pardon, me. No, wait, excuse me?" Tuck managed trying to remember both his manners and his quest. He paused and turned to get a better look at the chit who now stood at the street.

He had seen her before, that much he knew, but he couldn't quite place her.

"If you are looking for Lavinia, she isn't in," the woman repeated, a significant glance at the posies in his hand—pilfered as they were from his landlady's garden.

"She can't be out!" Tuck couldn't hold back his panic. "Demmit, where is she?" How could his uncle have let her leave with Ilford and his hired whelps still out there?

The lady before him seemed quite unscathed by his outburst. "They've gone to the Marchioness of Gosforth's afternoon in."

"The wha-a-t . . . a who-o—" Tuck's mouth fell open, words failing him. He came down the steps like an old man trying to get his bearing.

"Yes, rather what I said." The woman peeked up at him from her outrageously grand hat, and smiled, holding out her hand in a friendly fashion. "By the way, I am the Countess of Roxley. My friends call me Harriet." She looked him up and down. "You must be Mr. Rowland."

Roxley! That was it. This was the Earl of Roxley's infamous new bride. And just as outspoken and forward as everyone said.

"Why yes, I am Mr. Rowland," he replied, remembering his manners and bowing over her proffered hand. "My friends call me Tuck."

"I shall call you Mr. Rowland. Tuck can wait until I've chastised you thoroughly for making public wagers about my dearest friends."

"You'd best get in line."

"I never stand in line," the Countess of Roxley told him with a frosty lift of her brow and a merry twinkle in her eyes.

He slanted a glance in her direction. "No, I suppose you don't." He glanced back at his uncle's house, not sure what to do next. For in his pocket was a summons from Lady Gosforth as well. He hadn't been of a mind to answer it, but now . . .

Lady Roxley nodded to the house on the far side of the square. "Are you coming along?"

He certainly didn't want to face Lavinia at some afternoon in, before a gallery of London's most venal gossips, but he also needed to know that she was . . . oh, bother, he didn't know what he wanted her to be.

She had every right to be furious with him. She ought to toss a vase at him as she'd been threatening to do for a fortnight.

He wasn't unconvinced that she wouldn't. And then afterward, he wanted to tell her . . . to explain . . . how things had changed.

How he'd changed. How his heart had changed.

That he loved her.

Then in the middle of all this unfamiliar (and vastly uncomfortable) soul-searching, Tuck realized the countess had been saying something. "Pardon?"

"I assume you are here to see Lavinia."

"I am, well, I was."

"Excellent. Then you can walk with me to Lady Gosforth's."

Caught, for he could hardly refuse her, he nodded, and she struck a pace with a purposeful, determined stride. She rather reminded him of someone.

"You're from Kempton, aren't you?" he asked.

"I am," Lady Roxley replied.

"Are all the young ladies from Kempton like you and Lavinia?"

"A good portion of us," she told him with some measure of pride.

"I do believe I know your brother," he said.

"Which one?" she asked. "I have quite a collection."

"Chaunce."

She smiled. "You would know him. He's a complete scape-grace as well."

Then her expression turned thoughtful, and she asked, "Why were you so alarmed that Lavinia was out? Is she in some sort of trouble?"

Tuck gave her credit. Smart and perceptive. Roxley was going to have his hands full. That, or she just knew the Tempest sisters very well.

"She shouldn't be out."

"Whyever not?"

He added persistent to his list of traits. If these ladies from Kempton ever banded together, they might effect their own rev-olution of sorts.

He doubted the *ton* was ready for such a thing.

But he knew—given his experience with Lavinia—that the truth was in order. "It has to do with my wager with Lord Ilford."

She sniffed in dismay. "He's a perfectly despicable man."

"Yes, and he's hired a rather despicable pair of fellows to do some mischief."

Her eyes widened in alarm. "You won't let them, will you?"

"Good God, no! Mr. Bludger and his associate will never get close to Miss Tempest or her sister. I'll see to that."

The countess came to an abrupt halt. "Bludger? Did you say Bludger?"

"Yes."

"He's a deserter," she told him. "And a very evil man."

So Tuck knew. For the information the Honorable had gathered had left Tuck's blood chilled. But he didn't want to add to Lady Roxley's distress, so he merely said, "So Lady Wakefield asserted."

"Louisa is correct. She wrote to me that he'd been posing as a cook. Lord Wakefield is lucky he wasn't poisoned. My brother Benedict swore the man could taint boiling water by being in the same room."

"How do you know—"

She didn't wait for him to finish. "My brother Benedict—he's in the navy, a captain now—sails on the *Nemesis*. He writes to me all sorts of things my mother says are not proper subjects for young ladies. We—Louisa, Lavinia and I—always looked forward to his letters. Why they are nearly as good as the *Miss Darby* novels."

"Ah, that good," he offered politely.

The countess smiled approvingly. "I always had hoped that Benedict and Lavinia might . . . well, he was always fond of her, but perhaps it was because she is the finest bowler in two counties." She paused and studied him. "Did you know? She can throw a ball like no other."

"She has told me."

"Don't doubt it."

As much as he felt a bit of jealousy over the thought of another's admiring Livy, he couldn't help saying, "Wish your brother Benedict was here now—could use his help."

For it was in the back of his mind that Livy might well (and most stubbornly) refuse his help. But perhaps she wouldn't object or refuse the aid of an old acquaintance.

Lady Roxley tipped her head and peered up at him. "But Mr. Rowland, he can help you."

"How so?"

"Why he's here. In London. Benedict arrived two days ago."

Lady Gosforth's salons were well-known for being crowded—with every overbearing gossipy crone and matron from across the upper reaches of society.

If there was something to be discussed, dissected and most importantly, repeated, it could be found here.

So it was into this slithering, writhing snake pit of tattle that Lavinia and Louisa entered.

They'd been warned by Lady Aveley what to expect, and though they were used to the gossips of Kempton, nothing had prepared them for *this*.

Lavinia and Louisa followed Lady Aveley into the room, and when the lady stepped aside and revealed her charges in her wake, there was an audible gasp from several of the ladies in attendance.

But it wasn't all shocked gazes and furrowed brows, for there was Roselie perched on one of the settees and her hired companion, Mrs. Pratt, snoozing in a corner chair. Roselie grinned at the pair of them and eased over to make space for her new sister-in-law.

"Dear Louisa!" she exclaimed. "And Lavinia! How delightful," the viscount's sister declared, smiling at the other ladies around her, even if she seemed to be the only one sharing in this sentiment.

Lavinia sat down next to Lady Aveley, and after there had been introductions all around, the conversation sprang back to life as if it had never paused.

But to Lavinia's horror, the topic was none other than herself.

And Mr. Rowland's wager.

"I assure you, Miss Tempest," Lady Comber began, "we all have the utmost sympathy for your plight."

Heads nodded all around, though Lavinia had the sneaking suspicion it wasn't sympathy that was the reigning sentiment in the room.

"Alaster Rowland is a scandal," one of the matrons, Lady Nafferton declared with a sad shake of her head. "How he was allowed a voucher to Almack's, I cannot fathom. Why, I nearly left when I saw him admitted."

"Nearly," Lavinia thought she heard Lady Gosforth mutter.

Lady Comber nodded in agreement. "Well, if Ilford wins—as

it seems he will"—this was followed by a measured glance at Lavinia that said all too clearly there wasn't a hope of her attaining
any matter of redemption in such a short time. "You shan't see
Mr. Rowland in good company for some time to come. Lord
Comber says he'll have no choice but to leave the country. But
that is always what becomes of such fellows."

"It was a foolish wager from the start," another announced
from the doorway, and all heads turned to find Lady Blaxhall
standing there, coolly elegant in her half mourning and for a
moment there was a flicker of surprise as her gaze fell on Louisa.

But the viperish flash that instantly darkened her features was
quickly masked by an air of indifference.

For Lady Blaxhall had wrongly assumed that once her mourning was over, she would find herself as the new Lady Wakefield.

"Foolish?" Lady Gosforth replied as the widow made her entrance and took the chair beside their hostess, as if such an ele-
vated spot was her due. "I hardly see how you can say that, Lady
Blaxhall, when Mr. Rowland is more than halfway to winning his
wager. Lady Wakefield has proven against all odds that true love
will always win."

Lady Blaxhall blatantly ignored the dig at her own failed attempts to win the viscount's favor. Nor was she about to let the
matter pass. "My dear Lady Gosforth, Lord Wakefield's injuries
prevent him from being the best judge of character." The woman
turned and smiled at the new viscountess as if she had enjoyed
every word of a verbal sword thrust.

Lavinia cringed. For she saw the set of her sister's brow and
closed her eyes.

Louisa's words came out like honey. "I hardly see how a bullet
to the leg would affect one's judgment, Lady Blaxhall. But perhaps you assume—or rather had hoped—he would only be able
to think with his lower extremities rather than with his heart and
his wit."

Lavinia's gaze flew open about the same time Lady Blaxhall's
jaw dropped.

For her part, Roselie clapped her hands together, applauding her sister-in-law.

Nor was Louisa done. "Though it does seem to me that his injuries do color the judgment of those with no connection or concern for his welfare, or any due consideration for the service he gave our good King and country. Which I, for one, applaud and respect with all my heart."

But Lady Blaxhall hadn't been out in Society since she was of the tender age of sixteen for nothing. She shrugged off Louisa's set down without an apparent care in the world. "I just feel for your sister, poor Miss Tempest."

Lavinia's skin rippled with gooseflesh as the lady turned her icy blue eyes in her direction. "For who will ever want to connect themselves to a woman whose sister is married to a madman, and who will forever more have her name linked to a dreadful knave."

"He . . . I . . ." she began, stumbling to find the right words. Oh, bother she needed to get this right.

And not for herself, but for Tuck. For even as this vicious woman spoke, all Lavinia could hear was Mrs. Rowland's plaintive words.

He loves you, Livy.

And even if she couldn't forgive him for that wretched wager, she owed him a far greater debt for all he'd done since.

Lavinia straightened. "I hardly see why having my name linked to Mr. Rowland's is a detriment. On the contrary, I believe the gentleman has been the victim of judgments made in haste and from afar." And she paused and looked directly at Lady Blaxhall. "And out of utter ignorance."

"Miss Tempest! You astound me," Lady Oxnam exclaimed. "You of all people, who have been wronged so improperly by the man. How can you defend him?"

"My lady, what is proper?" Lavinia posed. "An arbitrary list of behaviors drawn up by people who have lost that spark of hope and joy that stirs one to live. Then we merely exist bound up in being accepted, in being proper. And who is it that judges all this?

People of narrow vision and hardly worth one's notice. I'd rather a man who has a spark in his heart and ventures much than one who gives little."

The room stilled, and all eyes were on her—some of them with a new regard and more than a few in horror at such heresy.

But it was Lady Gosforth who finally broke into the shocked silence.

"Well said, child. Well said." The marchioness looked around as if challenging any of them to naysay her.

Tuck started up the steps of the elegant town house, then realized he was doing so alone. He turned to Lady Roxley, who stood at the curb. "Aren't you coming in with me?"

"Oh, heavens no! I merely walked with you to ensure you arrived," she told him. "I know better than to go in there. Lady Gosforth is a veritable dragon."

"I thought you ladies from Kempton slew dragons as a regular course of business."

"Only the deserving ones," the former Harriet Hathaway told him.

"Still," Tuck replied. He'd never been to an afternoon in and found that he'd rather walk through Seven Dials with a beef-steak tied around his neck and towing a wagon of free gin behind him than face whatever it was that might be inside this perfectly respectable-looking address. "Didn't you say you were looking for Miss Tempest?"

So much for his attempt to recruit reinforcements.

She laughed at him. "I fear my time will be better spent finding my brothers. You do still want their assistance, don't you?"

"Yes," he agreed, squaring his shoulders as he glanced again at the imposing door before him.

For Livy.

"Tell them to meet me at my rooms at"—he glanced down at his pocket watch—"half past seven."

She nodded and set out on her own, her determined steps a reckoning and a warning.

He almost felt sorry for Chaunce and Benedict Hathaway.

Almost.

But for now, he had his own dragons to slay, so he strode up the steps and knocked on the door. The butler showed him into a salon done in blue, with gilded accents—that would be imposing all on its own, but the room was also filled with ladies.

He recognized most of them. The indomitable Lady Comber. Lady Oxnam with her lips pinched together. The sight of Lady Blaxhall sent a chill through him. He'd never liked the beauty to whom his cousin had once been engaged. And the feeling was mutual, for the widow's nose pinched at his arrival.

But this inspection took but a blink of an eye, for his gaze found its desired treasure, and he was struck by a shaft of longing that wrenched through him.

It had only been a few hours since he'd watched Lavinia depart, her lips pressed together, that terrible wrath in her eyes, but it had felt like a lifetime.

And now, here she was, surrounded by the fiercest gossips of London, and all he could do was pretend theirs was but a passing acquaintance.

That it wasn't something else tugging at his heart, leaving him lost in a maelstrom of his own making.

He wrenched his gaze from her and glanced around before he bowed low, realizing Lady Roxley hadn't told him the entire truth.

This was a veritable nest of dragons.

"Mr. Rowland," Lady Gosforth acknowledged. "You're late." Her brows rose slightly.

Ah, yes, the first matron to ready her flames.

Tuck took the marchioness's outstretched hand and placed a kiss upon it. "I fear my valet thought your invitation an unkind jest on the part of one of my friends." One glance told him she didn't see the humor in his excuse.

"Then you should keep better company," she told him, pulling her hand free.

Well, yes, he'd known that for years.

"Are those for me?" she asked, glancing at the flowers in his grasp.

He'd nearly forgotten he was holding them. "Why yes," he said, holding them out for her, his eyes straying momentarily to catch sight yet again of Livy.

And when he did, he found something unusual in her eyes. A pleading sort of look.

For him to stay or leave, he didn't know. Really didn't matter now, he was trapped.

Much as she was.

Lady Gosforth had taken the flowers, examined them quickly then handed them off to her hired companion. "Whether or not that is the truth, I'll take them anyway. Flowers are wasted on the young, and I am fond of bluebells."

"Then they were most certainly for you," he teased.

The old girl snorted. "My lord husband thought you a, and I quote, 'a bang-up specimen'—whatever that means. He didn't mention you were an incorrigible flirt."

"Hardly that, my lady," he demurred.

"That and more, I suspect. Then again, all I know of you, Mr. Rowland, is based on an alarming amount of gossip." This was followed by a *tsk tsk*. And a glance that asked, no demanded, an explanation.

But Tuck hadn't spent a good part of his life standing in the docket of shame without learning a trick or two. He waited her out, as if he had no idea what she might be eluding to.

Lady Gosforth waited longer than most, then barked a laugh. "Unrepentant to the end. I rather like that in a man. Though another lady might look aghast at such qualities." She looked him up and down again, then nodded for him to take the seat beside her.

"So whatever is it that you were all discussing when I arrived?" Tuck asked.

"You, Mr. Rowland," Lady Nafferton told him. "And all your sins."

Lavinia closed her eyes and wished herself well away from Lady Gosforth's salon. Dear heavens, it had gone from horrid to horrendous.

What the devil was Tuck doing here? And whyever had Lady Gosforth invited him?

And why hadn't his valet done something about that loose thread on his collar?

He looked as if he hadn't slept at all, all rumpled and barely shaved. She longed to go to him, to smooth back his hair, to straighten his coat, to wind her arms around his neck and let him kiss her again.

All of which was wrong. And improper. And not what she wanted, she reminded herself.

Not after what he'd done.

And yet . . . When he'd looked at her, she'd nearly gotten to her feet. Nearly.

And now he'd unwittingly walked into his own funeral.

"Yes, it was a most enlightening discussion," Lady Blaxhall added. "Though Miss Tempest had her own rather alarming opinions as to your character."

"I don't doubt that," he said though he didn't look at her.

Lady Blaxhall, who looked to be sharpening her claws, was about to say something else, but she was interrupted by the arrival of Lady Damerell.

The baroness was all aflutter, the lace on her cap and the fringe on her shawl all nervously dancing about.

"I've just come from Lady Rushbury's. There is a spate of speculation that this woman might be a Russian princess," Lady Damerell announced even before she sat down.

Nods all around the room indicated this wasn't a subject with which they were unfamiliar. But before Lavinia could ask,

"Who?" Lady Nafferton spoke up. "Russian? No, no, she was quite pretty from what I've heard. Decidedly English."

Lady Comber spoke up. "But the necklace she was wearing—diamonds and sapphires—says otherwise. Rare and old. And royal. I still maintain she is French."

"This hardly seems a proper topic," Lady Aveley pointed out, nodding at the younger members of the assembled guests.

But her comment was entirely ignored, especially now that Lady Comber had them all in her thrall.

"You were there?" Lady Nafferton sat up, aghast.

"Lady St. John is my mother's third cousin, once removed. I fear the connection is impossible to avoid."

Apparently the company was willing to forgive this scandalous kinship if it meant Lady Comber could fill in where the rest of the ladies lacked her first-hand knowledge.

"And what did she look like?" Lady Blaxhall asked, trying to sound bored, but even Lavinia could see an anxious sort of envy about her.

"So very fetching," Lady Comber told them as she basked in the attention, and to her credit, paused her story long enough to give her audience a moment of anxiety that she wouldn't continue.

But, of course, she did.

"Her hair is dark, with such a rich luster to it. Lord Comber remarked it was like a fine mahogany."

At this, Roselie sat up and tipped her head with interest, as if something had caught her eye. And it had.

She was studying Lavinia, a wry twist to her lips as if she was making a connection that had been puzzling her.

Reaching up, Lavinia pulled her bonnet down a bit. Then again, it wasn't as if Roselie would have been at Lord St. John's . . . So she couldn't have seen her . . .

Meanwhile, Lady Comber had smoothed her hands over her own elegant day gown and went back to telling her tale. "And her dress! Why it had all the markings of royalty, elegantly simple and entirely rich. I have never seen such sumptuous velvet. Oh, and diamonds sewn into the hem."

"Diamonds," one of Lady Nafferton's daughters whispered in awe, earning her a stern glance from her mother.

"That sounds like a waste of perfectly good jewels," Lady Gosforth remarked.

"I have heard there are already wagers as to who will discover her identity first," Lady Damerell added. "Why this mystery woman is the most sought after lady in London. Whoever she is, by tonight she could have her pick of suitors."

"Some unknown cardsharp?" Lady Blaxhall scoffed. "I hardly see why." The lady preened a bit, secure that she would continue to hold her throne amongst the *ton*.

"You know how it is, madam," Lady Gosforth said, looking down her nose at the proud beauty. "There is always some new, fetching young creature who comes along and usurps last year's crop. Or in some cases, the chaff from the previous decade."

Lady Blaxhall's eyes narrowed, and her smile tightened, showing just how she was no longer one of the pretty, dewy-eyed misses who so often held sway in the *ton*.

"Still, it is a mystery," Lady Damerell interjected. While she liked to stir the pot with her gossip, she wasn't one who liked it when the news boiled over.

"Wouldn't it be marvelous if she was a lost royal from the French court?" Lady Nafferton's other daughter said.

Her romantic suggestion was lost on the older matrons. Especially Lady Gosforth.

"A French cardsharp of royal blood? I give no credit to such nonsense," the marchioness snorted. "Lord Gosforth was quite firm on the point this morning, the lady is English. 'Fetchingly pretty,' is how he described her. And well-bred."

Beside Lavinia, Lady Aveley stilled, then began to cough. But no one seemed to notice, for they were all in a frenzy of speculation and theories, the whirlwind of conversations leaving Lavinia dizzy.

She didn't dare look at Lady Aveley, who had resumed her stiff stance beside her, nor did she dare glance at Tuck.

Instead, she did her best to shrink a bit into her seat. When she dared, she glanced over at Louisa, who, while looking composed, stole a glance at her sister.

They aren't discussing you, are they?

Lavinia slipped her shoulder ever so slightly. *Well . . .*

Louisa closed her eyes and appeared to be groaning inwardly.

Yes, this was rather like the aftermath of the infamous bunting incident.

"Lithe and elegant, I was told," Lady Nafferton confirmed.

"I for one applaud her!" Lady Damerell declared.

That stopped the chatter cold. Everyone gaped.

"Why Flora, how can you approve of such a thing?" Lady Nafferton said. "Gambling such sums and in that company." The lady sniffed, drawing her skirt back.

Lady Damerell tipped her nose in the air. "She cleaned out that wretched Ilford. Humiliated the man. Anyone who can do that, set him on his ear, has my open regard."

"Open regard for a thief?" Lady Blaxhall sat like she was having her portrait done—all straight and coolly regal. "Ilford says she cheated. Blatantly so."

"I thought she played with cool disdain and a sharp wit," Lady Comber replied. "But most importantly, I would love to know where she got that navy velvet—finest I've seen in years."

"That's it," Lady Nafferton said, sitting up.

"What is?" Lady Damerell asked her.

"Her gown," Lady Nafferton replied, as if the answer was obvious. "Who do you think was the modiste, Flora? Who might have done it up?"

This suggestion had the effect of baiting their hooks once again, and every lady in the room began dropping hers in the water.

"Madam Desmarais perhaps," Lady Comber suggested.

"Or that dreadful woman over on Clifford Street," Lady Damerell threw out. "She's all the rage though I've never understood why."

There were several nods in agreement.

"Then it is decided," Lady Nafferton declared, rising to her feet. Everyone else did likewise. "We shall canvass the modistes we know and see if any of them know who owns that gown."

"Oh, this will be exactly like being in a *Miss Darby* novel," Lady Nafferton's daughter said in an aside to her sister.

"I think you'll all be sorely disappointed when you find this imposter," Lady Blaxhall said as she rose, and made her curtsy to her hostess. "For it seems the *ton* is filled these days with ladies of questionable character and breeding." This was cast in the direction of the Tempest sisters, but no one was paying any attention to the venomous widow.

The notion of an expedition to every modiste shop in London had stolen her hold on the room. So the lady marched out in high dudgeon.

"Good riddance," Louisa muttered under her breath.

"I've never been overly fond of her either," Lady Nafferton confided. Then she brightened, and asked. "Now where were we?"

All too quickly the most likely shops were parceled out, and the company set out on their search, leaving the room nearly emptied.

Roselie and Mrs. Pratt followed behind the rest, the viscount's sister squeezing Lavinia's hand as she left. "All will be well, I'm most certain of it, Miss Tempest," she whispered, then cast a knowing glance at Tuck.

Lady Gosforth spied Mr. Rowland easing toward the door and caught him before he escaped. "Mr. Rowland, a moment. I would have a word with you. But first—"

She turned to her remaining guests, "Every week I declare I'm no longer going to have company, and every week I continue to open my doors to those cats," Lady Gosforth told them. She looked over at Louisa and Lavinia. "My dears, I beg you to do me a favor. Go upstairs. My chamber is on the second floor. One of the maids will be close by and tell her to give you my megrim powders, will you?"

The pair of them looked in unison to Lady Aveley, who nodded for them to do as they were bid.

And so they left, and Lady Gosforth turned to Lady Aveley. "I will have a word with them. Alone."

"I don't think—" Lady Aveley began.

The marchioness shook her head. "Gosforth has advised me of the situation. I will send them home in our carriage with William to watch over them. No harm shall befall them, or those villains will have to reckon with me. And Mr. Rowland, I imagine."

Lady Aveley pressed her lips together, glanced at Tuck, then nodded and took her leave.

Tuck drew a deep breath. For it was now only he and the marchioness. She returned to her chair and bid him to come close.

She reached over and caught up a box on the table, opened it, and pulled out a comfit. She offered the box to him, but he shook his head.

She shrugged, ate her treat and waited.

He did as well. Wary, he was no fool. He wasn't about to start unspooling the rope for his own hanging.

And, finally, the lady spoke. "So, Mr. Rowland, tell me why Miss Tempest should lend her favor in your direction?"

"Pardon?"

"You heard me, sir. Why should your suit be allowed?"

Dear heavens, at least Lord Gosforth had had the decency to ply him with a generous amount of brandy before he'd begun to press him for such personal information.

And then it hadn't been so much a press, but an unwitting spill. In his cups, he'd told the marquess everything Lord Gosforth wanted to know about Lavinia and as much as Tuck knew about her sister.

But here, in the clear light of day, with a bright shaft of sunshine from the nearby window cutting a path through his aching head, he had only one thing to say, the words that had eluded him so many times.

"Simply put, my lady, I love Livy."

CHAPTER 19

Louisa and Lavinia stood before a portrait in Lady Gosforth's boudoir.

It was like looking at a mirror. For there stood a pair of sisters, as identical as Louisa and Lavinia—but more revealing, sharing the same mahogany hair and blue eyes.

Louisa gathered her wits first and turned to the maid who was retrieving the megrim powders from a case. "Who are they?"

"Her Ladyship and her sister. But goodness, miss! Goodness." The girl gaped at the portrait, then at the sisters, crossing herself, before quickly ushering them out of Her Ladyship's room.

Lavinia took one last look at the painting from the doorway, her heart hammering.

How could it be? *Unless . . .*

"Does that mean what I think it means?" she asked Louisa, for she scarcely believed it herself.

Louisa rounded on her, pulling her to a stop. "That all those rumors were true? About Lord Eddows . . . that Papa isn't—"

Lavinia shook her head, for she didn't want to think of any other parent than their dear Papa. Sir Ambrose Tempest. He was their father. The only father they'd ever known.

"Lord Eddows died just before mother married Papa," Louisa said, more for her own sake, Lavinia suspected.

But she knew the rumors as well and glanced back down the hall . . . "So if Lord Eddows was Gosforth's heir . . . that makes Lady Gosforth our—"

Both of them glanced down the stairwell. *Grandmother.* Having never really had one, it was a rather formidable notion. Their mother's family had washed their hands of their errant daughter and her offspring years ago, and their Tempest relations had always been distant.

Now, it seems, they both knew why.

Louisa nodded. "Do you think she knows?"

"I think Lady Gosforth knows everything," Lavinia whispered back. She'd guess there was very little in London society of which the marchioness didn't have a full accounting and that she'd sent them upstairs with the very notion that they'd see the portrait.

"Whatever are we to say to her?" Louisa asked.

"I suggest we don't start out by calling her 'grandmother,'" Lavinia shot back. "Wouldn't that have been an *on dit*?"

Louisa smirked at her. "Might have quelled some of the speculation about this so-called Russian-princess cardsharp—or whoever she might be." Her sister's brow arched—much like Lady Gosforth's had earlier.

Oh, dear heavens! The resemblance was uncanny.

As for the mysterious woman all of London was seeking to unmask, Lavinia simply shrugged off that notion. "I fear that lady will never see the light of day again." When Louisa's brows arched a little bit higher, she hastily added, "I promise."

"And here I thought Almack's was the worst you could accomplish," Louisa muttered.

"It is hardly as bad as all that. Besides, I won an obscene amount of money last night. I won't need to ask Papa for extra pin money for the next ten years. And I didn't cheat like that horrible Lady Blaxhall claimed. I won fair and square—and it was ever so satisfying to best Lord Ilford."

Louisa whirled around. "More satisfying is that he doesn't know who you are." She sighed and looked over at Lavinia, trying to hold back a grin and failing miserably. "Serves that man right. He's a deplorable villain. More so because he is on the verge of ruining poor Mr. Rowland."

"Poor Mr. Rowland?" Lavinia could hardly believe her ears. "He wagered as to our worthiness!"

"Well, to his credit, he did wager that we are utterly respectable."

Lavinia threw up her hands. "So that makes it proper? Louisa, I think you've gone mad. Mr. Rowland has ruined everything."

"Only if you let it." Louisa huffed a sigh, as if she couldn't see what the problem might be. Then she took a deep breath before continuing, "Mr. Rowland's meddling is why I am happily married. I owe him a great debt. And so do you."

"Me?" Lavinia shook her head. "He is a knave and a rake, and devilishly improper and—"

But her words were stopped as Louisa whirled around and put her hand over Lavinia's mouth to stop her words.

And then she raised a finger to her lips and tipped her head toward the room beyond.

Tuck. His voice, full of emotion, said the words that Lavinia's heart longed to hear.

"Simply put, I love Livy."

Lavinia took a step back. He loved her? No, he couldn't. Her heart tangled up in a wild cadence. Now? He had to confess everything now?

Louisa glanced back at her from her spot near the doorway, her eyes alight, her head tipped just so to better listen.

"Eavesdropping?" Lavinia whispered, returning to her sister's side and catching her by the arm. "You know I don't approve. It isn't proper."

"But ever so enlightening," Louisa shot back, shamelessly listening to what Mr. Rowland had to say next.

For a moment, Lavinia wavered in that quandary of wanting to know and not wanting to know where Tuck's heart lay.

But curiosity won the day.

Oh, bother, Lavinia thought, moving closer and edging aside Louisa for a better seat.

It would hardly do to get this all secondhand.

"Love her?" Lady Gosforth barked a laugh. "You took her to one of St. John's Follies."

"As a matter of point, I didn't take her there. She arrived with someone else. I only went to fetch her home before she was . . ." He wasn't too sure how to phrase the rest.

Her Ladyship did it for him. "Yes, I can imagine the 'before she was' part. I'm not that old." The lady tapped her fingers on the arm of her chair. "And was she?"

"Was she what?"

"You know what I'm asking. Was she compromised?" The lady's gaze turned hawk-like as she watched for his reply.

"No." As the Honorable always said, if you have to lie, keep it to one syllable.

"Harrumph." The marchioness pressed her lips together and snapped her fan shut.

Tuck didn't know what to make of the lady's response. "You seem disappointed, Lady Gosforth."

"Well, I had hoped for another hasty wedding like her sister managed with Wakefield. Put all this gossip to rest once and for all."

The marchioness had yet to truly meet Livy, Tuck mused. She would always be in the maelstrom of gossip given her head-strong ways.

"Did you have a groom in mind?" he asked instead.

"Yes."

If the lady was going to hold her cards close, so could Tuck.

He decided to force her hand. "Your Ladyship has me at a disadvantage. Who do you think is worthy of her?"

"Well, you say you love Miss Tempest. So out with it, sir, are you or are you not going to offer for her?"

Tuck's heart lurched. Marry Livy? Spend a lifetime with her. Never had he thought he—Tuck Rowland—would marry. There were too many obstacles for him to wed.

Too many complications in his life.

And Livy deserved so much more than him. An honest man who would never drag her name into the scandal broth.

And so he told Lady Gosforth the truth. "I fear that is impossible."

"Why? All you have to do is ask."

"Waste of breath. She'll turn me down flat."

"You've kissed her, haven't you?"

"Pardon?"

"You heard me correctly. You've kissed her, haven't you?"

"Yes."

"And did you do it correctly?"

Correctly? Good God! Had she truly just asked such a thing? And did she honestly expect him to answer? He slanted a glance at her and found that, yes, she was waiting for his reply.

An afternoon being racked in the Tower would be preferable to this.

Nor did his lack of response hardly give the lady pause. "Well, never mind," she declared. "You have a reputation. You must know what you are about. If you've done it properly, and you love her, whyever would she turn you down?"

"Because I wagered on her honor. She quite despises me for it."

"Piffle. What lady worth her salt hasn't had her name put down in that dreadful book?" she declared. "You should have seen what they wagered about me."

And here Tuck thought the lady couldn't scandalize him any further.

Then Lady Gosforth leaned forward. "So you think she won't marry you? Mr. Rowland, I ask you this, have you've ever known a lady to change her mind?"

Those words gave him pause. He looked up at her, and she smiled at him, giving him a slight nod of encouragement.

But even if he wanted to marry Livy, why couldn't the lady see that it was, as he'd told her, impossible. So he asked, "Why are you pressing for this match when I have nothing to offer her?"

This was waved aside. "You love her."

"That, I assure you, will hardly pay the bills. My parents were proof of that."

"I knew your father, my boy," she told him, poking him in the chest with her fan. "And no man loved a woman more than your father loved his Jenny." She paused and looked him up and down as if seeing him for the first time. "You remind me of him."

"I don't know if that is a recommendation."

"Indeed it is. He and my son were friends. A pair of trouble-makers." She smiled at the memory. "I'm rather fond of trouble-makers," she told him, rising from her chair. "Marry the girl if you love her."

Tuck hastened to his feet. "I'd be more than happy to oblige you, my lady, but I doubt she'll ever speak to me again. And even if I could offer for her, I have nothing to recommend my suit."

The marchioness laughed. "Not if you kissed her properly, my boy. Not if you stole her heart."

As Mr. Rowland took his leave, Louisa pulled Lavinia back from the door and steered her sister to a nearby alcove. "Did he? Did he kiss you?" she asked once they were well hidden.

Lavinia looked away. She hardly wanted to admit it to Louisa, let alone to herself.

For to think about his kiss, the way it felt to be in his arms was to let herself fall into that dreamy stupor—the one where he continues to kiss her and she him.

And everything is . . . so full of passion.

"I know I shouldn't have, but it just happened."

Louisa took a step back, hands fisted to her hips. "Well I know how that occurs."

Her sister's confession surprised her even though Lavinia had well suspected that the viscount and Louisa had been alone far too many times before their hasty marriage. Still, she couldn't help but ask, "Is it like that with you and the viscount? As Lady Gosforth said?"

As it was last night with Tuck. When he'd held her. Touched her.

Down the hallway, she could see Tuck taking his hat and walking stick from the butler, and for a moment, he glanced over his shoulder, toward the stairs and up into the house, where she'd been sent on her errand.

He was looking for her, and it was all she could do not to go to him.

Not that Louisa helped matters, for here she was, a light of love glowing in her eyes. "Oh, yes, it's so wonderful. Very much so." Then her expression softened a bit. "But it wasn't easy to find our way. Piers has . . ."

"Difficulties," Lavinia supplied for her.

At this, Louisa nodded. "Aye. But his heart, I never doubt. His struggles I can only hope to ease them. Give him a home in which he can be secure once again." After a second, she added, "For always. And in return, he's given me—"

Security. A title. A respectable place in Society.

But when she looked at Louisa, she knew it was none of that. For if Piers had been the butcher down the lane, he would have still been Louisa's perfect match.

For together they were both made whole.

Together.

Simply put, my lady, I love Livy.

Oh, good heavens, was that enough? Lavinia wondered. And that he'd said it, and one might point out, to one of the biggest gossips in London.

Yet what good did that do her? She couldn't acknowledge that she knew his feelings. For to do so would mean having to confess that she'd been eavesdropping.

Yet. Again.

Oh, how Rowland would delight in that! He'd tease her mercilessly.

As well he should.

And then he'd kiss her.

As well he should.

Oh, but still . . . "I deplore that he made such a wager," Lavinia said.

Louisa, of course, could hear the reluctance in her voice. "And yet—"

"Oh, don't 'and yet' me. I will never speak to him again."

"Yes, but the real question is, would you kiss him again?"

"Eavesdropping?"

The question startled Lavinia and Louisa. They turned in unison—open-mouthed at being caught . . . by of all people, their grandmother.

"My sister possesses an incorrigible habit of eavesdropping. I have never approved . . ." But the marchioness said this with a smile. A fond one.

"My lady—" Lavinia began, glancing up the stairs, the portrait flashing in her thoughts.

The marchioness shook her head, then pressed her lips together, but not for long. She heaved a great sigh, as if a lifetime of sadness and regrets were leaving her. "I suppose you noticed when you were upstairs that we share a familiarity about us."

"We did," Louisa agreed.

"It was rather hard to miss," Lavinia said, then added, "but perhaps it is best not shared—at least not in public."

The marchioness nodded in approval. She gestured for them to follow her back into the salon, where she settled into her chair and bid the sisters to sit on the divan beside her. "I fear I've failed you both."

Lavinia glanced over at Louisa, then back at their . . . their grandmother. Oh, goodness this was going to take some getting used to. "I don't see how."

"Your mother came to me . . . just after my son died. Lord Eddows." She paused. "Have you heard of him? Of your mother?"

They nodded.

"Yes, well, she told me of her plight. I was not kind. In my defense, I was grieving. I loved my son—he was my oldest and my dearest—and his death so very sudden. So unexpected. And when she said . . . claimed . . ." Again that dismissing flicker of her hand as if she wished she could push it all under the carpet. But no longer. Lady Gosforth looked them both in the eye. "I didn't believe her. Wouldn't. Sent her packing. The next thing I heard, she'd married Sir Ambrose."

"Dear Papa," Louisa said softly.

Lady Gosforth nodded in agreement. "He is a credit to you both. He forgave and loved your mother as I should have."

"What could you have done?" Lavinia asked. "When a lady is in such a predicament—"

"You're correct. Nothing, I suppose. But when I saw the two of you—" She sighed again. "That night in Almack's—I was bowled over. And before I could get to you—" She looked over at them and laughed a little. "That was some debut, my dear girls."

"Yes, well, it wasn't our finest hour," Louisa admitted, straightening and smoothing her hands over her skirt, trying to appear the proper matron.

"Someday I will tell you the story of how I nearly burned down Lord Mayfield's conservatory. Oh, I was an utter disaster when I came out."

"You as well—" Lavinia gasped, feeling as if she had suddenly found a soul mate.

"And you play cards, or so Gosforth says," the marchioness said, her eyes alight.

Lord Gosforth! Lavinia hadn't yet made the association but now . . . no wonder he'd offered his carriage.

"I do," Lavinia said.

Beside her, Louisa groaned.

"Don't be that way," Lady Gosforth admonished. "I gambled my way into Lord Gosforth's heart with a very well played pair of queens."

Lavinia looked over at Louisa and smirked. Her twin looked ready to wash her hands of the both of them.

Not that Lady Gosforth seemed to notice. "Oh, how grand this is. I am going to delight in making you two the Toast of the Town, starting with invitations to our ball—tomorrow night. You will be my honored guests." She glanced over at Louisa, "That is if Wakefield is up to attending."

The words might have been snide from someone else, but they were kindly meant this time.

"I know he will be honored to meet you," Louisa told her.

And then Lady Gosforth sighed again. "I shall make up for lost time. I shall not fail you now."

"You haven't failed us," Lavinia told her, reaching across and taking hold of the lady's hand. "We have found each other when we were meant to."

"I've never asked for help before," Tuck admitted as his friends and new allies gathered in his small, spartan apartment. Piers, Brody, his Uncle Charleton, Chaunce Hathaway and his brother, the newly promoted Captain Benedict Hathaway.

Falshaw hovered in the background, wide-eyed at this unprecedented arrival of guests but doing his best to look ready to lend a hand if necessary.

It all rather took Tuck aback. "Yes, well, I don't usually find myself in such dire straits—"

Uncle Charleton coughed a few times.

"Yes, well, not the sort of predicament that requires assistance of this magnitude."

"About time you came to your senses and just asked," Piers told him.

"Wouldn't have it any other way," Chaunce Hathaway told him.

"Nor would our sister Harry," Captain Benedict Hathaway added with a laugh. "Besides, Miss Tempest is the finest bowler in Kempton. A rare gel."

Tuck liked the cheeky fellow on sight.

"That and," Benedict continued from his commanding spot near the fireplace, "a battle is won when all hands rise to the challenge." He raised his glass in a toast.

"Don't you sound all lofty and noble," his older brother remarked in a dry tone.

"You should try it some time, you taciturn old—" Benedict began.

"Um, yes, well," Tuck said, jumping into the fray. From what he knew about the Hathaway clan, they usually settled their differences with their fists, and he was certain his landlady wouldn't approve of a donnybrook in her building.

No matter how noble the cause.

"Shall we get started?" he asked when the door opened yet again.

The Honorable came in full of apologies for his late arrival and looking a bit disheveled. "Been combing my associates, my dear boy," he explained, giving his usually perfectly tied cravat a brush with his fingers. "Some of them were less than forthcoming. But anything for our Livy, eh? The gel's a dab hand with the boards. That, and I've grown rather fond of her."

So had Tuck, and he'd be damned if he was going to let anything happen to her or her sister.

After Tuck had explained the situation, with Piers, Lord Charleton and the Honorable adding their various tidbits of news, a definite picture emerged.

And it was grim. Bludger and his cohort Charlie had been ordered to snatch one of the sisters. After that, it was anyone's guess as to what Ilford planned to do, but not one of them held the opinion that it would be good.

"However do we stop them?" Lord Charleton asked, his brows drawn together in consternation.

"I find the best way to catch these sort of fellows is with bait," Chaunce Hathaway said.

His suggestion was met with immediate outrage.

Piers shook his head furiously. "If you think I'm sending my wife out—" He looked ready to rise out of his chair.

"—Or Livy," Tuck hastened to add—putting a steadying hand on his cousin. "I mean, Miss Tempest."

Even Brody waded in, "It just isn't done, my good man. Putting a lady in harm's way. What the devil are you thinking?"

"Hold steady," the newly minted Captain Benedict Hathaway chimed in, waving the others down. He looked over them all. "You aren't thinking this through. What is a lure if not a lie?"

There was an exchange of puzzled looks, while Chaunce grinned at his younger brother. "Just like the time we dressed up Quinton in one of Mum's old dresses and had him go racing across the green atop Father's new mount. Had the Kempton spinsters wagging for a month. Poor Mum!"

"To this day, Squire Martins still claims it was our mother on that horse," Benedict agreed, slapping his knee.

Chaunce glanced again at his disbelieving audience. "Who says we have to bait our trap with the real thing. This Bludger and his accomplice need only think they are about to make off with one of the Tempest sisters."

"They'll be surprised when they discover our deception," Benedict said. "But by then, it will be too late . . . for them."

The Honorable began to nod. "A shell game as it were. Nothing draws the unwitting in better." He paused, then remembered his company. "Or so I am told."

Tuck nodded as he began to see their plan unfold. But there was one nagging question. "Who on earth do you propose don a gown and prance about?"

And all eyes turned toward him.

"Oh, no!" he said, getting to his feet. "I'm not—" He turned on Piers. "'Tis your wife as well that's in harm's way. You put on a skirt."

"Not with his limp," Chaunce pointed out.

"Dead giveaway," Brody agreed with a hearty nod.

Piers shrugged in defeat—not that he'd even put up a fight. Then he grinned at Tuck. "You'll make a fetching lass. Perhaps Roselie has a gown you can borrow."

"I'm too tall," Tuck declared. "Won't fool anyone. Besides, I don't know a demmed thing about being a woman."

"You just need to get them to believe the lie, my boy. Like a bit of sleight of hand," the Honorable declared, pulling a coin from his waistcoat and letting it tumble and twirl through his fingers until it disappeared altogether.

The old fraud then reached over and plucked it from behind Brody's ear.

The Honorable winked at Tuck. "Walk as if you are on your way to your first ball, and they'll all want to dance with you."

"Oh, this I have to see," Brody declared.

Lavinia found herself wandering aimlessly about Lord Charleton's expansive London residence. Lady Aveley had gone to dine with her son and his new bride, and the sudden stillness of the house wore on Lavinia, leaving her a bit unnerved.

Nor had it escaped her that there were not one, but two new footmen about, and that Brobson had gone about the house double-checking that all the doors and windows were secured.

Something was afoot, but Lavinia had far too many other things on her mind right now.

She had a grandmother. Lady Gosforth.

And she wasn't truly Sir Ambrose's daughter.

Yet all that paled in light of Tuck's startling confession.

I love Livy.

He loved her? Oh, how could he say such a thing? Now?

Lips pressed together, brow furrowed deep, Lavinia didn't

know if she wanted to dash a vase at his head or run to his arms and let him kiss her again. Deeply. Thoroughly.

All of the above, perhaps. And not necessarily in that order.

She looked up to find that she was standing in the open doorway of the library, where inside Lord Charleton sat before his chess board, the pieces ready for conquest, but it appeared the baron's thoughts were far from the field before him.

"So, you are quite the card-player, I hear," Lord Charleton said when he spotted her turning to leave.

Lavinia paused and nodded. "Adequate."

"More than adequate from what I understand. You don't happen to play chess, do you?"

She shook her head. "That's Louisa's accomplishment."

"Then cards it is," he said, clearing away the chess pieces and taking a deck of cards out from the drawer.

They cut for the deal, and Lavinia took the cards after drawing a king.

"Stakes?" he ventured.

Lavinia thought about it for a moment. The baron had done so much for her and Louisa, that taking his money—even halfpenny stakes—seemed improper, so she suggested something else.

"The truth," she said as she dealt the first hand.

Charleton made a noise—a sort of snort and a laugh. "You've come to the wrong place. The truth is a rare commodity in London." He looked up and met her gaze. "Besides, those are high stakes indeed. You willing to take such a risk?"

She paused. For the first time in her life, she realized she had much to conceal. Her parentage. Her newly discovered grandmother.

Her feelings for a certain knave.

All of which would cost her much if she had to tell the truth.

"I suppose I will have to find out," she told him, dealing out the hand. All too quickly, she won, leaving the baron staring down at the cards on the table as if she'd conjured them out of thin air.

Not one to wait around, Lavinia collected her winnings immediately. "How do you forgive him, Lord Charleton?"

He didn't need to ask whom she meant. They both knew.

"Easily," he replied, shuffling the deck and after glancing at her, shuffling them one more time for good measure.

"That's it? Just easily?" she pressed, feeling as if she had just been paid in buttons.

He shrugged and nodded toward the cards on the table. "It's the truth."

She gathered up the deck, and when she won a second time, she asked the baron the question again. "I insist, however do you forgive him?"

"Because, simply put, there is nothing to forgive, my dear girl."

Lavinia laid her hand facedown. "He gambled away his commission money. People say he is a . . . a . . ."

Lord Charleton glanced up from his hand. "People say all manner of nonsense, Miss Tempest. Remember, I told you the truth is a rare commodity in London." He discarded and nodded toward her all-but-forgotten hand.

"Are you saying he didn't do those things?" Lavinia persisted.

The baron shrugged. "It is not my story to tell."

Lavinia discarded hastily, then realized she'd given away a pair of tens by mistake. She bit off a rather unladylike utterance, for she usually wasn't so careless, but her thoughts were awhirl.

Who was Tuck Rowland?

The man you love.

"I will say this," Lord Charleton began as he picked up another card and discarded, "if I have no issues with my heir's comportment and choices, why should anyone else?"

A shiver ran down her spine, for she knew this was a spark of the truth, what she'd been seeking.

"Oh, I won't disguise the matter—he's a madcap, impetuous fool most of the time, but when it matters, Alaster will go to any depth to do right by those he loves—even if it leaves him in the suds. Your godmother knew that, and I've realized it for some time."

Lavinia nodded as the baron's unwavering conviction settled into her heart.

It's all true, Tuck had said.

But was it? Was there more to the truth than the obvious.

"Is he in as much trouble as everyone says?" she asked as casually as she could, not even looking up from her cards.

"You shouldn't concern yourself with gossip," he advised.

"Yes, but if, say, I don't . . . shine as I ought tomorrow night, he'll lose this dreadful wager with Lord Ilford."

"As I said, you shouldn't give a thought to—"

"How can I not, when I—"

Love him. With all my heart.

She didn't say the words aloud, but when she did look up, the baron smiled at her.

As if he'd heard what was in her heart.

She was so distracted, she discarded again, this time giving up a straight and losing.

Staring down at her cards in disbelief, she gaped at Lord Charlton, who took his victory in stride.

He sat back and took off his spectacles, cleaning them with his handkerchief. "So Miss Tempest. The truth. What was the most startling piece of gossip you heard at Lady Gosforth's?"

And Lavinia had no choice but to tell him the truth.

CHAPTER 20

Lavinia glanced over at the ball gown on the bed. Pale silk done in an elegantly demure fashion. It was the sort of dress she'd dreamt of wearing all her life. And she was going to the sort of ball she'd always wanted to attend.

And yet, the entire evening held no appeal to her. Yes, she'd be received. Yes, Lady Gosforth would do her utmost to see that Society gave the Tempest sisters all due respect.

But one thing would be missing.

Him.

She flounced into a nearby chair and stared moodily at the grate in the fireplace.

Here she'd come to London with such high ambitions.

Spent years preparing for what was supposed to be a triumphant Season.

Instead, everything was inside out.

And mostly, she wasn't who she thought she was. Oh, it had nothing to do with the fact that her father wasn't Sir Ambrose. For that, in many ways, didn't make a difference. He was her Papa, and would always be. The dearest man ever, more so for all that he had given to her and Louisa.

But when she had thought she'd known exactly who she was and what she wanted, then along had come Tuck and ruined everything.

Not really ruined. Rather opened her eyes.

Is that so bad?

On the nightstand beside her sat the journal she'd kept all these years. Taking notes, carefully and deliberately composing her list of proper ideals on those crisp, clean sheets of paper.

Hours of devoted study and planning, she mused as she leafed through the pages and the all-too-familiar notes.

> *Proper Rule No. 18. When a lady strictly adheres to grace and manners, she shall be repaid in full measure.*
>
> *Proper Rule No. 43. The highest orders of Society are to be viewed with admiration and a sense of awe. For they are the guardians of order and manners and all that is gracious.*

Lady Blaxhall came to mind, and Lavinia snapped the journal shut.

Pompous, ridiculous notions, she now realized. Rising, she carried it over to the fireplace and deposited it in the cold hearth.

"Good riddance," she whispered as she turned her back on her old convictions.

That book, that wretched list had bound up her life in ways that would never have led to any true happiness.

When she turned, she faced her gown again. Oh, how she had thought this the perfect dress a fortnight ago when she'd ordered it, but now it seemed too proper, too staid—even though it was the first stare of fashion.

She glanced over at the clothespress and wished she could wear the blue velvet. Wished she could be that woman again.

For that woman wouldn't hesitate to do what needed to be done tonight.

There was a scratch at the door, and Lavinia bid them to come in—for it must be Nan here to help her dress, but instead of her maid, Mrs. Rowland came tentatively into the room.

"I don't know if I am welcome," the lady began, her hand still resting on the latch.

Lavinia's breath caught in her throat, and for a moment she was back in that carriage with the horrible icy truth chilling them both.

Yet now, Lavinia doubted that what she'd heard had been the entire story. No more than Tuck's mother was a simple, modest widow.

"I could use the help," she told Mrs. Rowland honestly. "Nan is a dear, but she hasn't your touch with hair."

"Years of doing it myself," Mrs. Rowland replied. Then she glanced over at the gown. "Lovely."

"Proper," Lavinia told her. "I only wish—"

"Wish what?"

"That I might be able to wear your necklace with it."

"But my dear girl, if you wear that necklace, everyone will know—" Mrs. Rowland paused and looked her up and down. "Are you certain?"

Lavinia nodded, making her choice.

For unwittingly, it had been Lady Damerell who had given her the idea when she'd said, " . . . *this mystery woman is the most sought after lady in London . . .*"

She'd be just that, and Tuck would win his bet with Ilford, though in the bargain, she'd most likely be ruined.

However, it was a wager she was willing to make.

If it meant saving Tuck.

Mrs. Rowland's eyes twinkled a bit as she smiled. "I had hoped you might be willing to gamble one more time." Then she opened up her reticule.

"This will never work," Tuck said, looking down at his costume. He desperately hoped everyone else would agree.

Sadly, they didn't.

"Come now," Piers teased, "you'll be the belle of the ball."

"Not funny," Tuck told him.

"I think you look quite elegant, Mr. Rowland," Lady Wakefield told him as she circled round him yet again, eyeing him from every angle.

He snorted and took another glance in the mirror. Oh, he'd rather be ruined than endure this.

Especially when Brody poked his head into the room. "Be still, my untamed heart. For there she is, my sun, my moon, my everlasting—"

"Continue, and it will be the last thing you ever say," Tuck warned.

"Scold," Brody replied.

"Be careful there, my lord," Mrs. Petchell told the baron as she handed a shawl to Tuck. "Some of us find that term offensive."

"And will lose you your dinner privileges," Lady Wakefield added, stepping forward to adjust the wrap that Tuck had no idea how to wear.

Good God! No wonder it took so long to get a lady out of her clothes. He shifted this way and that. He had enough layers on to think they were dressing him for a Russian winter.

Brody groaned but kept any further comments to himself though from the twitching of his lips, it was apparent the young lord had plenty more quips at the ready.

"This might work, my lady," Mrs. Petchell said, tipping her head and admiring their handiwork, for it hadn't been a simple task of fitting a dress around Tuck and making him look like a helpless young miss.

He was too tall and his shoulders too wide. But with a large pink bonnet and matching shawl covering most of his upper half and the lower half concealed in a wide skirt of muslin . . . and the yard in shadows.

He turned to get a look at himself and nearly toppled over, having caught his foot in the hem.

"Mr. Rowland, be careful. A lady mustn't step on her hem," Lady Wakefield warned, but the light in her eyes suggested she was enjoying this as much as Brody.

And Piers did his best to stifle a *guffaw* so it merely sounded like he was coughing.

Tuck took a deep breath, then a cautious step. And then another. None of them would ever let him forget this. *For Livy,* he told himself. *For her.*

"No, no, you mustn't skulk about. Just walk," Lady Wakefield told him, showing him by carefully and perfectly crossing the room.

"That looks much easier than it is," he told her.

"Just hold up your skirt," she advised.

"But don't show them your ankles," Brody advised, "for you'll have no hope then of fooling anyone." He tipped his head and did a careful examination of the hemline. "Then again, you just might find your dance card overflowing with eligible *partis.*"

"When this is over, I'm going to thrash you," Tuck warned him.

Brody leaned back, all smug satisfaction at his friend's discomfort, his hands folded comfortably together behind his head. "Not in that dress you aren't."

Tuck tripped and wobbled his way across the viscount's rear yard. While the new viscountess had managed a host of improvements, the gravel was uneven, and Tuck nearly pitched headlong into the tangle of roses near the gate.

He'd break his neck in this rig before he ever managed to lure Bludger and Charlie out of hiding. But he managed with a few careful steps to get through the gate to his uncle's well-maintained yard and breathed a sigh of relief that his uncle kept his pathways in good order.

As it was, everything around him appeared as it ought—the gravel raked clean, the peonies staked and tied after their recent and unfortunate encounter, and the corners all in shadows.

Even the mews beyond seemed to have stilled.

But he'd grown up in London and spent more than an ample amount of time with some of the Honorable's less-than-savory friends not to have developed a keen sense for when someone was lurking about.

And it wasn't just Brody concealed in the privy, or Chaunce and Benedict in the shadows of the gate, or Piers in the window above, with his pistol at the ready.

No, there was someone else about—for while all the rest of them were as still as mice, there was a rustle that shouldn't be there.

And by the time he was standing before Charleton's prized peonies, the hair on the back of his neck was on point. So he continued to feign a complete disregard for his own safety, bending over to admire the fragrant blossoms.

But unwittingly his gaze flitted up toward the window overhead, where to his shock stood Livy, gaping down at him.

That she recognized him was clearly evident, for she immediately swung away from the window in a great huff, and seconds later returned with a large vase in hand.

So this is how his life would end. With Livy finally smashing his head in with a stray piece of crockery and him wearing Mrs. Petchell's Sunday finery.

He could see the lurid inquest testimony now . . . published on the front page of every London paper. And probably half the papers in the country.

"Demmit," he muttered without thinking, and even as he uttered the curse there was the telltale crunch of gravel behind him.

Tuck whirled around.

Like a pair of river rats, two men all done in black, had stepped out of the shadows.

"Blimey!" came the response from the first fellow. "You ain't her!"

Tuck recognized him immediately. "Mr. Bludger."

Bludger sniffed the air like some feral creature, and, smelling a trap, he yanked a pistol out of his jacket and aimed it right at Tuck. "Oh, aye. So you know who I am. Then you'll also rightly know that if you move, I'll shoot."

And those where the last words that came out of the man before a large vase crashed right into his forehead. It sent Bludger careening backward into the villain behind him.

The two crashed to the gravel path, and before either of them could do much more than groan, Tuck's friends came bursting out of their hiding spots.

In no time, the pair were trussed up and in irons.

Benedict wrestled Bludger to his feet, then grinned at Tuck. "What did I tell you? Best bowler in Kempton."

Tuck turned around and saw Livy standing in the window, arms crossed over her bosom, and a triumphant look on her face.

Some bowler, indeed.

Yet he couldn't help but wonder whom she'd meant that errant vase for—Bludger or him?

CHAPTER 21

It was several hours later that Tuck glanced down at his pocket watch and realized how much time had passed.

He hadn't even had an opportunity to speak to Livy—for he'd wanted to see for himself that Bludger and Charlie were locked up tight before he let them out of his sight.

But on the way to the naval office to hand them over for desertion, Bludger had begun to sing.

Of all Ilford's business dealings and connections.

A treasonous list of associates and deeds that had Chaunce Hathaway ordering the carriage to the Home Office and commandeering their prisoners away from his brother.

"His Majesty's Royal Navy can have them when the Home Office is done with them," Chaunce had told Benedict.

And instead of protesting his brother's high-handed ways, Benedict had taken his leave of Bludger and Charlie with a cold smile and an even icier farewell. "Good luck, you foul rats. You'll wish you'd come with me."

After that, Tuck had waited outside the dank cells in the basement of the Home Office until Chaunce's superior, Lord Hower, or Old Ironpants, as Brody had muttered under his breath, had come to question the pair.

That interrogation had taken some time, and it was in the middle of it that Brody had come out.

"Lord Hower suggests you go see to Miss Tempest. I'm to go get Ilford. Seems he's been dipping deep and making friends in the wrong places to cover his losses."

Tuck fell into step beside Brody as they walked up the steps and outside into the cool night air. He drew a deep, long breath. "I'm coming with you."

"Can't have that. This is His Majesty's business now."

"I should have just called Ilford out that night at White's," Tuck said, shaken at how close Livy might have come to being harmed.

Caught in the middle of his reckless wager.

"Half-tempted to put a bullet in him myself," Brody said. "Hanging will be too good for him." When they got to the street, Poldie's brother looked over at him. "I hope I can trust that you won't mention my affiliation with—" He tipped his head toward the building. "Well, you know."

"You have my word," Tuck said.

"When Poldie died, and I inherited, I wanted to enlist. Take his spot. But my mother—well, you know my mother," Brody said with a shrug.

Tuck shrugged. The dowager was a most formidable woman.

"But then Chaunce offered to sponsor me, and I've been—" He stopped, lips pressed together tight.

"Probably better you don't say what you've been doing," Tuck said with a laugh. "Then if your mother ever interrogates me, I won't give you up."

At that, Brody laughed, then he nudged Tuck. "I hear Lady Gosforth is having a ball tonight. You should go see how Miss Tempest has fared."

Tuck hesitated. Part of him wanted to go—not over the wager but because he wanted to know she was safe.

But another part of him held back.

What if Livy was now being toasted from one side of the ballroom to the other? He didn't know if he wanted to see her being courted by every noble stripling and lofty blade in the city.

So instead, he said, "I doubt I'll have to worry about Ilford's coming to collect if she's caused another dust up."

"No, but I bet young Ardmore his next quarter's allowance that you'd make a Diamond out of her, and I want to know if I've won. You see, Tuck, I always had faith in you because my brother always did."

"Are you certain about this?" Mrs. Rowland asked once again, as Lavinia was the last to get down from Lord Charleton's carriage.

Instinctively, Lavinia's hand went to her neck, where the diamond-and-sapphire necklace lay, then looked up at the Gosforth town house. "Yes. I've made my choice."

"It won't be easy," Mrs. Rowland told her, taking her hand and giving her fingers a squeeze.

"I don't care what the rest of the *ton* thinks. Tuck will know. He'll know what he means to me."

And maybe then he'd say the words to her that he'd confessed to Lady Gosforth.

Simply put, I love Livy.

"And what the *ton* thinks of him?" Mrs. Rowland added.

Lavinia shook her head. "Tuck has proven himself beyond a doubt." She shivered at how close she or Louisa might have come to harm. "Even if he did what they say, he did it for the right reasons. I know it."

Mrs. Rowland got down and took both Lavinia's hands in hers and looked her straight in the eye. "He did do it. He did it for me. He took the money Charleton gave him for his commission and used it to get me out of Newgate."

Where once Lavinia might have drawn back from such a shocking confession, instead she stilled. "He saved you."

It was a statement. A truth.

What had Charleton said? . . . *Alaster will go to any depth to do right by those he loves . . .*

As he had tonight when he'd faced a pistol-bearing blackguard. He'd risked his life to help keep her safe.

All while wearing a dress. Lavinia smiled.

"Livy, child," Mrs. Rowland said, letting go of her hands and looking up at Lord Charleton and Lady Aveley, who were waiting at the top of the steps for her. "Do you love him? Do you love my son?"

Lavinia smiled. "I think that is something he should hear first."

Mrs. Rowland nodded, reached over and squeezed her hand one more time before she got back into Lord Charleton's carriage.

Climbing up the steps and entering the grand house, Lavinia found that she was in fact holding her breath.

For already, there had been more than one quizzical glance at her necklace.

Yet to her surprise, no one asked if she was the infamous and mysterious lady at St. John's Folly, but it seemed all of those who looked at her quickly came to that conclusion.

If not, their neighbor filled them in.

A stillness fell over the crowd as she stopped in front of her host and hostess. It was a moment that teetered between ruin and wonder.

Lord Gosforth grinned. "Ah, my dear Miss Tempest. Finally! I told my lovely wife that the moment I found you, I was going to engage you for another hand of cards. I must be avenged," the old roué declared loudly. And, with a grand flourish, led her off to the room set aside for cards, and all around them, conversations fluttered furiously back to life.

After she'd thoroughly trounced her host in three straight hands, Lord Gosforth pled off, saying, "La! Miss Tempest, you are a marvel and credit to your sex. I declare you the rarest of gems."

And that was all it had taken.

Instantly, Lavinia Tempest became the most sought after Diamond of the night.

High and low came seeking introductions. Oh, that wasn't to say there weren't some detractors. Matrons with daughters who were overlooked in light of the rush to catch Miss Tempest's eye.

And those previous Diamonds and Rarities who were edged off their pedestals were none too pleased by the arrival of this new star in their gilded and jealously guarded hemisphere.

But the tide had turned, and in the course of a few hours, Lavinia was consulted as to her favorite modiste, asked her opinions on the latest fashions, and, more surprising, had been proposed to three times.

Though one of those proposals had not been for marriage but an entirely different arrangement.

Good heavens, she mused as she sent the impudent fellow packing with a tart reply, perhaps obscurity and ruin wasn't such a bad bargain. It certainly kept the rogues at bay.

Save one. She glanced again at the empty doorway and sighed. If only . . .

Yet sometime later, her heart fluttered as if awakened, and she knew without looking that Tuck had arrived. And when he was announced, she glanced over her shoulder and spied him there in the doorway.

And he looked right at her.

The conversations around her faded. Nothing else mattered.

Tuck was here. Finally.

All night she'd envisioned this moment. How he would see her. That sly, teasing smile would turn his lips. His gaze would lock with hers. And then he'd push through the crush to gain her side.

And confess his feelings. *Livy, I love you.*

But, to her shock, his eyes fixed not on her gaze but on the string of diamonds and sapphires around her neck. And his expression hardened into a sort of cold fury.

She turned her back to the doorway, her hand at her neck.

And when she glanced back, he was gone.

* * *

What had Livy done?

Tuck couldn't believe his eyes. Yet when he looked again, there was his mother's now-infamous string of jewels around her neck.

When she turned away, he'd stepped into the crush, out of the limelight of the entranceway, still trying to grasp what he'd seen.

Wearing his mother's necklace . . . in plain sight.

After all he'd done to keep her safe, save her reputation (well, if one forgot those few interludes where he probably hadn't aided her cause—but this was Livy, and she was meant for kissing) but no matter, now it was all for naught.

Now everyone would know that she was . . . She that'd been . . .

Why it was ruinous . . . A disaster . . . It was . . .

He looked at her, then around the room, and realized something very different.

Yes, every eye was on her, and more to the point, she was encircled by every lordling, rake, and more than her fair share of the loftiest bachelors in London.

Tuck continued to circle the room, gaping at the sight from every angle.

Livy, his Livy was surrounded. The center of attention.

Adored.

Every man in this room now knew the secret he'd had all to himself this last fortnight.

That she was a rare and delectable gem.

And what shafted through him wasn't a sense of accomplishment or relief that he'd bested Ilford (who by now would be locked up in the basement of the Home Office) but a giant stab of jealousy.

She had been his. All his, and now she was lost to him. Far better gentlemen, men with titles and wealth and all the things she'd come to London to find, would now be hers for the choosing.

"Ah, Rowland! Come to gloat in your triumph!"

Tuck glanced over and saw Budgey grinning at him.

The fellow waved him over. "You've done it. But come now, you hardly look elated. You've won, by Jove! That you have!"

"Yes, yes," Lord Ardmore agreed, stepping forward to join them. "Masterful stroke of genius, Rowland. She's a pure Diamond. Quite literally!" He glanced over at Lavinia and shook his head. "Wish now I hadn't wagered against you."

Budgey was more to the point. "Wouldn't mind introducing me to the chit, my good man, now would you? Haven't been able to wedge my way to her side all night."

"In a moment," Tuck told him absently, crossing the room, catching her by the arm and tugging her away from her admirers—deaf to their protests.

And to hers as well.

"Tuck! Unhand me. Whatever are you doing?"

He ignored her and all the scandalized stares that followed in their wake.

He didn't stop until he came to the foyer, then steered her into an alcove, pulling the curtain closed behind him.

"What are you doing wearing that?" he demanded.

True to her nature, she ignored the obvious and answered coyly. "This gown? I thought the cut quite fetching." Her hands fanned out over the skirt and she turned a bit so he could see the entire ensemble. "Don't you?"

"Well, yes," he began without thinking, for the fabric clung to her curves exactly as he remembered them. But just as quickly he stopped himself and got to the point. "What I mean to say is, why are you wearing my mother's necklace?"

Once again, she was smoothly coy. "She was kind enough to loan it to me, and I could hardly refuse such a lovely—"

"Livy! You know what I mean," he said. "Everyone in this room will suspect you are— you were—"

"Dear heavens, Tuck. They don't suspect. They know," she told him, her eyes alight with passion. "That was very reason I wore it. Well, granted it was a risk, a wager, really, but it did the trick. I am the most sought after lady in London." She put her hands on his chest, her fingers splaying out beneath his jacket, running over his waistcoat as they had at St. John's.

And now the folly was his, for her touch, her words were lulling him into believing the impossible.

That he could love her without fear. Without recriminations.

"You've won your wager," she whispered, drawing closer, her lithe body brushing against his.

Dangerously so. For his breath seemed to have escaped him and the rest of him? Oh, it was far from lost—rather growing harder by the second.

Against every bit of desire he held for her, he pushed her back and crossed his arms over his chest, throwing up a wall against her charms. "Not at your expense. I won't have it."

He hoped she heard and heeded the stubborn determination in his words.

Hell, he hoped he heard them as well.

"Too late," she shot back, a look of irritation on her face, as if none of this was going as she thought it ought. "The deed is done."

What deed that was, he wasn't going to ask. Either she meant wearing his mother's necklace or his own ruinous behavior the other night at St. John's.

Tuck, oh, Tuck! she'd gasped as she came shivering and trembling into her release.

No. No. No. That had been his Livy. This woman before him, this Diamond was Miss Lavinia Tempest. And she deserved so much more than him.

So much more than a scandal-ridden rake.

Couldn't she see that she had everything she'd come to London for right in her grasp? She didn't need to settle for just anyone.

Especially him.

Nor was she finished. "Well, Mr. Rowland, if you are so worried about my reputation, then why do you keep hauling me into alcoves, unless you have an entirely improper motive?"

Of course she was correct. She had a bloody list after all.

He muttered a curse and yanked open the curtain, checking first that the way was clear, then hauled her back to the ballroom.

If he didn't know better, he suspected she was dragging her heels as he towed her across the large foyer, and more than that, appeared willing to utter a curse of her own.

So he decided to cut her off before she managed to topple her own success with an ill-timed venture into profanity.

"I wanted to thank you for earlier," he said, glancing over his shoulder at her as he came to a stop. "For saving my life."

"Oh, you think that vase was meant for that awful man?"

"I happen to know you never miss. At least so I've been told."

"Yes, well, I could hardly let him shoot you. While wearing what looked like Mrs. Petchell's best Sunday dress. Why, you would have bled all over it, not to the mention the hole." Her eyes sparkled slightly, mischievously. "Though I don't see why you changed your ensemble. I thought you cut a very striking figure."

"I did that to save your neck, I'll have you know."

"For which I am most grateful. But still, however am I to brag to one and all of your heroics without mentioning the lengths to which you went." Her brows waggled with delighted mischief.

She wouldn't. Tuck glanced at her. Oh, this was Livy. She would. "Not a word," he warned as they reentered the crowded room. "Don't you dare tell a soul."

It was bad enough Piers and company knew.

"Not even a snippet?" she asked. "Say for the *Morning Post* perhaps?"

"No."

"A good jest?"

"Not even." He turned his back to her and surveyed the crowd. Yes, most eyes were turned in their direction, as if waiting for something scandalous to happen. The band was striking up for the next set and several gentlemen looked ready to come back and challenge him for his place at Livy's side.

The lady herself was completely oblivious to all this.

"Then I suppose I will have to settle for a well-composed limerick," she was saying, pursing her lips together, her brow furrowed in concentration. "There once was a knave in a skirt—"

"Do you want to dance?" he asked. Anything to get her to stop.

To keep her from being stolen from him.

For he knew he wouldn't have her much longer.

"Dance?" Her eyes sparkled. "I thought you would never ask."

He led her out to the floor, amid grumbles and complaints that she had refused everyone else.

"Tuck, may I ask you a question?"

"Of course," he told her.

"Why do you like me?"

No, you have it all wrong, I love you. But he could hardly say that, so he feigned indifference, shaking his head. "Like you? Who said anything about liking you?" he replied. "You nag at me excessively. I suspect you cheat at cards—"

"I never—" she began, but he cut her off.

"You interrupt me. You're known to eavesdrop—"

"I never—" She didn't finish it, for he cocked his brows and stared her down, leaving the rest of her objection caught in the back of her throat.

"As I was saying, you are a dreadful minx, a handful, and I am happy to be done with you. From the looks of things, you will be someone else's problem in no time." They swung through the crowded dance floor, but to Tuck it felt as if they were the only two there.

"You don't mean any of that," she insisted.

"Of course I do," he told her. "Besides, you've done your bit. I've won my part. Helped you along the way. Now it is time for both of us to reap the benefits, starting with you and your"—he tipped his head and glanced at the card attached to her wrist—"next dancing partner."

"I'm not dancing tonight."

"Glad to know it," he said with a grin as he continued to guide her through the steps. "I personally don't see what all the fuss is about you and dancing."

"Yes, well, it only seems to work when I dance with you."

His heart pattered unevenly. They did fit. He knew it. And, demmit, so did Livy.

But couldn't she see how bad a match it would be? Eventually, something would go wrong, and she'd be caught in the middle of it.

"Well, it isn't too late to broaden your experience. Just look over there at Lord Spalford. He's been trying for the last few minutes to catch your eye. He'll make a respectably proper groom. And he has ten thousand a year and three estates. Fits that list of yours to a T."

"I only need one," she said. And she was talking about grooms. Though she did spare a glance at Spalford and immediately shuddered. "His ears stick out."

Tuck's eyes narrowed as he made a second inspection. "I suppose they do. Never noticed that before. How unfortunate." He slanted a glance over at her, then quickly looked back at the assembled guests. "Then smile in that fetching way of yours at Lord Elworth. He's only in possession of one estate, but I hear it covers a good portion of Dorset."

"Dorset?" Lavinia wrinkled her nose.

"You've become overly exacting."

"Discerning," she corrected. "If you haven't noticed, Lord Elworth, while professing to be in search of a wife, has spent most of the night looking at Lord Percival."

"Oh, bother. I had rather hoped you hadn't noticed that." Then he paused. "Just a bloody moment. However do you know about such things?"

She rolled her gaze upward, her lashes fluttering. Truly, did he think she'd grown up in a convent?

Tuck sighed and went back to his search.

His pointless search, she would have liked to tell him.

"Lord Apley?"

"Too dull."

"Lord Molescroft?"

Oh, good heavens. Now it was her turn to heave a sigh. "Are you mad?"

"Yes, well, I still maintain that the rumors about his first wife have been highly exaggerated."

"Tell that to Lady Molescroft, if they ever find her body."

"Mr. Ruscombe?" He just as quickly changed his mind. "Oh, no need to look there. He'll require an heiress if the rumors of his recent foray into horse racing is true."

She looked ready to say something, then changed her mind, her lips pressed together.

Before she could come up with another excuse, he added, "Though you are a dab hand at cards. You could keep him for years in the style he pretends to afford."

"Please, Tuck, just stop. Just dance with me. Hold me," she pleaded, and if he didn't know better, he could have sworn her eyes looked a bit moist.

Oh, demmit, she was going to cry.

And if he didn't know better, he suspected he might as well. That, or he could just continue to endure having his heart ripped in half.

So when the dance ended, he bowed over her hand, and said, "Miss Tempest, take good care with your choice. I trust you'll make it a proper one."

Bowing once, he turned and left the ball, not stopping until he got to White's.

It was any number of hours later that Tuck made his way up the stairs to his bachelor rooms. He had intended to drown his broken heart in a bottle or two or three of brandy, but when he'd gotten to his club, the entire room was awash with excitement over Livy's triumph, and the bets were already being laid as to whom she was going to marry.

It was the last thing he wanted to hear.

So he'd found himself wandering about, and in a wayward

moment had looked up at the sky and to his amazement, the night was clear and there were all the stars that Livy had dared him to look for.

To reach for.

He realized the only safe place for him on this wretched night was his own bed, but when he got to his apartment, he found the door cracked open.

"Falshaw? Are you in there?"

A crackle of foreboding ran down his spine. For there had yet to be any news of Ilford's arrest, so he moved quietly into the room. There was the soft glow of candles in his bedchamber beyond, while the front room remained in shadows.

Tuck slowly opened the drawer where he kept his pistol and drew it out. It wasn't loaded, but whoever was in the room beyond didn't know that.

At least he hoped whoever it was would be fooled by his bluff.

Quietly and slowly, he eased the door open, ready for anything.

Yet the sight before him couldn't have shocked him more. Left him disarmed.

Literally. For his hand dropped, the pistol slipping from his grasp and crashing to the floor.

"What the devil!" he muttered.

Lavinia looked up and smiled. "I thought you would never get home."

"What the devil?" Tuck repeated as he took a step closer.

"You told me to consider my choices carefully," she told him, glancing over at the chair in the corner where she had deposited her gown before getting into his bed. "I chose instead to make a wager."

"A wager? You've gone mad," he told her. "Put your gown back on!"

"If you insist," she told him, poking a bare leg out from beneath the coverlet.

"Oh, good God, you're naked," he gasped.

"Yes," she told him. "I am starting to think your reputation is highly exaggerated. For I wagered that you would already be kissing me by now."

"This is ruinous!"

"I know that. If anyone knows that, it would be me. It's Proper Rule Number 22." She paused for a second. "Well, it doesn't say to turn up in a man's bed if you wish him to make love to you—rather it is something a bit more pedantic." Then she smiled at him. "But as you can see, I'm rather done with rules."

"Livy, I can't . . ." he stammered, coming closer. "I won't."

But still he took another step as if he still wasn't too sure if this was all happening. "Who knows you are here?"

"No one. Well, save Falshaw. But he won't breathe a word of it."

"My uncle, Lady Aveley, they must be sick with worry."

She shook her head. "Hardly. They think I am spending the night with my sister."

Just as Louisa thought she was staying with Miss Stratton.

He raked a hand through his hair and shook his head. She could almost hear what he was thinking.

Demmit! What have I created?

He was about to find out.

She reached out and took his hand and pulled him closer, until she could curve her fingers around his jaw, feel the beginnings of stubble there. "Tuck, do stop complaining and make love to me, or I will marry Lord Apley."

"I thought you said he was too dull."

She kissed his hand, running her tongue over his fingers, between them, leaving him making a sort of strangled sound that only emboldened her. "He is. Though he said my eyes reminded him of bluebells."

Tuck sat down on the edge of the bed. "I already told you that."

Which was a vast improvement, in her estimation. She caught hold of his other hand and guided it to her bare breast.

"Yes, I know. I prefer it when you say it," she whispered.

And when you touch me, she wanted to add.

But she needn't, for his fingers began to caress her, while his gaze remained fixed on hers.

"I don't want to have to marry him, Tuck."

"You could have your choice of any of them, Livy."

"I think it's obvious that I have."

He leaned closer, his nose nuzzling at her ear. He inhaled deeply, then breathed out, warm and hot all over her neck, leaving her shivering. "Have what?"

"Made my choice. A most improper one."

He paused for just a second. "And you came to me?"

"You seemed the perfect man for the task."

And so he was.

For without another word, his lips crashed down on hers, and Lavinia Tempest knew that, in the most improper moment of her life, she'd made the perfectly proper choice.

Tuck yanked off his jacket, then his cravat even as he continued to kiss Livy. Touch Livy.

Good heavens, she was naked. In his bed.

Instantly, he was lost in a maelstrom of desire.

He'd spent the entire night composing a list of all the reasons why he couldn't have her, but for the life of him, with her in his arms, in his bed, he couldn't recall a single one.

Save the singular thought. *To have her all to himself.*

Now and always.

He finished pulling off his clothes until he was just as bared, and pulled her close, her silken skin warm to his, a contrast of heat and desire, the musky scent of her sex drawing him to her.

His mouth fused to hers, kissing her deeply, his tongue washing over hers, while his fingers sought that spot they'd found the other night.

The one that had left her trembling. And she trembled again

when he found it, running his fingers over the tight knot, her legs opening to him just as her mouth had. Ready, willing, and so very wet.

She moved beneath him, letting him cover her, writhing as he stroked her.

He wanted her so badly, he wanted to be inside her, filling her, but he also wanted to explore her, and it was that need, to see her, to touch all of her, that drove him to break off the long hot kiss that had forged them together.

"Tuck, please," she gasped, her hips riding up.

"Vixen," he told her, sliding down a bit so he could suckle at her breasts.

This time her mouth opened, but no sound came out, until her nipples were in tight, taut points and it was a single mew that came out of her, as if she'd climbed to an unexpected height.

He decided to push her just a bit higher and moved lower, so that his lips, his tongue was right over her sex, and when he parted his course, let his tongue replace what his hands had been discovering, she let out a different sound, even as her hands fisted in the sheets, and her heels dug into the mattress.

She arched up to meet him as he teased her yet again, his tongue drawing a slow circle around the nub.

"Oh, oh, Tuck, yes! Oh, yes."

So he did it again.

Lavinia arched upward, for never had she felt anything like this. His mouth over her, suckling her *there*—when he'd done so to her breasts it had been heavenly, but this . . . this was heaven itself.

His tongue pressed deeper, and suddenly she was rising and coming all at once. It came upon her so quickly, so swiftly, she gasped, and the world around her shattered.

And all she could hear was the well-pleased laughter of a knave.

"I don't see what is so funny," she told him, once she had finally come back down to earth—or rather the cozy confines of his mattress.

How and when he'd come back up to her, gathered her in his arms and was once again nuzzling her, kissing her neck, her ears, her hair, she didn't know.

Just so long as he kept doing it.

For already her body seemed to be reawakening, thrumming back to life in response to his touch, his kiss, the feel of his body entwined with hers.

She could barely tell where she left off and he began, save that he was warm and hard against her.

Very hard.

It was all well and good to have him kiss her and bring her to her crisis, but she wouldn't be truly and perfectly ruined until . . .

She shifted and turned so that she lay beneath him. Her hand reached down and touched him, marveled at the length, the thickness, and how much she wanted to feel him inside her.

As her fingers curled around him, running down the length of him, and she watched with a smug satisfaction as his eyelids half closed and his mouth opened into a hazy spiral of passion.

"Oh, Livy, what are you doing to me?"

"If you don't know, I can leave," she teased.

"Not now," he told her. "Not ever." And then he took her hands and pinned them yet again over her head.

She was hardly his prisoner, for she opened her legs to him, winding them around his hips, arching toward him. No, she certainly wasn't going to leave until she knew what all the fuss was about.

What had so many ladies writing guides to teach young ladies to avoid such situations.

She was starting to see why there needed to be so many volumes—for having Tuck torment her with his kiss, his touch made her wish she'd abandoned her list of Proper Rules years ago.

Or at least a fortnight ago.

"Love me," she whispered.

"I already do," he told her as he began to enter her.

"I know."

And while his brow arched slightly in surprise, he grinned at her and continued to move slowly inside her, letting her stretch to fit him. And when he came to her barrier, he breached it quickly, and she was lost yet again as he continued to move inside her.

This . . . This . . . hot and hard, riding against her . . . this was what all the fuss was about.

Lavinia ran her hands down his back, tracing the muscles there, hard and lean, and all the while he continued to move, his pace growing faster, and she met his thrusts with her own, arching up to meet him, her body taking that steep path upward, leaping forward with each thrust.

It was as if he was coaxing her, not that he needed to, for she was quite willing to come along.

Come with me. Follow me.

His hands continued to explore her, along her hips, drawing her up and closer, on her breasts once again, his fingertips tormenting her nipples, sending sentinels of desire racing through her limbs.

"Livy, Livy!" he began to gasp, as his cadence became a wild dance, thrusting into her, and he found his release, carrying her with him as she too tumbled over the edge and into his arms, breathless and quaking.

And with it, he murmured one single word into her ear, before he collapsed beside her.

"Mine."

Sometime later, Tuck brushed her tangled hair from her face. "You need to wake up."

"Again," she said, in a sleepy, pleased voice.

"I need to take you home. It is nearly morning."

She made a moue of disappointment and glanced at the

window, where the first light of day began to creep over the sill. "I suppose I must. I'm getting married today."

"Married?" Tuck sat up and gaped at her.

"Yes, married," she told him, leaning back on the pillows, one hand tucked behind her head.

"Then what the devil are you doing here?"

"I told you—"

"Yes, yes. Improper and all that rot. I thought—"

"You thought what?"

He shook his head as he tried to piece it all together. "I'll have a bullet in my chest for this."

"I doubt it," she replied with all the contented confidence of a house cat. Then she paused, her brow furrowing slightly. "Unless—"

"Unless what?" he demanded.

She waved off his protests. "Oh, never mind. It's a trifling thing."

"If it leaves me out on a grassy knoll at dawn with some irate lordling pointing a pistol at me for bedding his betrothed, then it isn't a 'trifling' matter to me."

She laughed. "How you go on."

"How I go on? You're the one who's to be married. Whatever were you thinking, coming here?"

Sitting up, Livy looked at him with those piercing eyes of hers. *The ones that went straight to his heart.* Which right now was feeling a bit pinched and battered. Here he'd thought—

Oh, demmit! Never mind what he thought.

But married? He knew this all was the point, but that was before. Before he'd . . .

"Is he titled?" he found himself asking before he could stop himself.

"He will be," she told him, glancing over at him.

"That's a fine kettle. Didn't you learn anything from my mother about marrying with only presumptive expectations?"

"I think I've learned quite a bit in the last fortnight," she said, curling toward him, her lashes doing that soft fluttering thing that tugged at his resolve to be furious with her.

Demmit, he was furious with her.

He was.

If only she'd stop looking at him like she wanted to . . . Again.

He shifted away from her and did his best not to look at her. "Well, if you had, you certainly wouldn't have gotten yourself betrothed to someone who *might* inherit."

She laughed. "And here I thought you of all people would approve utterly."

"Hardly. Can he keep you?"

"We'll manage. At least I'll manage," she told him with that utter confidence of hers. "I will remind you, I am a dab hand at cards."

"Oh, I've seen you manage," he shot back. "That gown over there would set me back another quarter."

"Now that you've won your wager, I'd say you could afford half a dozen of those gowns quite easily. And the shoes to match."

"Hardly. I have debts that must be paid off first."

"Listen to you!" She laughed. "How sensible you sound."

"I blame you." He glanced over at her. "Will you be happy, Livy?"

She smiled at him, the sort of glow that seemed to light the last remaining shadows in the room. "Excessively so."

"Will he be good to you? I won't tolerate it if he isn't—"

"He'll be perfectly decent. Though he will probably complain about the milliner's bill."

"With good reason."

"I won't mind."

"You won't? How is that?"

"Oh, Tuck, I love him ever so much."

At this, he got up and out of the bed as if pushed from it. She loved this man? What the devil?

"How can you? If you loved this poor fool as much as you claim, you certainly wouldn't be in my bed."

She laughed again. "What is wrong with you? I thought you wanted me."

He did. Looking down at her, he wanted her still. But suddenly. "All I've heard for the past fortnight is 'proper this' and 'true love' that, and now . . . What happened?"

"I fell in love."

It was so simple the way she said it. *I fell in love.* Like one might trip over the edge of a rug. Or decide between bacon or kippers for breakfast. Or catch a ballroom on fire.

I fell in love.

The problem being, he knew exactly what she meant. Because he loved her.

He loved Livy with all his heart. And now . . .

"I hardly call it 'love' when you spend the night in another man's bed. Who is this poor sod?"

"Tuck—"

"Who is he?"

"Alaster!"

"Demmit, Livy! Who is he? I'll shoot him myself and save him the misery of a marriage to such a faithless jade."

Instead of being insulted she smiled at him. "Mr. Alaster Rowland, I—"

He stomped back to the bed. "Livy! His name!"

She leaned toward him. "You, you great big oaf. I love you. And after last night, if you don't marry me, I'll shoot you myself. Or at the very least dash a vase over your head."

He paused and looked at her. "You would, wouldn't you?"

"Yes, Tuck, I would."

"I rather like living," he offered, as suddenly his future began to unfold before him. A future he'd never imagined for himself.

With Livy. At his side.

In his bed.

"It would be a waste of a perfectly good vase," he told her, climbing back into the bed and gathering her into his arms, not minding in the least that she'd led him on a merry chase.

"Especially since I rather like you," she said, once again the prim-and-proper miss.

Save that she was naked, and she was looking at him as if she would like to . . . again.

"I like you as well."

"So I've heard. That you *like* me. Though I heard it phrased a little differently," she pointed out.

His brow furrowed, then he remembered.

Lady Gosforth's afternoon in.

Simply put, I love Livy.

"You heard what I said?"

"Perhaps. Oh, bother, yes. All of it."

"You shameless jade! You were eavesdropping!"

"Uncle Hero says that information gathered in hopes of mutual gain isn't a sin."

Tuck wagged a finger at her. "Don't start quoting the Honorable to me."

"He taught me well."

"Too well."

He took her hand. The one that needed a ring. "Livy?"

"Yes, Tuck?"

"Are you certain about all this? About—"

"Everything?" She nodded. "Very certain. Or I wouldn't be here."

"You do know your own mind, I suppose."

"I wouldn't have—" She stopped, blushing again and glancing around at the rumpled sheets. "If I hadn't been most certain."

"Yes, well, there is that," Tuck agreed, kissing her nose and her lips. Then he pulled back. "You know, the Archbishop's office doesn't open for some time—"

She grinned. "Uncle Hero says to make every hour useful."

Tuck nodded in agreement. "Seems a shame to waste . . ." He kissed the nape of her neck and whispered how he thought the time should be spent.

The lady sighed. "Tuck . . . You *are* a knave!"

But she hardly sounded as if she minded.

CHAPTER 22

St. George's Church, London
A few hours later

"So you married him," Tildie said, smiling at the bride.

"Yes, it only seemed proper," Lavinia told her.

"Oh, my, it is all so romantic," the charwoman said, glancing yet again at the bouquet in Lavinia's hands.

And immediately, Lavinia held it out to her. "Please, take it, with my good wishes."

"Oh, but it is yours."

"I have all my wishes," she said, glancing over her shoulder toward the door where a tall, handsome man stood silhouetted in the afternoon sun.

"It does look that way," Tildie agreed. But the woman was as pragmatic as she was romantic. "Do you think he'll make you happy?"

But Lavinia was already walking toward her groom. She paused and looked over her shoulder. "Yes, most decidedly. In fact, I've already started a list."

At the mention of a list, Tuck eyed her as she approached. "What sort of list is this?"

Lavinia caught hold of his jacket, rose up on her tiptoes and kissed him. "A most improper one."